A BRAIDING OF DARKNESS

A BRAIDING OF DARKNESS

ANOTHER BEAST'S SKIN

BOOK II

JESSIKA
GREWE GLOVER

Published by: Pip & Plum Creative LLC

Supervising Editor, Proofreader: Cristen Cagle

Front Cover Design by: Miblart

Map by: Demi Hargreaves

Kintsugi-inspired Art by: Mitch Green

ISBN: 979-8-9875838-4-5 (e-book)

ISBN: 979-8-9875838-5-2 (paperback)

For My family of hooligans,
Damian, India, Phineas, and CocoMonster
My Wonderwall

Some content and themes in *A Braiding of Darkness* may be considered sensitive to some readers. These include violence, blood, death, sex, complicated relationship dynamics with possible infidelity, and grief. Neysa struggles with anxiety and post traumatic stress disorder. Events and situations in this book are, of course, fiction, magical, and at the mercy of vengeful gods, however, many emotions and the mental health ramifications are all too human.

<u>Aoifsing</u>
<u>Former Elders by province:</u>
Festaera: Paschale
Saarlaiche: Turuín
Veruni: Analisse
Maesarra: Feynser
Laorinaghe: Lorelei
Dunstainaiche: Soren
Naenire: Camua
Prinaer: Nanua

<u>Characters by province:</u>
<u>Saarlaiche</u>
Cadeyrn
Corraidhín
Silas
Magnus
Lina
Rhia

<u>Maesarra</u>
Saskiea
Ewan
Reynard
Cyrranus
Arneau
Etienne
Francois
Alan

<u>Laorinaghe</u>
Yva
Arturus

Farus
Xaograos

Festaera
Petyr
Tuso
Bestía
Kíra
Olek
Sergo

Veruni
Analisse
Julissa
Lord Dockman

Heilig
King Konstantín
Queen Marja
Saski (crown princess)
Arik
Ludek
Pavla (deceased)
Basz
Eamon

Aoifsing
COLLAPSED VEIL
Festaera
THE KEEP
Vascha Mountains
Prinaer
AEMES
HEMATITE
MINES
Dunstanaich
Saarlaiche
LAICHMONDE
Lake Gläch
THE ELDER PALACE
Veruni
BANIA
Laorinaghe Naenire
THE SACRED
CITY
Maesarra
En
Re
CRAGHEN
BISTAÍR
Ispil of Bogvi

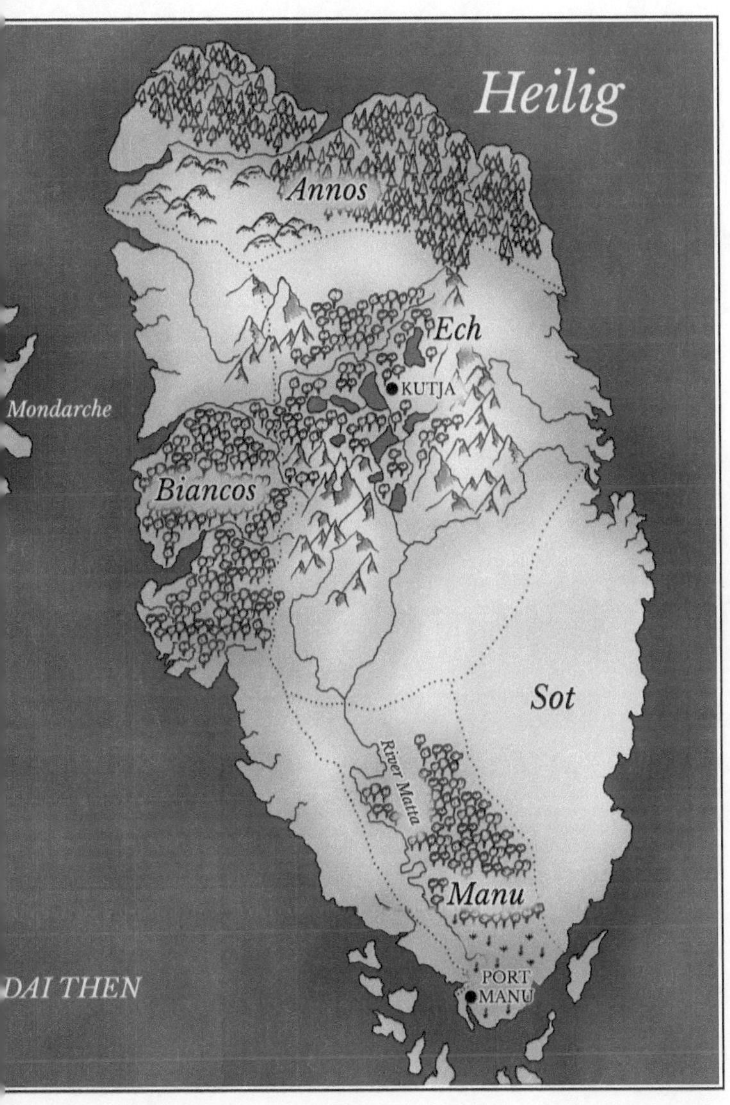

Heilig
Annos
Ech
KUTJA
Mondarche
Biancos
Sot
River Matta
Manu
PORT MANU
DAI THEN

PART ONE

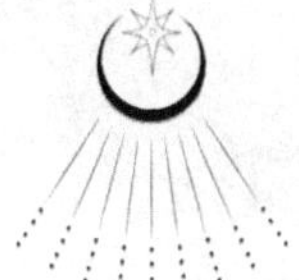

CHAPTER 1

NEYSA

Occasionally, I would catch his scent. A light layer of his rain essence around me, catching my breath every time. Most instances, the essence would disappear as soon as it appeared. Weeks of following mere mentions of a beast had us downcast. Many times, my *baethaache*, the beast within me—like the one Analisse forced from Cadeyrn—would become restless and sense him. I willed her to come out as I did when I was a child, but somehow, she refused. The day of the summit, I had a split second to decide how to act. How to play the events that unfolded once my mate became a monstrous version of our innate selves. Many pledged allegiances. Bestía, the platinum-haired general from Festaera, Kasscik of Neanire, Soren of Dunstanaich, Turuin of Saarlaiche. They all witnessed the dark magics used to tear Cadeyrn's self from its beast. Though my body wanted to wrap itself in despair and seek revenge, I knew that was why Analisse had done it. She wanted to show the delegates that we were monsters who would turn on them and I refused to give her the satisfaction. So, I walked out of the palace with Corra and Silas, having entombed my grief and become purpose

"

driven. I barely spoke. Basic functions were automatic, and my interaction with people was warm only when I had to represent our cause. In the evenings, I descended to a depth of grief too lightless and cold to support life.

Corra materialized before Silas and me as we sat around the fire. The days were getting longer, allowing more time to hunt him. Or at least what was left of him.

"I had a hawk come to me," Corra reported. "Messengers reported him in the north of Dunstanaich." We never said his name, I realized. 'Him' or 'It'. Perhaps trying to objectify this whole mess for us all. "Oddly enough, some have reported seeing the male. Someone recognized his markings."

That gave me pause.

"Do you think," I stammered, my voice like sandpaper from disuse. "He is fighting it and winning?"

"Perhaps," Corra said. "One farmer claimed a sheep was stolen by the beast. This is the first we have heard. Could be a load of rubbish, but it's worth considering. If the countryside starts getting razed, then we have bigger problems."

I asked how far we were from Dustanaich and Corra told me to wait for the next update. That update was from two days ago and the beast moves. We would head further north and see.

A week later had us in the center of Prinaer. I knew the quarries of stone here were immense and the gemstones harvested were said to be the most powerful in the realm. The *adairch dorhdj*, or double horn, I wore thrummed against me in a constant rhythm, like a second heartbeat. Corra had given it to me for Yule. It was once a present to her from Cadeyrn— a talisman of amethyst on one side, black tourmaline on the other. Corra claimed she realized it must have been given to her for safe keeping until Cadeyrn and I met. Met and fell in love. And mated. Before he was torn from me.

A hawk landed near Corraidhín as we cleaned up after a

meager evening meal of river fish and cheese we received from a sympathetic farmer. She read the encoded message and told us the Queen had a contingent of support from every province, but seers warned of a darkness moving in. The beast was spotted in Laorinaghe. Children happened upon it while it was sleeping, and they said it opened its eyes and stared at them as they backed away and it growled to the sky. Yet, it didn't attack.

My magic was in tatters, whether from the blight on our bond or from my own self-inflicted damper, I didn't know. I barely saw a hint of the white light, the electricity, or the heightened senses. It was almost as though I had shoved that cloaking back over me. Once again, I was wearing the skin of another beast. I couldn't even bring myself to try and speak to him through our *Cuiraíbh Enaíde*, the braiding of our souls that made us more than lovers, more than mates.

Corra said she would go to Laorinaghe ahead of us and we could head out in the morning, as she would follow the river in her dematerialized form. Corra and Silas could both dissolve into any moisture, allowing them to travel faster through their gifts than on land. Silas stayed with me, allowing his sister to move faster without us. She gave me one small, defeated glance as she became mist. I shucked off my boots, jacket, and various weapons, then slid into my bedroll. For hours, it seemed, I laid there thinking and not thinking in turn, trying to sort out what to do next. We couldn't stay in the countryside forever. In fact, we all knew that it was time to think about heading back to civilization. We needed to be present in the cities and towns. Needed to be amongst our folk, with or without him. My solitary life in the human realm wasn't looking so bad anymore. I would trade my anxiety attacks for this numbness. Loneliness for this abyss of helplessness.

Silas and I sparred every day to keep up our strength. He

taught me archery as well. His hands adjusted my hips, directing my body's angle for aiming my bow. Each kick of his boot against my heel was a gentle indication of proper foot placement. I did as I was told and became proficient, arrows flying true. He was patient and gentle, never pushing me to snap out of it, unlike his sister. Corra lost her cool with me one day after being fed up with my vacant company. She yelled and shoved me, telling me to get a grip. I simply shrugged and walked away.

Corra's leaving felt like a chapter's end. We would no doubt go to Laorinaghe, and from there migrate back to Saarlaiche or Eíleín Reínhe. The night pressed in on me and I began to hate the looming dawn. My breathing hitched and I started to feel my anxiety rising. It was better than nothing, I supposed. Buzzing filled my ears. Shuffling sounded behind me and Silas's warmth pressed against my back. His arms circled around me, and he tucked his head onto my shoulder, offering the comfort of a friend. For a moment, it felt like that hotel in Varna so long ago with Cadeyrn. I struggled for breath. As heat pricked up my spine and scalp, a light misting rain fell on us, cooling me down. I always overheated during my anxiety attacks, then was left shaking and cold in the aftermath.

For the first time in three weeks, I sagged. Exhaustion and misery finally had my eyes filling and a great sob came out. Silas's arms tightened around me. I felt his floppy brown hair against my face as he pressed his own into my shoulder. Ugly, racking sobs came out of me, churning my stomach. Still he held on, as if grief weighed heavy on him as well.

"This is it, isn't it?" I managed. He knew what I meant.

"Yes."

"Where will we go? I don't know where to go, Silas," I admitted.

"Your mother will want you with her," he answered quietly.

"I don't want to be there. I am not *that* princess. I don't know who I am anymore." I pressed my hands into my eyes.

"You are that princess. You are still his mate. You are who you always have been, *Allaine Trubaiste*."

"In the stories," I said softly, "the ones Cadeyrn's mother told him, *baethaache* could only be expelled if the male died." I swallowed. "Mine feels different. As a child I could summon her. He never could. Is his different? Is there any hope, Silas?"

"There's always hope, *Trubaiste*," he answered. "His power is different. Perhaps he needs to learn to separate his magic from that of the *baethaache*."

"I can't use my magic," I admitted to him.

"I know." He kissed the back of my head. "We could sense its absence."

"Is it gone? Am I . . . broken?"

"No! Dammit!" He turned me toward him and grabbed my chin. His face, shadowed by the dim firelight, was awash in anger. "You are not broken. By the fucking gods and *moinchai* shite. You have been through so much in such a short time. Your body is trying to protect itself. You have cloaked yourself," he said, staring into my eyes, "That's all."

"You have been through a lot too, Silas," I said, staring right back. "How do you not fall apart?"

He considered for a moment then cupped the side of my face. "I let my purpose be my shield. Instead of ducking behind it, I thrust it forward and move on."

"I heard you bedded your way across the battle camps. Is that what you mean?"

He rasped a laughed and pressed his forehead to mine. "That's one way. I could help you with that aspect if you insist," he joked. I smiled. Smiled. He felt the lifting of my cheek and poked me in the stomach. "See, you're in there, *Trubaíste.*"

I whacked his arm.

"I do love you, Silas." I said it in an amused way but meant it. He snorted. "I do. If it were the end of battle and I had to choose, I would save you over saving myself. Over saving the world, even." Well, that sounded really dumb. Thunder rumbled overhead.

"It's because of my glorious male body as you said. I know."

I laughed and laid my head against his chest, watching a streak of lightning cross the night sky.

"Yes, certainly it's because of that. That and the fact that every time I've fallen, it's you alone who has picked my sorry ass up."

"Weeel, you're so snotty when you fall apart. Someone has to do it. It's embarrassing."

I laughed again into his chest and breathed in his woodsy scent. A flash of lightning brightened the forest around us, and I felt a fluttering in my stomach. My magic.

"Silas," I whispered.

"I felt it," he said. I clutched his arm and there was another flutter. The sky flashed bright again, and my beastie purred. I smiled, looking at my friend, and touched my stomach. The brightest flash yet illuminated the sky, night turning to day. I counted to three and the thunder shook the ground. Electricity sparked through me, and I sat upright, Silas with me. White light surrounded us as I concentrated and reached toward the sky just as lightning flashed again. The bolt met with my hand and the electricity danced at my fingertips before fading away. I grinned like an idiot and tackled Silas to the ground and kissed his cheek over and over like an enthusiastic puppy. He laughed, then stilled. Oh. I had forgotten all the things he had admitted to me. His feelings for me.

"I'm sorry," I said, ducking my head.

"No. I am. It's just . . . Sometimes it's harder than others."

Shit. Needles of guilt crawled through my mind. Reminding me of how new this all still was for us all. Silas made space for me and my grief, regardless of his own.

"Thank you. For helping me. For always helping me." Like stars blinking in the sky, thoughts and ideas floated around my mind.

"I have an idea," I said, alighting on a thread. "You said there were temples to each element. I would like to forge my own."

WE CLEARED OUR CAMP, leaving only the fire. Around it we dug five additional holes and built a small fire in each. Silas gathered six stones from the riverbed and dried them off. He sketched rudimentary representations of the element to which each fire would be dedicated. I copied each symbol onto a river rock, scratching it with my dagger, along with the symbols I had carved in the stones while left in my captivity. From a piece of parchment we carried, I wrote a blessing to the elements and a promise to care for each. On the sixth stone, I scratched the same eye and dagger, and a heart with beastly wings, 'C & N' carved in the center. I had no real crystals to add to the makeshift temple, but I had my engagement ring with its large diamond and eight embedded gems: aquamarine sitting under the center diamond, emerald, amethyst, topaz, sapphire, moonstone pearl, peridot, and black tourmaline, which was on the underside of the band.

"These gems are the symbols of each province," Silas told me. I had known that yet didn't know which stone represented which province. Hadn't had time to find out. "Moonstone pearl is Maesarra. Aquamarine is Saarlaiche. Amethyst for Veruni, emerald and topaz are Neanire and Prinaer. Sapphire is Laorinaghe. Peridot is Dunstanaich, and black tourmaline is Festaera, because we all need protection from those fuckers," he explained.

I placed my ring just before the center fire, hoping no harm would come to it.

One by one, I walked from each fire, placing its stone and the written message in the flames, and reciting a prayer to find him and bring him home. Safely home. When I reached the center fire, I placed both the heart carved stone and the stone he had saved from my antics. Impulsively, I flicked out my dagger—the one Cade had given me for Yule—and sliced my palm. I heard Silas's sharp intake of breath and his extra plea to the gods. As I dripped my blood over the fire and over my ring, I recited my last entreaty to the elements, spirits who care for this realm, old gods, and whomever chose to listen at the moment.

"There was a time," I said aloud, facing the flames, "that nothing kept me tethered to life. I had lost all that I thought I'd had, and I had no purpose. When I met my mate and his cousins, seeds of life were planted in my soul. I breathed freely for the first time since I was a child. They are my family. I fell in love with my mate in a slow tangle of not understanding how deeply I could care for someone. I never knew," I sobbed. "I never knew I could feel like that. To want and be wanted and need him and have the barest touch make me come alive. I wanted years with him. I wanted . . ." My voice cracked, and I felt Silas behind me, placing his hand on my lower back. "I wanted children." I took a deep breath. "I am pleading with who or whatever is listening to help me find my mate, and I swear I will work to make this world a better place. I swear it." I squeezed my fist, and blood dripped out. I smelled the copper of Silas slicing his hand as well, dripping it in the flames.

"I swore months ago that you two would be together again," Silas began. "I swore to make that happen and twice now, you have been robbed of time. By my blood, Neysa, I swear we will get him back, and you will have your years together. On my life. By my love."

I pressed his palm to mine. The fires grew and burned ferociously for a moment, then settled. Rain resumed overhead, sending smoke in every direction, and I knew in my heart that it was searching for him. I leaned my head against Silas, our palms still together. As dawn tiptoed across the sky, the fires burnt to embers. I retrieved my ring, which was covered in ash and blood but not worse for wear. We went to each fire, and the ashes in each were concentrated on the same side. South. In the center fire, our rock with the heart glowed like a coal.

"You called me Neysa," I said.

"It is your name, is it not?"

"Yeah, but you never use it."

"Eh. Seemed like an occasion to be formal, what with the creepy blood-letting and all."

I burst out laughing and, after replaying the scene in my head, laughed even harder. "It was a bit dramatic, huh?"

"Let's just say, if I go missing, you had better think of something fucking memorable to top this."

"Don't go missing, my friend," I told him.

"Oh, I may, just to mess with you and see what you come up with. Maybe add costumes and such." I hit him on the leg.

We cleared our things and set off to Laorinaghe to find Corra.

LAORINAGHE WAS MOSTLY PEACEFUL, I had been led to believe, so we hadn't anticipated the threat. Lorelei had seemed incensed by Analisse at the summit. The summit where it had all gone to hell. I wondered often at the severity of the wound my mate took in throwing himself in front of my mother. Had he healed in his usual way, even though he was trapped as the beast? Silas and I met Corra at the rendezvous point we had discussed prior to her departure. It was on the edge of the city, on a hilltop that had a vantage point of the city proper and the sea beyond. Even from up here, we could spot it. Past the white buildings topped with blue and green roofs, which looked as if the city was a part of the sea itself, there were torches and soldiers along the coast. Boats were moored in a blockade.

Initially, we had thought this was in our favor—Lorelei amassing her forces to stand with us.

"There are wards as soon as one enters the city," Corra chimed, not bothering with pleasantries once we had caught up with her. "I figured out where the border of the wards is, and Silas, you and I can slip through. Neysa, you will have to stay out here."

"She can't stay alone. If there are wards and all that," Silas said, pointing to the soldiers. "Then there will be scouts up here. They are not ignorant of this landscape."

"I can stay hidden," I protested.

"You stand out like a dancing monkey in a public toilet," Silas commented.

"Where do you come up with this shit?" I asked.

"They were two incongruous things that came to mind. You understand the meaning."

"I agree with the sentiment," Corra said. "Though perhaps not the phrase. Especially without your magic, Neysa. What happened to you lot, anyway? What's with the scabs on your palms?"

I hadn't noticed the scabs. It was odd neither of ours had healed completely.

"*Trubaiste*, as you have your full magic back," Silas began, turning a pointed glance in his sister's direction. "I want you to stay hidden, near a bright, sunny place, aye? Should it seem that your hiding place becomes compromised, move to the bright spot and release the white light. We will make a run of the city and see if we can find out anything more. Meet you back here in two hours' time. If we do not return, you leave. Two hours, *Trubaiste*. Understand?"

I nodded, knowing he didn't believe me for a second.

He swore and grabbed my chin. "You go to Maesarra. Find Ewan. You go where it is safe. Do not come after us. Once you are within those wards, you are trapped." His sea glass eyes shot daggers into me.

"He is right," Corra said, adjusting her scabbard and daggers. "You are needed. Especially if we are all gone. Without you—"

"Without me, there's Ewan."

"I need you to see him safe," she whispered. "Don't ever tell him that or there will be hell to pay. Stay hidden. Stay safe. Two hours." They dissolved into mist, and only a smudge on the horizon told me they were moving into the city.

I ducked into a thicket of rosemary which butted against both a large tree and a boulder. And there I sat, shifting from leg to leg, waiting and watching the time. There were scouts. I could hear them mostly in the distance. The sun began dipping low, and ever-increasing shadows fell over the wilderness above the city. I fished through my pack and quickly ate a piece of cheese and dried meat, really wanting the apple but knowing it would make too much noise. I checked and rechecked my weapons. Two daggers sheathed on my gauntlets, short sword and scythe on either thigh, throwing knives on my bootstraps, long sword down my spine, and bow over a shoulder. Just before the two hours were up and I began to get twitchy, scouts started yelling to one another. I couldn't tell what they were saying, but there seemed to be a scramble to reach the city. The minutes clicked by, and at two hours the twins were nowhere to be seen. I unfolded from my rosemary hideout only to find a uniformed female stood directly in front of me. I covered a gasp and a stumble.

She seemed just as surprised to see me. We faced one another.

"Who are you?" she demanded.

"Neysa."

Her eyes went wide.

"The princess?" She shifted on her feet, and my hands shot to my weapons.

"What is the commotion down there? Why are there wards on the city?" I demanded of her.

"You shouldn't be here," she said quietly. "We are ordered to kill you. All of you."

"Ordered by whom? My mother is Queen. There is no law beyond that."

"Lady Lorelei. I will not kill you now, but I beg of you to leave." Crashing sounded behind us and two guards appeared. I tensed, and the female guard gave me a sharp, warning glance before turning back to them. "I have found a straggler from that caravan from yesterday," she announced to them.

"Kill her," one said. "I can't be assed to bring another one in for questioning. Plus, I want those weapons."

"Come and get them then," I purred, spinning and flicking two of my throwing knives at them. Each found their mark in the hip crease of either guard. This was beginning to be my signature move. They yelled and yanked the knives out, then sloppily launched themselves at me, swords swinging. Pulling my sword free of its scabbard, I ducked and slashed, steel hitting steel.

"Yva!" One yelled to the guard. "Kill her!"

"Yva," I said, thrusting my sword into the exposed armpit of the mouthy guard. He screamed and swore at me. "Either help me or attack me." She seemed to consider, honey-colored eyes mapping the scene. She even so far as took a step toward me with her blade.

Sharp steel nicked the inside of my arm. Blood ran freely into my gauntlet. Her face seemed too open for deceit as she watched my injuries with something like fear on her face. She tipped her chin slightly, a barely noticeable movement, and I knew she would side with her queen. Yva joined the fight and pushed against her comrades.

"Traitorous filth!" the quiet one finally chimed in.

"I will not follow orders that go against my Queen," she answered, and I saw her spin to gain momentum. Yva became a whirling dervish of movement before slamming into the quiet guard, knocking him into the next. Her movement reminded me of dust devils dancing on the side of the freeway in California. She drew back to spin again, and I allowed my electricity to surge through me into my sword and watched as the metal conducted the power through the guard's sword into his body. Because his compatriot had fallen against his shoulder, it took him too. They turned to ash. I stepped back, sword high.

"Swear your allegiance," I demanded, sounding nothing like the half-broken woman I was when I first came to Barlowe Combe. She sank to a knee and held her sword to me.

"I swear allegiance to Queen Saskeia and, by default, Her Highness, Princess Neysa." I gave her a quick nod and sheathed my blade.

"Why the wards?" I asked again. A roar so loud it made the trees tremble sounded from the city below. A roar that I had heard only once, right before powerful wings beat across the sea. He was here. I knew then why the wards. To keep him in. He could not change, could not access his non-corporeal magic. Prickles of the magic connecting me with Cadeyrn quickened my heartrate. Was it possible he was so near? Could I rely on my faulty heart as compass? "Do you know where he is?" I asked, voice shaky.

"He?" she asked.

"The creature," I said, and swallowed. "My mate."

"There are caves. By the beach. You won't be able to leave if you go in there," she warned.

"Then I will stay with him," I said, and took off at a sprint.

Chapter 2

Silas

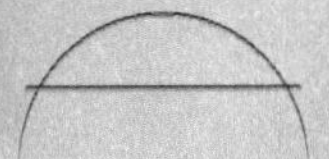

Of course he would have landed himself here. Cadeyrn said I was always getting into trouble, yet when he got himself in it, he was neck-deep in poisonous shite. I scented him as soon as we crossed the wards. Corraidhín and I got as far as the city center when we saw a protective circle. Salt and crystals dotted the streets. For just a moment, our magic vanished, leaving us heaving on the cobbled streets, and the light from the setting sun glared off the too-white buildings, blinding us. That was all it took to catch us. They knew they couldn't stifle our magic for more than a split second. A contingent of hundreds of guards surrounded the square.

"Any brilliant ideas, sister?" I asked, unsheathing my twin swords.

"None you're going to like."

It was too close quarters to lose our forms now. We would be more vulnerable during the dissolution. So, we held our weapons high.

"We are emissaries from Her Majesty the Queen," I said, my voice carrying. "We bear no threat to you."

"You trespass on the Sacred City. We have orders to dispose of you. Lady Lorelei does not recognize Saskeia as Queen," claimed a voice from the center of the lineup.

"Surely her lack of recognition is not shared by all of you?" I smirked, trying to catch a few shifty eyes. The whine of steel being drawn pierced my ears. "We are not alone, and your Sacred City will be a battle ground if you keep your loyalties to this insurgence. If you value your city and are for the good of all of Aoifsing, stand with us."

For a second there, I really thought most of the little fuckers would stand behind us. Gods know what they had been promised. A good half moved to face their peers in defiance.

"Yeah, well, that'll do," I said, and whirled, Corraidhín and I fighting back-to-back. I knew damn well we wouldn't make the two hours just as I knew Neysa wouldn't leave.

I had no idea how long we moved through the guards, but I was tiring and I knew my sister's magic was sputtering. I transferred some of my energy to her, the electricity in me vaulting from my veins to hers. In doing so, each pixel of the fae female dripped into salt water, building higher and more violent. She became the sea. A rogue wave, washing forty or so insurgents from the battle. I dissolved myself a bit and was able to move quickly through the confused lines of the onslaught, slicing and stabbing as quickly as picking weeds. Which I had never done, but in my blood-addled mind, it seemed about accurate. Bells began tolling, more soldiers rushing into the square. My sister's corporeal absence left another wall of sea water which took down hundreds more.

Then I heard him. That beastly little hellion roared so loud the whole godsdamned city shook. Blue roof tiles crashed down, and people ran screaming from their homes. I had no plan at this point. My magic was fizzling, Corraidhín's was as well, and my sword arm was nearly useless. The slice on my palm where I had sworn to Neysa to bring my cousin to her had ripped open, and the hilt of my sword bit into the opening. Blood ran down my arm.

Neysa, get the hell out of here, I thought to myself, wishing I had that connection she had with my cousin. For about a million different reasons.

"Cadeyrn!" I yelled, amplifying my voice so it carried across the city. There was a pause, then the battle commenced. Thundering footsteps sounded. The boots of a thousand soldiers. For fuck's sake. How big of a regiment did Lorelei have? Up through the streets, knocking buildings and soldiers down, I realized it wasn't a thousand soldiers, but one pissed off beast, dragging chains, headed right for us.

Fuck the gods, he was hideous. I was a bit envious. Especially as, even though he was bound and his wings looked as though many arrows had pierced them, he pushed through the crowd, culling soldiers until the remaining ones who stood against us fled. The beast looked at us, and I wasn't sure either Corraidhín or I was breathing,

"You do have a flair for the dramatic, cousin," I said before I could think of something better to say. My sister swore and shook her head. The beast huffed. Its eyes glowed and nostrils flared. It stepped closer to me and thrust his fucking great head into my bleeding hand and licked at it. I puked. Right there. Maybe because of the battle high or the fact that my cousin was now a bloody great monster, or maybe just the fact that the monster had licked my godsdamned hand. Once the purge settled, I saw that the cut had healed. His eyes were wild, casting about for . . . oh. Looking for *Trubaíste*. Her blood had mingled with mine.

"Do you know us, cousin?" my sister asked. His giant head cocked to the side. He huffed and sunk down. I wanted to take those fucking chains off him. I stepped forward and he growled. I held up my hands.

"Silas," Corra warned. I knew if the situation were reversed, Cadeyrn would risk everything to free me of chains.

"Cousin, I want to remove the chains. Will you let me? So you can get to Neysa." He became agitated and started whipping the chains around as though to break them. I ducked, covering my head.

"Stop this," my sister scolded him as she always did to us. "That's enough, Cadeyrn. Settle yourself and we can fix this."

He lay down, defeated. I snorted, and those huge eyes, the same color as my own, narrowed at me. I walked to him and lifted the chain. I knew he was a split second away from gnashing those fangs at me, but I ignored him, looking to the cuffs and the chains themselves to see where the weak spot would be. I brought my sword down on the chain and released the weight. He didn't move. The cuffs needed to come off, and we were on borrowed time out in the open city. Dredging up the last scraps of my power, I shoved most of what I had left of my power into the metal, filling them with enough exposure and mist to rust them completely.

"You can stop looking at me like that, you great shite." I spoke while I worked, just as he always did for me when he healed me. "I swore an oath to your mate." He thrashed a bit, knocking me down. "Calm down. Stop thinking with your cock. She nearly lost herself over you, you know. Lost her magic for a long while. I tried to convince her I would be much more suitable . . ."

"Holy fucking gods, brother," my sister swore. The beast narrowed those eyes again and snorted a great nasty sound that may have been a laugh.

"But, *Trubaíste* that she is, she decided that rather than spend her days with me in the forest," I continued, even though both he and Corraidhín growled, "she would build her own godsdamned temples in the middle of the forest. Temples, brother. She had me digging fire pits in the middle of the night, and called upon the Aulde Gods, the elements, the ghosts of the past, and everything in between to help her find you. You, you great hulking sack of shite." I could hear my sister sniffle a little. She never cried. I rusted one cuff so thoroughly that it broke apart as soon as my dagger tapped it. On to the next. "Do you know what she said—apart from that she loved me too?" I winked at him, and he snapped his teeth at me. Eh, too far, then. "She said that in her whole life—" I pointed at him. "Are you paying attention? In her whole life, she never thought she could feel the way she feels with you, you stupid arse. She said she wanted so many years with you and . . . maybe I shouldn't be the one telling you . . ."

"Then perhaps don't, brother," Corraidhín said, low and viscous. I ignored her.

"She said that she wants children with you. And she swore on her blood that she would do what is in her power to protect the realm if she could have you back." He swung his back as the cuff fell away and his chains were released. His great beastly head, nearly the size of my whole body, pinned me down on the cobbled streets. I probably shouldn't have said that about her loving me. Even though it was true.

"The thing is, cousin," I said, poking my finger into his leathery scaled chest. "She wants Cadeyrn back. So get your godsdamned shit back together and separate the beast from the male!" I screamed in his face, not caring by then if he ripped me apart. I swore an oath. He snarled, dripping bloody spit onto me. I thought I might puke again. It was that spit. By the gods, it was rank.

It was then that a rain of arrows fired down on us. I took one in the shoulder as I rolled, shield up. Corraidhín waved her arm and drowned the archers in the mist from the gathering night. I knew she was as spent as I was. We needed to get out of there. My cousin lay there, thirty or so arrows sticking out of him at various spots. Most through his wings, one in his chest, though it still rose and fell. There was one through the side of his face. Visions of when our parents were killed shot through my mind like moving pictures, giving me a last burst of strength.

"Fucking hell," I yelled. I tried to push him over. I tried to move him, but he was solid. Suddenly, he stood up and took off toward the water. We followed behind. He rounded on the beach where hundreds of soldiers lay drowned, victims of my sister's waves, then banked and headed for the cliffs. Eventually, we followed him into a cave. Torches lined the walls, and the brackets remained where his chains had been hung on the stone walls. This is where he'd been confined.

"Bloody hell," Corraidhín swore. "Silas, he needs healing."

He collapsed onto the sandy ground and passed out.

"He needs me," *Trubaiste* said from the cave mouth. Of course she bloody found us.

CHAPTER 3

NEYSA

There were so many arrows in him that I didn't know where to start. The twins were breaking them off and pulling them out as I applied pressure to the wounds. The one in his cheek made my heart hurt. Each shimmering scale reflected the last dying light of day. Our *baethaache* reminded me of the mythical beasts depicted in idyllic medieval tapestries. Wyvern-like with our leathery wings, yet softer in the face, like a dog. Cadeyrn's spiked terror in others, with the deep inkwell of its coloring and double rows of teeth which resembled glass shards. The injuries had him smeared in blood, panting and unconscious. I lowered down and placed my hand on his face, my beastie growling in response, beating her wings. I let them flare out from me, shielding him. The twins barked at me as the wings pushed them back. I covered him with my wings and laid down on the sand along his side. Had it been me, battleworn and bloody, his presence would have done more than any bandage could. After weeks of sleeping on the ground, the fact that it was sand did nothing to staunch the exhaustion pulling at me. I drifted asleep, my magic spooling from me in threads and ribbons, winding into my mate as he laid unconscious beside me, no longer a fae male, but a beast.

No dreams marred my sleep. I started coming to before opening my eyes and felt that Corra and Silas were not in the cave. Deep, even breathing sounded beside me. My wings had faded back into me, and I breathed in. My eyes sprung open.

Peridot eyes looked back at me. Not the eyes of a beast. The water colored eyes of the male who was my mate. Drawn cheeks and thumbprints of shadow smudged under those eyes in stark contrast to his too pale skin and raven hair. A painful lump caught in my throat.

"Cadeyrn?" I asked quietly. I reached a hand up slowly to touch him.

Please tell me you haven't forgotten me, I said to his mind, brushing the tip of his ear with my fingers, and his eyes closed. A sound came out of him that was more of a croak. Red stained his cheeks. I had never seen him blush. The color lit his eyes aflame.

I haven't used my voice in so long.

There are vocal warmups you could do. Like A-E-I-O-U. Red leather, yellow leather. It helps your singing voice...

His mouth was on mine.

That's not a vocal warmup per se.

To hell with the vocal warmup, he said, keeping his lips crushed against mine.

Silas rounded the corner then.

"Is everything . . . Oh. Well, that's a change," he said. "I'm not sure you're in any shape for any of that, cousin," he teased. A snarl ripped from Cadeyrn.

"I'm in fine shape . . . cousin," he managed to choke out, though his voice was grainy and rough. Silas snickered, and Corra walked in.

"Sorry to interrupt, but we are in an enemy city and there is a female dressed in the livery of Lorelei's guards saying she knows Neysa and swore allegiance to her. Am I killing her or is she telling the truth?"

"Yva. Yes, she fought her kinfolk with me."

Corra made an agreeable sound and left.

"We have sent hawks warning our known allies and have called for aid," Silas informed us as he tossed clothes at Cadeyrn.

"Lorelei was here," my mate said. "She personally set up the wards. I couldn't get out and I was injured enough for them to shackle me. She sat by me for days. Time was difficult. I was me but not. How long has it been?"

"Nearly a month," I said softly, my voice hinging on a sob. He swore, low and vicious. I watched as he pulled on the trousers and tunic, strapping weapons to himself. "What now?"

"Do you remember the story I told you? The one my mother used to tell about the *baethaache* who flew all over playing spy?"

"What have you been up to?" I asked. His answering smile was devilish.

He had visited the domain of each representative, individual of influence—whether financial or political—and military personnel. Information gleaned in his shadowed *baethaache* persona from those visits would clue us in as to where we could place our trust in the coming conflict. He had been planning to take to the seas and monitor Dockman's marine affairs when magically launched spears and arrows brought his beast down just off the coast of Laorinaghe. My hand stayed over his heart, fingers feeling every beat, almost uncaring of the success he had.

AN OFFICIAL AUDIENCE was requested with Lorelei and her ministry. Yva gathered known resistance to the Elders. Most residents did not understand what their representative was doing in sealing off the city. Having her guards under instruction to kill the royal family was a surprising and unprecedented course of action. We walked through the streets offering warmth to people and speaking of an Aoifsing with representation from the people. By noon, a messenger found us with an invitation to join Lady Lorelei for dinner. Our hawks had come back as well, bringing news of forces at the ready in other cities and a regiment on the way to us. They wouldn't arrive until tomorrow or the following day, so we were on our own until then.

There was an inn near the sea where we settled for the afternoon, Yva agreeing to bring us clothing to wear to the dinner meeting.

"What did I look like?" Cadeyrn asked after bathing. He stood in front of a clouded mirror, a worn towel wrapped about his hips. "I know I had wings. And I saw talons."

I stopped finger combing my wet hair and walked to him, tucking my own towel in under my arms.

"You were magnificent." I looked into his eyes. "Shall I show you?" He took my hand and I pressed it to his face, showing him my vision of him.

"What if I hadn't been able to change back?" A weighted question. One which I didn't know how to answer. So, of course, my lacking social skills cracked a joke. A bad joke.

"I would have had a pet all the other kids would be envious of." He frowned, and I held onto his hand even as he turned away. "There is no magic stronger than this," I said, my electricity crackling between us, meeting his heat. "What's between us can shatter this realm if we let it. And if I had to let my beastie take over, then so be it." He stilled and focused his eyes on me.

"No. You do not change for me. You do not change for anyone. Silas said . . ." He coughed. "He told me about the oath you swore." My eyes were clear and met his as he held up my palm, grasp gentle, voice knowing. "He told me some of what you said . . . during the oath, I suppose. It's foggy as I was not exactly me. I smelled you on him—your blood, that is— and he was able to bring me back." He stopped and fidgeted with the thigh holster that was sitting on the wooden table beside us.

"What did he tell you?" I asked softly.

"He said you wanted children. With me." He didn't quite meet my eyes.

"I want everything with you. I understand if you don't— or can't."

Slowly, he turned back to me, a crooked smile softening his face.

"Don't be stupid, Neysa," he said with a twinkle in his eye. "Shall we get a head start on that now?" he asked, pointing to the bed. I tugged him closer using his towel, but then there came a knock at the door. We laughed.

"Typical."

Yva brought us two options each to wear. She included old livery underpinnings to stash in our packs in case we had to take off, plus formal wear and something casual.

"I didn't know what royals might want to wear," she admitted.

"Oh, Yva, we aren't picky." I told her. Cadeyrn changed into the formal wear, which was a cobalt blue jacket that buttoned up the front with black trousers that tucked into his boots. I saw Yva out and turned to begin dressing myself but stopped dead looking at Cadeyrn. I had never seen him wear color. Ever. Not that I was complaining. I could live my life and enjoy him in his black, grey, and white, but the cobalt on him was striking. He finished buckling on his various weapons and caught me staring, slack-jawed.

"What?" he asked, confused. I shook my head and ducked behind a screen to slip my dress overhead.

"I have never seen you wear color," I called while doing up little gold buttons here and there all over the top of the gold dress.

"I have worn color . . . just . . . not often."

"Well, it suits you. Although, really, what doesn't? It must be hard being so gorgeous," I teased him. He snorted and muttered something I couldn't hear.

The dress itself was ankle length with slits up the side to mid-thigh. The bodice came up in two separate pieces to cover my assets while buttoning in four spots between my ribs, then more little buttons under the arms, linking the bust to the back of the dress. I knew Yva was my sort of girl when she said she threw in some bronze gauntlets she 'found along the way'. I slipped them on and moved from behind the screen to tend to my hair in front of the tiny mirror. It was still mostly damp, but the temperate air was letting the waves form without frizz. I twisted small sections back away from my face, and, as I lacked pins to secure it, I tied the length of my hair in a low knot. It wouldn't last the evening, but that didn't worry me. When I turned to grab my own sword belt and daggers, Cadeyrn stood right behind me.

"This dress is fit for a queen," he said, running a finger down the material, making me shiver. I cleared my throat.

"If we weren't running late, I would show you how the skirt splits." I lifted my leg and propped it on the table to strap on a couple more daggers. The material fell away. He growled. "Oh, look. That's how."

"I think I'm closer to my beast than I knew. We really should have taken a bit more time alone before all hell breaks loose."

I laughed and pushed onto my tiptoes to kiss him quickly before pulling him out the door. The twins were waiting outside the door, dressed similarly to us. It was Silas who spoke up.

"You two will never be able to fight in those dresses."

"I can fight in anything," I answered. "My boobs might come out; but I can still fight."

Silas and Corra roared and Cadeyrn rolled his eyes, which made me laugh. He then smirked at me.

"That's the spirit."

CHAPTER 4

NEYSA

Cypress trees lined the road leading to the palace in the Sacred City of Laorinaghe. As we neared, palace guards lined the drive and the steps into the building. The gate rolled up, and we were admitted, walking four abreast through an open-air atrium with potted citrus and olive trees sprinkled around merrily bubbling fountains. A guard asked us to follow him up a wide, winding staircase to the next level, quite a way up. We followed further into the palace, along the terracotta floor, through arched doorways lined with flowering climbing vines, and into a dimly lit dining room.

"Welcome to my home," a voice called from the archway. Lorelei stood, a half-smile on her face. She tsked. "It is generally regarded as poor form to upstage the host with your attire. Or do they not teach that in the human realm?" she asked, clearly speaking to me. Her eyes zeroed in on my engagement ring and narrowed, though she had seen it at the summit last month.

"I was limited in my selection at such short notice and wanted to be sure to honor, not upstage, my host, my lady."

She laughed at my response. "You're learning to play the game quite well, it seems. Such a change from the last time I saw you." She walked around us in a predatory circle, running a finger along Silas and Cadeyrn's shoulders.

"Corraidhín," Lorelei said. "You are looking well. You have been sneaking around my city for the past few days, my spies tell me. Find anything of interest?"

"I am happy to begin that part of the discussion, my lady," Cadeyrn spoke with dangerous quiet. "Though we were under the impression that this was a dinner."

"Ah, the *cuídvsite*," she said to him, walking over. She placed a finger on his jacket, and it took everything in me not to rip it off her for calling him a monster. "I miss my pet." She pouted and turned away, walking to Silas. Cadeyrn stiffened beside me.

"You may sit by me. Your reputation precedes you." With that she walked to the table. I was ready to rip out every honey-colored hair on her head and peel the golden-brown skin from her face. Cadeyrn's hand shot to mine and squeezed before speaking mind to mind through our bond.

Control it, Neysa. She's baiting us all.

I'm going to kill her for the pet comment alone.

That's only because you wanted me for a pet first. It's pet-ty jealousy.

Oh. My. God. That was the worst joke in the history of jokes.

It certainly was. I may throw myself from the parapet over there because of it.

I stifled a laugh and sat down next to Silas, Cadeyrn coming to sit across from me. A salad with hard cheese and dates topped with marinated olives was brought out and placed before us. We picked at the course for a few minutes, and I was almost embarrassed by the amount of bread I was eating.

"Lorelei," Corra spoke. "I do love that gown. The color

suits you very well." The mint green chiffon did look lovely on her skin. I would admit it even though she had had hundreds of guards attack us and kept my mate as a pet. Right now, I pictured a slowly spreading stain of blood across the material. "I like it almost as much as that yellow you wore on summer solstice all those years ago. That yellow was . . ." Corra let her voice get a bit smoky.

"Hmm. Yes. Thank you, Corraidhín." Lorelei turned to us.

Salad plates were cleared, and a terrine of ground meat and potato was brought out. We ate again in silence.

What do you think she's doing? Stalling for time? I asked Cadeyrn in my mind.

I am not sure. I think Corraidhín is sussing it out.

Silas has been unusually quiet as well.

I agree. Let's sit tight and see what happens. His eyes met mine across the table.

Good, because this is the first meal I've had in ages that didn't need to be skinned first and I really want dessert.

You know what I want? My mate's voice darkened, and I looked up, but he continued pushing the meat and potato onto the back of his fork.

Couldn't imagine. Ugh, I couldn't even pretend to say that without a shiver.

I'm sure you could. Watercolor eyes met mine as I saw his throat bob with his swallow.

Peanut butter cookies?

Yes. We both smiled, a shy smile meeting me across the platters of food. I'd wished he had sat beside me.

"So, Lorelei," Silas crooned, leaning toward her. She pushed her ringlets back over her shoulder and cocked an eyebrow at him. "Do you not have an entourage? We dine alone with you."

"I thought it best to have you all to myself," she purred, placing her hand on the table between them.

"I'm not complaining," he drawled. "I was just wondering if we could have a private tour of . . . the palace." Something changed in her face, and I wondered if he pushed his leg into hers. She flushed.

"We shall see," she said, her voice rough.

I felt Corra's magic slip out in drops and beadlets. I sensed I was missing dessert. Cadeyrn shifted, and an ember of his power slipped around me like a second skin.

Did you just shield me? I asked him.

Something is up. Are you ready to engage her in conversation?

"Lorelei," I said. "While I am glad you enjoy my friend's company, tell me. What are you trying to do here? There was no ultimate rule over Aoifsing. The provinces were still going to run mostly independent of one another. Why put a death order on my family?"

"Better question," Corra chirped in. "Where is Lorelei?"

Cadeyrn swore, and I could feel his power snaking toward her, unraveling whatever spell was there.

She laughed nervously and rang a bell. Three chairs shot back, and I followed suit. Guards entered the room, effectively cornering us.

"Do not come closer," Cadeyrn said to them in a voice that promised death. "She is not your Lady Lorelei, and she threatens the life of your queen and princess."

"Kill them all," Lorelei, who was not Lorelei, ordered. They stepped closer, faltering a bit.

"For centuries, this province has lived in peace. Why now would your representative choose to sever ties with the rest of Aoifsing?" my mate asked them. One bloodthirsty guard charged from the back and it set them all off like a pack. The four of us slammed our power into them. A relative hurricane of force took out the whole lot of them. More boots pounded down the hall. Silas threw the table against the door, blocking it for the moment.

"Who are you?" Corra demanded.

"She is Julissa, Analisse's sister," Silas offered. "I knew her scent was different from Analisse. I knew hers rather intimately." His words sent a shot of raw anger through me.

"Where is Lorelei? Have you killed her?" I asked.

"Bah. No, no. She's too useful. I bound her tongue and powers. She was so frightened of you, *cuídvsite*," Julissa said, pointing at Cadeyrn. "When she slammed around in her cell too much and drew attention to herself, I would dump her in your cave to silence her." Holy shit. "Mostly, though, I need to keep her alive in order to keep the spell going."

The guards were beating against the door.

"You have to know that this won't end well for you," I said.

"For me? Oh, girl, you are sorely outnumbered. Though I was hoping to have a bit of fun with that one." She pouted at Silas. The door broke; the table splintered. She lashed out at Corra, who was nearest, and Corra dissolved before her and spun around the female in a waterspout, trapping her within.

"Guards of the Sacred City!" Cadeyrn called them to halt. "We have not come to harm anyone here. This female has been impersonating your Lady Lorelei. She is not who she claims to be and is the sister of the witch, Analisse." There was a murmur through the males in front of us. "Stand with us and help to find and free Lorelei. Stand against us and you will be killed. There will not be another warning."

Corra's waterspout sputtered out as Julissa's magic pounded against it. The guards took one look at Julissa and saw only Lorelei. They advanced. Cadeyrn moved first and swung his twin swords forward and back, cutting through the soldiers like they were nothing. The movement and speed with which he fought put mine to shame. Nevertheless, I followed him, stabbing and slashing as I went, my skirts swaying. The twins fought behind me, blades, water, and a compound of power that throbbed against me. I reached Cadeyrn, and we pressed our backs against each other, still fighting.

"Princess!" Julissa called. "I thank you for finding a traitor amongst my ranks."

I spun and saw that she had a knife at Yva's throat. Silas was closest, and I called him. He dropped into a slide and kicked the legs out from under both Yva and Julissa. Yva jumped to her knees only to take a sword to her side, making her fall again. I lunged for Yva and tried to staunch her bleeding as I pulled her out of the fray.

Silas had Julissa by the hair and pulled her hands behind her back. He walked backward to the throne room behind us and reversed up the steps to the dais. Corra and Cadeyrn were still taking down soldiers, though I noticed neither were making killing blows.

Get to the dais, Cadeyrn told me. *Stand beside Silas.*

You had better be right behind me. That better not have been a cryptic last words 'stand beside Silas' comment.

No, I just meant to literally get your ass up there.

So we did. By the time we had all made it up, Cadeyrn brought up a wall of impenetrable heat between us and the regiment beyond.

"Soldiers of the Sacred City," I called, fumbling and shaking with adrenaline. "This female is not your lady. She is wearing a cloaking spell to seem like Lorelei. She claims to be keeping your representative captive to keep her spell going. She held my mate captive here as well, forcing him to remain as a *baethaache*. I lay no claim to your lands. Find Lorelei and we will right this."

Cadeyrn finally unraveled the spell. As it shed, Julissa remained, the dress hanging on her thin frame. Where Lorelei was average height and full figured, Julissa was tall and statuesque. The soldiers all stopped and gasped.

"Find your lady!" I commanded.

Most of them dispersed to track down Lorelei. Some stormed the dais, eager to get a hold of Julissa.

"It is up to your lady to decide her fate," I said to them. "If you would assist in keeping her bound?"

"Your Highness," they intoned and bowed. That will never not be weird. I can count on one hand the times my name was said correctly at Starbucks, and here, everyone drops to their knees for me.

We sat there for over an hour waiting. Cadeyrn went to help find Lorelei while the rest of us stayed to contain Julissa. Yva's bleeding stopped as Silas kept a hard pocket of pressure against her wound.

"For the future, soldier," he said to the female, "I'm not one for too much color in my wardrobe." He gave her a silly smile, gesturing to his dark green jacket and brown pants.

"Duly noted. Next time, you can use your own coin to purchase your colorless wardrobe."

Oh, I did like Yva.

"Duly noted," he answered.

I saw Cadeyrn walking up through the hall, Lorelei in his arms. My heart sank. *Please be alive.* At the threshold, I saw movement. He set her down, and she walked, slowly and painfully, toward the dais. Her honey gold ringlets hung limp against her brown skin which was sallow from malnutrition. The dress she wore hung in tatters from her once voluptuous body. Anger flared in me. We stood in waiting before a large set of open windows facing the sea.

"This is the witch," Lorelei stated, voice vacillating between a rasp of what I assumed was her natural voice, and the higher pitch of Julissa's. "Bring her forth. If you please," she added with a slight bow to me. Corra and Silas kept Julissa bound and stepped forward. "You have led my folk to death.

You have caused irreparable damage to families and the sacred heart of their city. What have you to say, witch?"

Her voice belied a strength I knew was waning.

"My sister brought me with her here," Julissa insisted. "Before the summit when she was to meet with you. Your trust in her allowed her to take you captive and cloak me to be you. Her imprisonment and the stripping of her lands was unexpected. I am now without a home myself. I was victim here just as you were."

Lorelei tipped her head to the side and studied Julissa. She whipped a hand across the female's cheek and drew blood. Then whipped another across her chest.

"You caused chaos and destruction. You will not live." She swiped once more, and a deep gash lay across Julissa'a throat. Lorelei pulled the imposter off her feet and threw her through the open window, down to the rocky beach below. The moment was so brutal and drenched in wrath that I looked away. My mate caught the Lady of Laorinaghe as she swayed and nearly fell.

"I apologize for any destruction we have caused when the soldiers attacked us." I put a hand over my heart and faced her. She waved me off.

"It is done, Your Highness," she said softly. "My weakness for a certain woman led to this." She turned to Corra. "Was it you who figured it out?"

"She did not remember the summer solstice," Corra said with a wink. Lorelei chuckled.

"Ah. One could never forget that summer solstice."

"No, lady. I shall always have fond memories of your yellow dress."

The lady blushed, lighting up her sickly pallor.

"I thank you all and bid you to please stay here as long as you need."

"My lady," I called to her. "Yva is one of your guards who

was stationed beyond the wards yesterday. She saved my life and helped us today. She is quite loyal."

"Indeed? Your Highness's recommendation bears much weight. I shall see to her promotion myself."

Corra offered to escort the lady to her chambers along with a small contingent of guards. Cadeyrn and Silas walked Yva to the infirmary where another healer was brought to Yva as her injuries were not life-threatening. The throne room cleared out.

I was tired of these palace battles. Tired of throne room disasters. Just tired. The week I spent in Aemes doing nothing consequential with Cadeyrn before the summit seemed like a distant dream. I slumped onto the ledge of a fountain, facing out toward the sea. Gold satin spilled around me onto the terracotta floor. It was blood-splattered and torn. I looked down and adjusted the bust. I did not come popping out, which was surprising, but the top was soaked in sweat and blood, making me quite indecent. I didn't care. Slices and bruises marred where my arms were exposed, and my elbow ached. An old tendonitis issue had cropped back up. I knew it was because I had been gripping my sword too tight, and in the back of my mind I wondered why my fae body wasn't healing it. I needed to remember to have Cadeyrn tend to it. When he wasn't immersed in healing himself and everyone else.

"Your Highness." A soldier appeared and bowed at the waist. "Are you alright? Might I get you something?" He spoke softly, like I was a wounded animal. I tried to summon a smile, but I'm quite certain it was more of a grimace.

"Thank you, but I just needed to sit. Could . . . would you get me some water, please?"

He started to turn but stopped and offered his own canteen.

"If it doesn't offend, I would offer you mine whilst I fetch a pitcher for Your Highness."

I took the offered canteen with thanks.

"What is your name, sir?" I asked.

"Xaograos, lady," he said with a deep bow.

"Thank you, Xaograos. You are very kind."

"It is my honor to serve." He left his canteen with me and walked through the hall where bodies were still being carried away. So many had to die tonight. For what? They were all loyal to Lorelei and yet they died for that when we were all on the same team. I couldn't let that train of thought continue. As I stared out at the sea, a woman appeared before the alabaster railing. At first, I thought her a servant as she was dressed in homespun, a kerchief on her head. I wiped my eyes with the back of my hand, no doubt smearing blood across my face. The woman's form wavered, and I realized she was a spirit. I swallowed, a bit unnerved, and she smiled at me kindly.

"There will be trying times ahead," she said to me. I didn't know if anyone else could see or hear her. "You will face obstacles both friend and foe, but your path does not shift." A monologue so similar to the old woman in Peru last year. "Trust yourself. Do not lose heart, for that is where your true strength lies. Time shall alter you. Time shall wear on you." She began to fade.

"Wait!" I called. "What obstacles?"

"Many trials. If you keep your faith, you will persevere." She faded completely.

"Bloody hell," I muttered, hanging my head. I felt Corra slump next to me.

"My tits came out. Yours?" She asked. I smiled.

"Nope. Yours are bigger, though."

"Huh. Oh, well. You okay?"

"Can I let you know?"

"The others aren't back yet?" She pushed at a large puncture in her thigh. It was healing already, but an inch or so off would have hit an artery. I shook my head. "What did the ghost say?" Trust Corra not to beat about the bush.

"The usual. Trust yourself, blah, blah. You're going to encounter many horrible things, but it's okay because you are warm and fuzzy, etcetera."

"Och, that old chestnut."

"So, summer solstice."

"Lorelei would never have forgotten that."

"How long ago, Corra?"

"Twenty, maybe twenty-five years ago? Not sure."

"You two would have been quite a pair. The eyes on you two alone . . ." I said, nudging her with an elbow. She chuckled.

"Alas, we were not meant to be."

"What happened?"

"The truth is that I did not love her as she loved me. I loved her, and we were quite compatible in the bedroom, but I was missing something vital. The same feeling that stopped every relationship I have had in three hundred years." She was being so open. Corra rarely spoke of herself. She kept it all tightly sealed despite her intrinsic warmth. I didn't want to press her for details but wondered if she knew how deeply Ewan cared for her. It was not my place to say. He felt she would never settle down. "I am in love with Ewan," she said finally. "I think he is what has been missing, but I don't know if . . ."

"He was hurting. When we were gone. It took him a while to tell me. But we shared a common grief. He told me that he told you to move on. For your sake."

She stared at me.

"He didn't want you to feel like you owed him anything. But he said he loved you, Corra."

"Well." She sat up straighter. "I shall speak to him, then." She patted my knee. Xaograos brought a pitcher and cups and set them next to us. Corra grabbed the pitcher and chugged from it, then passed it to me. I followed suit, and a distinctly male chuckle sounded.

"You two are quite a sight." Cadeyrn took the pitcher from me and drank as well, then passed it to Silas. "Come, you lot," my mate said, offering his arm to help me up. "You're injured?" he asked, nostrils flaring.

"It's nothing." I turned my arm over and held it out to him. He unclipped the gauntlet, and a gash ran along where the top of the gauntlet met my skin. There was a decent amount of blood, which was likely why I felt as faint as I did. Rumbles of anger flittered through his touch as he held me a little closer. Quickly looking down at me, I caught a flash of that beast, vying for permission to escape. His exhaustion and anger held a tenuous chain to that beast. I hooked a foot around his ankle. A slight token of our here and now. An anchor in the tempest.

"I've found us quarters for the night." He covered my arm with his and led us away, his healing magic working its way to pull the skin back together. I turned back to the guard, who waited patiently, and handed him his canteen.

"My gratitude, Xaograos. I hope you can rest this evening."

"Your servant, Your Highness," Xaograos said.

Cadeyrn inclined his head to him in thanks.

"You want to tell me about the ghost?" he asked me as we walked through the tiled hall. I knew he would have seen or sensed her through our connection. I always had trouble controlling what I projected when I was exhausted.

"Maybe later. It was all fortune cookie mumbo jumbo."

"I believe that reference is somewhat lost on me, but I

assume it was typical oracle perils and heartache ahead but be true to thine self . . . ?"

"Precisely," I told him. I put my head against his shoulder as we walked. "We never do get to just stay in bed as long as we want, do we?"

"It will happen. I promise you."

CHAPTER 5

NEYSA

Another dress ruined. Another night I would spend without clothing. The satchel Yva packed us with the underpinnings was still in that inn by the sea. After bathing and scrubbing the blood from my skin, I thumped my head back onto the pillow and half-heartedly pulled the sheet up. The air was temperate enough that it was cool without being cold, warm without being uncomfortable. I wished Cadeyrn would hurry. After nearly a month without him, all I wanted was to feel his warmth around me. To breathe again with our souls entwined. A year ago, I would have said that was the biggest load of rubbish I had ever heard. A year ago, I would have sworn that love was fickle and insubstantial.

"And now?" my mate asked from the door to the bathing chamber, a blue and white towel slung low across his hips. My mouth went a bit dry.

"Now I know you are a part of me, and I want and need you as much as I need breath."

He used another towel to dry his hair. Every muscle on

49

him was pronounced and cut from his skin, his chest honed like granite.

"High protein diet worked out for you, then?" I teased a little breathlessly.

"Sorry you missed dessert," he said quickly. A little too quickly. I just looked at him and sat up a little, the sheet falling down. His eyes moved from my face and left trails like the sun on my skin. They travelled down my neck and collarbone, to the rise and fall of my chest, my peaked breasts, my stomach. I watched him move a little closer to the bed, the planes and tucks of muscle shifting as he walked. I saw that his hand was shaking a little as he ran it through his hair and reached back to grab the back of his neck, a gesture so familiar to me that my heart ached.

"Are you hurt?" I rasped, suddenly nervous. He gave me a shy, crooked smile and sat on the edge of the bed next to me. I reached for him, not wanting to be apart any more than absolutely necessary. Our fingers entwined, and something ancient settled in me.

"No, lady," he said in that rough voice that sent me spinning. "A little nervous, I suppose." He huffed a laugh. As tired as I was, I smiled. As beaten down and aching, and hungry again, I smiled. I smiled because we were together here. For all my hoping and praying and searching, I really hadn't been sure it would happen. When I looked into those clear green eyes, I saw every hope and prayer and answer staring back.

"Come here," I whispered and sat back. He scooted further onto the mattress, and I lifted the sheet for him to come under and into my arms. Within the circle of my embrace, I held him against me as he had done for me. When was the last time he slept and felt safe? Certainly not in that prison cave. Likely not the entire time he was trapped as his *baethaache*. His cheek pressed against my chest, and his arms went around my waist. I kissed the top of his head and tightened my own arms, then linked my legs through his. It couldn't have been more than a minute or so before I heard his breathing slow and I felt his heartbeat even out as he fell asleep. I could keep first watch tonight.

Tapping. Tapping like a beak on a windowpane roused me from a deep sleep. Bright, warm sunlight flooded the room.

"My lady," called a voice behind the door. More tapping. A cough. "My lord?"

Cadeyrn raised his head and grumbled, still half asleep. Normally, any noise would have him up and in a crouch. I brushed my lips across his silken dark hair and began extricating myself from our tangle. He mumbled a protest and tried to hold on. I chuckled and slid from his grasp and edged from the bed. Grabbing the grubby remnants of my dress, I held it in front of me before opening the door slightly. Xaograos stood in a clean uniform, looking fresh, if exhausted.

"Your Highness," he said with a bow. "Apologies for disturbing you. There have been reports of ships. A fleet gathering in the Sea of Saen Daíthaen." The Sea of the Old Gods.

"Not friendly, I take it?"

"Not likely, Your Highness. The Lady of Laorinaghe and your companions are preparing to gather in the council room."

"Please tell them, Xaograos, that we will be there shortly." He bowed and left. *What the hell am I going to do with Cadeyrn?* I stared at him sleeping facedown. His powers must have been in desperate need of recharging. Perhaps shifting back into his fae form really depleted him. I stood twirling a strand of hair around my finger, trying to figure out what to do about my mate and what to wear. Pulling the sheet from the bed, I wrapped it about myself, toga style. It looked utterly ridiculous, but I wanted to get to the council. Someone could find me clothes then. Cadeyrn was going to be so pissed I didn't wake him. Oh well.

Along the coast between Maesarra and Laorinaghe, near the Ispil of Bogvhi, sat a fleet of ships from Veruni and additional ships, flying an unknown standard. Messengers rode in that morning from the South bearing the news. Corra received a hawk informing her that the naval fleet was preparing to sail and that we should remain here. Shelter in place was the official recommendation. Everyone debated who undersigned the threat. The main players, Paschale, Feynser, the former Elder of Maesarra, and Analisse, were out of the picture. Analisse was imprisoned under the palace on Eíleín Reínhe, the Queen's Isle. Something in my gut sloshed thinking of Reynard's parents and their vehemence towards us. What we faced now seemed to be an enemy standing beside us. Silas scrubbed at his stubbled face and kept blinking his eyes as though he, too, was completely worn down. He asked questions about exact locations, sea depth, known military officers in Veruni, and so on. Yva stood guard near Lorelei and was given instructions to call in commanding officers in her lady's guard to bring intelligencers, and I finally pulled her aside and asked if she could use her very unmilitaristic skills to bring us clothing again. Corra dissolved momentarily and came back in, having received another message by hawk.

Turuin had raised soldiers (what was left, as Saarlaiche had volunteered so many during the uprising against the Elders since they were fiercely loyal to Cadeyrn) to defend the coast-line. Additionally, he stationed ships in formation off the coast, facing off with several craft of unknown origin.

"Fucking hell," Silas swore. "At least between Western Maesarra and Saarlaiche, we know there is some defense. Corra, get word to Soren and find out what is going on in Dunstanaich."

"My border guard has neither heard nor seen anything out of the ordinary," Lorelei stated.

"With all due respect, my lady," Corra interjected. "Based on the events of days past, we need to ascertain where loyalties really lie here. As in, in Laorinaghe, both within and outside of the city."

Lorelei swallowed audibly but nodded. I could imagine she was infuriated. Not so much with Corra but with the entire situation. Just as Cadeyrn was infuriated. Cadeyrn, who I could feel coming in at the moment, his heat preceding him. We turned toward him.

"Good morning, princess," Silas teased, winking at his cousin. "Sorry, *Trubaíste*. No offense." He winked at me as well. Cadeyrn came to stand behind me in his blood-stained trousers from last night, no shirt. What a pair we made.

I like the look, I said to him. He leaned down and kissed just behind my ear.

It got cold after you stole the bed sheet for your own fashion needs. You could have woken me.

You clearly needed the rest. I couldn't have you falling asleep on me again today. It's a blow to my self-esteem.

I can assure you, I am fully recharged.

"What have I missed here?" he asked aloud.

I filled him in, and Silas gave him notes we had taken and messages we had received. Lorelei motioned for two guards to come to the table. They twisted two knobs in the center and pulled back leaves of the wood to reveal a map. Compartments on either side held pieces to place on the board like a chess game. Silas moved the pieces into the formations we knew were out there.

"How do you—do we—does one," I stammered, waving my hand, "determine location here? Apart from general magnetic pole directions like North, South, East, West? Is there longitude and latitude? How would one pinpoint exact locations?"

"Do you remember when you asked me if this is an alternate Earth?" Cadeyrn asked me.

"Quite fondly. I loved watching you squirm."

"I did too. Very entertaining," Silas added.

Cadeyrn shot him a half-hearted glare. "I told you it was the same universe, but a different realm. Well, it is, but it's not. As you may have noticed, the stars are different. We are at a magnetically separate point in the universe."

"So, like a different planet?" I asked.

He pinched his nose. "No. Remember the folds?" he asked. "We are within one of the folds. So rather than being one blip in a plain of vastness, we are a blip within a fold. Does that make sense?"

"Not to me," Lorelei admitted. I smiled at her.

"So, Earth, the solar system, and galaxies I knew growing up are all within one fold? Then here—Aoifsing, the lands across the sea that are so super mysterious that no one really knows them, the stars above that are somehow written upon our skin—these are all within a different fold? And the universe itself is the folded blanket?"

He agreed with my assessment.

"So, what does that have to do with positioning?" I asked, looking at the map.

"Magnetically, it is different here. In terms of true north, the pole shifts. We have different magnetic fields and, while overall it stays the same, the grid system we use loosely cannot be relied on one hundred percent."

"So, there is no equator because the demarcation line bounces in a sense?"

"Yes."

"So, it's a crap shoot as to how you would place armies on this board?"

"Oh! I watched a documentary on casino games!" Corra exclaimed. "In this case, it would be more of a roulette shoot. Or game? I don't remember. However, the magnetic fields here tip and rock, so where a continent is may change based on how the magnetism shifts. Like a ball on a roulette wheel. Well, they would be on a map, that is. They don't scoot around on land or sea." She summoned a droplet of water in her hand and let it wobble around before it settled.

I think I followed where she was going with this.

"So, could we make a line grid and use Universal Transverse Mercator coordinates to pinpoint locations if we knew the median magnetism in the area?"

"In theory, yes," Cadeyrn answered. "The grid would shift but we could have a percentage of room for error based on the known magnetism within a given part of the grid." He paused and looked at me. "How do you know about military coordinates?"

"Military history analytics helped with my trading. Remember I told you I did a dissertation on it?" I answered. "Anyway, if we knew where a regiment was or would be, I think it may be possible to use the magnetism to contain it to a particular part of the grid, thereby hedging the forces. If we could establish a geographic locator code like the military uses."

"If we could, that would be quite handy," Silas said, pursing his lips.

"What we don't know is the topography of Heilig, the land across the sea," Cadeyrn added.

"Really, I am flabbergasted that no one knows anything about the 'land beyond the sea'. I mean, really. It's irresponsible."

"Well, actually," Lorelei chimed. "We do know a bit." We all turned to her fully. "I have been there with Analisse." She flushed and placed both of her hands on the table and blew out a long breath. "Your mother, Princess, hails from a family across the sea."

AN AFFINITY for water was not common in Aoifsing, Lorelei explained to us. Those of the mist, like my mate and his cousins, were an isolated group, and as of now, the bloodline had come to a stop. That was the closest that those of Aoifsing come to a water affinity, apart from Feynser, who gained his affinity after being sworn into his Elder position. A half millennia ago, Lorelei explained, a young king and queen were called to Aoifsing. They were drawn here to fulfill a need to balance the *taerra* magic—the magic of growing things—with that of the water running through the world. Aoifsing was stagnant in its growth, and it was felt the gods delivered these monarchs to the lands. Across the sea, fae were known to have a wealth of power in water magic. The royal family set off on a quest of sorts to imbue their gifts to a new land.

"Eíleín Reínhe had been a stone isle," Lorelei continued her history. "It was windswept and covered in rocks and boulders with no wildlife or foliage to speak of."

The newcomers, Lorelei told us, sheltered there during a storm. Once the winds and rain had passed, a wild bloom swept across the rocks and sand-blasted island, as if in welcome. The queen touched the ground, a hand on her swollen belly, as she was near to delivering, and claimed the island was hallowed ground. There they would build a bridge to this new land, keeping the isle close to their hearts. As things didn't always work out the way we would like, the home was not ready for children, and the queen needed a midwife. They were summoned to the interior of Maesarra, where the most revered midwives and healers were located. Twins were born, a male and female, who grew up between the Isle and Bistaír, their estate in Maesarra.

This family brought new life in the form of both the children, who possessed powerful gifts for water magic and oraculoís (the ability to use one's mind to communicate). Consequently, the landscape on Aoifsing began to thrive once again as it had in centuries past. Though they had no true claim to rule, it was widely accepted that they held the key to the natural prosperity of the land.

"What happened to their homeland?" I asked Lorelei. "If they were monarchs when they arrived here, who maintained the rule in their lands?"

"I was part of the decision to ask them to come here and help balance our magics. The queen had a sister to whom she handed over her rule. Perhaps fifty or so years ago, Analisse and I were sent by Queen Saskeia to see how the lands were faring. We have very little communication with them, as there are wards stitched throughout the very atmosphere of the archipelago which surrounds the great lands. We carried with us specific instructions and stones to allow our passage."

"When was Saskeia crowned?" Cadeyrn asked. I was wondering the same thing.

"Roughly three centuries ago. Her parents, your grandparents, abdicated the throne when the children were of age. Your grandmother became very ill. It is widely believed that she was poisoned. When she passed, your grandfather allowed his immortality to wither away. They were both friends to me, and I mourned their passing. Analisse grew up alongside your mother. Her own father was the original Elder from Veruni. Your uncle, Konstantín, became the King of Heilig and your mother's liaison to the lands."

"Why does no one say the name?" Silas asked.

"There is power in knowledge and names, and perhaps your mother and uncle never fully trusted us all—with good reason—so they kept the name secret. Only Analisse and I were given it and permission to travel there."

"And Lord Dockman," Cadeyrn added. She nodded.

"That is more recent. Trade became necessary."

"What did you find on your journey there?" Corra asked.

"I love my lands here. Laorinaghe is my pride and the child I never had. However, I found that I did not want to leave Heilig. The beauty was astounding. It is a land of many rivers and bodies of water where the flora bloom in extravagant explosions of color. My senses were saturated day and night. It is no great surprise that your mother is as beautiful as she is— as you are as well, Princess. It is as if the land itself is incapable of mediocrity."

"What of Konstantín?" Silas asked.

She sat back. "He is beloved by his people. They have a council similar to that which you are trying to accomplish. We were welcomed to the lands and treated as compatriots. Analisse made many acquaintances."

"We need to pay Analisse a visit," Cadeyrn growled. Deep within me, I snarled, wanting to shred the succubus apart.

Silas was arranging ships on the board. Seeing the known fleet positions and the formation, I reached out and touched the ship at the forefront. A vision barreled into me, sending mind and body into a maelstrom.

Ewan riding to us. Blood. Waves. A hole blown in the

archipelago, ghostly soldiers marching through, my mother's eyes looking back at me, glazed over and unseeing. Dead. A hand reaching to me. Analisse sitting on a stone dungeon floor, smiling.

"Shit. Grab her feet, Silas. Neysa. Look at me." Cadeyrn was speaking. I was aware that I was shaking violently with cold, as though ice water ran through my veins. My body arched up and my back cracked. "Look at me, my love." He held my face in his hands and blew. I tried to focus on him.

"Watch her neck, Cadeyrn," Corra warned. "She is shaking too much. Neysa, darling, grab onto Cadeyrn. You need warmth."

I wanted it to stop. Needed it to stop. I ached with the force of the convulsions, and I had never been so cold.

"*Trubaíste,*" I heard Silas say. "What did you see? Let us take that away from you."

I sent the images to Cadeyrn. He swore, and I heard the shouts of his cousins as heat flared around us.

"Corraidhín, send a hawk. Tell Ewan to return to the palace and take soldiers. He needs to secure his throne. And by the fucking gods, someone get her some proper clothes."

Gradually, the convulsions eased, my mate's warmth covering me.

Secure his throne. Ewan's throne. The queen was dead. My mother was dead. I could feel it in my bones.

SHUFFLING feet and a cacophony of voices surrounded me. I was vaguely aware of lying on a velvet bench or chaise. There was a cloak wrapped around me and a blanket draped across my legs. I sat up, grunting in pain.

"Don't move too quickly, darling," Corra said. "We aren't sure what cracked in your back, and Cadeyrn wanted you awake before he healed you."

"Did you send the hawk?" *Ewan's throne.*

"I did." She grabbed my hands. Hers were icy, likely having just shifted from mist. "I am going to leave and try to find Ewan. I want to accompany him back and help in any way I can."

I nodded.

"He's so strong, Corra," I said. "Tell him I'll be there as soon as I can. Give him . . . give him this." From the center of my palm, I dropped a single aquamarine. "Tell him I found it in my clothes after we collapsed the Veil. Have him add it to his crown."

Corra kissed my head and walked off. We were wasting time. I couldn't keep sitting here like a useless lump while the world fell apart. The problem was that I couldn't move my legs. Holy shit. Panic crept up. The knot in my chest had me in its vice again. Breathe, Neysa.

Cadeyrn. I called to him. *I can't move my legs. Where are you? I can't move my legs.*

I tried to let an electrical current flow through my legs like a power line. If I could shock them like an AED machine, they might work. Somehow, I managed to send out a simultaneous trickle of electricity and a deluge of water and shocked the hell out of myself. That was the most water I'd ever released. Given my mother was dead, I suppose her power transferred to me as well. Every ounce of the female who I had only just gotten to know, had become a part of me now. Me and Ewan. Once again, my body rocked and slammed back into the bench, vibrating with electricity. Silas started to walk over. I flung my hand out to tell him to stop, and a lash of lightning shot towards him.

"Shi-fuh!" he yelled, diving out of the way. "The fucking gods, *Trubaíste*!"

"Don't come near, Silas. You have too much water. I can't control this." I wrapped my arms around myself.

"What the fucking hell did you do?"

"I tried to shock my legs into working."

Cadeyrn walked in. He raised an eyebrow at me.

"Causing trouble?" he asked with a quirk of his mouth.

"Don't come close. I'm out of control." I stuttered the words, electricity rocketing through me, water dripping from me as well. I didn't know how much longer I could deal with this without turning my brain to porridge. Cadeyrn stepped closer. "Please. I don't want to hurt you." He stood next to me and started to lean over. I screamed as lightning erupted from me. He caught my arms and pushed his fire into me. Immediately, the powers receded, and I calmed.

"Now, what's this about your legs?" He leaned over me, his hair slipping forward and brushing my forehead. I was trying to let him in. Let him soften me into relaxing, but my panic crept up. Tears slipped out and ran down my face and my lip quivered.

"Hey. None of that. I can fix it. Scoot over, bed hog," he teased. I pushed up onto my hands and shoved myself over. His hands gently rolled me to the side, facing away from him. His deft fingers touched and flicked at my back like he was playing an instrument. When he got to the lower back, I stopped feeling him. My breathing caught. I felt nothing below my lumbar spine area.

"Did you realize that when you first came to Barlowe Combe, I had no idea what to do with you?" he asked, a smile in his voice as he worked on my back. "You infuriated me and made me need a cold shower in the same moment."

"And yet . . ." I complained, bad-natured.

"I know. I knew, or thought I knew, how you felt, and yet

I wouldn't accept it. I thought surely you wouldn't want this life with me. In Rila, when you touched that tree carving . . ." He trailed off. "I felt you. A longing in you, and the thought that you might never be loved. And I wanted to burn the fucking forest to the ground to spite everything that had made you feel like that. Because I loved you, and I didn't know how to say it. Old as dirt and I felt like I was a lad."

I snorted. Sounds of Silas's footsteps told me he had left the room. From the hall he yelled to call if we needed anything.

"So, while I thought I knew, I am male enough that I was sore Silas had you. I was pissed he loved you and had you and I was standing in that frozen forest knowing you thought you were unloved and I couldn't make myself tell you otherwise." He stroked my back along my spine, and I let my wings stretch out across us. Prickles of feeling returned. A wash of heat alight at his touch. "Beautiful," he murmured. The wings receded. "You know now?"

I turned and looked up at that world-ending beauty in him.

"I mean, I should hope you are aware of my feelings, mate?" he asked so seriously that I smiled.

"I'm getting the idea." I kissed his chest. "There's always room for enlightenment."

"Neysa," he began. "About your vision."

"Let's wait until we hear from Corra."

"We can't. We must discuss it." He pulled on a strand of my hair.

"Not yet, okay?" I whispered. His arms slid around me. "Ewan doesn't want to be king."

"Most of us don't want the lot we are given," my mate answered. I looked him in those glassy green eyes. I knew how his fate weighed heavily upon him. Today meant one step further down the road to his birthright. Now our fates were intertwined. Or always had been. "We make the best of it." He tucked that errant strand of dark hair behind my ear.

"And you?" I asked carefully. "Would you have chosen all this had it been offered to you?"

"Every second of it."

"Can I tell you something? You don't have to say anything. I just want to tell you." He nodded and moved his fingertips up my arm, still testing and firing up the nerves. "When Ewan and I were across the Veil, trying to find a link between the stones, the Veil, and those who could cross, he mentioned bloodlines. He made a comment about you both being from the mist fae, and yet had healing unto yourself. Ewan said that you were the start of a new era and that any offspring you had would likely be so strong they would be the cornerstone for all fae. I held it together fairly well whilst we were there. I really did. But when he said that, I felt like everything living in me was yanked out. I knew . . ."

Ugh. I stopped and blew out a breath. Get it together, Neysa. "I knew then that you would have to move on. You needed to provide a next generation." He shook his head. I put my fingers to his lips. "I made Ewan swear to keep to the outer crescent of the stones. I had lost too much already," I choked. "I expected it to kill me." There. I'd said it.

He swallowed, and his heart was racing. Anger shone in those eyes. Anger with me, I realized with a bit of a shock.

"I knew based on the chemical constituency of the stones, the Veil, my blood, all of it, that it would be so volatile that it would close the damned Veil. But I knew it would destroy me too. I did it to save him and you, and my friend, Shannon. She was my only friend, and she had a family."

I was blubbering a bit now. Not quite crying, but in hysterics. Tears failed where panic reigned. "It was our only chance to make it right. My mother must have seen it happen —or seen me realize it. Ewan and I both had dreams the night before. That's why she came to us. She gave us all of her magic and that's why I'm alive. And that's why she's dead. She depleted her magic, and because of it, she was murdered." *My fault. It should have been me. She would have lived, and you could have gone on.*

"What is wrong with you?" he barked, pulling away from me. I jerked like I had been slapped. He stood glaring down at me.

"Me?" I felt like a pumpkin that had been scooped out, the innards dumped on the ground. All that I had held in, all that I felt, laid bare.

"You were sacrificing yourself. We could have found another way. I knew it. I *knew* you would do something like that when I let you go."

"You did not *let* me go, Cadeyrn. I decided to. I had to. I was expendable here and needed there."

"Expendable? Bloody fucking hell, Neysa. Survivor's guilt is one thing. You should hear yourself. A little self-worth for fuck's sake. We would have found another way!" He pivoted, heat coming off him in waves. My fingers clutched the sheet.

"You tried to find a way for almost a hundred years, Cade! I found the way. I needed to collapse the damned thing, and you were needed here."

He whirled to me. Lights flickered in the room around us.

"To be a prize stallion? Nice. Thanks for that." His hand raked through hair still mussed from sleep. "You gave up. You decided to get it over with and gave up."

"What did you do, huh? You nearly let yourself die on that battlefield. That much you told me. And what I saw for myself, while you slept, is that you got steaming drunk for weeks after. You were letting females all over bloody Laichmonde touch you." I didn't add the one I saw kiss him in that alleyway. He might not have taken another to bed, but there were females following him and Magnus around for weeks. He stood, wide, wild eyes looking at me.

"I wasn't the one out socializing and flirting every night, Cadeyrn." I shouldn't have said that last bit. I didn't even hold it against him, nevertheless, it came out like a slap. His head reared back, eyes wide.

"I don't know what I'm supposed to do or say to you," he said, his voice barely audible. "It's never right. It's true, though. I did want to die out there. I only fought to keep everyone else alive."

"What do you think I did?"

"The difference is that I didn't make that final call. You did. You said, 'Fuck it' and sacrificed yourself. I kept fighting." His arms crossed and uncrossed over his bare chest. "Yes, I got drunk. To get you out of my head. Everyone was telling me to get on with it and take someone to bed. Everyone except Silas. I had wished you loved him and never gave me the time of day so I didn't feel like death was kinder than what I was feeling. How about that?"

"Well, I suppose that would have been easier for everyone, eh? Then you could have got on with it, stud." And that's about when I shoved my foot in my mouth. I was a walking talking maelstrom. I stood up, tripping on the stupid sheet around me. What did it take to get clothes in this place? His nostrils flared and chest heaved as he stood stock still. He looked utterly defeated. And I wanted to take it all back.

"Cadeyrn."

"I don't know why we bother," he spat, quietly and viciously. Every thought went out of my head. Nothing but screaming, empty silence filled the space where I should have said something. He turned on his heel and walked away. I dropped the sheet, wrapped the cloak around me, and made my way through the other door. Silas stood there, arms crossed. I braced myself for a snarky comment, but he just stared at me like I was someone else entirely. My traitorous lip wobbled as I looked at him.

"Did you honestly think you were expendable?" he asked in a whisper.

I shrugged.

"You made this mess, *Trubaíste*. You two need to fix it. Stop destroying each other."

I walked past him toward my room, my head hung like a wounded animal. "Maybe we shouldn't fix it. Maybe we shouldn't bother."

Distant, rumbling thunder and a driving rain began outside the balcony doors. I didn't care. In my heart, I knew I had been the one who destroyed everyone. My parents' marriage. My father died protecting me. My brother grew up an orphaned slave because of me. Caleb gave up on me years ago. It wasn't his fault. I was a shell of a person. Not even a person, as it turned out. Even Cyrranus, the former Elder Guard who nearly got himself killed for me. And my mother. She gave everything she had for Ewan and me to get back safely. She likely even knew she would be killed. And I never even had the decency to call her mother. Why would anyone bother with me? I was as worthless as they came.

CHAPTER 6

NEYSA

In my room was a pile of clothes. Everywhere I went, I had to find clothing based on the charity of others. I was sick of it. I didn't have anything of my own, apart from the aphrim skins which I knew Reynard had made for me. I dropped the cloak and slipped into a loose pair of black silk trousers and a matching fitted cami. I snatched up a jug of wine from the table, along with my weapons, and left the room. Yva stumbled as I crashed out the doors to the private apartments.

"My la—Your Highness," she said.

"It's Neysa. That's all. Do you drink?"

"Pardon?"

"Do you drink wine, Yva?"

"Yes, though not on duty."

"Good. You're off duty now. Come with me."

I stalked down to the beach and swigged from the jug, then passed it to her. She took a cautious sip while I picked up my sword.

"Would you like to spar with me? It's not a command. Just a question."

"I would rather not . . . Neysa. It could cause trouble for me."

Fair enough.

"I'm not holding you here. You have the rest of the afternoon, evening, whatever it is, off. You are welcome to stay and drink with me, or you can go home to your friends and family."

Spinning my sword felt so good. I lashed and swept, rolled, flipped, did all the stupid shit my father told me would be the death of me. Who cared at this point? I chased waves from the water like a dog and would flip, then throw my dagger into an escaping glob of seaweed. The seaweed made me think of Ewan. I didn't know what to think about him. About him and Corra. That was none of my business, yet I still let the concern get caught in my tangled web of mental vomit. Yva and I passed the jug back and forth until it was empty. She was giggly, which made me laugh, because she seemed like the least giggly person I had ever met. The legs of my trousers were soaked through, so I took them off and continued my swordplay in my cami and black underwear. There was no one around, and my bathing costumes in the human realm were far more revealing than this. I wondered if I actually did fit in more there than I did here.

Thwack. I threw another dagger. If there were another Veil, from what I gathered, I would be the only one with the correct biochemical makeup to pass through it without incident. Thwack. The dagger hit in the center of the already speared seaweed ribbon. I could cross back. Let everyone get on with it. Thwack. I pulled the three daggers out and walked back to my position. The reality was that I wasn't needed here. I got Cadeyrn back. He could carry out his birthright. Ewan would rule. Analisse would die. I had promised the skies that I would work to make this world better. Running full speed, I did an aerial over a large rock, landing in the calf deep water, then threw my sword at the shore. It stuck into the ground exactly where I had been standing. I noticed Yva, swaying a bit on the beach, staring with an open mouth. I bowed. If I left and stopped messing up everyone's lives, I would be making the world a better place.

A wave smacked me on the back and careened me into the rock, face first. My nose exploded in pain. I pulled out of the water, laughing like a lunatic.

"Shit!" Yva yelled, sprinting for me. I waved her off as I made my way out of the shallows.

"I'm fine. It's a nose. It'll heal." She grabbed my wet trousers and held them to my face. There was a lot of blood. I was very drunk. She swayed as well. "That was a lot of wine." I stated the obvious.

"I haven't eaten today. You?" she asked.

I shook my head no.

"Maybe we should go get something."

"I don't feel like going back there." Not to mention there was a copious amount of blood running down my throat into my stomach. Face wounds bled like crazy.

"We could go to a tavern?"

I could just see us in a tavern. Her livery and my being soaked through, drunk as college kids. I wasn't reckless enough to invite that kind of trouble.

"Maybe in a little while."

"I realize I'm overstepping, Your Highness." I glared at her. "Neysa. But may I ask what is wrong? I saw your mate as well. He was . . . *Aedtine Aimschire*." Fire weather. An accurate description, I'm certain. "Lord Silas as well. I asked him if he needed anything, and he snarled at me. Then apologized."

That sounded about right.

"I am a glorious fuck up, Yva. I am ressponssible for countless deaths and the ruin of ssso many lives. All because I exist. Plus, I'm sssocccially inept." Crap, I'd started slurring. "I shhhould leave Aoifsssing."

She looked alarmed.

"Forgive me, but I see no reason that would rectify anything. Would your mate and friends not find that unbearable?"

I shrugged in answer.

"Perhaps for a time. They are all better off without me. Trust me. I have multiple degrees." I stood and rolled my shoulders. "Okay, I'm ready to go for round two. Ssstand back, please."

Thwack. I tossed the dagger at a plant and pinned the blossom through the pistil into the dune behind it. Not that drunk then. Thwack. I let another fly. Where the hell did it go? My third shot from my hand. I heard it land but couldn't see it. *Okay, I've lost two.* I stumbled up the dune looking for the daggers. Where the—

"You could kill someone like that." Silas had a dagger in each hand, the blades cutting into his palms. Shit.

"Oh my God. SSSilas, I'm ssso sssorry."

He passed them back to me and wiped his hands on his pants.

"They'll heal. Who ate your face?"

"Giant shark," I said. He smirked.

"Corraidhín watched this thing called *Shark Week*. She wouldn't go near the water for a year." Corra and her documentaries. "You seem to have lost your trousers too."

I headed back down the dune, weaving back and forth. Yva looked at me in alarm after noticing Silas.

How many weapons had I brought down? One sword . . .

"Fix it," Silas commanded in a voice he never used with me. Three daggers . . .

"I can't. I make everything worse. I am better off leaving." No, four daggers. Where was the fourth? Crap. I hoped it wasn't swallowed by the ocean. I dropped to my knees and pushed at the sand.

"Bullshit. Fix it." He toed my foot. *Where is my dagger?* "You two have dealt with so much and are so in love it makes me physically sick."

I wanted to be sick right then.

"Stop, Silas. Leave me alone." *Where's the dagger?* It was the one I threw first then moved towards . . . Yva held it out to me. I gave her a sheepish smile.

She winked and started jogging up the shore. Silas watched her go. Four daggers, one sword. I could have sworn I had something else. Maybe I shouldn't have drunk that much. With weapons. I sat back on my heels thinking about what I was missing. Silas squatted down next to me.

"He would be better off without me," I admitted. "I shouldn't have come back. It's been nothing but trouble."

He smoothed the salty hair away from my sticky mess of a face.

"You don't believe that."

"No? Then why is it you are always finding me and trying to get me to make it work? I ruin everyone's lives. Everyone I love. You can't deny that." I pointed at him. "I messed you up a little too."

"Of course you did. I jumped in headfirst, though. I'm still alive."

"For now," I grumbled.

He chuckled.

"I'm serious. I needed to die to collapse the Veil. It is a scientific fact. Not Ewan. Not any of you. I did. I was doing it willingly. You all would have been fine. Life would have gone on. It had been over a month. Cadeyrn would have been well into getting over it. Instead, my mother gave us every drop of her magic to keep us alive and get us back over. Everything.

And now she's dead. Ewan is probably a target now. It's all because of me."

"One, Cadeyrn would not have been fine. He was getting sloppy in his fighting. He was dying alongside me after facing Paschale. Do you think having a week of binge drinking meant he was getting over you? I fucked half the legion and I still didn't! And you weren't even mine to mourn."

Oh.

"So, no. We are not better off without you. If you don't give a shit about us, then do it for Ewan."

"Ewan was enslaved for thirty years while I had a warm home and a father who loved me. Who died for me. I wouldn't blame Ewan if he decided that his first job as king is to wipe me off the map."

"Oh, please." He waved me off.

"Silas, I don't want to wreck anything else. When Corra said I was an abscess, she was right. I wish . . . I wish I could have realized how to seal the Veil before everything went to shit. It would have been better for everyone."

"Feeling mighty sorry for yourself, Princess?"

"Don't call me that." I tried to snarl, but it came out as more of a slurp. It felt like my nose was turned inside out, a cartoonish sketch of a female.

"I will call you that when you're acting like someone who can't handle her shit. If you don't want to be that person, then get it together and be that troublesome disaster I know and love. Might I remind you that you swore an oath to the gods and fuck knows who and what else? Make it better."

"What if it's better without me?" I looked him in the eyes, my own spilling over with tears. My broken nose wasn't healing due to the seawater. I felt it swelling more as I fought the tears that wouldn't stop coming. My right eye was swelling shut.

I looked down at the ring on my finger. His mother would

not have wanted her only son to marry and mate with me, considering the damage I caused. My shoulders were curved inward. I couldn't stop the damned tears, and I wanted Silas to leave. If he was going to call me princess for falling apart, so be it. I could get my shit together later.

"Come, *Trubaiste*," he said softly. "Let me take you back up. It's getting dark." He lifted me. "We wouldn't want any more sharks to come get us." I stopped fighting and let him steer me, picking up my weapons as we went. "You're going to walk through the palace in your knickers?"

I shrugged, but he handed me the wet and bloody pants. Fine.

It seemed a lot further walking back up. Maybe because I just expended roughly the amount of energy I would have when I did MMA fighting. Plus, the wine. Thank the gods for being fae and metabolizing alcohol fairly quickly. We passed through the vine-covered gates to the palace with its hanging blue and white tiles, and into the foyer on the main floor. It was empty, apart from a few guards. Up the stairs into the residential apartments, I hid my bloody face as we passed more and more guards. In the open central room near the corridor to my chamber, Cadeyrn was speaking to two soldiers and Lorelei. He stopped when we walked in. Lorelei gasped and hurried over, clicking her fingers for servants to bring things. I shook my head, which felt like there was an actual shark attached to it for all the weight and swelling.

Cadeyrn stood staring at me, breathing heavily, his jaw tight and ticking.

"What. Happened?" He addressed the question to Silas.

I snorted, which sent a clot of blood flying from my nose onto the lapis medallion inlaid on the tile floor. The blood began running freely again. Cadeyrn stepped closer, as if to heal me. I stepped back even though my face hurt like hell.

And my legs. I looked down. Hmm. They were battered as well.

"Shark," Silas reiterated what I had said. He knew it was a load of crap.

"Shark?" Cadeyrn exclaimed. Lorelei yelped.

"Fucking great one at that," Silas said, pressing his lips together.

"No. I was joking," I said, my voice nasally. "It's fine. My face hit a rock. I'll live. Good night."

Servants rushed back in with linen, gauze, and tinctures.

"Thank you," I said to them, taking the supplies.

"I'll take them," Cadeyrn said, his voice strained. I made myself meet his eyes, and I felt like I could die right there.

"I've got it." I turned away, my stomach flipping in on itself.

"Shall I clean your weapons, Your Highness?" Xaograos spoke. He took them from me. I walked slowly on my own, then heard Cadeyrn call after me, not even bothering to speak mind to mind.

"Let me at least heal you. Please." His voice was like a rubber band pulled taut. I stopped, then blew out. "Please, *Caráed.*" *Caráed.* My heart. I squeezed my eyes—my eye— shut.

"Fine." I left the door to my—our—room open. He had to have been spent from healing my back earlier. An abscess. That was what I was. I stripped away everything good from everyone. I was swaying a bit. More from hunger at this point, but I had no real desire to eat. He caught my arm, keeping me upright.

"You were drinking?" An easy question. No judgement. "Yes."

"Did . . ." He cleared his throat. "Did someone push you into the rock?" I nearly snorted again but wasn't keen on another clot shooting out.

"No. I managed it all on my own with the help of a wave."

"You were swimming?" He looked confused and concerned. It reminded me of Cuthbert.

"I was . . . It doesn't matter."

His nostrils flared, and he took a deep breath as if to steady himself. Hands were on my face. I closed my eyes. That zapping and tingling sensation wound around my nose and eyes. Then he looked down at my legs and touched them one at a time, knitting the cuts back together. It was done in less than twenty minutes. I supposed our powers worked in tandem.

"Your orbital bones were shattered. You could have lost an eye. Plus, your nose had a lateral fracture. It felt painful."

"It was." I walked to the bathing chamber and began shucking off my clothes. "Thanks for healing me." The door shut, and I ran the bath.

As soon as I lay down in bed and had his scent around me, I couldn't stop the tears. It was the opening of flood gates. The compounding loss I felt and couldn't shake. Night dropped its curtain over the sea. The room was cast in shadows; only three dim lamps were lit. I sobbed into the pillow, wishing the pain to go away. I knew enough from Psych 101 to know I was sinking into a depression. Knew I was enabling it with my self-loathing. The sheet was clutched in my hands so tightly, my nails bit into the skin of my palms. To stifle the sound of my sobs I bit into the pillow, tearing the fabric. Shuffling, like someone standing up from the ground, sounded from the other side of the wall. The door clicked open.

Ugly sobs flowed and I tried to reign them in and bury my head deeper into the pillow. The side of the bed depressed. I felt him shift closer to me. The heat from his hand warmed through the sheet and my chemise as he hovered it over my side, like a question. My shoulders rocked through another embarrassing sob. That must have been answer enough, because his hand came down on me and he slid against me, tucking me against him before I had a chance to protest. Our bodies lined up, back to front, and he pressed his face against the back of my head. We stayed that way for an hour, maybe more. I couldn't stop crying. He didn't stop holding me.

"I didn't mean it. Any of it. I'm a shit," his strained voice said to the back of my head.

"I'm . . ." I sobbed again. I couldn't catch my breath to speak properly. "Corrosive. I strip away everything good."

"Corrosive? No, no, my love. You are everything that matters."

I had my entire face in the pillow.

"Why *do* you bother?" I asked, pulling my knees into my stomach and trying to staunch the ache.

"Because I love you. We love each other more than anything else in this life. Your parents, your brother, are not your fault. Terrible things happen. We have each other." I let myself put my hand next to his. He immediately threaded his fingers through mine. "Neysa." There was a catch in his voice. My back pressed into him, and I grabbed his other hand in mine. "You said to me that night in Bulgaria that you hoped that I could find peace and be happy. I have. With you. Only with you. I don't want you to ever question that. No matter how mad you get at me, or how much of a shit I am being. I am happy with you like I have never been in my entire life. And I am old."

"Are you sure?" I whimpered like a child. He laughed.

"Yes, *allaíne caráed*. I am quite sure. You?"

I laughed a little through my seemingly endless tears.

"I am yours alone."

"As I am yours," he said, kissing the back of my neck. "Just so we are clear, I had no intention of furthering my bloodline without you. If I were to have a child, it would be with you only."

"I would say we should start working on that now, but it seems war is upon us."

"Yes, and I would wager you have eaten as little as I have today."

I let him in to see what I had been doing on the beach for hours. He flipped me over on top of him.

"You truly are *Allaine Trubaiste*." A beautiful disaster. He called me the affectionate name Silas had for me. "You didn't show me the wave, though."

I cringed and thought back to it so he could see. He swore and sucked air in through his teeth.

"Bloody hell." He kissed my nose and eyes and ran his mouth down my jaw. "If I promised I would feed you soon, could I steal a few moments of your time, *caráed*?" he asked, moving that mouth along my neck.

"Just a few?"

"Perhaps more. I haven't had the pleasure of your full attention for a month. And I missed you terribly."

"Take your time."

Silken locks of hair trailed across my stomach, following the path his mouth made. I pushed my hips up into him, and he grasped me under my backside, pulling me up to his mouth where he explored before moving back up to my chest and neck. The chemise came off along with his clothes. I pulled him to me and claimed his mouth with mine, nipping hard enough with my sharp incisor to break the skin. My tongue found the drop of blood and sucked at it. He groaned and pushed against me. The month apart, the fighting, word of death, the argument between us, our hunger, and everything else that built like a tidal wave crashing into us that day, made us too desperate for one another to take each other any slower. We joined and moved quickly, soaking in all that we had missed and needed while we were apart.

CHAPTER 7

CORRAIDHÍN

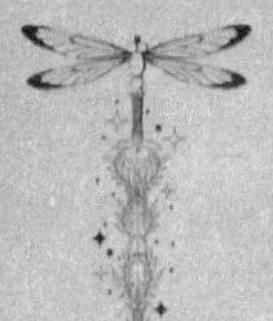

When I was small, my mother had told me I had a secret gift of knowing someone's heart. She trusted my intuition better than anyone else because I could read intention. Ewan, however, I could not read for so many years, and I wondered if it was because my heart knew his and blocked him out. What I could do, though, was find him anywhere. I could locate him through any drop of water or heaviness in the air. What that meant for us, I did not know and refused to think about. I needed to find him and get him to a secure location to keep him alive. All we knew from Neysa was that the Queen had been murdered and Ewan needed to secure his crown. As I left that palace in the Sacred City, I could hear all hell break loose between my cousin and his mate. I don't know how he didn't know she had prepared to sacrifice herself at the Veil. I suppose that was my gift, though.

As I travelled the skies and waterways, my magic was depleting. I hoped to get to him for long enough to explain. Once that was done, I could try to recharge. Even though I truly hated seeing Ewan when I was so thoroughly disheveled.

Perhaps halfway through Maesarra, I felt my powers spluttering. Awe, hell. He had to be close by. I felt his water affinity. If I could latch onto that, I could release my magic a bit and become a part of his, if only to have enough left in me to speak. It was a long shot, but I could try. Using the gift of sensing Ewan, I found him and tried to attract his magic. I hoped it wasn't an intrusion. Once his magic came close enough, I dissolved into it, like rolling with a wave. Except that I became like a bottle caught in a swell and was tumbled over and over in his magic, dragged under and pulled into him for miles and miles. When I became mist, my body flowed sensually in the water and air, fluid and soft, but in his magic, I was cast into a stormy sea. It was as if Neysa's lightning and his water affinity were awash together—a veritable typhoon. Not even Silas and I had a presence like this. Never in my three centuries had I allowed myself to be given over completely to anyone else's magic. Not once had I become this vulnerable. Fitting that the first time I did so, I became debris amid a shipwreck. Rolling and tumbling and being cast about for countless minutes or hours, I lost my grip on myself and stopped feeling. I was only unarticulated existence, riding his power until I landed atop Ewan, soaking him through in my noncorporeal form.

"What the hell?" he yelled, jumping up. I was a sad little puddle on the ground, and I had regained enough of my true self to realize that I felt truly ridiculous. Additionally, I was having a bit of an issue gathering my power to get my body back. I pulled from the ground. Voices other than Ewan's sounded from around the campfire. *Please don't try to kill me on sight.* Silas and I were always at our most vulnerable as we dissolved and reestablished our bodies. Pulsating power pushed into me, prodding.

"Corraidhín?" he yelled. "Holy gods." His power pulled at me more, and I gained my body and collapsed onto him.

Utterly naked and looking like a drowned kitten, I tried to make the best of it and flipped my hair back.

"Hello, darling," I managed before passing out.

Whether Ewan took my news of Neysa's visions well, or if he was spiraling down into a mad fury, I wasn't certain. I still did not know him as well as I would like. Despite his being the first male I had ever wanted to keep. For centuries, I flitted between lovers. Some I loved, of course. Lorelei, for example, was a treasure. Thinking of her still made my toes curl. Yet I knew I could never give myself to her fully. There had been plenty of males who caught my eye for a time, but truly, once the chase was over, I was bored. If I were being completely honest with myself, I was far worse than my brother. He never cared for the chase. He just wanted the catch. Then he would let them go. Like those documentaries about the American men who would go catch and release fishing. They never ate the fish. What was the point of getting dressed up in those hideous outfits to spend a day swatting flies on your neck, and you still didn't eat what you caught? Well, I was quite certain my brother ate before the release, so perhaps not a true analogy. I really didn't care for fishing either way.

Then came Neysa. Poor sod. I had never seen my brother so dumbstruck as he was the day after she had lain with him. Gods. I wondered when he would get over her. If ever. I had hoped that Lina would help on that front. She always made my own mouth water. Yet he still wasn't quite there. With Ewan, though, I saw a future. I wanted him. I wanted to keep him. I did not like his silence on the matters afoot. I motioned for him to say something. Anything.

"It still makes more sense for me to head to the Sacred City and present a unified front. Do we even know the state of the Isle yet?" Ewan sat across from me, his elbows braced on his knees. I had dressed in his spare shirt and a pair of breeches, and now sat sharpening my knife. Normally I could change the molecular structure of everything I had on me, like clothing and weapons, but this time I was so fully given over to his power, everything but my dagger dissolved completely.

"I have sent hawks to make sure our fleet is ready. There have been more revelations," I told him, willing those bright mossy eyes to look at me. He looked up briefly and scowled.

"Of course there would be. What now, Corraidhín? My mother is dead. We are under attack from who the hell knows what or who. You came splashing into me, having infiltrated *my* power. So, what else?"

Well then. I was speechless for probably the first time in my life, so I sat back and bit my lip, staring at him. Infiltrated his power? He thought I had breached his power for my own fun? Gods it was the worst experience of my life. Well, there may have been others, but still.

"Well?" he pressed.

"I tried to get to you as quickly as possible. The situation seemed dire enough to warrant it. I assure you, I meant no offense, Ewan." I spoke quietly, not liking the feeling in my stomach. This was new to me. Perhaps all the water contained an amoeba or parasite that now lived in my stomach. Gods. I wished I had never watched anything on the American South.

"And I appreciate the haste, Corraidhín, but you have yet to elaborate on the latest."

"Your mother descends from a monarchy in the lands across the sea," I began. I told him all that Lorelei had divulged.

He stood abruptly.

"I can't believe I am hearing this. So, we may be fighting an entire land mass and their armies? We stand no chance of winning. Of surviving. And my sister?"

"I left before she was healed. I am certain she fares well. Ewan, please."

He whirled on me.

"Ewan please, what?" he barked at me.

I growled in his face, teeth bared so hard, my canines tore my lips. I would be godsdamned before I let him speak to me that way. His eyes rose with rage as color bloomed on his face, reminding me so much of Neysa.

"We move to Laorinaghe. Tonight. Send hawks to gather forces with Soren and Bestía of Festaera. She answers to you lot, does she not?"

I nodded.

"Good. We need their ships and whatever nightmares Paschale has been brewing in that festering cesspool of a province. I want us all together and planning this out. What are you waiting for? Get the damned hawks in the sky!"

I stared him down for another minute, warring with whether I should just leave or tackle him to the ground and ride him until he had a rosier outlook. I decided I was far too upset with him to do that. Shame.

"I will send the hawks and escort you back to Laorinaghe because I promised Neysa I would see you safe . . ."

"I am not a child. Do what you like." He dismissed me and turned away.

"You are certainly not, Eóghaín, King of Aoifsing." He faced me at that, a distraught look on his face that was shuttered over in a blink. "Yet you are reacting as though you are. I shall keep my word to your sister, whom I love. Know that had I not given my word to her, you would be pouring water from your boots for a month to come, and I would be gone and bedding the first good-looking fae I came across. I do not take well to being spoken down to, boy king."

I knew that had him in a twist as I could hear his heart ticking a thousand beats a minute and his own power casting a grey twilight over the camp. Perhaps this was why I never bothered to get involved with anyone of consequence. I passed Cyrranus and licked my lips while giving him a raised eyebrow.

I knew there was no way in Mother Aoifsing he would take the bait, but it was fun to goad them all in my fury. I suddenly remembered something.

"Neysa handed me this." I walked back to him and dropped the aquamarine in his palm. "She said to be strong and put this in your crown. She believes in you. For the record, I did too. I am, as humans say, on the fence now."

He snarled as I stalked off.

Chapter 8

Neysa

Corra's hawk arrived within a day of her departure, so we converged in the Sacred City to present a unified front. Cadeyrn agreed, though we were all concerned by the tone of Corra's correspondence. She said Ewan was not himself. She told me to not hold her to oaths from now on. I hadn't realized I held her to one. Within another half day, hawks arrived from Bestía in Festaera and Soren of Dunstanaich. They were all readying forces. I went to the archery range to meet Silas, but found Yva, not dressed in her livery, but wearing simple, practical clothing. Her shots were outstanding, and I stood watching for a few minutes before approaching her. As with any skill, especially in weapons training, learning from multiple instructors garnered more success.

"I know you didn't want to spar with me when I was drunk, but how about giving me pointers on archery? It's a skill my father left out of my training."

She lowered her bow at my question, and even from behind I could see her amusement.

"It would be my honor, Princess," she teased. "That flip

over the rocks was worthy of a ballad 'round a campfire. Until the wave, of course."

I laughed. "Yes, until the wave. I apologize if I put you in a strange position."

"Not at all, Neysa. I had . . . fun. It has been a while since I enjoyed myself. My head was pounding a bit this morning, though, and I don't have a healer attached to my hip as you do." She winked, nocked an arrow, and let it fly. Straight into the center of the target.

A whistle sounded behind us, and we both turned. Silas swaggered over, his bow slung over his shoulder.

"Impressive. Has my *Trubaíste* found a new archery instructor?"

"Great skill comes from many masters. Or so say the cat posters in the human realm."

"I shall take your word for it, but I do relish you calling me master."

I laughed and prepared to take a shot, willing my nerves to quiet.

"Show me, Yva," Silas said, rolling her name off his tongue with just the slightest bit of heat. "How you would correct her stance and form."

She shot her eyebrow up, quirked her mouth as if to say 'challenge accepted', and moved to me.

"Neysa, you have the basic stance down. Your feet are parallel to your target, but you tend to let your right foot turn in. It likely doesn't affect you in anything else, but comes from running, I should think. You over pronate because your calves are so tight. You run on your toes?" I nodded in a daze. "It isn't a big deal, and you are quite skilled at self-correction, but it keeps your stance a bit off. In an ideal situation, you would be lined up perfectly with your target and your feet would be perfectly straight. In real life, however, we would be releasing arrows quickly, at a clip, and on the run. For our purpose today, let's have you line up and try to pull your feet out of the pronated stance."

I was shocked at her direction and looked at Silas. His mouth was hanging open, his eyes wide.

"Question," I asked both of them. "I have gotten okay at hitting my mark from my normal stance. However, I was practicing from kneeling or an otherwise situational stance and couldn't hit the damned thing for love nor money."

"Show me your kneeling," she said.

Silas muttered something that sounded a lot like "I've tried that one before," but I ignored him. I knelt on one knee and released my arrows, missing my shot.

"Now, tuck tail," she told me. She walked to Silas and gestured for him to kneel as well. I nearly peed myself as he looked completely confused, kneeling alongside her. She pulled his hips backward and pushed up so his backside was slightly elevated. I copied the stance and released my arrow. It found its mark dead center. I grinned at her and caught Silas's eye as he fixed a bemused, lopsided grin on Yva.

"You can stand up, Lord Silas," she told him before turning back to me.

He looked so flummoxed that I burst out laughing.

"What? Did I do something?" she asked, suddenly less confident.

"No, no," I said, wiping my eyes. "Lord Silas isn't used to being told to kneel then being dismissed." She turned a thousand shades of red and, to my surprise, so did Silas.

"Apologies, my lord," she said to him with a bow. He snorted and waved her off.

"I am not your lord, Yva," he said. "Though I might not be opposed to it." He winked and clapped me on the shoulder before walking away, saying he had to check whether any other messages had come through.

"That was interesting," I told her.

"How so?" she asked, self-consciously tugging on her unbound honey brown hair.

"Oh, nothing." I winked at her and started to nock another arrow when we heard a commotion. "If this is your day off, you might want to leave now before you get sucked into whatever that is about." She narrowed her eyes at me, and we set off at a jog into the palace.

"HE's HERE, Neysa. It's going to take a hot bath, a full bottle of wine, and quite possibly a willing participant to get me in a better mood." Corra stormed through the courtyard in male clothing, looking much worse for wear. Ewan and three guards, including Cyrranus, were several paces behind. Ewan looked briefly toward Corra and brought his attention back to the rest of us.

"I don't think she will actually find a willing partici-pant . . ." I started.

"I don't care. Brief me," Ewan said, voice clipped. Cadeyrn and I looked at each other.

"Bestía mobilized forces. Soren set his fleet southward. The guards in Eiléin Reínhe have asked what we plan to do with the island and—" Cadeyrn coughed and held my hand. "Her Majesty. Not to mention Analisse, who is in the dungeon." Shit. I had forgotten that. "We assumed you had gone back. Until Corraidhín sent a hawk."

"As I told Corraidhín," Ewan said hotly, "it made more sense for us to convene here and prepare. I am told there is much to our family history."

I nodded at him and brought him inside to discuss away from the others.

Care to talk about it? I asked him silently.

Not particularly.

Something happen with Corra?

Are you not getting the not particularly part?

Geez.

We have a lot going on. I just want to know what is causing unrest among us. Yesterday it was Cadeyrn and me. You should have seen it. He gave me a side eye. I showed him some of our argument, Silas, the daggers, the beach, the wave. He widened his eyes and smiled slightly. *So, you see, we have to keep each other in check.*

It's just a lot going on. Our mother. Then Corraidhin infiltrated my magic. It's just a lot.

I stopped and turned him to me, which was difficult because he was much taller and broader.

You're going to do just fine. I can't think of a better king. Plus, I'll always be here to annoy you. I mean, have your back. I hugged him though he remained still.

I don't want this, Neyssie. I am a foundling. I wasn't good enough to keep with you or our parents, so how am I good enough to rule? I don't want it. Any of it. I want to be left alone.

Before I could stop him, he walked off. I stood, trying to breathe over the breaking in my heart.

I FOUND Corra with Silas in her chamber, swigging from a bottle of wine, lounging in her dressing gown.

"It seems you had a day yesterday, Neysa," she said in greeting when I walked in. I smirked and squeezed her bare foot, which was propped on an ottoman. "Your brother was a right arse to me. I am releasing myself from keeping watch over him."

"He is having a hard time, Corra. Give him a little bit to sort himself out."

She waved the bottle at me.

"Do you know how many times I have given my heart to another?" she asked. "Never. I have allowed myself to be vulnerable to another and release myself to their power just this once. And it slapped me in the face. Actually, I wanted to slap *him* in the face, but I did not and you understand my meaning."

I sat down next to Silas on the settee.

"I suppose that was an interesting experiment three hundred years in the making. Well, moving along now," Corra chirped. Her forced cheeriness left a sick feeling in my gut.

"Corra," I pleaded. I wouldn't tell her what Ewan had trusted me to know. So, I just patted her foot again and left. What a mess. Neither Corra nor Ewan were any semblance of their usual selves, and my head was pounding on and off since the night on the forest floor. Poor Silas having to deal with all of us.

Dockman sent a hawk informing us of a host of ships moving across *Saen Daíthaen*. Cadeyrn found Ewan training outside and delivered the message. I watched from the terrace above. Corra stepped next to me. She was still in her dressing gown, yet looked perfectly put together otherwise, from her shiny slightly waving hair to her lined eyes and rosebud mouth. I saw Ewan scrub his face and throw his hands up. Cadeyrn placed a hand on his shoulder, which was shaken off.

"See what I mean?" Corra intoned. "He's an arse."

Of course, with the fae hearing, the two males looked up at us. Ewan stared daggers at Corra.

"I am done with him," she spat and left.

"Have them confront the ships. We need to know what's happening. What would you do, Cadeyrn?" Ewan asked my mate.

"It is not my call, Majesty, but I would have one or two of Dockman's ships confront the fleet. Perhaps have a scout or two in the air if he has them."

"How the bloody hell would we have a scout in the air?" Ewan asked.

"A hawk with mind affinity. Or use me."

"No," Ewan and I both said at the same time.

"I could go," Cadeyrn said. "Put me to use."

"You're not going." Ewan said. "Your little beast stunt this past month nearly killed my sister."

Cadeyrn became very still and looked Ewan straight in the eyes.

"Then tell me your plan, Ewan."

"I don't have a plan. We are all fucked. Between my sister's weakness for you and your cousin, your monstrous temper tantrum, that succubus imprisoned near my dead mother's body, and Corraidhín's obnoxious possessiveness, this whole fucking realm is primed to fall. Do any of us have any idea what is going on? I mean, truly. Why are Neysa and I in line for this throne? We aren't even from this place. Send the hawk. Tell Dockman to figure some of it out and get back to us."

He pivoted to walk away, but Cadeyrn pulled him back. Ewan swung out to hit him. Cadeyrn dodged it, and in one move had Ewan backed against him, arm around his throat and his knees kicked out. I sprinted down. By the time I arrived, Ewan was on his knees and Cadeyrn was talking him down.

"I understand your grief and frustration. I understand your questioning what is happening, because believe me, we all are. What I do not understand, and will not tolerate, is your chastising my mate or my cousins. We were all thrown into this mess. I didn't ask for my birthright any more than you did, and yet here we are. I like you, Ewan. Quite a bit. I will stand beside you and be of service so long as there is mutual respect. That goes for respecting my mate and my cousin as well. Are we clear?"

As I came up behind them, I saw Ewan nod.

"Good." He let him go and offered a hand to my brother. We all looked skyward as a hawk swooped in, no doubt looking for Corra. Rushing to find out the message, the three of us stomped inside. Corra stood scowling.

"I suppose I should get dressed now," she said. "There is a host moving on foot through Prinaer. Bestía said they circumvented Festaera and her border patrol. We aren't sure who it is, but they move aggressively. Bloody hell. Can I get some food around here?"

Lorelei summoned a servant to prepare dinner, giving Corra a quizzical look. I needed to expound on the idea I had yesterday before the visions, so I asked everyone to meet in the war room.

Based on the knowledge we had of the hosts being provided to defend Aoifsing, we could be at a serious disadvantage. Especially seeing as there seemed to be an additional force moving against us from the sea. Not knowing our enemy was really starting to piss me off. Cadeyrn sent out messages to all his contacts to gather forces and store provisions.

"We need to catch them off guard," Silas announced. "They know we know they are coming, and I would bet there are smaller units moving at a quicker pace than the ones we have eyes on."

"Special Forces," Cadeyrn clarified. "Mobilized combat teams that are sent ahead of the host to . . . lighten the load. Make surgical strikes."

I looked to Cadeyrn.

"I want to look into what Neysa was saying yesterday about hedging the forces in. Silas, do you remember when we had to fight the militant faction that tried to overthrow the Elders?" Silas nodded in confirmation. Cadeyrn turned to the rest of us. "We were sent as a small reconnaissance team to sort out who and what we were facing. It turned out we had a few hundred militants to contend with, and there were maybe twenty of us?" He addressed the question to Silas.

"I remember hearing this story when I was young. My chambermaid had seen you two after the battle and had quite a crush on you, Cadeyrn," Ewan interjected.

"It's because you walked in all pissy and battered, screaming for ale. All the females swooned." Silas winked at him. I laughed, and my mate quirked a smile at me.

"I digress," Cadeyrn went on. "One of their scouts found us and sent up an alarm. We could either try to retreat and outrun them, allowing their forward progress to the Elders."

"You probably should have," Ewan grumbled. Lorelei snickered.

"Not all of us were evil, your Majesty," she said to him.

"Or," Cadeyrn continued, "we could hedge them in. Silas and I split into two groups and led each around the outer edge of a small valley. Actually, come to think of it, Reynard, that slick weasel, was useful that day as well. Silas and I each sent out our shields away from us, around the perimeter of the valley. Reynard ran like hell toward the center, luring the militants into the valley. We closed the shield and unleashed hell on them where they couldn't escape."

"If I recall, you did sustain some losses and you may have been partially gutted yourself?" Lorelei asked. Cadeyrn waved her off. I blanched thinking of it.

"Point being, we made it out and the faction was eliminated. I see, Cadeyrn, what you are getting at. You want to trap them." Silas strummed the table and looked at the map. I was afraid to touch the pieces again. "We may not be able to rely on the same topographical advantage though."

"That's why I think we should look into Neysa's idea," he answered.

Everyone turned to me. I took a breath and tried to explain. We would need to mobilize our forces to lure the advancing army to a more reactive area. Prinaer stood out as being a good place if we could get there in time. From what I had been told, it contained many crystal mines. Perhaps we could find one that had magnetic properties like the tourmaline. Regardless of that idea, we could pick an area and set up a magnetic field within it.

"There are mines of hematite in central Prinaer," Ewan blurted. "I saw the location in Saskeia's journals. I remember from our research in the human realm that hematite contains the highest levels of iron out of any terrestrial rock. She also had procured many stones, which she sent with me. Hematite, iron nickel star stones, and peridot. She knew." He shook his head and yanked at the collar of his jacket.

"What are the star stones?" I asked my brother.

"Magnetic rocks. Like chunks of metal that come from the sky," he explained.

"So, we think we could use the stones to generate a current?" Cadeyrn asked.

"Exactly," I answered. "Corra, are you able to decrease temperature?"

"A bit. Not drastic. It's easier if there's moisture involved that I can freeze. I am more of a ceiling fan than an air con." She winked at me. I saw Ewan swallow. "Lorelei can, though. She can drop the temperature even in the hottest moments."

Oh, Corra. Lorelei looked a bit uncomfortable given the company but agreed that she could indeed cool the air. I explained my plan and said we should head out as soon as possible. Ewan was the first to storm out of the room. I looked at Corra and pursed my lips. She lifted her chin and raised a single eyebrow at me. Cadeyrn walked over to her and started to say something but stopped like a wall had been erected between them. She met his eyes and sucked in her cheeks. He cocked his head to the side and backed up a step.

"Corraidhín, would you follow me out for a moment, please?" Cadeyrn asked. She nodded and walked out.

Silas twiddled his thumbs and stared at the war table. I walked over and placed my hand on his back. He smiled and turned to me.

"Clever plan, *Trubaiste*. Don't let it get you killed. Even if you are the only chemically accurate whatever you called it."

"I won't if you won't," I promised. "Pinky swear?" I held up my pinky to him and hooked his with mine.

"Only if I don't have to admit to saying 'pinky swear,'" he laughed.

Corra and Cadeyrn came back in. She was red faced and looked on the verge of tears, though I'd never seen her cry. She pointed at me.

"Not a word to anyone outside this room," she told me in a tone that brooked no argument.

Corraidhín is with children.

I brought my hands to my mouth. Based on the thoughts careening in my head—happiness, fright, questions about her power and being a part of this fight, and finally, her relationship with Ewan—I knew hers must be worse.

"Before you say anything, yes, I am fine to fight. No, I am not telling anyone. I refuse to have this be an inducement. Life goes on. Yes?"

I agreed, feeling my heart ache for my brother who lost everything he ever cared about—from me, to our parents, to Corraidhín—and gained only a crown. The one thing he didn't want.

CHAPTER 9

After a full day and night of travel, Reynard caught up to us in the company of roughly five hundred soldiers from Maesarra. He had left another two thousand to defend the coastline. Units were coming from Saarlaiche, closing in on the time we would likely meet with the opposing force. Soren and Bestía travelled from the north and were planning to arrive behind the enemy. Corra kept close by my side. She and Ewan wouldn't so much as look at one another. I tried to move close to him to chat, but when he saw who kept close to me, he kicked his horse on ahead. I sank onto my bedroll in our tent that first night and groaned. Everything in me ached. I was dreaming of soaking in a large hot bath. The tent flapped back and Cadeyrn ducked in, kicking off his boots. He chuckled seeing me face down.

"Not liking the roughing it part this time around?" he asked.

"I think I'm better at it when I'm trying to find you. My misery and determination alleviated the awfulness."

He sat beside me and ran a hand along my back, then

under my jacket and shirt. I made some small sound that had him sniff a laugh.

"Are you worried about the fight?" he asked.

"Yes. What if I was wrong? What if they are expecting the plan? What if it gets one of you killed?"

"Ah. Not yourself then? Just us?"

"Mostly, yes."

He snorted, pulled off my boots, and rubbed my feet. Then worked his way up my legs.

"You should probably sleep fully clothed in case we get surprised," he said, his voice getting rougher. I flipped onto my back and looked at him.

"I figured as much." Propping myself on my elbows, I watched as his hands stroked along the length of my leather pants. "Are you worried about anything?"

"Of course. I worry about keeping you safe. About making sure Corraidhín is okay."

"Not yourself? Just us?" I teased him.

"Mostly, yes." He climbed on top of me and claimed my mouth fiercely. I dove my hands into his hair and wrapped my legs around his waist. Stupid leather pants. His palm moved over my arms and chest, fumbling with the hooks on my jacket.

"I thought we should keep our clothes on, General," I breathed. He pulled back and stared at me, those green eyes raking over my face and the open jacket. When he spoke, his voice was several octaves lower and laced with darkness. I shivered.

"I'm certain that would be the safest idea," he said. "I'm willing to risk it if you are."

He unlaced my pants as I fumbled with the toggle on his. Our hands found each other as I slid closer and kissed him. Flipping me over onto my knees, we made use of the cramped space as best we could, and he roared loud enough to wake the camp. I went over the edge at that roar, feeling the heat and power rolling from him into me. I was panting and still pushing back against him as he laughed and kissed up my spine.

Whatever we face, Caráed, we face together. Never doubt that.

I love you, Cadeyrn.
And I you. Always.

AN HOUR or so before dawn, scouts came tearing into the camp. A regiment had moved overnight and taken the high ground that would offer us no advantage. Our plan would never work if we couldn't get them off that ridge. What's more, if we were stuck beneath them, our losses would be catastrophic. Ewan found me as I was strapping on various weapons and sheathing my twin swords across my back. He was bedecked similarly, a shield on his arm as well.

"Well, that was a good idea," I told my brother, pointing to the shield.

He shrugged.

Dammit, Ewan, give me something.

"Can you feel it?" he asked. I stopped and tried to block out the sounds of the camp dismantling, the sing of weapons. It was faint, but I felt it perhaps a couple miles out. A tug on my psyche, like the pull of the tourmaline. I looked at him, eyes wide. "Any idea what it is?"

"No, but I can go see."

"We can both go."

"Ewan," I warned. "You are needed here. Plus, what if it's a trap?"

"This whole thing is a trap. We knew that and have tried to play it to our hand."

"Please stay here," I begged. *Stay and look after Corra.* I guess that was the wrong thing to say. He glared at me with a simmering rage.

She can take care of herself just fine, Neysa. And she has made it quite clear that she is done with me.

Oh, Ewan. She is not.

"I am coming with you. I want to know exactly what it is. And where you are," Ewan said.

Cadeyrn walked up to us, glancing between the two of us.

"Everything alright?" he asked.

"There's a tug," I answered. "We both feel it. We need to find out what it is, and if it can help us."

He nodded, meeting Ewan's eyes.

I kissed him quickly and stalked off with my brother toward the direction of the pull. Once we had crossed the tree line and walked into the depths of the forest, the tug became stronger. I grabbed his hand, and the pull was exacerbated with our energies connected. I felt the urge to run toward it, and yet with what the coming days or weeks had in store, I knew it was wise to conserve some energy. Out of all the crystals I had located since I crossed paths with Cadeyrn, the tourmaline was the strongest. It made sense, as it was the protection stone and had pyro-electric properties in line with my own. Tourmaline was called the stone of the goddess Heícate in Aoifsing. The one which could contain and control magic, just like the goddess herself. The further Ewan and I walked toward that draw of power, the more forceful it became. I focused on my *adairch dorhdj*, harnessing the protection in it. Ewan looked at me warily.

"That was from Corraidhín?" he asked, feigning nonchalance. I nodded. "It retains her scent. She . . . has changed."

"Ewan."

"Don't, Neysa. What shall be, shall be."

I wish I hadn't promised Corra. I wished I could tell him what I suspected was true. I finally understood what Corra meant in the wagon when she told me some things were not for her to tell me. Though we were friends, she had known Cadeyrn and I were mates, or *Cuiraíbh Enaíde*, and would not tell me. Some truths needed to be heard from the place from where it came. For Ewan and Corra, if they were mates, they needed to realize it on their own. Perhaps Ewan was so much like me that he was blocking it out. Perhaps they too were mates? I could see pain coming off him like drops of sweat. Through whatever bond he and I had from being twins, Ewan's distress was a visible, tangible thing to me. I only hoped we would all live through this battle.

My head was swimming with the effects of whatever was pulling us. The forest was still night dark, though dawn was approaching. No moon or stars lit the oppressiveness around us, but I knew we had found the source of that pull. Standing a hundred or so meters west of the two of us was a cliff face several hundred feet high. At the bottom was a cave mouth. We steeled ourselves and entered. The entirety of the cave pulled at us from every direction. Our weapons strained against the pull.

"Hematite," Ewan breathed, touching the walls. "The entire mountain is hematite." He looked at me. We sprinted for the opening and took stock of the breadth of the mountainside. It stretched for a mile or so north and south, blockading the west. "We need to lure them here."

I agreed and tried to open communication with my mate.

Cadeyrn.

Neysa, we don't have much time. Scouts are reporting forward teams approaching us.

You need to come here, I said. *Lure them here. We have to move our plan. I can explain more when you get here, but I need*

Silas and Lorelei first. Keep Corra on the fringe. She won't want to be, but the risk is too high for her.

On my way. Shields are going up.

I was marking positions on the ground using rocks and looked up to find my brother staring at me, lips so tight they had gone bloodless.

"She's with children," my brother said. His nostrils flared. I saw him straining to breathe. "I heard you tell Cadeyrn to . . ."

Shit. I bit my lip and opened my palms to him.

"Say something. Yes or no. Please."

"I cannot. I'm sorry."

He slammed his sword into the earth, resulting in a tremor across the forest. Well, that might lure them.

"Why wouldn't she . . . ? Forget it. You won't tell me."

"I swore I would not."

"Fuck it all to never. The only good thing I have ever done in this life and I crushed it."

"It's not gone, Ewan. Go to her. As soon as this is over."

He scrubbed his face and roared, pulling water from the tree roots and causing a few to topple over.

"Control it. Use your rage for battle and passion for your mate."

"What did you say?" he asked. I tapped my foot, warring with whether I should tell him. He stalked closer. "What, Neysa? This is my life we are talking about."

"I think you may be mates," I blurt. "You are so much like me and pushed her away when you lost your sense of self."

He staggered in a circle. A howl sounded from the north. We looked up to see hundreds of yellow eyes glowing in the darkness.

"Shit," we both said.

I could really use some reinforcements right about now, I told Cadeyrn.

What's happened? We are en route.

Lupinus. Hundreds of wolves.

Child's play. You two took them on before. He was joking, yet there was worry in his voice.

Howling resounded from every tree and hollow. Why did they have to be so damned creepy sounding? We raised our individual powers. Ewan drew the water he had summoned, and I linked my electricity into it. Threads sparked between us. We held the connection as we separated and backed up, stretching the current between us. A positive and negative. Wasn't that what I learned in physics? When you jump a car battery, opposites attract, right?

I don't understand a single thing you are blathering about in your head, but I trust it will work, Ewan said to my mind. As we stretched the current between us, several hundred meters apart, we both walked perpendicular to how we had been walking, creating a veritable horseshoe of electricity. The current flared, becoming stronger, and from the edges the magnetic pull of the hematite began to waken. A wolf lunged for Ewan and he swiveled, nearly dropping the connection. I could feel him panting from the exertion, but he carefully slipped a dagger from his thigh, and as the wolf came at him again, he threw it, spearing the animal through the eye. The rest of the wolves howled and descended toward us.

This might not be the right time to tell you this, but your eyes are glowing, he told me. Uh oh. I reached into myself, feeling for a thread to this problem. My beastie fluttered, anxious and ready to be let out. I didn't know if I could hold the charge while letting her fly. But if I had a link to the lupinus, then perhaps . . . I focused on them. Unfortunately, as I started that, three or four decided to attack us. I dropped the connection. Shit. The magnetic power trembled around us. Ewan drew his sword and slashed at them. At least ten more joined the fray and I quickly swiped and stabbed with swords.

Arrows pierced the furred creatures. I didn't have a chance to look around as we fought more and more, but I knew Reynard was around somewhere, backing us up.

"Oddly glad to see you, Reynard. Last time you ambushed a fight of mine, you shot my friend." I heard Ewan snarl and saw him brutally decapitate a wolf. I shuddered. "I like being on the same side."

I heard him chuckle.

"Glad to be of service, little mouse." In a blink, he was standing beside me. Christ, he was fast. With him trading his bow for a sword, we fought together. I spiraled deep into the link I had to lupinus and gave a single command.

STOP. They halted and sat. Okay, that was super strange.

"Whatever you did, it worked. Your eyes are still glowing."

YOU ARE MINE. YOU HEEL TO ME. YOU ALL WILL FIGHT FOR ME. SPREAD OUT AND SERVE. They all listened. Every wolf slunk off and melded into the predawn darkness. I slumped over. Ewan put his hand on my back, then he turned and threw up. I felt sick myself seeing the gore.

As though the forest bowed to him, Silas showed up near us with barely more than a rustle of leaves. Lorelei trailed behind.

"Do the trees do your bidding too, God of the Forest?" Reynard asked Silas. My friend smirked, shoving his sword into the ground as he had that day on the beach in Barlowe Combe. I remember how sexy I had thought he looked. And how much I had wanted to pummel him.

"Only if I ask very nicely," he purred. Pressure built overhead. It was time. Ewan and I took a deep breath. Cadeyrn arrived and began unleashing his shield. Reynard moved to a high tree, still within the boundaries we had marked. Thirty or so other archers moved to similar positions. My brother and I reinstituted our play from earlier, with me harnessing Silas's unstable weather. It would be hard for my mate to keep his heat to a minimum, but for the magnets to be as powerful as possible, we needed the temperature to be low. Soldiers had set the iron nickel star stones on the eastern border. Silas and a few other fae with shielding abilities took to the south to blockade the clearing. The north was open, allowing room for the advancing troops to pass. Once the stones were all in place, plus the extra hematite and peridot Ewan had brought from our mother, I latched onto Silas's power, and we forged the magnetic field that would fence in our enemy. Together, Ewan and I formed an iron core, strengthening the field. The more fae that moved into the field, the stronger the magnetic field would be. Cadeyrn was cloaking the bulk of our army, allowing only a hundred or so to show, inviting the adversaries to the party. We held for another ten minutes. Waiting was draining me. *Keep it together, Neysa.*

Then I locked eyes with my brother. We felt it. Icicles spearing in like daggers. Arrows slamming into the shield.

Paschale had been building a horror show up there. I don't know who is controlling it now, but the ghost soldiers and ice spears were a hit in the last battle, Cadeyrn said to me. Holy fucking hell.

You sure Bestia isn't controlling them? You trust her? I asked.

Um.

Cadeyrn?

I'm sure. She and I . . .

Oh, for Christ's sake.

It was a very, very long time ago. We fought together and were involved.

Well, maybe she's pissed at me and wants to send some ghostly ice daggers at my ass for having you.

I . . . don't think so.

No?

Just then one of those ice spears pierced the ground an inch from my foot.

Next time, could I be debriefed prior to the situation?

Yes, Your Highness.

Fuck off.

He laughed.

Hundreds of Festaerans laden with ice daggers stampeded into our trap, followed by strange beasts with exposed veins that glowed in the greying dawn. Ewan and I ran the same as we had earlier, creating our horseshoe of electrical current. Lorelei dropped the temperature to unfathomably cold. By my command, the wolves picked off the enemy as they neared. I felt each of the wolves' losses like a splinter in my finger. We knew the moment the magnetic field had been fashioned completely. Soldiers kept coming, and Cade finally unlocked the full spectrum of our forces. Arrows rained down on the enemy; swords clashed and spun. My brother and I had to keep to the center, out of the melee. Most did not get close enough to me for fear of the electricity I harbored. Some tried and died the instant their steel contacted my power. Each time they did not stay away or die instantly, however, I sustained another injury. Ewan was dealing with the same thing. Almost like death by repeated paper cut. It was maddening.

All around us, the battle waged on. The stench of death hung over us all, trapped in this vacuum of our own making. Blood and innards, feces and urine. I was freezing and feeling my power splutter here and there. Ewan's eyes went wild for a second, and I knew Corra had appeared.

"Get out of here!" Ewan snarled at her. A wave of warriors launched into us, throwing us all back. Corra became mist and drowned the lot of them in one fell swoop.

"Sorry, darling," she said, becoming slightly more corporeal. "What was that?"

I snickered. Ewan had a murderous look on his face, but it broke a bit as he tried not to smile. Thank the gods.

Dawn broke over the eastern front, showcasing the carnage around us. Through the strewn bodies and clashing steel came a very not-dead Feynser followed by an equally not-imprisoned Analisse. Feynser locked onto me. Corra tried to come closer, and he sent a wave of water at her, dispersing her mist. Ewan screamed.

A little longer, Ewan. Hold it steady and we can get out of here.

"Did you think you could get rid of us that easily? You are so young, my dear," Analisse cooed. "Sorry about your mum." Analisse began screaming, and I knew a lance of heat hit her. She screeched like a banshee.

Sorry. I couldn't not do it, Cade said to me.

"Many thanks to your papa, Reynard, for my release," Analisse drawled, casting her gaze about in search of the archer. "You two truly aren't on the grandest terms, are you?"

"Perhaps," Reynard hissed from the cover of the tree canopy, "that's because he is a murderous sycophant who delighted in torturing me for a few centuries." An arrow caught her sleeve, pulling her arm back and hitting Feynser in the jaw. She snarled and ripped the lance from her shoulder.

The water level rose. Our warriors were panicking. There was too much electricity around.

Get everyone out, Cadeyrn. Wait for us on the northern end. Be ready.

Dammit, Neysa, he answered, but moved as many of our fae out as possible. Feynser picked several retreating soldiers to drown as they ran. It was disgusting. I was losing a hold on my power, and I felt my brother in the same predicament. We had to do this quickly.

"There is someone from far, far away who is quite keen to meet you," Feynser said to us. "It's really too bad the ships you thought were protecting you are the very ones that are destroying your hope to hold the throne, young king." He raised his hands and pulled water from every pore in the earth. Rather than a wave as our mother had summoned, Feynser used Silas's weather system against us and caused a super cell. Rain, winds, and pressure collided to form a tornado. Bodies, limbs, blood, and weapons swirled, dancing on a wind driven point near the ground. All around it, particles sucked upwards into the cyclone.

"Silas!" I screamed. "Get out!" I felt him running toward us, spearing for the exit. A knife thrown into his neck knocked him down. I screamed and, from a distance, heard Corra do the same.

We go now, Neysa, Ewan said to me.

Run for Silas. Drag him out. I will keep the fence up and follow you.

You are not dying in here, Neysa. Do not pull that shit again.

No. But I will hold this as long as possible. Get Silas out. He's dying. I could see blood puddling around my friend as he choked around the knife in his throat. Silas's booted feet were scrambling in the dirt, heels flinging grit in every direction as he kicked. The thought of Silas going down curled its fingers into my windpipe, cutting off air. Not Silas. Ewan sprinted, keeping his power up. Bloody hell, he was strong. He grabbed a hold of Silas under the arms and dragged him toward the northern opening. Blades flew. I spun and sent my throwing knives into the bushes. Reynard followed my lead and began picking off more and more hidden threats.

"What do you say, my dear?" Analisse asked, taking a step toward me in the waist-deep water surrounding us, as the winds and rain lashed at everything. "You and me?"

Out of the corner of my eye, I saw Ewan and Silas cross the line. Arrows started spinning in an arch from only a short distance from where Reynard perched. I took my eyes off Analisse to see why. Glimmering in the early light, Corra was spread out on the ground, barely corporeal. Shit.

The look cost me. Analisse lunged. I parried but caught a dagger in my side. Oh fuck, that hurt. She pulled her dagger back, my skin and muscle attached to the blade, and licked the length of it, eyes twinkling in delight. I started to sway, shifting backward. Reynard dropped from the tree, fast as an adder, and grappled for purchase on Corra, trying to pull her away. She couldn't die there. With any last scraps of power I had, I spun the light from myself, casting the scene in a complete white out. Another scream sounded and the freezing temperature stopped. The air became heavier and warmer like the late spring morning it was. Lorelei. Her power slipped from the world in the brightness of this nightmare. The atmosphere was a phone line gone dead. A soul had been removed. Guilt riddled me for her people losing her. Still, I ran for Corra, blood gushing from my wound. Reynard struggled with lifting Corra. I spoke to her, trying to get her to hold on. Together we heaved her up and ran for the border. At the edge, though no one could see, I was yanked back.

I felt Analisse's mouth on me, pulling blood from my wound. Nails and fingers pried the ragged edges of my laceration, her teeth worrying at the flesh, sucking more and more blood. Agony soared through me everywhere her fingers and mouth dug. Bone and muscle tore, the action audible even in the thick of all that was happening around us. At first there was the warmth of my own blood and her saliva coating my sides and dripping into my waistband. Once she had chewed deep enough, nerves must have severed, because I didn't feel much at all.

I was losing consciousness quickly. *Think, Neysa.* Analisse was so enraptured with drinking from me, I took the moment to release the thin dagger from my wrist and drive it into her temple. She stilled. I pulled it out and stabbed it back in again and again. Then I rolled and stabbed her through the heart and screamed and thrashed and stabbed her for everyone she had hurt. For my parents. For Cadeyrn. Pulling my sword from my back in a fit of pure rage, I brought it down, severing her head. Meters from the exit seemed like miles.

I don't think I can make it, I said to Cadeyrn through our minds.

Like hell you can't.

Cadeyrn ripped through my magic, tearing across the white out, hefted me over a shoulder, and sprinted out of the field. I brought down the white. Trapped within was Feynser and a small battalion of his soldiers looking bewildered. Cadeyrn set me down and turned to the force field we had created. His unleashed heat and mist ignited everything at once in the trap. Fiery water spouted like hell geysers, sparking flames and boiling mist in arcs around the enemy. That power. Feynser bowed and began surrounding himself with his water to fend off the heat. Ewan and I released our hold on our power, and the heat from my mate warmed the magnets, which destabilized the field. Magnets could not stay stabilized without the cold. Nothing needed to be trapped anymore anyway. Nothing would survive. And so, Cadeyrn walked into that firestorm and became the fire and mist itself. He dissolved into it all and incinerated Feynser where he stood in his pocket of steam.

MY BROTHER WAS CROUCHING over Corra, snarling and trying to figure out where she was injured. I crawled toward Silas. Cadeyrn and another healer pulled out the knife and tried to staunch the bleeding, but he was still choking and spluttering. My mate came back over and dropped to the ground, feeling for my wound. His hand came away soaked with my blood and tissue matter. I was rasping for breaths and couldn't see.

"My two troublemakers here," Cadeyrn said to me softly. "Let's get you sorted. Shhh, cousin. Don't be pushy. Your bleeding has stopped, at least." I felt Silas grab my hand and squeeze. I opened my eyes and saw Cadeyrn swallowing repeatedly, his jaw ticking. All three of us were hurt. His whole family. My beast rumbled. I couldn't quiet her. She broke free and separated herself completely from me. Ewan shouted an expletive and watched her soar, then land next to him. He tensed, but she laid her wing over Corra and chirped quietly. The beast was always protective of my brother, so helping his mate must have been in the job description. Slowly, Corra's form appeared. She was stark naked and slightly rounded in the belly. Cadeyrn worked on me, knitting the wound together. I saw Ewan tentatively place a hand over Corra's belly and another hand on her cheek.

"You ridiculous, wild thing," he said to her through tears. "What were you thinking?"

"Oh, you know. A flashy entrance and all that." She tried to wave a hand.

"I am going to marry you and take you away and make you my queen and love you. Even if you protest. I will have my sister's beastie carry you along. Got that, Corraidhín?"

She laughed and patted his cheek. Aforementioned beastie seemed to fade into the trees, perhaps knowing that it was time to once again become one with me.

"Oh, you love me now, do you?" she asked.

"I have always loved you. I just had to convince you that you loved me back. And I was a horrid twat for the way I treated you."

I turned away, giving them privacy in this forest of so many. I could finally breathe, and as my mate worked on Silas, I met his eyes.

"Are there any more coming? Did it work?" I asked.

"Yes, it worked, you silly sausage," Corra piped in. "Gods, you two will give me grey hairs, and fae are not known to get grey hairs, so beware my wrath!" she teased.

"I need a hawk," Ewan said. "We need to send word to Turuin. He needs to defend the incoming ships and attack Dockman's fleet." Cadeyrn swore. "I think our world just expanded," Ewan said, hanging his head.

Chapter 10

Neysa

Consciousness was a fleeting thing. Once Cadeyrn had closed my wounds from both Analisse and the incessant slashes from various weapons, I had fallen into a sort of oblivion. As I woke, I heard the water close by and felt Silas asleep next to me. His neck wound was severe. I knew Cadeyrn lingered close and could hear him pacing now and again, speaking heatedly to someone. Why was I still struggling to keep my eyes open? I tried to speak, but nothing came out. What was going on? Burning pricked in my side where Analisse had torn the dagger wound open. I knew some wounds took longer to heal and some needed more recovery time. However, I felt like tent stakes kept me on the ground. How many godsforsaken injuries could I manage in less than a year? There was a damper on my power. I couldn't summon light or open the connection to my mate or brother. My beastie was gone, and come to think of it, Cadeyrn was unreachable. No breath came easily and my heart raced. Dirt scraped under my fingernails. I could move my hands. I slapped them on the ground.

"You're awake?" Cadeyrn knelt beside me. I could see him lower down but couldn't turn my head. "You can't move?"

My hands slapped the earth again. A second set of boots scraped beside his.

"Did she not heal?" A female voice. I knew that voice yet couldn't place it.

"She did. Perhaps I missed something," he mused. Hands moved over me. "Neysa, touch me with your right hand if you can hear me." I did as he asked. "Touch me with your left hand if you cannot speak." I did so again.

"What is the problem, Cadeyrn? We need to move them shortly," that female voice intoned. I wanted to pull her hair. He growled. A fair female came into view. *Bestía*. In my addled state all I could think about was how she and Cadeyrn had been involved, and now she hovered over my compromised body. She had piqued my defenses that first time she opened her mouth at the summit on Eíleín Reíne. Had someone told me she was the one to kill my mother, at this point, with her standing so close to Cadeyrn, I wouldn't have questioned it.

"Neysa, I think Analisse tainted your blood. I cannot be sure, but there seems to be a restraint on your power and your body, not allowing mine to fully heal you. Touch my right hand if you understand." I tapped his hand. "Good. I cannot speak to you mind to mind." I tapped his hand and squeezed my eyes shut. That link was based upon our mating. I couldn't feel that either. He touched my hand, brow furrowed in what I took for worry. "I think there may have been a constraint put on our bond. Do you feel that too?" I tapped his hand. "I'll work on it. We need to move you to a secure location. Our forces need to get to the coast. I may need to go as well." I tapped his left hand. *No, no, no.* "What? You don't understand?" Oh, for Christ's sake. *Don't go. Not without me.* He looked up at his companion.

"She's delirious, Cadeyrn. Allow her to convalesce while

we see to the coast." Something hot and not at all magical boiled in me at that statement. Pulling her hair out one strand at a time while I poked holes in her seemed like a good idea. I heard a grunt next to me and knew Silas had woken. Cadeyrn scooted over to him and spoke with his cousin. A shadow passed over me, and a fair female came into view. Her platinum blonde hair was braided and hung over her shoulder, brushing my face as she bent over me. And she smiled. An adder's smile. I started slamming my hands in the dirt, flicking it from my left hand at her. Her cold thumb pressed into that hollow spot between my collarbones as she winked those glacial, nearly lashless eyes at me. Cadeyrn called over.

"She's having a fit. I'm going to check on my soldiers," Bestía said. As she turned to leave, the Festaeran kicked the ground cover onto my hand. This was not good. I scrabbled for Cadeyrn. A hand wrapped around mine. Not my mate's. Silas. I squeezed repeatedly.

"I'll take you both to the wagons," Cadeyrn said to us. "We can travel together to Maesarra. I will leave you in Bistaír and head further." I squeezed my eyes shut. No, no, no. I felt him over me before he lifted me up and carried me to the wagon. Cadeyrn looked down at my face, his expression empty and distant. Not like the male whose soul mine knew as its own. As he laid me on the wagon floor, a strange sort of look came over him, and he simply walked away. I was thrashing inside. I needed to figure out what had been done to me. To us. Silas was brought in next. He was walking on his own, albeit slowly. My friend crawled over to me and took my hand as he laid down. I was squeezing as hard as I could and tapping my finger on his.

"Och, *Trubaíste*. I reckon you are trying to tell me something," he said. His voice was a rustle of leaves on concrete. "I don't know what yet, but we will figure it out. I recognize that . . . the penguinness is gone." I crushed his hand in mine. "I swore an oath, remember. Do not worry too much."

There was nothing to do but worry. However, my body had other ideas, and I slipped back into that odd sleep.

Two days on my back in the wagon had me wanting to annihilate everyone. Little by little, feeling came back to my extremities, starting with my toes and feet. By the evening of the third day, I could sit up and speak. Weakness wracked every part of me, my disposition suffering along with my body. Silas helped around camp and was even training for short periods of time. He watched Bestía and constantly muttered about her being a Festaeran demon. Cadeyrn brought me meals and offered to help me to see to my basic needs but left me alone beyond that. It humiliated me enough that I refused his help. He became more distant each day.

The stench of old wood and the tang of my unwashed body and dried blood permeated my senses in the wagon. Just as I had felt when word of my mother's murder came, the abyss of emptiness I was encountering had me in a vice grip. I couldn't allow Bestía or Analisse, may she rot in seven realms of hellfire, the satisfaction of seeing my downward spiral. So, I ate and spoke and walked and tried to retrain myself. It was useless to swing a sword yet. Each morning before dawn, when the world was at its darkest, I strapped on my thin dagger, left the camp, and did endless sets of squats, lunges, army crawls, and the like to strengthen what I had lost. Accessing my full power, like our mating bond, was still out of reach. However, each morning I would make a point to call upon the lupinus. They allowed me to walk amongst them. Even without my cache of power and the benefit of my swordsmanship, I had a small feral army of my own.

A fortnight after the battle in the magnetic field, I attempted pull-ups on a branch perhaps a couple feet above my head. Initially I swung myself up to stare out over the canopy of forest and plains that stretched toward the coastline of Maesarra. These were my lands. I would claim them and hold them with my brother no matter what. Lorelei died defending her lands. My mother died for hers. If kin had indeed come from across the sea, I would meet that head on as well. There were no birds in song as I sat on my branch like the *paitherre moinchai* Silas called me, my lupine brethren scattered below, keeping watch.

It was said Analisse was the reason my gifts had abated and my healing compromised, but I was absolutely certain Bestía had more than a little to do with it. In fact, though my fae powers were buried, my female instincts were on high alert. Bestía was trying to ruin me, starting with capturing my mate's attention. I could have my wolves tear her limb from limb to see if that reestablished my magic. However, did that make me a monster akin to her or Analisse? I thought it might. Perhaps soon enough, I wouldn't care. For now, I was better than that. I slipped down the branch and hung, packing my shoulders into place, and began to pull. Four pull-ups in, I felt a slight tearing of my stitched skin, and I dropped to the ground. Too soon. As I made my way back to the wagon, I heard a rustling between the tents and stiffened.

"Your Highness," Cyrranus greeted me. I wondered what he had been doing. Or who, rather. It wasn't my concern. "May I help you back to your wagon?" No one but Ewan knew I had been trying to retrain myself.

"Thank you, Cyrranus, but I should be fine." I hoped. He leaned closer. Close enough to share breath.

"You smell of blood. If you are not looking to draw the

attention of a certain male, then perhaps get to your wagon quickly." He pointed to my side. I felt it and swore. Indeed, the skin had fully ripped. Shit. "I see that there is a vileness here. Something has settled amongst us, and I know it has frayed your mate as well."

"I have no mate," I spat without wanting to. I had a mate. But he was so distant and unresponsive to me, my grief and anger forced my tongue. I wanted to throw up, but that would just tear my skin more. Plus, I needed every ounce of nutrition I could get.

"Thank you," I forced. "You have always been kind to me."

"You always have my loyalty. Know that." He turned and walked back between the tents.

I slunk to the wagon and climbed in, hissing from the sting of taking off my jacket. Fae healing, both my own and the extra abilities Cadeyrn offered, had become so common-place to me that having this wound not heal was humbling. Having my magic cut off felt as though I were constantly chasing phantom limbs. If I could not use my powers as they had been meant to be wielded, then I would train until I was a new sort of beast. I touched my stomach, missing the flutter of my *baethaache*. She had stayed with Corra and Ewan. Was Cadeyrn's still within him? I stifled a sob. Confusion at the mating bond's absence, I could understand. Yet his indiffer-ence to me was something else. It was as if he were . . . oh. Bewitched. As the thought processed, I pulled my shirt over my head. It would need washing. If he were bewitched, what was her endgame with him? Essential oils next to a small basin of water sat near me. I took two cloths. One I used to quickly wipe myself down and freshen up. The other I used to clean my wound and staunch the bleeding. Lina had told me that using frankincense followed by lavender helped to clot wounds. I dropped each on the torn skin. Circles of possibility ran through my mind of whether Cadeyrn were sentient behind the enchanted wall Bestía had mortared in his mind. Was he tortured and trapped, feeling as hopeless and helpless as I felt?

These physical wounds, as mortal as they were, paled in comparison to my detachment from Cadeyrn. These physical wounds served as mascots of my emotions. Crude representations of an all-encompassing love now unattainable. The scar ran the length of my side from the underside of my breast all the way around my rib and into my oblique muscles. Bitter crimson lines streaked like veins from the tear, while red puffiness formed the perimeter of the injury, making every movement hurt. I knew infection when I saw it, yet there was nothing anyone seemed able to do.

As the canvas flap opened, I expected Silas to come through. Where he had been, I didn't want to know. It was Cadeyrn. My heartbeat tripped at seeing him. Even now, our bond in shreds, facing all we were, one look at him and my hands started shaking from wanting to touch him.

It might break me. When you pull away, I had said to him that night in Cappadocia. I didn't know how right I had been. Every time we were separated, each time I thought I had lost him. Every fight, misunderstanding, and now this utter disregard for me, pulled at each of my seams. I kept trying to stitch myself back together, but I didn't know if this time it would be possible. Everything was unraveling. I stared at him as I held an arm across my bare chest, the other hand pressing a linen to my wound.

"What have you done?" he asked, his voice like frost. I closed my eyes and counted to five before answering.

"Apart from being stabbed and torn open by a succubus and having my magic ripped from me?" I blinked at him. His eyes were shuttered, then he rolled them. My gut clenched. "The wound reopened. Again."

"Shall I look at it?" he asked. I tensed at the thought of his hands on me, yet I agreed. He slipped into the wagon, and I moved the cloth, still covering myself out of some self-preserving sense of modesty. His nostrils flared as his hands moved along the cut. Memories of sitting in the dining room in Barlowe Combe after Peru rushed at me like a storm surge.

You're like this great ocean . . . all I want is to drown in you. His words clanked around in my head. Drown in me. Please come back to me. I was shaking as he felt around the torn skin.

"Is it painful?" he asked, eyes on the wound. I didn't answer. I couldn't trust myself to speak. Finally, he looked up for an answer. His eyes met my own, which were filling with grief. For a brief second, I thought there was a softening in his. I could have sworn I felt a pulse of wanting. I reached out and touched his face. He jerked back. How the whole camp did not hear the violent break of my heart at that rebuke was beyond me. I quickly scooted back and threw my filthy, blood-stained shirt overhead, hissing with the pain.

"You need to rest and heal," he said.

"No," I answered. "I need you." He started at my statement. "What happened to you, Cadeyrn? To us? Maybe our bond has been smothered for the time being, but my feelings for you haven't changed. You can't say the same, though, can you?"

He looked at me with that impassible face.

"Perhaps a female healer would benefit you." That was all the answer I received as he left the wagon.

"What were you doing?" I heard Bestía's pinprick voice ask him from a few feet away.

"Nothing."

No, I supposed not. Blood still leaked from my wound. Pain still lanced my side. A female healer. Lina.

"Were you in the trash tent?" Bestía asked, knowing full well it was my wagon. Cadeyrn was silent but for the scuff of his boots on gravel. "Gods she stinks of death."

I jumped from the wagon and ran for Corra's tent. Cadeyrn and Bestía were on my heels.

I turned to them.

"Fuck off, you two," I said, giving them an obscene gesture. Bestía laughed. Silas rounded the corner of Corra's tent, an oatcake in his hand.

"Silas," I called. He shot the others a look and ducked into Corra's tent with me. "Shield, please."

He threw up a cocoon around the four of us. Corra looked at me quizzically as she lounged against my brother on a bedroll. They were beautiful together: Corra's auburn hair and glowing skin and Ewan's bronze-flecked dark hair and liquid emerald eyes. As much as I was hurting, something softened in me that they had each other. Ewan finally had someone to call his own, and Corra had love after centuries of it escaping her. I wished Yva was with us. Another female on our side. She had felt it her duty to return to Laorinaghe and see to her fellow provincials.

"I need to send a hawk to Lina. I need her to figure out a tincture like the one she gave us in Laichmonde. A magic shield or protector. Something that can sort out what is happening to my power and . . ." I would not cry. I was done with tears. There was no more room for them in my fight. Silas placed his hand on mine.

"I can do it now." Corra sat up.

"Wait a bit. Bestía is watching. We have to be careful."

They nodded.

"I think . . ." I began, not wanting to sound like I was simply a jealous ex. "She may have bewitched Cadeyrn. Is that even possible?"

"I couldn't understand why she was here to begin with," Silas said. "She pledged loyalty, yet the contingent of soldiers she brought with her have come out relatively unharmed and the Festaeran nightmares we dealt with were independent of her? It stinks of something. I saw her watching you, Trubaíste. I've been around loads of jealous females, but the look on her face was something else entirely."

"Anyone can see there is something off," Corra said with a shrug. "Call it my female intuition, but I think she's been trying to get Neysa out of the way."

"I say we get rid of her," Ewan whispered. "I have no qualms whatsoever. I shall take council on the matter but know that it is my position. She has used aulde magic on you both. I can feel it."

"Did she?" I asked. "Perhaps. Or perhaps Analisse drained me of my magic. Perhaps Bestía is conveniently here at a time when my power is gone, and my bond with Cadeyrn too," I said, the last with more than a little waver to my voice. Rain pattered overhead, ticking on the roof of the tent.

"What is between you and my cousin was not magic. It was you two. Love. It is not natural to go from one breath to the next and have one's heart change completely. Whatever the case may be," Silas added, "Analisse was working with Feynser, and I would put coin on our Festaeran friend being in that happy arrangement too. Magnus sent me a message from the coast of Saarlaiche. He is in position to do whatever we need of him. Including overrunning the Festaeran forces. *Trubaíste*, perhaps it's time we put on a little show like we did in Bania." Magnus being Silas's oldest friend, it was a great comfort to him to have the fellow Saarlaichian male working with us.

The rain strengthened. I knew what he meant, and I knew how hard it had been for him. The show we put on trying to convince Analisse and her loyalists that Silas and I were together to get me out and back to Cadeyrn—back to my mother—altered something in him. The offer meant that much more to me because of it. I leaned my head on his chest in thanks. Knowing they all held suspicions about Bestía calmed the voice in me that said I sounded delusional. There had to be some great plan linking the Festaeran with Analisse and Feynser. But two of that circuit were now dead. The final death. So, who was Bestía working with?

"I don't want to put you in that position again, Silas. You are not a pawn, and I refuse to use you. But I love you for offering." I kissed his cheek.

Corra bolted upright. "No, Neysa. I believe we have all been made pawns. It is time to be queen. The queen uses her pawns to protect her king. Plus, you know, Silas and I are knights. But not like Elton John kind of knights. Like the ones in those documentaries I watched on finding the Holy Grail and the order that disappeared. Templars, I think? We should name ourselves. The Knights of something or other. I don't know. You figure it out. Ewan, be a love and fetch me breakfast."

Despite my poor disposition, I had to laugh. Silas watched me, searching my face for an answer to Corraidhín's statement. I nodded to him, and I knew he understood I would play along again. One more time.

To break the spell between us, I turned back to my brother. "She hasn't made herself a meal in three hundred years, Ewan. Good luck." He gnashed his teeth at her playfully, then left the tent to do her bidding.

HAWKS ARRIVED with messages from Turuin that Konstantín, the king of Heilig, had made it through his blockade safely. Messages followed Turuin's from Konstantín, that he came as a friend to Aoifsing requesting an audience with his kin. Both sides agreed to reconnoiter in a small village on the coast of Maesarra. Corra made certain the exact location was not passed on to Bestía or her soldiers, which, at the very least, bought us time in the planned rendezvous point without any diversions. The situation made it so that I was not deposited in Bistaír as planned but travelling along with the campaign to the coast. That morning we had decided to play our cards differently with Cadeyrn. It took four more days on the road to reach the village where we were to wait for our meeting. Each day I stuck close to Silas, leaning on him and making everyone think I needed more physical support than I did. The longer she believed me infirm, the more leverage we had to pick apart her plan.

Cyrranus sought me out the first night we arrived in the village.

"I have been played for a fool more than I care to think about and, contrary to my history, I am no fool. I recognize your caged animal actions and I want you to know that I can help in any way you need. I do not care much for your mate, and the way in which he is treating you has not softened my regard for him. However, the situation seems . . . less than characteristic of your relationship." He held his hand and sliced the palm with his spare blade. "I swear to uphold my loyalty to you and your brother. I repent for my actions earlier in the year and wish to make amends. I am in your service." He knelt on the ground and offered his hand to me, life source running free and dagger held aloft.

What the hell was I supposed to do with it? Shake it?

"Rise, please, Cyrranus. I accept, but quite honestly have no idea what to do with a bleeding hand. Any guidance?" He smirked and took my hand. Kind of gross. I didn't know him that well.

"Your acceptance is sufficient. The land has heard my pledge to you." He stiffened and looked over my shoulder at where footfalls sounded.

"What's going on here?" Cadeyrn asked. Feeling his heat

near me sent my body into a frenzy. I was quite sure everyone could sense it. My cheeks heated.

"Nothing," I answered just as he had that day outside of the wagon.

"It certainly looked like something. Cyrranus, your hand is bleeding. You have gotten it on her Highness."

I turned to face him. Cyrranus stepped to my side. Cadeyrn's eyes snapped to the male standing at attention near me.

"Is there something the matter, Cade?" I asked. His eyes narrowed. Since we had been together, I had only called him Cade when I was angry with him. And in that moment, I knew he was not really my Cadeyrn. "You don't seem concerned with my life any other time."

He stared at me, then Cyrranus. For a split second, it was as if the shutters came down in his eyes and I could see the male I loved so fiercely. I fiddled with the engagement ring on my finger, and my hands dropped nervously to my side. He caught the motion and his mouth opened slightly. I couldn't so much as breathe.

Where are you? Then Bestía came up behind him, and the moment passed.

"So cute. Neysa is cavorting with the help." She ran her hand over Cade's chest. I pulled back and delivered a one-two punch, knocking out her tooth and crushing her nose. Her slight frame hit the dirt.

"I believe the address you have forgotten is, 'Your Highness,'" I spat at her. "You have been permitted here only because I have not given the order to kill you. Yet. Do not test me further." I turned to leave, but her voice caught me. She raised it.

"Do you not think that killing me because your betrothed no longer wants you is a bit monstrous, *Your Highness*?" she asked with a smirk on her bloody face. The entire camp was watching us now. Silas had come up to me and taken my hand. Ewan's sword was drawn, as were many others. I cocked my head, assessing her, then squatted down to peer into her face.

"You're a witch," I said, low and dangerous. "You stink of deception and rot and everything decaying in this world. If my mate wants me away from him, then so be it. If you threaten me or the integrity of my brother's throne, I will put you down with no regard for my monstrosity. I can be the assassin, the monster, the darkness that one day snuffs you out."

She spat on the ground and smiled.

"Then you will never figure out how I did it," she whispered so low that only I could hear her.

I released the dagger at my wrist and pointed it right between her eyes. Cade's hand came down lightly on my shoulder. Briefly, there was a soft zing in the connection. I snarled at him in warning, and he snatched it back.

"You have no mate, Your Highness," she whispered. "Who are you going to be now?"

"I am who I have always been. My own beast. Watch yourself, you sick piece of shit." I walked away, pulling Silas along with me. Not more than two or three paces from where Bestía and Cade were standing, Silas turned me to him and pulled me into an embrace, his hands on my face. My heart was racing. I touched my forehead to his.

"That's my girl," he said to me.

Cadeyrn had said that to me. I wanted to vomit. I wanted to cry. I wanted to stick my blade in my own heart. None of that would do anything for our situation. The air became unbearably hot, and a snarl ripped from Cade as he helped Bestía from the ground. They walked from the center of camp into the village. Bestía's blatant disregard for me, for her king, for the obvious scheme she was pulling was maddening. But she was right. Until we figured out how to undo her damage, our hands were tied. Even Ewan couldn't stop her so long as Bestía's spell—or whatever she was doing —was a mystery. We could only watch and observe her. Make certain she had no access to critical intelligence—but only watch her.

"Cadeyrn seems to be warring with something inside of him," Cyrranus offered.

Silas snarled. There was a whole lot of snarling going on.

"Of course, he is," Silas snapped. "My cousin would rather die for his mate than see her treated this way." He stopped and realized he had put a wrench in our plan. "Fuck it all to never."

I put a hand on him.

"I can play the game, my lord," Cyrranus told Silas. "I understand the play and the risk."

Silas nodded at him and took me to an open field at the edge of camp.

Just as I was about to ask what we were doing, he pulled the twin swords from his back and tossed me one. My side kept splitting open. Almost every morning when I snuck off to train, it ripped. Angry red lines speared from the wound toward my heart, indicating blood poisoning, but there was nothing I could do so I ignored the pain. I wasn't sure I could even play dress-up with a sword, and I admitted to him that I wasn't sure I could manage it. Silas stalked over to me. Eyes from the camp followed us, many fae following our tracks. He bent over and kissed me. Slow and devilishly. I looked up at him, stunned. Wild wickedness danced in his eyes. I had to laugh. We stepped back from each other and began a dance of swords.

"My lady," he drawled. "I have missed these daily romps with you."

He lashed out.

I spun and knocked his sword with mine. Pain lanced up my side. His eyes widened. I shook my head. I would rather put on a good show. Cade's presence came to the line of voyeurs, yet I didn't spare a glance for whether Bestía stood beside him in the place where I should have been.

"You do always know how to take the edge off of me, Silas," I crooned back and whirled. Spiraling to the ground with more speed than anticipated, I came up under his sword, flush against his chest. He laughed and leaned down to nip my ear. I ducked and dove between his legs, rolling behind him. The seam of my wound opened completely, the side of my torso feeling like my insides were barely contained. It wouldn't be long until everyone saw the blood seeping down. I winced from the pain.

Silas, his back to the crowd, mouthed whether I was okay. Lips quirked in a forced smile, I ran full speed at him. The side of his blade arm knocked me back several feet. An "oooh" came from the crowd. He stood over me, whispering an apology. Just as he was about to put a boot on me, I rolled, then kipped up to standing. Oh, Christ. I nearly passed out. Fever was overtaking my body, causing shaking and chattering teeth. He crouched, ready for an assault. Feet dragging along the ground, I circled him.

"I always look forward to having you under me, *allaíne Trubaíste*. It's always such a pleasure."

"Then come and get me." I kissed the air and ran the opposite direction, barely able to see. Being fae and worked up, he wouldn't be able to resist giving chase. My wound was bleeding freely, and I suspected if I didn't see to it soon, I might lose consciousness. Again. Boot steps came up and I stopped short, jumping to face him. So quickly I didn't register it happening, Silas picked me up and had me on my back in the grass. His sword stretched from his hand away from us; his other hand pinned my arm.

"Do you yield?" he asked loudly and breathlessly. Then quieter, "Gods, *Trubaíste*, you are bleeding. Can you even get up?"

I shook my fuzzy head.

"Wrap your legs around me." I did as he said. "Ready for a good show?"

I smiled weakly as he stood with me wrapped around him and walked us back to the camp, his hands on my face, trying to transfer energy to me. There were mutters of "I thought she and Cadeyrn were mated?" and "Yeah, well, that Festaeran bitch has done something to him."

A trail of warmth followed us.

CHAPTER 11

NEYSA

Ewan stayed in Silas's tent, field stitching my side while we waited for a healer.

"How many times has this opened, Neyssie?" my brother asked softly. Every time it opened, it ripped further. The scar stretched down to my hip now.

"Nearly every day."

He and Silas both hissed. I'd needed to train. Needed to show everyone I was just as good without my magic and without my mate. The healer pushed through the tent. She tsked at me and worked slowly, knitting the skin together, pulling the infection from the tissue. Her dressing worked better than Cade's had on this wound. Whatever magic held our bond at bay kept him from healing me as well. It wasn't the wound itself, but the lack of conductivity between us. The lightning was gone. I was panicking again. Additionally, without my magic, there was not enough siphoning off of my energy and I had no ability to restore my sense of self. Wet rasps of breath racked my lungs like staccato beats of a metronome. The healer shushed me. When in the history of shushing had shushing ever worked? I was ready to punch her in the face as well.

"Now, darling," Corra soothed. "Ama needs to work. You must try to still. Use your clever breathing thingy. I will tell you a secret. I am thrice as powerful now as I was before. When the time comes, you and I can destroy anything and everything you wish. It will be that girls trip we wanted when we so unfortunately ended up in the godsdamned cloud forest eating meat bars and getting shot at. We can raise hell and kill Bestía an inch at a time, starting with her pinky toe. I may even be able to find some wild horses to run with. But for now, lovely, sit still and allow Ama to work."

I knew that name.

"Ama?" I asked, looking to the healer, who pulled back her hood. She smiled at me.

"Always in trouble, I see," she teased. I laid my head back and stilled for her.

The sun was close to setting by the time Ama finished. She began dozing in the corner, too spent to make her way back to wherever she slept. Staring at the ceiling, I began singing. Maybe I was delirious, but in that instant, I missed music. My father always used to tell me to crank the volume or sing when I was upset. I had forgotten that. He loved off-beat music with strange chords I'd never understood. I'd had bands and songs I loved.

Lyrics, normally sung in low-fi with electric guitars and violins, spilled out of me, telling tales of lovers believing impossible things between them. Songs from a band I used to see in L.A. Alone in that tent, feeling so alone in every aspect of the word, it was as if every lyric of every song I had ever loved applied to my ridiculous life, even though I was sure there was never anything like my life. Still, I kept singing. Song after song. As though music were a stand-in for my powers, giving me release.

Ama woke and checked my wound before leaving. Corra walked in and out. Voices carried through the camp. All the while, I stared at the ceiling, not allowing myself to shed any tears, and I sang. My voice was horrid and scratchy, yet I felt every bass line like the amplifier was next to me. The sun had set and a lamp was lit in the far corner. Sounds from the camp quieted; still I sang these stupid songs. Songs which had filled my days while I studied or commuted or ran or cooked dinner or stood in my shower while I struggled to breathe through countless anxiety attacks. Here I was, in another realm, fighting a war, losing my powers I had worked so hard to master, dealing with Cadeyrn, and wishing I had music beyond what my own parched throat offered me now. I didn't want to think about how much else I could lose.

After what felt like hours, I stopped singing. I pulled my knees into my chest and knew my wound had finally been healed. In turning, I saw Silas sitting in the corner, near the lit lamp, his red-rimmed eyes on me. The tent pushed open, and Cade walked in, seeing us both there. Heat flared around us.

"What is going on?"

"Is that your catchphrase now, Cade?" I asked sourly, voice like fingernails on rust.

"There was blood in here. What has happened?"

Silas unfolded from his seated position and stalked to his cousin, controlled and lethal.

"What happened is that you never healed your mate and didn't realize it. She's had a festering wound for weeks because you are allowing yourself to be bewitched by that *cuídvsite.* You are still rational, Cadeyrn. Use your godsdamned brain."

"She would not have torn the wound had you two not been engaged in such brutal foreplay. Or did it tear in the throws?" Cade asked, a flare of green fire in his eyes.

Silas visibly shuddered, restraining himself from attacking his cousin.

"I hope that question keeps you up at night," he said instead, then walked to me and stroked my face possessively. I leaned into the touch. Cadeyrn's eyes followed the movement. He swallowed.

"Konstantín has arrived. I expect he would like to speak with his kin." Before he left, Cade looked at my hand where my engagement ring still sat. "Unless you want to invite questions, you might want to take that off."

Howling in the distance echoed my feelings. I knew my eyes must be glowing, yet Silas said nothing. I stood from the table where I had been laid and pulled on my boots and jacket. Before leaving the tent, I saw a necklace made of raw rose and clear quartz. Each crystal was left jagged and harsh, hanging like icicles from a silver chain. In touching the crystal, I was shocked that a vision came with it: Ama placing it there and dropping a crystal into the pocket of Cadeyrn's trousers. I clipped the necklace around my neck and left.

Chapter 12

Silas

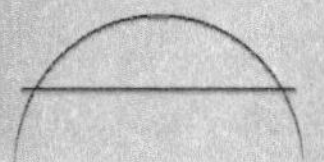

What sick fucking twat would play those games? I had my run of debauchery and enjoyed it very much. But what had Neysa done to deserve all she had gone through? If I didn't know my cousin and all he had withstood, and the fact I could clearly see that Festaeran demon had scrambled his thinking, I would have killed him. Neysa may not have loved me the way I would have liked, but part of me wanted to take her far from that mess. Far from the death and intrigue, and to have kept her quietly with me. But that was a drunken daydream.

Standing by and watching Cadeyrn with Bestía while Neysa hung her head and accepted it was torture. Ewan, the beautiful little sod, had threatened to kill the Festaeran bitch several times. I tended to agree, but my sister and Neysa said to hold out and see how to dismantle the enchantment. Funnily enough, I'd heard rumors that Bestía had been slain in the battle in which I nearly died. Inaccurate dissemination of information, I supposed.

Neysa thought no one saw her as she snuck past me every morning to train on her own. In the beginning I would follow her and watch. Watch her anger over not being able to do what she could months ago. Watch her improve. Watch her bleed and scream and cry out in the woods where no one could see her. Apart from me. I thought I had scented Cadeyrn one morning. In the trees near me. No one knew what to do to wake him from this spell. It was as if his memories had been wiped clean, along with their bond and Neysa's powers.

Once we had decided to play our scheming parts again, I knew deep down that eventually Cadeyrn would be overcome with seeing his mate with me. I knew her scent and desire would wreak havoc on him. So, we played the game. She let me kiss her and hold her and sometimes, I told myself, it seemed like she was okay. Until the night after Ama healed her and she sang. Fucking gods, what weepy, emotional songs they had in the mortal realm. She sang for hours about the *"beautiful corpses of this destroyed humanity"* and all that kind of rubbish. Some of those songs she sang would haunt me. Fucking hell.

Reynard, the weaselly little shite, had become my closest ally. His speed allowed him to run messages between towns for me. I had to corral our supporters without Bestía and her legion getting wind of it. Kasseik diverted his regiments, and rather than come to us and deal with the wreckage we were amassing here, I had them reroute and merge with Turuin. Eventually, I'd see us joined, but when the head of our army was enchanted by an enemy posing as ally, I couldn't take the risk.

I hadn't sent for Lina days ago when Neysa asked. I hated to involve her in everything. She would have been taking a great risk, leaving her business, and she was still pissed at me. It had seemed like every time we had a go, I took off and left her. Not to mention the fact she blamed Neysa for quite a few of the trials of late—from Cadeyrn's and my injuries to my leaving. Even though there was no one I would have trusted more to figure out this spellbinding bullshit Bestía pulled, I couldn't do it. So, I'd sent for Ama instead.

Our weapons were meticulous, because every frustrating, raging minute when I walked away from Cadeyrn or Neysa, I cleaned them. I even cleaned others' weapons.

"Silas." Neysa snuck up on me. I was so used to her scent from the wagon, I hardly noticed. I set the sword aside and looked at her. I hated how her eyes saw right through me. She had lost so much weight, but still it was that face that undid me. "If I don't hit something right now, someone is going to die a slow and painful death."

"What can I do for you, *Trubaíste*?" I stood and held up my hands for her to punch. She knocked them half-assed.

"That whore keeps making snide remarks about my smelling of blood and sweat. If I kill her now, there may not be a chance to break the spell. So, I need a distraction."

As she spoke, I saw my cousin come around the corner with the whore in question. Every time he saw Neysa, it was like he had never seen her before. I pulled Neysa to me and leaned into her neck and sniffed the length of her. She shivered, and I nearly growled at it. Gods, I wanted her.

"They are coming this way. Are you up for a bit of theatre?" I whispered in her ear.

She answered by putting her arms around me and grabbing my face to kiss. Fucking hell. I wasn't expecting that, and I backed her against the wagon, pressing my body into hers. I knew she felt the heat come off of Cadeyrn. He didn't even seem to notice it, the poor sod. None of us knew whether he was bedding Bestía or not. They had a thing a hundred years ago. It was casual, I remembered. He never seemed bothered about its ending. I pulled away from Neysa's mouth, knowing I had to stay my course, even though reattaching myself to her was the only thing I wanted to do.

"Silas," Cadeyrn called. "I have need of you."

I turned slowly to look at him, my hand twirling in the escaped hair from Neysa's braid. His eyes caught the movement. I saw it then. Another flash.

"It looks as though *she* has need of him as well, my love." Bestía's words could have been a gut punch to me as hard as I felt them hit Neysa. Against me, where they couldn't see her, her shoulder caved, and she bit my shoulder to keep from crying. I wanted to kill them both.

"I can spare you this moment, Silas," Neysa said, rallying herself. "Feel free to bring me back that whore's head. In flames." She beamed an evil, beautiful smile. I walked away, pushing at my trousers.

"Where are our reinforcements?" Cadeyrn asked. "Turuin was supposed to be here before us."

"As far as I have been told, there was a storm off Saarlaiche which delayed the travel a few days. Turuin even lost a ship," I lied through my teeth. Normally, my cousin could see right through my lies. This, however, seemed to appease him. I needed Turuin to stay offshore and offer back up if shit went tits up on our end.

"You need to let them know," Bestía said to me, "that we are being patient, but our patience has its limits."

The flaming head seemed like a bloody great idea right now.

"Pardon me, lady," I answered, gritting my teeth. "But you do not give me orders. Come to think of it, Cadeyrn, why exactly is she here?"

"She aided us in battle and is a part of our collaborative defense."

"She did fuck all, cousin," I barked.

She hissed.

"The battle was a success due to Neysa and Ewan's plan. You go worry about whatever you worry about these days, and I shall uphold my responsibilities. As always."

"Go warm your little bitch's bed, underling," Bestía spat. I started to lose control; rain came down in great sheets.

"I should say the same to you, but gods know, there is no warmth anywhere in your body." I stalked off to find Corraidhín and secure the hawks.

Chapter 13

Neysa

Turuin opted to hold the sea line of defense, staying offshore while we all gathered in the village to meet the King of Heilig as he disembarked his ship. Dark mahogany hair like mine and my mother's was in a shaggy crop on his head. Though he had a spray of freckles like Ewan and I, his face was very fair, his eyes large and a deep olive.

As siblings, we faced him and bowed in welcome. He did the same. The meeting was to take place in a private home in the village. Our host graciously offered to vacate completely so we could reside there for the duration of our stay, but we all opted to stay in camp. Bestía walked alongside Cade, her hand on her sword, like his consort or second-in-command. The air was tense as we settled into the drawing room of the comfortably appointed home. Konstantín looked me over, no doubt noting the hollowness in my face, the lack of color from fever and trauma.

"Are you well, Your Highness?" he asked with what felt like genuine concern.

"I am presently, Your Majesty. I have recently healed from

the last battle in which Analisse of Veruni both stabbed and drank from me. The wound was difficult to heal."

His eyes widened as he sat forward.

"I was told you have a mate and are betrothed," he asked me. "Is your mate not present?"

I swallowed. This could have been planned better.

"That would be me, Your Majesty," Cadeyrn answered. I found my voice.

"King Konstantín, my mate, Cadeyrn Bowden of Saar-laiche." The words tasted like ash on my tongue, and to anyone who knew me, sounded much the same. It seemed to placate his curiosity, so he began to tell us of the strife in his lands.

Ten years ago, the ruling party of Heilig decided to allow certain trade ships to enter the archipelago which protected the lands. Heilig was completely surrounded by these enchanted islands and they served to protect the people for millennia. In recent years, the Lady Analisse, her commander Lord Dockman, and several others travelled often to Heilig for trade and pleasure. Unrest began in the larger cities, and the fae of Heilig protested the royal line having been given to Aoif-sing. The visitors only recently pledged to bring back their royal heirs and provide the lands with fae who might breed more power in the land.

"I came to beg you to consider establishing a presence in Heilig," King Konstantín began. "While en route, we were ambushed by Lord Dockman and a fleet of ships. We managed to get away, and though the ship with Dockman himself was sunk, I witnessed his being hauled onto another boat."

We sat back. Something didn't sit well with this story. Where would Dockman have gone and where was the seed of deceit? With the Heiligan king or within our own ranks?

"His Majesty and Her Highness must remain in Aoifsing for the time," Cadeyrn said. I looked at him in shock. Why did he feel he needed to answer for me or Ewan?

"I understand this to be quite surprising," Konstantín said, splaying his hands in supplication. "I come bearing no ill will. I left these lands long ago so my sister could rule. She and I were very close, and it was quite hard. You both favor her so much. You, Neysa, remind me of my daughter, Saski. All I ask is that you help keep the peace in your homeland."

"Who blew through the archipelago?" I asked, remembering my vision.

"Phantomes were called from the darker, aulde magics. Part of the unrest. Phantomes were released in some villages as well. Many lives were lost. You see, it has become quite a problem."

"Those phantomes. Where did they go after they blasted your wards?"

"I don't know," he admitted.

I turned to Cade and reached to show him the vision in my mind, even so far as touching his arm. He looked down at me with indifference, and I withdrew my hand. Bestía snickered and coughed as though she swallowed water wrong. Thank you, Corra.

"Cadcyrn," I said. "The ghost army you fought. What did they look like?"

He watched me for a hair of a second.

"Wraiths. Barely there, yet capable of tactile assault. They moved through their own army—that of Festaera and those who fought alongside them, without causing harm, yet were as deadly as corporeal warriors against us."

"Phantomes," Konstantín confirmed. Ewan swore.

"And have you any means to dismantle the phantomes? Can they be eradicated beyond killing the one who controls them, like Cadeyrn did?" I asked.

"We have mystics and necromancers who can fell many at a time. Though we must find who controls the intent. Our mystics are very skilled, but this type of warfare is older than most." Aulde, dark magic.

"Have you any mystics with you, Your Majesty?" I asked.

"Seven."

"I should like to speak with them directly."

"Of course." He motioned to one of his guards to fetch the mystics.

Having mystics at my disposal sparked a plan in my head. I leaned into Silas and whispered to him so only he could hear. He stood and left, returning with Cyrranus and five guards of our own. Konstantín looked alarmed at first, but the guards all moved to Bestía.

"What is going on?" Cade asked.

Honestly if that question came out of his mouth one more bloody time, I was going to hit him.

"Bestía, you are being detained by the rulers of Aoifsing and Heilig." I looked to Konstantín, realizing I might have overstepped his authority. He tucked his chin once. "You will remain in custody until I have deemed you not a threat." Which was not bloody likely. My boots stomped on the rug with enough force to make the mantel vases teeter.

"On what grounds?" she asked haughtily.

"Conspiracy against the crown," I answered, ticking off the offenses on my fingers. "Accessory to murder. Deviant use of dark magic. Shall I go on?"

"This is absurd," Cade remarked.

"I love you more than life itself, Cadeyrn. But so help me God, if you say anything else that makes you look this stupid, I will lose my shit."

"You see, she is jealous. This is a lovers' spat. She is upset he chose me," Bestía said.

Silas's hand on my back steadied my rage.

The mystics entered the house with a small faction of guards. I thanked them for coming before they looked at me and then at each other. The plan which had formulated in the preceding moments had so many iffy factors, yet it seemed like my best option.

"What has been done to you, child? Let us look." They spoke as one.

Goosebumps ran up my arms. Silas and Ewan flanked me.

"You have been spelled. Bound by your own magic." They tilted their heads side to side in synchronized creepiness. "It cannot find its way through." They turned their heads to Cadeyrn. "You must see her to release her."

"This is bullshit." Cade stormed out.

"I have one question at the top of my list," I asked. "If I kill the one responsible for spelling me, will the spell be broken?"

They seemed to be having an internal conversation.

"That one has been long dead," they intoned in unison.

Shit. Bestía laughed.

"Stupid girl," she said.

"How do I break the spell?" I begged. Silas threw a shield around Bestía, keeping her from hearing their answer. Bless him for the forethought.

"Face the one who fears you. Be the one who holds you. Embrace that which seems foreign. Speak as though you can be heard. Find those who dance to your song." They quieted and left the room.

"Any code breaking skills on that one, Neysa?" Corra asked.

"Fucking hell," Silas swore.

Bestía laughed from the other side of the room.

"So, may I go now?" she asked. "My lover has left. Analisse is dead. Good luck." She began to choke, water bubbling from her lips. *Lover. My Lover.* Bestía calling my mate her lover created a rising tide of tar like hatred in me. I didn't know if she and Cadeyrn had been together intimately yet. I hoped I would have sensed it. Scented it. Something. Still.

"Corraidhín, love," Ewan remarked.

"Sorry, darling. My hormones are getting the better of me."

"Keep her contained," I commanded. "Your Majesty, I will help in any way I can. As you can see, we face an internal threat. Please know it is sensitive in nature."

"Of course," he answered.

PASSING SMALL SHOPS AND HOMES, I stalked back through the town. It was a quaint, happy village. Cats lounged on balconies; warm light lit the windows. Bistaír, my family's estate, was mere miles inland from here, and I had yet to see it. Tonight, I needed to get to the sea. Just north of the harbor was a beach covered in shells and washed-up coral. I ran to the shore and pulled my boots off to sink my feet in the water. Breathe.

Movement to my right had me spinning, daggers out. Cade raised his hands.

"If you say 'what is going on' again, I swear I will throw this dagger at you."

He actually chuckled.

"I didn't mean to scare you. I came to breathe in the sea," he said.

Of course he did. Just as I had.

"Why don't you see it?" I asked.

"See what? We had a mating bond, I will admit. It is gone now, and I am free to feel as I would like."

I could have eaten hot coals and felt less pain.

"And you as well. You are free to . . . dally with Silas."

"So, everything. Every feeling we had. Every touch. Every promise. You chalk it all up to a bond that has been removed?"

"Yes."

"Ah. Stupid me. I suppose then that the thought I had in Rila was correct. I will never be loved. As I love you."

"I am sorry. I do not mean to hurt you this way. Truly."

"Will you humor me a moment?" Trying to speak as though every breath hadn't been stolen made my question torpid. Still, I would not cry. He shrugged in the darkness of the beach. I stepped closer to him. Alarm shot to his face. I touched his arm and moved my hand up the length while my other hand moved to his stomach. He tugged at my hand to pull it away, heat flaring slightly. Tightening my grip, I stroked his face and hair. Everything in me trembled. Rumbling came from deep in him. Whether it was his *baethaache* or just a response, I didn't know. My lips touched his neck as I stood on tip toes. Even with my height, he was at least six inches taller. I kissed his salty skin softly, then pulled away. His hands fisted and I saw his eyes were closed, but I walked away before he could say anything else.

"I don't know why I bother," I said.

A NECROMANCER, a sparring ring, *Araíran-aoír* nut flour, sugar, eggs, vanilla, five clear quartz, five rose quartz, and a hot bath. Like the start of a bad joke, I stood in my tent with my knights of whatever and spewed a list of what I needed. On our way to an inn, Silas gave me a searching look. I knew I smelled of Cadeyrn after pressing against him and likely my desire in that horrible moment. I did not want to talk about it. Talk about getting a couple of blocks away and throwing up until my sides ached. I wanted to bathe and wear fresh clothes that were not covered in blood. Yes, I should be sleeping, and I told Silas he should be as well, but I had a plan, and it needed to be done quickly.

Inquiring about a necromancer in a small village was a delicate matter. Of course, no one knew of one. *No, no aulde magic here, Your Highness.* In speaking to the most respected healer, I impressed upon him the need I had for a necromancer to free our realm from a plague. I also asked for groceries, new clothing, and underwear to be sent to the inn. So really, the knock on the door could have been anyone.

A father and sleepy young child stood waiting to be invited into our room. They carried two parcels. The father handed them to me and blurted out that we could not speak to anyone of his child's abilities. I explained we may be able to cloak the child, but we needed him to help us. They would stay the night at the inn.

I bathed quickly, barely long enough to enjoy the water on my skin. Buckling my weapons over the fresh leathers my mother had made for me gave me a sense of power and purpose. I lined my eyes with a kohl pencil and braided my wet hair back. Dressed and ready, Silas and I stomped down the stairs of the inn to the kitchen.

Hours later, a few soldiers dragged the two most ostentatious chairs we could find in the village down to the field I commandeered as a sparring ring. Dawn painted lazy lilac stripes across the sky, dragging its languorous fingers through the horizon in slow, teasing strokes. Dread filled my gut in that early hour. In these muted watercolor minutes, everything could turn around or be blown to hell.

Cadeyrn stood amongst a few males near the cook's fire, drinking tea and listening to their stories. *Bannocks and tea, Neysa. Focus.* The morning was warm already with a humid breeze coming off the sea. I left my jacket in my tent, wearing just a fitted cotton tank with my leather pants and boots. The new necklace from Ama hung below my clavicle, above the *adairch dorhdj*, which sat above my modest cleavage. My hair had dried in waves from the braid and, until I had to get in that ring, I was wearing it down and loose. From the braziers I lifted a kettle and poured water into a tin cup. Chatter stopped when I came round, but as I sipped from my cup and waited for the bannocks to cook, the chit-chat resumed.

"It's 'ere," one male pointed just below his elbow. "It gives me shite whens I use me sword 'an whens I pull sommin' from the wagons."

I recognized the soldier and his Dunstanaich accent.

"It's called tendonitis, Griffin," I told him. He looked surprised I knew his name. They all turned to me. "I have it as well. Hurts like hell in your grip, right?" He nodded. "It's very common. For me, it's worse when I grip my weapon too tightly. The bits that hold your muscles and bone together get inflamed—like, they swell, and that's why it hurts. Try some of this on it." I reached into my shirt and pulled out a tin of salve Ama had made for me. It had lemongrass, calendula, lavender, and something else I couldn't place. He caught the tin as I tossed it over.

"Awe, your 'ighness. I couldn't be taking from ye," he said, his cheeks darkening.

"Please. I insist. Can't have my warriors in pain." I winked at him and turned to Cade. "Remember how bad mine got after we sparred that day in the woods? Oh, and after the fight in Bulgaria?"

He narrowed his eyes at me and blinked several times as

though he were trying to remember. Griffin rubbed the salve on his arm before handing it back to me with thanks.

"Let me know when you need it again, Griffin, okay?" I pushed my mass of hair over my shoulder and rubbed some of the salve on my own elbow and shoulder, working it into the kinks there as I drank my tea.

From a distance it was the same Cadeyrn. He was easy and encouraging with his soldiers. Refined elegance and sun-bronzed fair skin. He had trimmed his hair and still shaved every morning. Broad shoulders pushed at his leathers from centuries of daily training. I noted all the blades he had on him that I had strapped on him myself at times. Even the hidden ones. I guess we hadn't known each other that long, but it had felt so real. It had been so real. It was to me, at least. Every small moment when I stared into those eyes that swallowed me whole. Every touch and tease. The way his heat would rise when I pressed my hand into his back or touched his stomach. The way he made me feel when his hands went into my hair before he kissed me. The quips and whispers between us. The way we bantered and were content to lay all night, talking of books and nothing consequential. All these little details I cata-logued in the short time we had been granted. The last time we slept together, the night before the battle, came to me as vivid as the first time in the hollow. I wasn't hungry anymore and stood holding the warm bread as I stared off in the distance, thinking about the male mere feet away. The soldiers he had been speaking to left, and he turned to me, sensing or scenting a change in me. I glanced his way, then back into nothingness.

"Did I heal your elbow in those times you mentioned?" he asked me.

"Yes. Well, after our fight I avoided you for a couple of days until Reynard attacked me in the woods. You offered then." I smiled a little. He looked up at me from lowered lashes. I honestly could have had him right there in the middle of the godsdamn cooks' area.

"I don't remember. That's odd."

"Do you remember when you healed me after Peru? My broken rib and shoulder?"

He shook his head. "It was kind of you to offer your salve to that male."

It seemed like he was avoiding the question.

"I don't like to see anyone in pain."

He nodded. "I don't remember after Peru. I'm sorry. I suppose things have been busy."

It was a gentle letdown. I swallowed and set the bannock down for someone else and swigged the rest of my tea before steeling myself.

"Cadeyrn. If there's nothing left between us, then I should give this back to you." I pulled the ring from my finger and placed it in his hand, folding his fingers over it.

"Keep it," he said. I smiled sadly at him.

"I only wanted it for one reason."

"What was that?" he asked quietly.

"To be yours." I walked away before I could say or do anything else.

Chapter 14

Neysa

Today, I would play queen. Today, I would sit beside Ewan in his crown, and I would pretend for the life of me that I was running the show. Today, I would fight like the warrior queen I had to become. Ewan and I lounged in our ostentatious chairs on the field that was laid out with clear and rose quartz outlining the shape of an a*dairch dorhdj.* Two thrones borrowed from stately homes. I hadn't seen Reynard in days, yet he sat along the length of my armchair, perched like an elegant cat. We drank wine and called Cadeyrn and the others over. Full fighting leathers completed my get-up with a touch of dark lip stain. Once everyone had been brought down, Cyrranus showed up with Bestía. Cade looked confused and stood before our makeshift dais.

"What is the meaning of this?" he asked.

"Of what?" Ewan asked back with an air of innocence.

"Why have you brought her here?" Cade asked.

I stood, wine in one hand, and came very close to him. "I want to have fun, and we can all spar together and drink wine."

"Are you mad?" he asked me. Likely.

"So, question is. Who fights first? I know. You and Bestía. Silas and me."

"It's a trick. She is going to try to kill me, Cadeyrn," Bestía said.

"Oh, please. Were I to want to kill you outright, you'd be dead. Isn't that right?" I smiled, sick and saccharine. "Let's go. All of us in the ring." I grabbed Silas by his jacket and pulled him along. Cade looked so pissed I nearly laughed.

Cadeyrn and Bestía squared off and began to dance around each other—strike and parry, block and thrust. He removed his jacket, the heat getting the better of him. My mouth went dry looking at his chest and back. Wine did not help in this heat. Removing my own jacket and Silas doing the same, we began our own waltz. I was distracted but didn't care much. I wasn't trying to win against Silas. That wasn't the point of this. He managed to get behind me and wrap an arm about my sweat-soaked abdomen and the other held his sword near me. Our bodies were pressed together, sweat slicked and panting. I looked at Cadeyrn sweating and caught his eye. Bestía took advantage of his distraction and cut his arm. I hissed and she smiled. Though Silas kept me in check, I stared at Cade. Between the press of Silas and looking at Cade, warmth built in me.

"Do you yield or shall I have you on your back again, Princess?" Silas purred. I moved my free hand up his thigh in answer.

Cadeyrn. I kept trying to reach him. I gave myself over to the warmth building in me from watching him, Silas near me, and I projected that to Cade. *Watch me.* My hand clenched on Silas's thigh. I could feel him pressed against me, his heart racing, though outwardly, Silas remained unruffled.

In two moves Cade had Bestía down and disarmed. Cyrranus and the other guards kept her there. Cadeyrn looked at Silas and me. I wrapped my leg around my friend and spun in his sweat-soaked arm, then pushed us both down. I sat on top of him and pressed into his chest. Cadeyrn's eyes were on us, I could feel them. The heat was oppressive.

"Do you yield?" I asked Silas, my mouth just above his.

"Whenever you want me to. Shall we do it here?" He cocked an eyebrow at me.

I stood and bowed before Cadeyrn. "Ready?"

"You can't be serious?" he asked. I pushed my lower lip out in a pout.

"Why not? Let's dance."

He moved so fast I didn't see it at all. His sword lay across my chest, his other arm holding a dagger to my throat as I faced him. Hmm. I looked him in the eye and smiled.

You could just take me here.

He shook his head as if to dislodge a fly. His dagger dropped a fraction, and I knocked it away with my elbow, earning a smarting cut, then kicked him backward. As he stumbled, his hand darted for my arm and pulled me to him. I pushed as hard as I could and knocked him down. My knees were on either side of him, hands on his chest, my thin dagger out. A wicked gleam came into his eyes, and a smile spread across his face. Uh oh. I shoved down harder and pressed myself into his body, my face inches from his. I felt a response in him and a rumble. He flipped me over and had a knee pinning down one of my legs, his mouth latched onto my neck like a wild animal, teeth slowly puncturing the skin. I didn't know what to do. My arms were pinned above my head and his breadth of power poured into me.

Kill me then. I felt a bite that instantly healed, and he slowly slid from me, coming to kneel beside my heaving form.

I knew you'd pull away. Eventually.

His head snapped to look at me, my hand shading my eyes from the sun.

"What does that mean?" he asked me.

Slowly, I turned to him. *Can you hear me?*

He gave one curt nod. I couldn't breathe. *I made you cookies.* Holy shit, Neysa, really? That was what you chose to say? *Even though you've been horrible to me.* A smile ghosted his lips.

"Cadeyrn," Bestía called. His head shot up and looked at her. He started to stand. I grabbed his arm, and he tried to yank it away, so I tackled him. Full on, ungraceful, Texas Friday Night Lights-style, headfirst tackle.

"Now, Ewan!" I screamed. Chanting and a childlike voice rose above the din of onlookers. The crystals surrounding us glowed in the morning light, casting beams of pinkish light between us and Bestía. I hoped I was correct in assuming she had been dead and come back, just as Feynser had. The necromancer was there to unravel the tethers holding Bestía to this realm. What a fate to contend with as a child.

I wrestled with Cadeyrn, who had a solid upper hand, then brought my own mouth onto his neck and bit down with just enough pressure to show I was serious, but not enough to break skin. We were godsdamned fae, and I would claim my mate. I pushed on his arm and set my hand on his stomach. Heat rose between us. The chanting and child singsong voice got louder. Cadeyrn's hands went into my hair, and I grappled for him, driving my knees into his inner thighs. He took my face and crushed his mouth against mine so hard my teeth sang. His kiss was nothing I had experienced before. It was animalistic and closer to feeding than desire. As though his very life depended on that kiss. Teeth caught on my lips and tongue. Blood slithered in my mouth. Both his and mine, mingling. I couldn't see or think as I was lifted off the ground and carried away. I knew Silas followed close behind, and Cadeyrn pulled from my mouth to snarl at him loud enough to make the tents shake.

A wall of flame, courtesy of Cadeyrn's gifts, blocked us off from the onlookers, and an avenue in the middle of blue flames opened for us as we rushed along. His hands clawed under my vest and tore at my skin. I dragged my nails down and over every inch of skin I could find purchase. We were covered in each other's blood and sweat and everything came alive in me. Once in his tent, we crashed and dropped to the ground in a heated tangle. Distantly, there was a screech, and I knew Bestía was succumbing to the necromancer. Cadeyrn tore open my vest and his hands were all over me. We pushed out of our trousers and paused for the slightest second, both crazed and shaking. I launched myself on him and pulled him on top of me. I raised my hips until he was fully sheathed, his growl turning everything in me molten. I went over before I was ready for it to be done. He slowed and brought his lips to my ear, touching the pointed tip with his tongue, then whispered, "I remember all of it now."

He slammed his mouth and body into mine again and thundered a moan that reverberated off every tent, wagon, and structure in the vicinity. The beast and Battle King staking his claim.

We were a mess. As much as I knew we had to go back out there and deal with Bestía and the necromancer, I wanted to stay and lick each other's wounds until they healed. Entranced, I watched some of the gashes I caused on Cadeyrn's chest knit back together, leaving just a smear of blood behind. He ran his fingers and mouth over my scratches and gouges, healing them. His long fingers touched the scar from Analisse and ran a trail up the length of it. His skin became hot to the touch, his jaw ticked.

"I couldn't even heal you?" A low, sandpaper rasp of a question.

I turned, not knowing if I could even have this conversation. The crystals of my necklace fell to the side of my neck when I shrugged and looked away. He lifted and straightened them across my chest.

I still loved you, I told him. *Every second I watched you not feeling anything for me. Watched you with her. It was cruel. I thought . . . I thought that surely you could feel me. Feel something for me.* I looked up, the tent ceiling rippling with refracted light. *With or without the bond I thought you'd still at least know me. Want me.* I hated admitting that. That I missed being wanted. *But everything was gone.* I kept talking, his catching breaths the only other sounds.

You didn't feel. Is it . . . is it just chemical for you? Just a preordained animal need? I asked, still staring away. Because if that was all it was, that was not how I wanted to go on.

I think . . . that's what she intended it to feel like. So you would always question it. He was able to respond to me again, and he gently turned me to face him.

"All my memories of us were gone," he said aloud. "It was like you were just this person who appeared with my cousins. I knew we were supposed to have been mated, and I didn't understand it, because I didn't know you. There were times I would start to . . . feel something. When I walked into Silas's tent and smelled your blood. On the beach, I wasn't sure what had hit me. When you gave me back the ring, in my head I knew I shouldn't feel anything, but something inside was screaming at me to pull you back, to say something. So, no, it is not just some preordained notion.

"It is a deep, fucking, soul-ending love I have for you." His hand raked through his hair. "Even though the strongest magics were used to tamp down our bonds and feelings—my feelings. I felt myself falling for you over and over again anyway."

I refused to cry. Of course, that meant I had to keep my damned mouth shut. Screams and wails were coming in a constant wave from outside. We really should get out there.

"Say something," he begged me. I turned to look at him. He knelt next to me, fully exposed, head lowered like a weeping angel.

"What finally flipped the switch?" There was a cold note to my voice. I knew it hurt him, but I had tried these past weeks to build a shell around myself to survive. He reached forward and touched my stomach.

"When I had you pinned down," he murmured, embarrassed. "I could hear every beat of your heart and heard you speak to me. Then . . . you said you knew I'd pull away. It was like a bucket of water was thrown on me. Something started screaming at me. So, really just you. You 'flipped the switch,' as you say."

A particularly loud and awful screech sounded. We both sat up and gathered our clothes. Leather pants were horrendously difficult to put on over sweaty legs, but duty called.

"Good of you to join us," Silas yelled over the screaming of the dead who answered to the Festaeran demon. His chuckle resounded through the high-pitched chanting of a child no one could see. For a split second, I was rooted to the spot, taking in the scene. All over the field, coming up to just beyond the crystals, were reanimated bodies trying to surround Bestía and bolster her reserves. A veritable generator of life from which Bestía was siphoning energy. She knelt with arms flung wide, eyes bleeding, arrested in a state of suspended animation.

You were right, Ewan said to me, and I heard him. Which meant my magic was fully back.

"I usually am," I yelled back to him smugly. He grinned

and tossed me my sword. I spun it gratuitously, making Cadeyrn roll his eyes.

Every now and again, one of the dead would break through the line and one of us would sever head from body. Bestía's platinum hair had turned white and wispy. I walked to her.

"Neysa," Cadeyrn and Ewan both growled.

"Face the one who fears you. Be the one who holds you. Embrace that which seems foreign. Speak as though you can be heard. Find those who dance to your song," I said to both of them in our minds. Darkness was as much a part of me as the light I harbored. From the day I was taken from my mother and brother, I had a heady, nearly impermeable darkness in me. It fed my drive, my soul. It kept me from breaking. I would not apologize for my darkness. I would stroke it and listen to it. I would never again allow myself to be vulnerable to someone or something like Analisse or Bestía. Perhaps that did make me a monster. I stood before the female who had stripped my magic, my light, and my love from me, and gave myself over to my creature tendency. I was fae, not human. I was beast. *Baethaache.* Where was my beastie? I cocked my head to Bestía and knew my eyes cast a yellow glow. Wolves slunk from the tree line and surrounded the field. The onlookers and soldiers gasped. I commanded the wolves to take down the dead. And they obeyed. Crunching, screeching, wet, ripping sounds drowned any voices as the wolves met with the dead. Splinters of loss hit me from my charges who were killed. In mere moments, however, the corpses were felled. Konstantín and his mystics stepped toward me.

"How long ago was she dead before she came back?" I asked them.

In unison, the mystics answered. "Four cycles of the moon, daughter of the between."

That was an interesting answer.

Bestía smiled, blood pouring from her eyes and nose.

"I had him. I nearly freed him from you. Who would want that crown of darkness you possess?" she cooed in a lilting, spun sugar voice.

"Is the necromancer nearly finished unravelling her spells?" I asked. The mystics looked to one another in silent conversation. Good grief, they were unsettling.

"It is done. She is ready to be finished, she who is held in darkness," they sang.

Ewan stepped to me, Cadeyrn on my other side, Silas at my back, and a host of lupine subjects in the field behind us.

Find those who dance to your song.

My brother, my mate, my Silas, my wolves. They were all my darkness and salvation. Together we would pull ourselves from the catacombs of what we had endured. Together we would forge a new light. Not to drive out our darkness, but to illuminate different paths through. I angled my sword to take out the female who nearly destroyed everything. Part of me hated Cadeyrn for letting her. I knew he was spellbound, but it hurt me.

"So, she is ready to be put down?" Cadeyrn asked all of us.

The mystics all bowed.

"Battle King," they sang. "Consort to the one held by the Goddess of Aulde."

My skin crawled at their deference and implication. Without a moment's delay, Cadeyrn lunged forward and severed Bestía's head from her body and set the corpse aflame in blue fire. Silas sent a wind to scatter the ash. I gasped for air as the last dregs of her spell fled.

The necromancer stopped. I felt the child leave, relief washing over me that the cloaking of the child necromancer worked. No need to destroy another life. Cadeyrn set fire to all the dead who lay across the field, his vast power finding an outlet.

My wolves kept at a distance yet held me in their sights. Cadeyrn walked toward them, his weapons sheathed, and he knelt before the line, bowing his head to my charges. They sunk down to their haunches in return. It was an eerie sight to behold; in this field, on this morning, all of my world and particles had come together.

In turning, I saw the seven mystics facing me, each holding out an item. I walked to them. As each handed her item to me, she bowed. A magic coated bean or seed, a wand of selenite, quartz, pyrite, a seed pearl, a gold thread, and a polished red stone like garnet or ruby.

"Daughter of darkness and light. Paladin of the Veil. Queen of *Taeoide Gaellte* and *Aedtine Aimschire*. We honor you and beseech your assistance in the lands beyond the sea. Come to us, across the waves. We will be waiting." Just as they spoke in unison, they turned and walked away. Konstantín looked at me and sunk to a knee.

We took council once more at the home in which we had met only yesterday. It could have been a lifetime ago. Though we knew the main players and had dealt with them, we had not figured out some of the supporting roles and who held them. Bestía had indeed been killed in the final battle against The Elders. She had been a double agent so to speak for Paschale, but was working with Feynser and Analisse to eradicate The Elders for their own gain. Who had brought her back, we still did not know. We assumed their ultimate goal was to rule Aoifsing amongst themselves. Why Analisse promised to bring Ewan and me to Heilig remained a mystery.

None of us were naive enough to trust Konstantín at his

word, however genuine he appeared. I believed the threat against his family—my family—was real, and against it, he sought our help. How closely knit his ambitions were to Analisse's, however, was yet to be determined.

I felt so very tired. In five days, we would set sail for Heilig. I hated leaving without Ewan and Corra, yet I knew it was the best and safest option. Who I was and had been were spinning around each other like cars on black ice. I left the house, seeking the sea, and stopped to watch a family playing along a beach.

"I want you to know I am incredibly creeped out by those mystics and the shit they said to you." Corra came up alongside me and threaded her arm through mine. "However, if it makes you feel any better, I knew you were the heir of Heícate, the Goddess of Aulde, long before today. And it didn't scare me. Even being the goddess of darkness and magic. The mystics, though . . ." She shuddered.

I laughed, but a loud sob tore through me as well.

"Oh, darling. I know. This has been too much." She pulled her arm from mine and wrapped it around my side.

"Who am I, Corra? That answer has changed six times in the last year. How can I be anything to anyone without knowing who I am?"

"Look at me," she said in the authoritative voice she used on her brother and cousin. "That answer has not changed even once. Only the accessories have changed. You are Neysa. You are your mother's daughter, making you a princess. You are your father's daughter, giving you life and light. You are heir to the goddess of magic and darkness. That's fabulous, by the way. You are Cadeyrn's mate and queen and lover and friend. His world. You are Ewan's sister, and my friend, which is by far the most important." I laughed through my ugly crying. "You are everything to Silas, which is sometimes an issue and may need revisiting. But I feel you both need one another to traverse this world and the next. None of these things changes *who* you are. Now, go stare at the ocean or whatever it is you lot do. But do be careful of sharks; I watched this documentary on them for a week straight. Ugh. Or here's an idea. Do everyone a favor and lock yourself away with your mate until you two cannot walk."

"In case you didn't know," I told her, "I love you, Corra. You're quite good at this helping me get my shit together stuff."

"I know. What do you think I've been doing for the lads these past three centuries?" She walked off, her hand upon her tiny, rounded belly.

I sunk down into the shell-covered strand and opened my palm. In it was a seed pearl, given to me by the first mystic. An offering to the Protector of *Verraige*. The sea. Perhaps I was asking for safe passage. Perhaps I was giving thanks for the gift of knowing I could breathe near the ocean. Whatever the case may be, I let the lapping water lick the pearl from my hand and swallow it into the depths of *Verraige*.

Shells crunched behind me. One by one, they will come, I thought to myself with a smile. It was the beginning of a children's story my father used to read to me. I couldn't remember the tale itself.

"*Trubaíste*," Silas said. I looked up at him and smiled. "Quite a day."

I stood and hugged him fiercely. He laughed and hugged me back, his scent wrapping about me.

"The cookies we made are in the room. I could get them."

"Promise me something, Silas," I said into his chest, breathing in his woodsmoke scent.

"Anything," he answered, voice gruff.

"That you will always believe in me. Because you have the clearest soul and biggest heart of anyone I've ever met in either realm, and if you believe in me, I know I stand a chance."

"Your mate will always believe in you," he said carefully. "Silas."

"Of course I will always believe in you, *allaine Trubaiste.*" He kissed the top of my head.

"Corra thinks that, for whatever reason, you and I need each other. Do you believe that? I think we both know I need you. I would have fallen off a cliff of my own making a million times had it not been for you. Do you feel like you need me?"

"Like the air I breathe." His voice was hushed and could have been carried away in the waves. "Your mate is waiting for you. Better hurry, lest I steal you away into the forest and keep you for my bride." I smiled at him and reached up to press a quick kiss on his cheek. "Och, you stink!"

He made a face and waved a hand in front of his nose. I sniffed myself.

"Remember when Corraidhín said you and my cousin were like penguins?" he asked. I did. Before we left for the Isle, she said she saw a documentary on animals who mate for life, and Cadeyrn and I were like badgers and penguins. Silas leaned in and winked at me. "The penguins are back."

Chapter 15

Cobbled streets drank in the late afternoon sun as I made my way through town. At first glance, it was a small fishing village, but the further I walked I realized it must be a resort town. Many shops, cafes, taverns, and boat rentals lined the shore. It could almost be human, but for the way colors danced in dizzying arrays, the spectacles the flowers put on, and the fae I encountered who were equally beautiful and fearsome. I was raised to see people for who they were and appreciate cultures and colors for the beauty in our individuality. In Aoifsing, I saw it as no different. Were we any less lovely because we had pointed ears or elongated canines? Decidedly not. Going back to that inn on the other side of town was what I was supposed to do. What I needed at the moment was to wander. To think without being injured, or scheming or . . . Christ, I hadn't eaten today. No wonder my leathers were loose. Weeks of anything I ate tasting like dust from the crushing despair had kept me from holding onto any weight.

Polished wood columns and wide shutters opened to the street of the inn I had procured on this side of the seaside town. Balconies hung over the water and dripped with climbing vines releasing the intoxicating scent of jasmine. Luxurious and simple in its decor and atmosphere, it felt like the kind of hidden gem one might find in the Caribbean. Next to the inn was a dressmakers. I ended up purchasing four dresses and sandals. In my head, I was pretending to be on holiday. A careless tourist spending coin and decompressing. By the time I had eaten my third pastry and bathed, having changed into one of my new dresses, the town's folk were whispering that I was here and patronizing businesses. Everything in my body ached to be by the sea, so even the restaurant in which I chose to eat had tables on the edge of the rocky shore.

Only a trickle of a breeze moved across me as I sat sipping a sparkling rosé while picking at a breadbasket. The breeze felt heavenly on my bare shoulders. Ribbon-like straps held up my dress, meeting at the fitted bodice, which contoured my torso until it hit at the hips and dropped to the ground with open sides, allowing ventilation in the warm, Maesarran air. Black silk looked dramatic, yet the dress seemed to call to me. I had scooped my hair into a topknot, secured with pins, and still wore the two necklaces.

It wasn't that I was avoiding Cadeyrn, though it may have seemed that way. I needed to be on my own for a bit and not be in a war camp or a palace under siege or on a quest. These last few hours were likely the only time I would have to do this for a long while. Sailing for Heilig was not something I wanted to do. In fact, the thought angered and exhausted me. I wanted to just be for a while. Wanted to figure out what being me was. Especially in this place. As that thought presented itself to me, I realized I did want Cadeyrn to be a part of this discovery process. Admitting to myself that I hadn't been entirely sure after the days' events made my stomach clench in consternation. Really, I was a mess of confusion and self-doubt. He was my mate. Even when the bond was stripped and he didn't know me, I felt him. I always felt him and knew. So, after keeping my thoughts closed off all day, I sat back at my little table by the sea and opened them back up, reaching out to find him.

There was a restaurant in Malibu that everyone used to go to, I said to him. *It was a touristy place with buckets of shrimp and slices of pie the size of my head.* An awakening, softly amused acknowledgment of my words came across. *It was where people in L.A. took out-of-town guests because it was on the ocean and all that. My dad and I had another little place we liked to go a little farther north. It was less crowded, and I think it was really only patronized by the people who lived in the vicinity, because it was tucked kind of behind houses and hung over the Pacific. It felt a little bit like the cafes in the South of France.*

It sounds lovely. His response had a smile in the tone, though his voice was rough.

We would go often, and they knew us there, I continued. *It was the first place I went after my divorce. They didn't say anything to me but gave me a small slice of chocolate mousse cake. Then Dad died, and I went there again. They gave me that cake again. Well, I assume it was a different cake, but the same type, you see. I realized after that, ever since I was little, whenever Dad or I had a rough day when we were in California, that's when we would go there. And so often, Dad ordered the chocolate mousse cake. He likely had quite a few rough days. So, intermittently, for twenty-five years or so, this little place north of Malibu was where Dad would take us when things got heavy.*

Did you go there when you went back to fetch the amethyst dagger? Cadeyrn asked.

No. I just got tacos. A soft chuckle came through. *Because all I wanted at the time was to get home to you lot in England. The only thing that really weighed heavy on me was who I am or was becoming and how you fit in that picture.* Silence. Then a rough answer.

And all I have given you are more weighted questions.

Do you have questions for me? I asked, thinking he may question the ruse with Silas.

Only if you want to answer them. I am certain I have many to answer for you.

Would you have dinner with me? I showed him where I was, further opening the link.

Give me a few more minutes. I'm finishing up here. He showed me what he was doing. A group of ten or so children stood around him in a courtyard while he showed them how to properly hold and swing a sword. Their eyes were bright, and they were soaking in being given lessons by Cadeyrn. I missed seeing that softness in him.

Take your time. I'll be here.

PACING myself on the wine while I sat waiting was a bit of a problem. Staring at the sea, piercing my second sight into the depths, spun me away from this picturesque town, and I saw the colors below the surface and could feel the varying pockets of warmth and cold. Felt the soft cloud of sand on the sea floor and the ripples from the bump of waves. As though I were swimming for the surface, I pulled up from the sea to growing warmth around me. Cadeyrn stood a few feet from the table, watching me. He had changed from what I had seen him wearing. He was now clad in a simple white shirt with his sleeves rolled up in the heat and black trousers shoved into boots. I smiled at him in the coral-tinged light of sunset, and he sat in the chair across from me. Everywhere his eyes hit on me I felt a trail of warmth and a whisper of his rainlike scent as though it were a scarf being teased over my skin. After a time, his eyes found mine.

"You are so beautiful," he said finally.

"Having a bath and fresh clothing makes a difference."

"It doesn't matter what you're wearing."

I looked down at the table and fiddled with my glass. A server came over and bowed to Cadeyrn, filling a glass for him. I had ordered a plethora of dishes, from pasta covered in shellfish to mussels in a lemongrass broth. We ate until near bursting. Though our conversation wasn't deep or meaningful, we chatted about little things, and I realized these were more of those small moments I craved.

The dishes were cleared and another bottle brought out.

"I heard your singing in the tent. I sat outside for quite some time, thinking you must be a siren and that's why I kept getting pulled to you even though I didn't know you. How ridiculous is that?" His eyes were so wide, and his mouth was quirked comically. I laughed.

"With my voice? Especially last night? I'm the worst siren ever. Lure unsuspecting warriors with my scratchy emo rock songs."

He snickered and finished his glass.

"Smelling the amount of blood that came out of that tent had me in a blind rage."

"Yes," I drawled, wine easing my nerves. "'What is going on?'" I teased, mocking his voice and accent with those words. "Holy smokes. You kept asking that over and over. Drove me mad."

"I was a lost puppy. I truly had no idea what was going on." He smothered his own laugh. "It feels so stupid now. I feel so stupid." He scrubbed his face.

"You were violated," I said seriously. Though for some sick reason, I just burst out laughing. Horrified, I covered my mouth with my hands and ducked my head into my napkin but still laughed hysterically. The table shook a bit, and I looked up to see him laughing.

"I'm sorry. This is so inappropriate." It took me three times to say that, my eyes streaming tears from giggling. His mouth was trembling at the corners, and his face was flushed from laughing so hard. I took a deep breath, attempting to quell the outburst, then sipped my wine, but it ripped from me again and I sprayed the wine across the table, narrowly missing Cadeyrn.

"It's like an affliction," I gasped, my cheeks hurting. I hadn't laughed in months. Not really.

Our server brought a third bottle of wine out and set it down saying it was on the house. He also set down a small silver bowl of chocolate mousse.

"They didn't have mousse cake," Cadeyrn explained, sobering slightly from our fit.

"Chocolate mousse is actually my favorite dessert. In Paris, I would order one in every single restaurant. I gained like ten pounds every trip."

"I want to know everything about you." He looked at me, still flushed. "If that's okay with you? I want to know your favorite foods and scents and songs. Everything you think is important and likely what you find trivial."

"And will you tell me about yourself?" I asked, raising an eyebrow.

"Anything you want to know." We both sat back and sipped from our fresh glasses of wine. I wasn't ready to spoil the mood with questions about the past few weeks.

"I miss music," I said, looking out at the calm water. "I never realized what a big part of my life it is. I always used to have it on at home. Dad and I used to play it all the time growing up. I went to concerts regularly. L.A. has all these small theaters where bands played and I liked doing that.

There were three or four bands I saw every time they toured. So, while I don't necessarily miss doing that—they were all good memories. Well, not all, but most."

I thought of the night I had gone alone to a show because Caleb was busy. He ended up following me and made a scene outside of the El Rey theater. The worst part was that, as embarrassing as it was that he caused so much drama, he had actually come with a girlfriend. I had enough wine in me now to where I wasn't sure if I had projected that memory. From the look on Cadeyrn's face, I suspected so.

"Anyway, what I miss is the music itself."

A group of fae walked by, dressed up and happy. Males and females, heading out for the night. They smiled at us and continued down the boulevard. I wondered where they were going.

There are taverns and nightclub-like places that way. We could go if you want, he offered.

In a little while. I'm happy sitting here for now. A breeze blew in, cooling my sun-warmed skin. I closed my eyes and let it flow over me. The sun was nearly set, the world darkening slightly. The past month I had spent dreading the darkness. I hated being in my tent or in the wagon, not knowing where Cadeyrn was or what he was doing. The worst part was knowing he had not cared where I was. It took me a minute to restructure my feelings on the oncoming dark. When I opened my eyes again and took in the soft lights twinkling on the bay, the townsfolk coming out to dine or dance, the warm lights in windows, the male before me, there was a shift. Like the darkness inside me, the night was nothing to fear anymore.

"You figured out the riddle the mystics told you. May I ask how?"

I sat forward and looked at his face in the dying light.

"It wasn't exact. I kind of guessed and took chances. 'Face the one who fears you'. I figured it was Bestía. After all, I was the only one who could bring an end to her. 'Be the one who holds you,' I had to keep it together. Myself. Keep myself together. If I didn't think objectively, and it was hard, nothing would change. 'Embrace that which seems foreign.' Using my lupinus gifts. It was the only power that remained in me." I mused over that to myself for a moment. Perhaps my lupinus gift was a link to both realms. A power existing within me which kept me toeing the line of the fae and human realms. I pulled my eyes from where they looked down at fidgeting fingers.

"Plus," I continued, "we had decided as a group that Silas and I would . . . pretend. I hadn't wanted to, but Corra told me it was time to be queen and protect my king. So I had to use my knights." I smiled a little.

He did as well but looked unsettled. I continued.

"The next one was easy. 'Speak as though you can be heard.' I kept trying to talk to you. In my mind or in person. I just kept trying. For so long it had been like speaking in a vacuum, but I kept trying. 'Find those who dance to your song.' I have my fair share of darkness in me, Cadeyrn. I know that. It makes me volatile and emotional. It protects me. Ewan has it too. Perhaps we all do. When I looked at us standing there in that field, I knew Silas accepted my darkness, and I hoped you would too. So, I used that hope and knowledge and I just went for it." My voice was a little raw. It had been such a long day, and I was fully drunk. Yet I didn't want this to end.

"You did well."

We were silent. My head buzzed, and my limbs felt liquid.

"When we were younger, Silas, Magnus, and I used to go out to the clubs. It's not too different than in the human realm. We . . ." He paused and coughed a laugh, giving me a sidelong glance. "We were quite a trio. I think that's why Magnus tried to get me to be that male again when you were gone. We drank until we were sick—which is saying something. We can handle our alcohol fairly well. We had companionship. It was next-level debauchery."

He rolled his eyes gloriously. I gave him a look that said I wasn't surprised. By God, he was something to look at.

"There was this one night." He ran his hand through his hair, then grabbed at the back of his neck and looked at me. I bit my lip. "I have no idea how much we drank. Gods. Magnus got this idea—he was always shit stirring—to replace the musicians. I don't play anything. Silas really doesn't either. He was schooled on the viola, yet all he really did was cause the livestock to run."

I laughed.

"So, we got up into the little box where the musicians play, and handed them our drinks, telling them to take a walk."

"What did you play?" I leaned forward, chin on my hands.

"This instrument called a síarnan. It's similar to a guitar but plays deeply like a bass, and you keep beat on a skin on the back like a drum. It's, well, complicated, and I was horribly drunk. We did a whole set of shit music like that until we were kicked out. For whatever reason, a whole gaggle of folk followed us—males and females fighting for our attention. It turned into a full-on brawl because males and females were upset that their partners wanted to come home with us. Turns out, Magnus took some half-cocked love potion he stole from Lina and put it in our drinks. It took us all night to lose the following."

I was laughing openly. "I'm quite sure you would have had some offers regardless."

"Not with how poorly we played," he laughed.

"Let's go find one of those clubs," I said. We paid for the meal and took to the streets, following some of the folk along the boulevard. A block or so after the restaurant, Cadeyrn's fingers brushed mine in question. I walked a little closer to him, feeling my blood spike, and touched his fingers back. He laced his long, calloused, beautiful fingers through mine. Holy God, just his hand in mine made me dizzy.

The interior of the club was dark with small fae lights bobbing from the ceiling and in corners. Instruments played songs that were upbeat and entrancing. I smiled, bright and happy for Cadeyrn. He answered mine with one of his own, and I swear my heart stopped completely. Not that we needed any more, but he left to get drinks. Others were on the dance floor, and I joined in, moving to the music. I had to pick up my skirts so they wouldn't get stepped on, and tied the sides in a knot, exposing my legs. Cadeyrn stood at a table, watching me dance.

Come here, I said to him.

I rather like watching you. I am not the only one, either. I laughed aloud because as he said that, a female came up to him and placed her hand on his arm.

"You have beautiful eyes!" she yelled over the music and din of voices. He smirked.

"That's what my mate tells me." He pointed to me. She pressed her lips together in embarrassment and mouthed an "I'm sorry" to me. I waved a "no big deal" and kept dancing, moving with the crowd across the floor. I lost sight of Cadeyrn as the crowd shifted, and then I was on the opposite side of the room. My skin was getting sticky with sweat from dancing. I found him again; he was still standing against the high table with untouched drinks. A lazy smile greeted me, and he blew slightly, sending icy wind at my neck and chest. I moaned a bit.

"What do you want to do?" I yelled over the music. Though there was no stereo or DJ, the music was loud and permeated the establishment as much as any human club. He shook his head. I stepped closer to him, instantly wishing we were somewhere more private. Instead, I wrapped my arms about him and pulled him to dance. We moved to the music and let it hold us in its trance for a few songs. He leaned into me and took my hand.

"I didn't do anything with her," he yelled. He knew I knew who he meant. "She was persistent. Called me 'lover'. I didn't do anything. I want you to know."

I pressed my head to his and nodded. He caught my bottom lip in his and pulled at it.

"I know how it looked with Silas," I said. "I know you saw us kiss. It was to try . . ." I smoothed at his collar and ran my hands along his broad shoulders. "To wake you up."

His eyes found mine, amused. "It worked."

We made it about half of a block after leaving the club before I pushed him against the wall of a building and kissed him senseless. My skirts were still tied up, and the heat around us was near suffocating. I drew back and gulped down air. He was breathing hard and exhaled theatrically.

"Wait. Before we go any further. I have a confession," he told me. My hands stilled on him. "I hope that tray of biscuits was for me, because I ate the whole thing." I yanked him to me and fastened my lips to his, walking backward toward my inn. An inn further from the others. We backed into the doorway and pulled apart, as a couple exited, chuckling.

"This isn't even our inn," Cadeyrn said, making to turn. Pulling a key from the folds of my dress, I grabbed him and pulled him further in the building and up to our room. He marveled at the room that hung over the water. The dark wood floors and white linens matched the woodwork and jasmine on the balcony. A fountain bubbled in the corner of the room, and the breeze danced through the curtained windows.

"Nicer than the other, I think," I said. He walked to me slowly. I drank in his powerful body and the way it shifted as he moved. Heavy-lidded mountain stream eyes raked over me as he moved closer. "My favorite song is about a letter being

written to a lover saying he wished she could have been the one
—thought she was the girl he'd always dreamed about, but the
make believe ran out," I told him, swirling my finger in his
palm.

"That's . . . very depressing," he said.

I laughed.

"Yes, I told you I was dark. My favorite scent, apart from
the ocean, is the smell of rain. Whether it's the way it smells
coming down in winter and mingles with woodsmoke, or how
it smells steaming from a thunderstorm in summer when the
world needs to cool down. It smells like you."

He stepped closer still, standing in front of me, and put
his hands into my hair and pulled the pins holding the top
knot. My hair fell, and his hands dove through it and ran
down the length.

"Tell me more."

I closed my eyes, trying to think, and leaned into his hand
on my cheek.

"When I was seventeen, I had a boyfriend who wasn't very
nice to me. He wore this horrible cologne—something or
other 'Noir,' and I will always associate it with him. That is my
least favorite scent."

"Did he hurt you?"

"He pushed me once. I slammed an elbow into his face
and kicked him in the chest, breaking a rib. So, no."

Cadeyrn chuckled. Fingers trailed over my collarbone and
touched the crystals at my throat. He leaned down and kissed
my shoulder. I brought my hand to the back of his head and
twined my fingers in his dark hair.

"More. Please."

"I ran away from home once. Not to get away from my
father. I felt bad about that. But I was sick of the kids in
school. Sick of the boys who stared at my chest and made up

stories and the girls who believed them. I was fifteen and looked older."

"How far did you get?" he asked, kissing my other shoulder and lifting the strap on my dress, simply running a finger under it.

"Spain." He snorted and had me confirm it. "We lived in England that year."

"Why Spain? Why not France, since you have a clear problem with chocolate mousse?"

"We had been on holiday in Spain the previous summer, and there was a boy who worked near the house we rented."

"Completely ridiculous," he said, smiling against my ear. "Who follows someone to another country?"

I whacked him.

"He had this black hair that fell into his bright blue eyes . . ."

"And did you find him?" Hands trailed down my back and along my waist, as his mouth moved along the side of my neck. I leaned my head back, giving him access to my throat.

"Yes. It took me forever to get to Barcelona. My flight connected in Brussels, which was dumb. Anyway, I looked like a bedraggled cuddly toy when I arrived. He said he didn't remember me and introduced me to his girlfriend."

"Ouch." Teeth scraped my throat. The memory of his teeth at my throat hours earlier had me arching to him. "What did you do?"

His heart was racing, and the colors of the room and the lights from outside were swirling in my vision.

"I called my dad to pick me up."

"From Spain." Not even a question.

"From Spain. He did. My swords were taken away for a month."

Cadeyrn laughed again, lifting both straps and pulling them slowly from my shoulders.

"Tell me about you," I said breathlessly, undoing the buttons of his shirt from the bottom up. Sea breeze blew in the balcony doors, momentarily cooling our heated skin.

"I trained Magnus on the sword," he began, undoing the tiny buttons on my back. "His and Lina's father died when they were very young, and I am maybe a hundred years older."

"Negligible age difference to be sure," I teased, bringing my hand round to his backside.

He growled.

"So, I think, and I never found out for sure, but I think Silas put them up to this. We had been training for a few hours one day at their home outside of Laichmonde. I was a bit of a hard ass on Magnus." He drew a line down my arm and held my hand to his mouth.

"You? Can't imagine."

He nipped my finger and promptly had it in his mouth. I gasped and pushed against him.

"Magnus was perhaps twelve or thirteen at the time. He asked me if I wanted to see his father's swords. He said his mother told them they could use them if they learned properly. So, I agreed and followed him to a woodshed at the edge of their property." He lifted the dress by the shoulders and pulled it off my arms, letting the silk swish over my arms as it laid me bare for him. I was thankful I had gotten new undergarments. He stopped talking for a moment and stared at me. I put a finger under his chin and lifted it, meeting his eyes, and nearly getting lost in them.

"Keep going," I whispered. His hands traced my new scar, and heat flared around us. Lace ties held my underwear together at the hips, and he looped a finger through the tie and cocked an eyebrow at me. "What was in the shed?" I asked, breathing so hard spots were forming. His chest rose and fell as often.

"Swords. As he said. But there was another door, and Lina

opened it and told me that inside it was the best one of all. So, like an idiot, I walked in. And they shut the door and barred it. It was a safe room of sorts."

I started laughing, my chest bouncing against his. "How long did it take for someone to find you?" I asked through giggles. He was laughing and brought his hands up to the lace bralette and removed it.

"Two days." He ran a thumb around the edge of my chest. I undid another button on his shirt.

"You must have been very hungry."

"Starved. Eventually, Corraidhín dragged Silas by the ear and had him let me out." Another button. I lifted the shirt open a bit more, running my thumb over the bumps of his abdominal muscles.

"Did they get in trouble with their mother?" I asked.

"No, no." He shot me a cat-with-a-canary grin. "I upped their training and made Lina join too. It was far worse a punishment. I don't think either has forgiven me."

I answered his grin with one of my own.

"I want to see you smile for as long as I live," he told me. I undid the last button and pulled his shirt off completely. On a silver chain around his neck hung my engagement ring. I touched it lightly. I hadn't seen him wear it earlier today.

"I cloaked it. When you gave it back to me. I told you it had felt wrong. So I wore it, but cloaked it so she wouldn't see."

I leaned my head against his chest and pressed a kiss to him, then smoothed my hands down his sides and wrapped my arms around him. He held me.

"What is your favorite anything?" I asked. He rumbled against me. "Apart from *that*?"

"The scent of crushed leaves in autumn when the sea air blows through the trees. That sounds a bit sad. The way your skin smells when you get out of a hot bath. Reading. The time to read and sit. Peanut butter cookies, thanks to you. Those pork dumplings you get in Hong Kong. The sea and everything about it."

I nestled my head against him and ran my hand along the inside of his waistband. He traced circles on my lower back and pulled the tie from my underwear. I backed up and sat on the bed.

"Your boots are still on," I said, low and gravely. As I blinked, they were off and in the corner. I sat up, stunned, and pushed at his trousers as he climbed over me. "However did you do that, mate?"

"Particle transference," he growled. He tugged open the other tie.

We moved together slowly, and I left strokes of electricity along his face as we rocked. He shuddered and had alternating blankets of warmth and cool mist laying over our bodies. Pushing up on my elbows, I kissed his eyelids and along his cheekbones. He held my face in his hands and kissed me, stopping all movement and relishing in the kiss itself.

"I told you that no matter what happened, to know that I love you and you are my mate," he said, voice thick. "Never doubt that. I am sorry for what happened."

"It was . . . harder than I could handle. I thought I was tough and could keep going. I kept trying to be strong and hear you say to never doubt you. Yet . . . you didn't even know me. I couldn't even eat. Stupid girl, right?"

He ran a hand along my ribs and shook his head.

"Never stupid. Just . . . mine," he said softly. I staked claim to his lips and brought him further to me until there was nothing in the world but the two of us and the magic between us.

ONE DAY we would sit on a balcony, and it would be ours. It would be where we settled or where we were for lengths of time. Above all, it would be where we chose to be. Sleep was so needed, but I felt panic at having this night end. This was how I wanted us to be. This was what we deserved to have together. When I first attempted to open to Cadeyrn and let him in my mind to see the visions I initially had, I started by picturing myself sitting with him and telling him inconsequential bits and pieces from my life. As though I knew what I longed for. I had felt so much in those moments that it scared the hell out of us both. Here we were on the coast of Maesarra, pretending to be on holiday, and not awaiting a sea voyage to an unknown land. Our bodies were pressed in close, squeezing onto the chaise on the balcony, surrounded by jasmine. *We might need a beach house*, I thought with a yawn. A rumble of laughter jostled me.

"I wouldn't mind that," Cadeyrn answered. "You're tired. We can sleep."

"No." I said it too quickly.

"I won't go anywhere."

"I know. I just don't want this night to end." He pulled my hand from under the sheet that wrapped us together and held out the ring he removed from around his neck. I held out my finger and sniffed a restrained cry. The metal slid over my finger and settled in. My mate took my hand and kissed the knuckle above the ring.

"Let's not wait. On anything."

I turned in his arms and looked into those eyes.

"I'll need a dress."

He smiled against my mouth.

Chapter 16

Neysa

Setting sail across an unknown ocean, for an unspecified task and an unspecified length of time, made me more than unsettled. This was not the honeymoon either of us would have chosen, and leaving behind Corra and Ewan made my heart ache. Silas swore that Turuin and Kaseik would defend my home, and that the forces gathered amassed to far over a million. He was confident enough in them that he felt comfortable leaving with us. Even still, the previous days passed far quicker than I would have liked.

The morning after the defeat of Bestía and her ill begotten army, Cadeyrn and I found the others and announced our plans to wed that day.

"You need a dress," was the first thing that had come out of Corra's mouth. Cadeyrn rolled his eyes at us and murmured something like "she could stand there in a fishing net and still be beautiful." Corra splashed water in his face and told him he would acquiesce to every wish I would ever make because he caused hell for me for weeks.

"I'll do my best," he said, and flashed me a dimpled grin.

Once the town caught wind of our planned nuptials, there

was a bustle. The dressmaker I shopped with the previous day tracked me down and insisted she be the one who provided my dress. Children covered the sidewalks of the boulevard in flower petals, and local vintners scrambled over our wedding wines.

"And here I thought we were doing the equivalent of eloping and not making a fuss," I grumbled as I was pulled away from discussing with Cyrranus whether he would be staying on with Ewan and Corra or whether he was planning to accompany us across the sea. Silas sauntered up behind us and poked me in the ribs.

"Did you truly mean to keep a low profile? In their eyes, royalty is marrying in their town. The bunting is stringing as we speak," he teased me.

"It seems like a lot of hoopla when there are so many pressing matters at hand."

"That, *Trubaíste*, is exactly why it should be celebrated. As you did for my cousin, you both are bringing light upon a dark time. They want to set up this hoopla, as you call it, though I have no idea what that means."

"Oh, you make pretty speeches too, my Silas." I nudged him with my shoulder. "Cyrranus was saying that he will stay on with Corra and Ewan."

Silas nodded.

"Gratitude, man," Silas said to the male. Cyrranus sketched a quick bow and left us. "I wonder, *Trubaíste*, should I do the same?"

I started to panic. He held up a finger and raised both eyebrows.

"Before you say anything, just listen."

I pressed my lips together and was breathing through my nose. He explained that there would be a time in the coming months that Corra would be more vulnerable, and Ewan would be preoccupied with her, his crown, and the new babes. Silas felt as though he may be of more help with them than he would be with us. Especially now that Cadeyrn and I would be wed. I loosed a breath and took his hand.

"I will support whichever decision you make. I see a definite advantage to your staying on. But, Silas," I continued though he was looking off a ways, "don't leave because of me. Especially since we don't know what we are facing. Who we are facing."

"Are you worried?" he asked.

"Listen. It seems to me that every time I turn around, something awful presents itself. By my count, each and every time that has happened since I came to meet you lot, you, Silas, have held me together. I am worried. I'm terrified."

He pulled his hand from mine and scrubbed at his stubbled face, then looked at me sidelong. The weight of that gaze, his measured countenance, had me fidgeting.

"So, you are asking me to stay? With you?" Yes. No. Ugh.

"I'm asking you to consider both options. Perhaps with a little bit of sympathy for my tendency to attract trouble." I wasn't being fair, and I said as much. He laughed but it was forced. Those glass green eyes narrowed at me, and he began tapping his booted foot. My heart matched the beat, waiting for his response.

"You are aware that I could never deny you?" I wasn't, but now I felt really guilty. "I told Cadeyrn you two will certainly be the death of me."

"You don't have to answer right now. Think it over. Speak to Cadeyrn and Corra."

He agreed, and we walked together to the inn so I could get ready. I stopped short outside the doors to the inn and turned to Silas.

"It's tradition in the human realm for the bride's father to give her away to the groom. Would you . . . Can I ask you to do that? For me?" His mouth popped open in a little 'O', voice rough with emotion when he answered.

"It would be my honor, Neysa." I hugged him tightly, and in touching his jacket, a vision swam into my head. It was of Cadeyrn, telling Silas that if it was my choice, and I did not wish to take him back, he would not stand in the way of Silas and me being together. I gasped for air, pulling from the vision.

"*Trubaíste?*" Silas asked me, worry clouding his face. "A vision?" I nodded. "Anything I should know?"

I kissed his stubbled cheek and made for the door. "Only that you and Cadeyrn are hands down the most admirable, true-hearted, and beautiful males ever." I had to walk away before he saw the tears coming down my face.

Is everything okay, Neysa? Cadeyrn's voice.

I believe so. I want you to know that I love everything about you.

Silence.

That's oddly cryptic; but okay. May I mirror the sentiment? I'll see you in a little bit.

I WORE white for my marriage to Caleb. My father was unimpressed by my choice of fiancé from the beginning, and even so much as asked me if I was quite certain of marrying Caleb just as we were about to walk down the aisle. Doubt made my knees weak the entire walk.

This time around, with my mate and the surety of what I was going through with, not only did I choose to forgo the aisle bit—it wasn't a custom here anyway—I wore a dress that was the color of candlelight, embroidered with gold. The shoulders had capped tiny sleeves made entirely of dripping gold and silver beads and crystals. The beading travelled across the chest and dove down into the gathered satin of the bodice. The silk satin dress skimmed across my midsection and dropped to a puddling mermaid train befitting of the seaside venue. Ama curled my hair and left it half down, fastening in combs and barrettes that gave the illusion of being a chandelier in an art nouveau French nightclub. In a last-minute decision, I pulled the ostentatious diaspore earbobs from the satchel I carried everywhere. When I was taken in Cappadocia, they were in the pocket of my dressing gown. Somehow, seeing them on me in this dress, they seemed to fit. If nothing else, it would make Cadeyrn laugh. All in all, I was pleased with how I looked, and was in a bit of a mad tumble to be with my mate and soon-to-be husband.

Silas fetched me from the inn, and a carriage brought me to the beach where we had stood not two nights earlier. As I came across the shell-encrusted beach, a large crowd gathered both on the shore and along the boulevard in either direction. I had eyes only for Cadeyrn. He was dressed in a fitted black suit, still a few weapons bumping out from the fabric. I smiled at him.

"I believe this is where I give you up, *Trubaíste,*" Silas said roughly, kissing my cheek and once more on my hand as he passed it to Cadeyrn. A thrumming of electricity passed swiftly between my friend and me.

"Thank you, brother," my mate said to his cousin and took my hand. "Perfect," he said to me. "Everything about you is perfect."

"Down to your blood type?" I said nervously, then giggled.

He looked at me oddly.

"It's a line from a song. Sorry." I smirked at him, and he chuckled.

"Have you met the wood sprite in the earrings yet?" he whispered.

I leaned in and whispered back. "She's a right little mischief maker."

Oh?

Hid my underpinnings so I was forced to forgo any at all. Oops. Heat flared around us.

"Are you lot finished with the innuendo?" Corra called over.

And so we were wed by the captain of a ship from Saarlaiche, presided over by Ewan, and sealed with a meeting of lips which sang a hundred songs of hope in my blood. After the brief ceremony, we all descended on a large restaurant and drank sparkling wine until the effervescence permeated the atmosphere. Cadeyrn and I held our glasses to toast, our matching silver bands glittering in the soft lights. As the wine touched my lips, I was once again struck with an immersive vision.

Beasts swarming an area. A discarded and dented crown, splattered in blood. Lands with rivers and small inland seas. Energy. So much energy. A pull to me. To Cadeyrn. Rippling in the air. A Veil, clouded like looking through fumes—but it was failing. Allowing things to pass into this realm, but not from the human realm. I slumped forward in my seat, and Cadeyrn caught me before my head smacked the table. Folk around us gasped. Our family surrounded us in a protective circle. I looked at my husband in shock, then sought the eyes of Ewan, Corra, and Silas.

"There's another Veil. In Heilig. Something is wrong with it."

Ewan swore viciously.

"It is not your sacrifice to make, Neysa," Ewan said, swirling grey building in the air. "Not this time."

"No, it is not," Cadeyrn agreed. "We will figure it out and deal with it."

Corra whimpered. A sound I would never have thought could come out of her.

"I will be back here, and I will meet my little niece and nephew or whatever they may be. I promise you. We will all be back here." While I didn't know if it was a promise I could indeed keep, I knew that keeping my family together was my top priority. To do that, though, we needed to sort out this new Veil.

Two days after our wedding, Silas and Reynard joined us aboard our vessel headed for the land of my mother's parents. Many trials ahead indeed. On this voyage, I planned to take advantage of every moment in the suspended time frame that was sea travel to be with my mate. Whatever waited for us in this land of beauty and water magic, our purpose there would imbue us with obstacles and peril. I stood at the helm of the ship and cut my palm, allowing my blood to drip into the sea. An offering and an oath.

The blood ran freely. Cadeyrn and Silas rushed to meet me.

"I swore once to do what is in my power to protect these lands, and I will uphold my promise as I swear to the elements that I will return safely with my family." Both cousins pulled my dagger from me and sliced it across their own palms in turn, echoing my pledge to return.

"Fucking hell, *Trubaíste*. What did I tell you about the theatrics?"

"Only that they had better be spectacular if you went missing. I'm just proactively dramatizing things. Besides, it's fun to see Cadeyrn get all hot and bothered when my blood is shed."

From the depths of the sea to the skies above came a long sigh and a feeling as though the world itself were bracing for theatrics of its own.

PART TWO

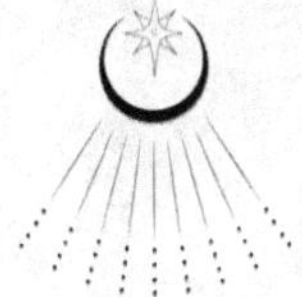

CHAPTER 17

NEYSA

A green so green, it was blue. The entirety of the coast had a scarf of opalescent green, which met the shoreline in a majestic kiss of color like the scales on a mythical beast. Passage through the archipelago had been a harrowing marathon of moving within the parameters of the natural wards imposed upon the landmass itself. Konstantín gave us strict instructions on how to make the passage, which involved invoking both mine and Cadeyrn's magic. The power I was able to draw from the sea itself had strengthened throughout the course of the voyage. Yet my inherent raw power seemed to need both my mate and Silas to harness it. Since that night by the campfire while we searched Aoifsing for Cadeyrn's beast form, my magic seemed to require Silas's nearness to function optimally. Nearly a month had passed since we set sail from Maesarra. Though the time on the ship was a borrowed pause in the chaos that we had been thrust into, the wounds of what we endured were still a bit jagged.

Cadeyrn's power burned in a steady throb around him almost constantly. As we neared the archipelago, he released the damper and was a stanchion of heat and flame. Tendrils of my power found his and latched on, fusing together as a part of our *Cuiraíbh Enaíde*, the braiding of our souls that lived deeper in us than even our mating bond. What none of us had anticipated was that my power seemed to request buttressing from Silas's now. As Cadeyrn stood on the prow of the ship, my magic twisted and curled with his. Silas stood near me as well, his magic looping and stitching itself through mine. During the first week of being in close quarters on the ship, the males were butting heads over this new revelation. I myself had always felt that though Cadeyrn was my husband and mate, I was connected to both his cousins almost as strongly. By the second week aboard the ship, Silas could barely look me in the eye. Our past, our closeness, his guilt with Cadeyrn, all built to an uncomfortable reality we would need to address once off this blasted vessel.

Similar to the haze of the Veil, the forcefield of magic around the archipelago that surrounded Heilig was a murky, tangible thing. With our three powers synced, the wards admitted us, allowing a slow crossing through the haze. Months ago, in that war room in Laorinaghe, before Bestía, before Lorelei had been killed in the battle on that magnetic field, I had had a vision of these lands. Of this archipelago. Between the fortifying islands and the shoreline of Heilig, the waters were placid and clear. Our ship glided noiselessly through the straights toward that teal shore.

Twinges of apprehension fluttered in my stomach. Cadeyrn slipped his arm around my waist and drew me closer. His scent wrapped around me like a blanket as I laid my head against his chest. He knew I resented having to come here. What I wished for us was to be able to live peacefully in Aoifsing and perhaps start a family as my brother and Corra were doing. Ewan, though, now had the responsibility of the crown he resented as much as I resented coming to Heilig. What a pair we were. Breathing deeply, I tried to quell the rising anxiety in me; my mate pressed a kiss to my head.

"We have made it through worse," he said quietly. I tightened my arms around him.

"Technically, we have no idea what we are about to encounter so it's quite possible this will be much worse than what we've dealt with in the past," I countered. He chuckled and made small circles on my side with his thumb.

"I suppose. Though it will have to top murderous ambushes in jungles, Bulgarian dams, kidnappings across realms, near ablation of your body in a magical and chemical explosion, attacking aphrim, battling Elders, having our souls torn apart—twice—lupinus attacks, magical impotence, impalement, blood poisoning, deaths of our parents . . . Am I missing anything?"

"Cracking my spine from a violent vision?" I grumbled, nestling closer to him. His thumb stroked up my side and brought my face closer to his. I looked up into his watercolor eyes, the shade between an aquamarine and a peridot, and felt my stomach flip over. My hand went to the flat of his abdomen, and an answering rumble came from his *baethaache*. His face came down to mine, lips parting to kiss me softly. I turned to him and wrapped my arms around his neck, holding on for perhaps the last time before we disembarked.

You're stronger than anyone I've ever known, Neysa, my mate said to my mind. *I don't believe this ordeal will change that. If you need reminding of that strength, feel free to exert your dominance over me any time.*

I laughed against him and pinched his backside.

I will hold you to that, Mate.

We have some time before landfall . . .

"It will be a blessing to get off this floating stink boat and be away from you lot for an extended period of time,"

Reynard drawled from the cabin door. "Gods above, I hope the males of Heilig are as good-looking as your family, Little Mouse."

"A compliment, Reynard?" I gasped. "From you? I'm shocked."

"Mm. Don't let it go to your head, Mousey." He winked and strode for the helm. The captain announced land fall, so we gathered our belongings in preparation for this journey to the lands of my grandparents.

SILAS

A TASK. I needed a job to do, if only to get my mind off what we had dealt with the past months and the mental mayhem from being on this bloody ship for three weeks. Stepping onto dry land made me want to run for miles to get out of my head. My cousin and *Trubaíste* likely felt the same.

The day after our tryst, we agreed to put it all behind us. The day I knew, without a doubt, that she was Cadeyrn's mate —even before he did, the poor sod—I made the mental note to get on with it. That day in Bania after Analisse, when I knew . . . I knew Neysa wanted me, and I don't know which of us it killed more. Then she kissed me goodbye. It was the longest I had ever been out of control with my magic. Lina wasn't stupid. She still took me, knowing full well I could never love her as I loved my cousin's mate. My sister knew there was a connection between Neysa and me that was more than my simply being a stupid bastard who couldn't get past wanting to bed my own damned cousin's mate. Neysa couldn't leave it alone any more than I could. I had thought the answer was in staying behind and looking after Corraidhín and Ewan and the babes. Until *Trubaíste* begged me to stay with her.

The night in the forest when I swore on my blood to bring back my cousin, Neysa's magic came back when she connected to mine. At the time, I couldn't bring myself to say anything, but the pull we always had to each other turned into a solid, necessary element in that single moment. Fucking hell. It wasn't until we were all stuck on the godsdamned boat for weeks that there was no way around our bond. Cadeyrn tried to ignore it. He did a bloody great job of it, but his mate was connected to me, and I loved her as though she were my own. How was any male supposed to get past that? How was I supposed to get past the only female I had ever really loved being mated and married to my cousin? My brother, really. Where did that put me? I couldn't very well walk away when our powers were connected. I hadn't even been able to look at her this past week. By the time we disembarked the boat, I was out of my mind needing to get away from her. Thank the gods that Konstantín's envoy, whom we had dealt with in Aoifsing, was waiting with wagons just off the dock.

"Basz," I greeted him, grasping elbows. Cadeyrn and Neysa came up behind me. Reynard was no doubt scouting ahead. I wouldn't be surprised if the little weasel jumped ship and swam ahead just to show his speed.

"Lord Silas. Your Highness." Basz inclined his head to us all.

"Bah. I'm no lord. Just Silas."

"I'm afraid your journey to Kutja includes another boat. The wagon shall take us just up the road where we shall take the river barge inland."

All of us groaned.

NEYSA

WHILE THE THOUGHT of another boat made me want to hide and refuse to come out, once on the barge, it was clear that this experience would be a far cry from that of the sea voyage. Polished wood decks surrounded the vessel in three levels, punctuated with copper pillars. Seating areas dotted around the main deck, and it looked as though there were covered dining set ups on the next. Basz explained we would be on the barge for two nights as we moved inland toward the capitol of Kutja. Then he said the magic words: bathing chamber. Not chamber pot, privy, or bucket. Basz gestured to it with irreverence, yet as soon as I saw where it was, I passed my weapons to my mate and walked directly in. Behind me, Cadeyrn and Silas snickered. A servant was already filling the large copper tub, steam billowing out in glorious, humid puffs. As Ama had done for me the first day in Bania when I was covered in a hundred different kinds of filth, I grabbed a flannel and wet it, scrubbing my skin raw and cleaning my nails before I sank into the glorious heat of the tub. I covered my face with my hands, attempting to quell the rising panic about being in Heilig, dealing with phantomes, and figuring out what was going on with Silas and me. And my mate. Holy burning hell I had a real problem. We hadn't all spoken about it in detail. It was uncomfortable for each of us, yet at some point we needed to assess this. Just not yet.

Twilight was falling when I made my way to the dining area on the second level of the barge. Staircases twined from the starboard side, opening onto a spacious deck with a large round table set with baskets of bread and bottles of wine. Once out of the bath, I had donned a simple white slip of a gown, needing to be out of restrictive clothing. A stunning female poured my wine as Reynard slipped into the chair next to me. He had regained so much color in the past weeks. Cadeyrn worked to heal in him what Paschale had destroyed. Weeks at sea under the sun had even bronzed his skin. With his color returned, the fine-boned structure of his face was revealed.

"Mousey," he said, sipping from my glass before his was poured.

"Look at you, Reynard, all clean and handsome."

He started, not expecting that. I wondered briefly if he had ever really been complimented. The more time I spent with him, the more I realized I liked him. He was witty and fun, and seemed to genuinely enjoy being with us all.

"What must it be like, Mousey, having those two males ripe for the taking?"

And then he said stuff like that, and I wanted to drop kick him. However, I knew a diversion when I heard one. He was embarrassed by my compliment and tried to deflect it.

So, I leaned toward him and whispered, "It can be quite . . . hard, at times." I winked at him, and he snorted. "In fact, it is quite a . . . slippery situation if you . . . come to my meaning."

He clinked glasses with me and laughed heartily. It wasn't a laugh I had heard from him before.

"I guess you are more fun than I thought. I'd still take them both, though."

It wasn't his fault. He didn't quite understand the situation, so I ducked my head while I sipped the light white wine.

Of course, both of the males being drooled over happened to crest the staircase at that moment, and Cadeyrn coughed.

"Not going to happen, Weasel," Silas said, plucking a bread roll from the plate before he sat opposite to me. Cadeyrn slid onto the seat on my other side and trailed a finger down my arm in greeting. I leaned into him, breathing in his rain scent.

Basz joined us and debriefed on what had transpired since we last spoke with Konstantín, who had left after arriving in Aoifsing. We had entered Heilig from the south and were travelling northeast to Kutja. Along the west coast, and further north, there was more unrest brewing, yet it hadn't made its way this far south. We could convene with the royal family and begin to travel round, doing a show of face. Between the wine and the low light, my mind drifted whilst I stared out of the open sides of the barge. Trees of varying species and size banked the river, small waterfalls and boulders littered about. Lights of colors I couldn't catalogue were shining from the trees and water, reflecting off the river current in a mad frenzy. It was hypnotic. I stood and walked to the railing, holding my wine.

"What are they?" I asked aloud, not bothering to turn to anyone. Basz came alongside me and pointed outward.

"In essence, they are simply pockets of light. Energies converge in this land. When the air and atmosphere itself cannot hold onto it any longer, pockets of light and color burst, shining for days at a time. It is seen more in the less populated areas, as energy transfers between fae when we are together. Therefore, it is absorbed rather than it bursting."

Awe must have shown on my face. Basz smiled, pleased that his land had elicited my reaction. I looked to the male beside me, feeling the eyes of the three at the table. Basz had a serious face with golden eyes setting an amber glow to his dark skin. Every angle, from his cheekbones to his chin, was sharp and chiseled, making him look like a digitalized rendering of a beautiful male.

Lorelei wasn't lying when she said this land was full of beauty. Thinking of the Lady of Laorinaghe, my heart gave a great thump. New representatives must be chosen to spear the provinces onward. I had left a letter of recommendation for Yva, the Sacred City of Laorinaghe guard who had fought for me. Cadeyrn and I agreed that she would be a fair delegate should she wish to embroil herself in politics. In the distance, a few pairs of glowing eyes stared at me across the river. I inclined my head to the lupine creatures. Warmth neared me, and I smiled over my shoulder as Cadeyrn came to stand beside me, an arm about my waist. Whether he was clean and polished as he was now, or roughed up and war-torn, my husband was breathtaking. I pressed a kiss to his shoulder. His peridot eyes smiled down at me. Every time we had a moment of relief or rest, some disaster showed up knocking.

"Tell me, Basz," Cadeyrn began. "How does Konstantín fair?"

Silas shuffled to us, his woodsmoke scent pulling at my senses.

"Well, Majesty. He has kept his immediate family—your family, Your Highness," he added with a nod to me, "within the palace and grounds. Just precautions."

"And you, Basz?" Silas asked. "Have you seen the trouble areas yourself?"

Basz regarded Silas. "Some, my lord. I was sent with a group of soldiers when we heard of the phantomes in the north. I witnessed the destruction they caused, and upon taking our leave of the areas, we were blockaded by mobs angry over the dwindling protection magic."

Perhaps, like the crystals needed to diffuse the Veil in Aoifsing, there was a more concrete reason for the release of the aulde dark powers. I touched the raw rose quartz shards hanging on my chest below the *adairch dorhdj*, the double-horn pendant I wore. The crystals warmed to my touch—and with a pulsing beat, I was thrust into a vision. The first I'd had since our wedding night nearly a month ago.

Haze and grey-tinged air clouding a tree canopy. A dented crown laying amongst the ashes and ruin of a structure. Blood. So much blood. Phantomes moving across the barrier to the human realm. Winds and waves. Cadeyrn on his knees in battle black, head hung in grief. A sword stretched from another hand coated in blood and filth. The sword is etched with rune-like markings—one I saw in Barlowe Combe. The cuff of the jacket is ruched up to reveal a tattoo of a single marking that looked like an arch with a looped squiggle bisecting it, a single star in the middle.

I choked on my breath, feeling my dinner rise inside me. Cadeyrn's arms grabbed my shoulders and brought me to the railing. The nausea subsided but the vice around my chest clenched.

"Let it out," my mate said softly, his healing gift trying to feel for the anxiety's cause.

White lights spun from my body, bathing the deck in an incandescence. Basz swore. Just as quick, the light spiraled into me. Black spots danced in my vision. As I began to pass out, Cadeyrn called to Silas for help. Soft mist blew around while Silas wrapped an arm about my middle. Lightning shot from us both. I heard Basz exclaim as he drew a shield around himself. Finally, my breathing opened, and I collapsed on Silas. Turning in his arms, I yanked at his sleeve, needing to see for myself. He attempted to push my hand away, but I snarled, and he stopped resisting and looked away. Just above the inside of his wrist was the tattoo in my vision. Both of my hands covered my mouth as I stumbled back into Cadeyrn. Silas was still looking away. I looked at my mate and pleaded with my eyes.

"What does it mean?" I asked Silas.

He shook his head once and looked at his cousin, cocking his head to the side. Their eyes locked and Cadeyrn nodded. Some unspoken conversation that their centuries together made possible.

"Please," I begged and grabbed at his jacket, pulling him closer and pounding on his chest. His head still turned from me, he embraced me, and I felt his breathing quicken. Seeing his arm on the ground, covered in blood, and Cadeyrn kneeling on a battlefield, I understood what I had seen. And as the realization dawned, I knew I had projected the vision to Cadeyrn. His heat flared and he dropped his wine glass, the smashing glass a distant bell toll.

No. A single denial from Cadeyrn. His own thoughts were blowing through my mind.

Cadeyrn, Silas, and I excused ourselves from the company and walked to our rooms. Once the door clicked shut, Silas's shield came up around us, barring any listening ears from eavesdropping. I slumped against the desk.

"Where was it?" Cadeyrn asked, a cold steel note in his voice. The assessing general.

"Are one of you going to tell me what this is about?" All humor in my friend had gone.

"I don't know," I said. "I feel like it must be here, yet I'm not sure."

"Fucking gods, you lot," Silas swore. "Tell me."

I yanked him to me and placed both hands on his face, about to tell him to go somewhere safe. His eyes widened; his mouth gaped like a fish.

"I saw it. I could see it. Your vision." He pulled my hands from his face and stormed out of the room.

I slid to the ground and placed my head in my hands. Cadeyrn sat beside me.

"I'm sorry," I whispered. "I didn't mean to . . . I don't try."

I looked at my mate, his dark brows drawn together, eyes somber.

He touched his forehead to mine and kissed me. "Don't apologize. I understand. I mean, I don't. I really bloody don't understand what is happening. But I know you don't either."

This male beside me meant the world to me. His nearness sent jolts of wanting through me. I wanted nothing more than to be with him for as long as we could live. Yet, I could not live without Silas. Physically. My power was linked to his. What did that make me? In my vision, I saw him dead. If he were dead, then surely I would not survive long. Where did that put us?

"As my cousin would say, 'knee-deep in poisonous shite.'"

Sunlight streamed in the small windows of our room, waking me with the dawn. I stretched and rolled to Cadeyrn. His eyes opened, sleepy and unfocused. The sight of him in the morning, tousled and warm, had me writhing against him. Slow and tauntingly, he moved his hands up and down my back.

"You should go to him," he said softly, running his hands through my hair. "He likely needs you."

"Cadeyrn."

"We'll figure it out, Neysa. We will. Go to him. I can't imagine what it must be like for him. Perhaps for you as well." I swallowed and kissed his chest once. Twice. "For the record, this is my favorite way to wake up," he told me, matter of fact.

IT ALWAYS SEEMED redundant to knock on a door with fae. Between the hearing and scenting, chances were they knew who was coming. Silas, I knew, could sense me from a distance. It was a part of whatever was between us. I still wished we weren't on a boat. As luxurious as this one was, none of us could get away. Though after the vision I'd had, I didn't want to let him go far at all. He scoffed when he answered the door and turned back into the chamber. Perhaps I had woken him as it was still early. He stood in loose pants and no shirt, his brown waves in a bit of a mad tangle. I thought about pulling my fingers through them to detangle, but quickly shook off the thought. He poured water from an ewer and swished his mouth before swallowing.

"What can I do for you, *Trubaíste*?" he asked, folding his solid, ripped arms across his chest, tattooed side facing inward. "Did you not get quite enough this morning?"

A slap. That's what it felt like. My lips curled and wobbled at the same time, pissing me off. He hadn't asked in a teasing manner like he might have another time. It was a barbed question. One I resented.

"Piss off, Silas."

"I would, but I'm stuck on a fucking barge."

The glass crashed onto the wooden side table. Never had Silas spoken to me like this. My nostrils flared in and out as I weighed whether to walk out. Then the vision came back to me.

"What is the tattoo?"

He filled another glass of water, draining it. "A symbol from the aulde language."

"I gathered as much. What does it mean?"

He scrubbed his face and looked out the small window. I backed up a step. Maybe I shouldn't have come. Maybe he didn't want me to be here. Really, why would he? Maybe Cadeyrn knew that and was a bit sneaky in ushering me out. Maybe—

"Stop, *Trubaíste*," he said roughly. "You're sending all that mental vomit to me."

"Oh, fabulous. Do I get any privacy in my own head these days?" I leaned my forehead against the wood paneled wall. He chuckled.

"Though if you must brush my hair out, I wouldn't say no."

I smiled. "Shithead."

"Always." He held his hand out to me. "Come here. I'm a bit worse for the wear this morning, Princess. Took a bottle of wine to bed last night."

"Did it treat you well?" I stood in front of him.

"Took full advantage of me and left. And now I've a pounding head."

I wet a flannel, then rummaged through his pack to pull out the bottle of peppermint oil that Lina had given us months ago. Three drops on the wet flannel soaked in, and I touched it to his forehead and temples, then the back of his neck.

"That's what you get for taking strangers to your bed," I teased. The peppermint was bracing and helped wake me up more. His eyes watched me, throat bobbing before pulling my hand away.

"Thank you. That helps," he said roughly.

"Tell me." He knew what I meant, but I turned his arm over to look at the tattoo. My thumb brushed it, making him shudder.

"Destruction or disaster. It's the same word. And love." He looked at me sidelong, sea glass eyes narrowed. I exhaled, not knowing what to do. "Tosser who did it fucked up. Was supposed to be the symbol for 'bloody great warrior.'" He gave me a lopsided smile. I choked a laugh. Disaster. *Trubaiste*.

"When?" I breathed.

"The day of the . . ." He waved his free hand. "Thing with Bestía."

I nodded absently.

"You were planning to stay." He made an agreeable sound. "I asked you to stay with me instead. I'm horrible."

He laughed and kissed my hands.

"*Trubaiste*, I don't know what the hell is happening here, but I don't want to cause trouble for you both."

Stay, I thought. Stay and be safe. The thoughts popped in my head like directives. Stay with me.

"I will." He answered what I hadn't said aloud. I stepped to him and wrapped my arms around him tightly. "I knew you couldn't be near me without wanting to jump my—"

I whacked him on the arm. "Cad."

He chuckled against my hair.

NOTHING WAS ordinary in this place. Lorelei's description was correct. Even the rock faces through which the river wound had swaths of flowering vines and ivy draped here and there like accessories. Just before moonrise on our last night aboard the boat, I took supplies to an isolated part of the observation deck, hoping to be alone. From my basket I pulled a small copper bowl, gems, smudging sticks, and frankincense oil. The barge had emerged a few hours ago into a wide section of the River Matta. Basz explained that the waterway we had started on merged from the narrow mountain pass with the

River Matta, and where the leg we were on flowed to the capitol while the leg we moved away from headed to the sea in the northwest.

The seven mystics who sailed with King Konstantín revealed that I was the heir to the Goddess Heícate, guardian of magic and darkness. Each mystic gifted me an item. The seed pearl I had released to the sea before leaving Aoifsing. I knew each additional gift would have its own indicative feel for how and when it should be used. Under the full moon, I felt the need to scry for a vision using the golden thread one of the mystics gave me. The air was chillier as we made our way further into the center of Heilig. Small pillars of clear quartz surrounded me where I sat cross-legged. Seven drops of frankincense fell onto the glassy surface of the copper bowl of water. Calling on my gifts, I isolated the electric charge I carried with me and concentrated on willing the charge to my fingers to spark the sage smudge stick. Around me, the crystals wobbled and vibrated, filling with energy. As though a small window opened in me, a jolt sparked from my fingers, dancing atop the sage until the smudge stick caught fire. I smiled, pleased with myself. For a few short moments, my hands moved the bundle through the air around my circle, and then I blew the fire out, dropping ash into the bowl.

Concentrating on my heartbeat, the rhythmic thump set the tone as I peered into the water, allowing my mind to wander. Questions popped in and out, and I let them flow. In the ripples of water, I saw faces. *My brother and Corra; Bixby and Cuthbert; my mate, walking away, smiling back at me. My own face, turning and crumpling. A female with dark hair like mine. Basz shielding me from something. Lances of pain. That dented, bloody crown again. Looking down at myself with a rounded belly, strong hands covering mine. Fingers entwined, above two heads on a pillow, that tattoo showing.*

Distantly noting my body in the here and now, I lifted the

golden thread from the mystics and dropped it into my palm. I called out to Silas in my mind, then hands were upon mine. Electricity and mist swirled, lightning brightening the skies around us.

My cheek scraped against Silas's stubbled face. His woodsmoke scent heightened my senses. It was fully dark. I held my breath for a short moment before opening my eyes, hoping Cadeyrn wasn't here. Gods only knew how this looked. No one but us, I confirmed. I lifted myself from the male under me and held my pounding head.

Cadeyrn. I was scrying and released a bit of energy. Silas found me. I'm fine.

Be careful. Come back to bed soon.

"You know how some people are messy eaters?" Silas asked from the wood deck. He propped himself up onto his elbows, stomach muscles rippling with the movement. "I've come to think that perhaps you are a messy magic wielder. You can't help it. You just explode like the sad bastards who get food everywhere." I picked up bits of ashy sage and flicked them at him. He lifted an arm, and his power dissolved the sage midair. I dove forward and straddled him, grabbing his arm.

"Oh my God, Silas," I said, holding up his forearm. I felt him breathing under me and knew I should move but couldn't make myself. Above the tattoo marking on him, perhaps two inches in length, was a single gold line. The metallic of it shone even in the darkness. He stared at it.

"It's the thread from the mystic," I said, though he knew that. Tingling electricity still surged through me, running through the veins in my arms. His eyes zeroed in on my right forearm, and he pushed up the sleeve of my sweater. In the same place as it was on him, a gold thread stretched across my skin. A snapshot in my mind of a squiggle—the same squiggle as Silas had inside the arch on his arm, etched onto a stone and into the dirt in that forest in Prinaer. The symbol for the

Taempchal a Caráed. The temple for the element of love. The face of the mystic who had given me the thread showed in my mind, smiling, knowing I understood now. I looked at Silas. Emotions ran across his face like credits on a screen.

Cat-soft footfalls sounded, and warmth entered as Cadeyrn came over to us.

"I have it as well." He lifted his arm. He was in pajama trousers and no shirt or shoes, as though he jumped from bed and came to us. We three sat, knees bent, looking at our matching golden lines, wondering what in all the realms to do now. Silas broke the silence.

"I came out because it seemed like there was a request for my power. Like a knocking at the door in my mind. I knew it was Neysa, so I allowed her to take it."

Ah. The window opening, allowing electricity to come through.

"I came out to make sure she was okay, Cadeyrn." He turned pleading eyes to his cousin.

Cadeyrn patted his hand.

"I need to write down what I saw." I stood. Perhaps it made me a coward for walking away when we should all be addressing this, but I couldn't sit there with my husband and talk about a thread of love that imprinted itself upon me and another male. I simply couldn't.

CHAPTER 18

NEYSA

Palaces made me jumpy. There. I said it. This past year, every palace we had been in, including my childhood home on *Eilein Reínhe*, we had to engage in a battle of sorts. Whether it was having my arm torn open by Paschale in Festaera, the full-scale mayhem at the Elder Palace, the battle with Analisse's sister, Julissa, pretending to be Lorelei in Laorinaghe, or the night of the summit when Cadeyrn's *baethaache* was forced to emerge and he disappeared in the skies, it seemed well within my rights to be twitchy about entering another palace. In a foreign land with questionable allies and formidable dark magical enemies, every shadow made me suspicious.

Basz and his guards led the way forward from the barge onto the walkway into the palace. The building itself sprawled for acres. It seemed to be more of a walled city than a palace with fully separate keeps and ramparts. The overall facade was not of a fortified castle, however, but of a majestic property with serious attention to detail. Guards lined the walkway, holding their shields and weapons at the ready. They had been under attack, I reminded myself as my adrenaline spiked. I felt my mate's hand move toward mine as he brushed my fingers once. Near the walls, foliage spilled along the banks of the loveliest moat I could have imagined, glowing with orange flowers. We continued walking in, Basz leading the way. Once we crossed a grassy plain inside the walls and came to the steps leading to the palace itself, he turned to us, gesturing upward.

"For the time being this is the only entrance to the palace itself. There are wards on all other exits. You understand the reason behind it, I'm sure."

I'm calling bullshit, I said to both Cadeyrn and Silas. I assumed they could both hear me. I still couldn't hear Silas speak mind to mind, but at least he could hear me.

Yes, my delicate princess, Cadeyrn responded with a smile in his voice. *I'm quite certain this is the only exit they have allowed us to use.* A brief flare of light and electricity surged through me. Luckily Basz had his back to me, though I'm sure he felt the flare, so I quickly kissed my mate to cover it up.

Stealthy, mate. The old kissing in an alley cover up?

I touched his stomach in response, which made his heat flare.

"Oh, for the love of males in armor," Reynard exclaimed. "Spare us all. Or at the very least, include us all."

Basz laughed good-naturedly.

"Sorry, Basz," I said to him. "It's all still a bit new." He only smiled and said he and his mate likely acted the same in the beginning. As we walked up the slate stairs to the main palace door, I shot my hand back and squeezed Silas'.

He hesitated, then squeezed back.

Sweat and grit covering him, Konstantín and four others rushed toward us from a balustrade inside the building. The three males with me tightened in a protective blockade, which might have pissed me off had it not been kind of sweet.

"Your Highness," Konstantín called, out of breath. "We weren't expecting you until much later. I apologize for my appearance. We were in the training ring when I heard you had arrived."

"Not at all, Your Majesty. I'm sure we are looking a bit ragged ourselves."

"May I present my children." He turned, revealing two males and a female, all dark-haired and olive-eyed like Ewan and me. "Arik, my son. Saski, my daughter and the heir to my throne." We bowed to them. "My son and intelligencer, Ludek." The darkest of the three royal children bowed to us and smiled at Basz. There was a tangible connection between the two, and I guessed he was Basz's mate. "My wife, Marja, you shall meet later. She was married before me and birthed two children; Ludek being her eldest. Pavla was killed leading scouts in the north this past autumn. My wife still mourns."

"Our condolences, Your Majesty," Cadeyrn said to the king, placing his hand over his heart. The others were looking at us like we were their next meal.

Konstantín sighed.

"The rumor is that you lot are impressive in the training ring. Might we get a glimpse of that whilst you're here?" Arik asked us with a wicked gleam in his eye.

I grinned at him. "As soon as I've slept on solid ground and had a few full meals, Your Highness, I would be happy to stretch my limbs."

He said he would show us to our chambers himself so that we could get started on the rest.

Nothing was helping me sleep. The breeze coming in through the windows, as chilled and perfectly night-kissed as it was, felt wrong. The wards on the balcony door and windows let the air in and out, but I knew we had no access to the night itself. Trying not to panic when sleep-deprived, more or less trapped, built itself into a bubbling angst. Cadeyrn fell asleep beside me, and I stared at him, bitter he found it so easy. Did he not feel trapped? What about Reynard and Silas? They were probably all asleep, not bothered by the sensation of being stuck.

Breathe, Neysa. Inhale for five, hold for seven, exhale for nine. I repeated the sequence four or five times, then willed a soft projection of light to the tin tiled ceiling. Using the cadence of my breathing, I watched the light expand and contract as though it breathed along with me. It slowed my heart rate after a time, and the anxiety subsided slightly. Turning to my sleeping husband, I watched his breathing as though it were my own. Gazing at his chest as it rose and fell, my eyes trailed the scars that showed in certain light. Injuries that he never properly healed or allowed to scar, like the split on his lip from when Silas hit him. In sleep, his full bottom lip pouted and made him look almost childlike with his long dark lashes fanned against angled cheekbones. So much for controlling my breathing. It hitched watching him, so I scowled at him for being able to sleep and for being so beautiful it made my breathing trick useless.

"You could wake the dead with the intensity of that scowl," he said without so much as moving. I stuck out my tongue at him, and a small smile played at his lips. "If it makes you feel any better, I've sussed out how to dismantle the wards on our windows, the rear gate to the training ring that leads to the stables, and the door to the kitchen garden. I wouldn't suggest trying unless we are in check, as there will be a big fuss. But it can be done."

"How?"

I didn't even know when he had time to figure it out. Dinner had directly followed our arrival and included a taxing few hours wherein Queen Marja blamed Ewan and me for her daughter's death. She stated in no uncertain terms that had my mother sent us there years ago, the blight on their land would never have happened.

"She could not be bothered to travel here once. Not once! Our gifts need tethers. We need to often be in close proximity to those with whom we share bonds," she said, breathless and rushed. My eyes caught Silas's and shifted away quickly. Konstantín covered his wife's hand with his own, giving it a squeeze. Her face pinched and I saw Ludek's gaze shoot to his mother's hand. Her long, dark fingers tangled in a grip far tighter than a loving gesture would require.

"I dare say," Konstantín beamed, voice and smile brighter than the overall mood. Dirt and sweat still clung to his face from his sparring, and had he not been crushing Marja's hand, I may have liked him for the casual statement he made in welcoming us with no pomp and circumstance. "Enough talk of bygones. We have welcomed a new era. Niece, I am so pleased to have you here assisting us in our plight."

Marja scowled at him, her dark eyes narrowed to slits. He may be using excess force, but she was not laying down for it.

That is a dynamic I would rather not have to endure for very long, Cadeyrn said to me through our bond.

Tell me about it. Seems like Ludek is the only one who reacts.

The male cattycorner from Marja watched his mother until she gave a barely perceptible nod. She immediately turned her ire for her king back to me. *Great.*

"I will say this once," she began. "My husband is not over fond of displays of emotion." With all eyes on the king, he sat back, drinking from a blown glass goblet of wine. Ludek sat up taller, as though preparing for something. I wondered what his gifts were. "My Pavla died. A violent, lonely death. She died because of the blight on these lands. Saskeia could have built upon my king's magics. Possibly even Saski and Arik's magics. Together they could have *helped us,*" she sobbed. "Instead, she sent you to hide in another realm and refused to reveal her heritage."

Uncharacteristically, I kept my mouth shut and allowed the implications. Her children eventually stepped in and apologized, but it did absolutely nothing to improve my feeling about being here.

The memory of that dinner had me on edge enough to refuse any hint of sleep. Cadeyrn's voice in the lightless bedroom brought me out of my reverie.

"The wards are tied to individual spell casters, so my gift was able to see a spell signature on each we passed. The training ring and likely a few in that vicinity are linked to Arik. Our windows are linked to the queen. The kitchen was linked to someone we haven't met yet. There is a heavy spell signature of Basz, but I haven't been able to isolate what and where."

I sank back onto my pillow and exhaled into the darkness. "The idea being that should one of them leave or be harmed, the other signatures are different?"

"One would assume."

I made a silent snooty mimic of his tone and vernacular. He reached over and flicked my nose. "Does it make you feel better to make fun of me?"

I made a noncommittal sound. His arm reached over and pulled me against him, where I laid my head in the crook of his neck and shoulder, breathing him in. I traced my finger on his chest in a small circle, listening to his breathing and letting his scent dance with mine until sleep finally found me.

Dawn saw me up and out in the training ring, trying to get in a few circuits before everyone else awoke. While the ground of the ring was gravelly dirt, the walls surrounding it were ivy-covered and glowed blue in the predawn light. An iron gate closed off the far side beyond which was more foliage and the sounds of rushing water. That must be the gate Cadeyrn said had Arik's signature.

Setting stones at various angles and tracing lines into the dirt, I used the lines and stones for agility drills. My feet hopped and scooted, shimmied and pounced from one stone or line to the next over and over again. Once done, I sprinted across the ring, jumped into a handstand against the wall, and threw my torso into handstand push-ups. On the boat we trained daily, but freedom of movement was not a benefit of sea travel.

Slow, melodramatic clapping sounded from the gate where Arik stood leaning, his sword belt hanging from a hip. Long sword, two daggers, throwing knife in his boot. Likely a hidden weapon or two.

"I see you're waiting for me, then?" he asked. I bowed quickly, and he waved me off. "Let's be done with the titles, shall we? I couldn't care less, and I have a mind that you feel the same."

"Good morning, Arik," I said with a smile.

He grinned back and unsheathed his sword. I did the same, pulling twin swords from my back. We walked a circle around one another, taking our measure.

"What is breakfast like here?" I asked.

"You seem quite invested in your meals." He lashed out. I turned slightly out of the way.

"I am. One of life's greatest pleasures." I stabbed forward. He easily slid away.

"What, may I ask, are the others?" He stroked the trimmed beard on his strong jaw.

"Oh, I'm sure you can guess. Dogs, wine, sleep, sex."

He barked a laugh, and I caught his sword between my two and arced all three to the right. His eyes went wide as he attempted to step back. I moved forward and caused him to stumble. Seizing my advantage, I opened my swords and rolled so I was back-to-back with him, then turned and held my forearm dagger to his throat.

"So, about breakfast, cousin?" I released him. He was laughing and panting a bit. Silas and Saski stepped from the shadows of the doorway into the palace.

"Did you let her win, brother?" Saski called over, a slight sneer on her face. She too was wearing black flighting leathers, and I made a mental note to see if I could order a set like hers. They had ventilation patches like fish gills, under the arms and behind the knees. She carried a curved blade sword, similar to a scimitar, with a hilt fashioned to look like a great bird with open wings. She was taking stock of my weapons and stance, looking eager to try her luck.

"She bested me, sister. Perhaps our conversation took a distracting turn." He winked at me, and I bowed. Silas snorted and tugged on the braid I had pulled my hair into.

"*Trubaíste*," he said. "Ready for me?"

I nodded, and we started our typical dance around each other. The same we had done nearly every day we had seen each other since that first little spar on the beach in Barlowe Combe. His twin swords kissed mine and our energies struck through them. Above us, clouds rolled in and thunder boomed. There was a collective gasp from our audience, which seemed to have grown by a few, but I didn't turn to see.

Show off, I said to Silas in my mind. He smirked and raised an eyebrow at me. I did the same as our blades came together, crisscrossed to the point of having to call a draw. His left hip dipped ever so slightly, and as I was keenly aware of his body tells at this point, I knew he was about to drop down. As he tilted, I let go of my swords and flipped sideways over his back, wrapping my legs around his waist, and reached for my short sword. Silas's hand beat me to it and pulled my sword from its thigh holster, tossing it away with a growl. The growl had my toes curling in my boots, and light spilled from me, meeting with the yawning light of early dawn.

His back straightened, and I let myself drop from him, hitting the ground hard, and rolled. He picked up his sword again and tossed me mine. I kissed the air between us and heard chuckles from the outskirts of the ring. The morning dew seemed to inch its way into every crevice of my leathers. Taking a minute to pull off my jacket while Silas did the same, I whooshed a breath as he charged me. He was in a battle crouch, pushing forward with his head. I jumped to the side, and he caught me around the hips, pulling me down under him, laying my arms straight above my head. I inched my knee up slowly, as I had in my chamber in Bania.

"Ah, ah, *Trubaíste*. Not falling for that one again." We were both breathing in great gasps. "Yield?"

I thought I needed to show a thing or two to this audience. My partner smirked, sensing or hearing my thought, and gave me the slightest give as he deliberately slid his bare chest off me. Holy gods. Cadeyrn was off riding with Konstantín, or this could have been awkward. Silas's smoky scent was like incense around me. I took a pause, then quickly shrunk into a tight fetal position before rolling out from under him and flipping him on his back. My nails drove into his palms, right on top of the scar we both still had.

"Do you yield?" I asked.

His fingers curled into mine. Though he laughed and agreed, I saw a burning intensity in those sea glass eyes. Saski walked to us, a sly smile on her olive-skinned face. Her face was much like mine yet slightly darker. There was really no question we were related.

"That was quite a performance," she said.

I pulled my knee over Silas to stand, straightening my tank top. I felt Saski's eyes go to my arm.

"What does it mean?" She pointed to the golden thread imprinted on my forearm and the matching one on Silas'. I cleared my throat, looking around for water.

"The thread was gifted to me by one of your mystics. It found its way onto my skin."

"And his as well. Curious." She walked to Silas and touched his arm. I could see on his face he was not happy to have been touched that casually. Yet we were guests in this castle. I stepped between them and answered.

"Yes. On Cadeyrn too. It is a bond between the three of us."

"The three of you? Or between you and both males? Interesting."

"I wouldn't touch that, Your Highness," Reynard said from the shadows. "Trust me. I've tried."

I winked at him. Saski's mouth curved into a viperlike smile. Oh, lovely. Another one like that.

"It would never work between us, Weasel," Silas said, brushing dust from his thighs.

"Come, sister," Arik called. "I've promised our cousin a breakfast fit for royalty."

Everyone began filing out as I picked up my weapons and

dusted them off. Silas handed me my jacket and said into my ear, lips grazing the shell, "Good match."

My blood heated, and suddenly I wasn't hungry. I was nauseous and needed to bathe. And perhaps find my mate. So, I stomped off to my chamber.

Cadeyrn had returned and was finishing cleaning himself up as they had gone riding through boggy forest plains. I tossed my blades down when I entered and made a straight line for him. He laughed and let me push him against the wall.

"Did you lose?" he asked.

"No." I pulled his clothes from him with a marked growl and toed off my boots and trousers. He pulled me in, and I claimed his mouth while I yanked his backside to me. He kissed me fiercely and started to move against me, then stopped. I lurched forward, trying to keep going. His eyes narrowed and mouth pressed into a thin line. I made an impatient sound, but he shook his head, nostrils flaring.

"I think perhaps not," was all he said before turning away.

"Cadeyrn."

No. He pulled his shirt overhead and buttoned up his jacket. I stood against the wall, mostly naked, burning with desire, and shaking from cold rejection. He paused before walking out of the room.

"I won't touch you if your lust is for someone else." Each word was slow, quiet, and decisive.

"You needn't pretty yourself for us, cousin," Arik called as I walked into the dining room. I had taken a very cold bath and dressed in my aphrim skin pants and a grey on black damask patterned jacket. The jacket had a stand-up collar with full length tails and skirt split and opened in the front. Perhaps because I was in a mood to be reckoned with, I lined my eyes with a rim of kohl and stained my lips darker. Reynard muttered a plea when I walked in.

"I hope I didn't keep you waiting. I was filthy."

Reynard leaned to me and whispered, "You look more like the heir to the Goddess of War and Death than the Goddess of Magic. Tone it down, Mousey."

I nodded once and accepted a plate to fill with pastries and bacon, fruit, and something that looked like the love child of Greek yogurt and whipped cream, dusted with cinnamon. Cadeyrn was seated near Basz and Ludek, on the opposite side of me. Saski was next to Silas, engaging him in conversation.

"It intrigues me that you were trained to fight as a human," Ludek said to me. His voice was almost delicate, like movement in the night. I wasn't dumb enough to think it made him less formidable a character. He had a deeper olive skin than his half siblings, and warm, rich brown eyes that seemed to be everywhere at once yet felt concentrated on me.

"My father saw to my training from a young age. I took to it well enough."

"I like the way you moved. It was like . . . controlled chaos. A beautiful destruction."

Silas and Cadeyrn both coughed.

"I'm sorry. Was that out of line?"

"No. No. Thank you. I think. I'm sure the males who spend time with me would tend to agree with you. About the chaos part, at least." I grinned to put him at ease. "Were you born in this area, Ludek?"

"Far from here, actually. My father was a council head in our land. Heilig is broken into lands rather than provinces, but it is essentially the same as Aoifsing. The land we are from is called Sot. I can show you a map later if you'd like. I hear you are somewhat of a scholar."

I told him I would love that.

"I will be in the library in the afternoon. Join me. Unless, of course, you need as much time to get ready for the party as my sister does." He saluted his sister with his juice glass. Confusion must have shown on my face, as it did on my mate's.

"Our father has arranged a party tonight with our trusted friends and courtiers. It won't be too formal. Entertainment, dancing, and surprises," Saski explained.

I wanted to groan. I didn't like surprises.

Cadeyrn left the room with Basz and Arik without so much as a thought to me, though both males accompanying him bowed to me.

"So, it does bother him, then?" Saski asked.

Whipping my head round in shock, I looked at her. Electricity crackled in my extremities and the water glass on the table boiled, shattering the glass. She laughed and clapped, reminding me of Reynard when I'd first met him.

"I did wonder."

"I know I am a guest here, yet I would advise against any remarks like that or assumptions about my mate and me." I crossed my arms on the table and leaned forward. She was openly smiling at me, lighting her eyes and freckles. "I have come here at an inconvenient time, having endured more than you may know. If at any time this arrangement does not suit me, I will leave and let you sort out the problems internally. Understood?"

"She means no harm, Neysa," Ludek assured me. "She tries to push the limits with everyone. We understand your terms. Don't we, Saski?"

She was still smiling but agreed. Silas held a hand for me to follow him out.

"What?" I snarled at him once we were in a private courtyard.

"What happened?" he asked.

"She pushed me."

"You've been pushed before. That's not what I mean. What happened when you left?" he asked. I couldn't meet his eyes. He opened his mouth to ask again, so I started talking.

"He wouldn't touch me. Because . . . because I guess, he scented . . ." I flapped my hand. "And you." I covered my face with my hands, utterly embarrassed. He swore. "I wish Corra were here."

"Me too."

BASZ FOUND me wandering the inside grounds of the castle an hour or so after breakfast. It was so unlike castles in the human realm and most of what I had seen in Aoifsing. Plaques along the walls of an exterior wall told tales of kings and queens, warriors, and villains throughout Heilig history. Etched in bronze was a depiction of a woman holding a book while waters rose around her. When I felt Basz near me, I asked about the plaque, as it had no explanation.

"She was a great queen from many generations ago. A different bloodline than you, I believe. These lands were in peril. Her people hungered and sickened. An entire generation had gone without reproduction—which, in our terms, was a few hundred years. Magics died, and eventually the plant life grew tired." He had a voice for tales. Deep and musical with the slight slip and shuffle of his Heiligan accent.

The queen ascended her throne after her parents slipped into the next life. The population was dwindling, and she felt she must try to do something. Her gift was considered useless to most, as she could turn foliage to metal—gold, silver, bronze, copper. No one cared for a monarch with only the ability to make more riches. Left on her own, she fled the castle to find an answer.

Trails of the plague led her. She followed the path of hungry people, drooping flora, and parched ground. In the center of Heilig she found a cave. Deep within the cave was an ancient pond. After months of searching and on the verge of death herself, the young queen sat by the pond in the cave and submitted to an exhaustion beyond any she had ever known. Glinting images on the pond's surface came to her. In the surface of the water, she saw the future of her kingdom. It flourished and prospered with her and her family alive and well. She at first thought it a cruel joke. She couldn't imagine being well enough to walk out of the cave, let alone stand for generations as a figurehead.

When she raged, her gifts manifested into something greater than she had imagined. The queen threw herself into the pond, distraught and alone. The water evaporated around her, turning into silver along the shores. Within a short time, all that was left was a veritable tub of silver, holding a queen and a book. She picked up the book and, at her touch, words appeared.

Sitting on the metal bottom of the pond, the queen read for days, absorbing knowledge and prophecy. In the power of written words, her magic grew. As she read, veins of silver rushed through the lands, purifying the ground water. After, the queen stepped from the cave, squinting in the dim light of dusk, and held her hands aloft. From the depths of the ground rose a well of water. Two trees beside her turned to metal and attracted an oncoming lightning storm. The elements met and, within the storm, the queen submitted to her lands, pleading with the elements to save her people. In the silver-soaked flood, she was drowned and flushed from the center of the land mass. Some say she was found dead by a young necromancer, who couldn't bear the thought of losing her. Others say the necromancer was her soul partner, hidden within the drying lands until their powers needed to be braided together.

"Either way, no one knew for certain, but the young queen returned to her palace with a mate, finding the paths leading her home alive and thriving. Though she had no remarkable gift, somehow, through that which she did possess and her sheer will alone, she saved the lands. She is Heilig. The heart of our lands. Its life blood." Basz finished the tale, and I was lost in the story.

"Did she ever find out what caused the sickness?" I asked, turning to the bronze rendering of her story.

"Some say a curse. A mystic who turned against the people. Others say a natural way for things to start anew. An unpopular opinion is that the boundaries between this world and the next thinned, allowing elements on either side to convene and attempt to eradicate each other."

Like the Veil. I turned to him, wide-eyed.

"What do you believe, Basz?"

"I have never been one for popular opinion." He gave me a small smile.

I touched the bronze, feeling its smooth bumps and reliefs. As though drifting on the sea, I was cast into a vision.

Reading until my eyes burned. Elemental symbols swirling in the air like snowflakes. Electricity crackling through a forest. A box, sacred and old. Within the box, photos of visions past—Silas's dead arm. Cadeyrn kneeling in the dirt of a battlefield. The dented crown. A hand closing the box. Rushing water. A hawk.

Slumping against the wall, I came out of the vision. Basz crouched near me, asking if he should get Cadeyrn. I told him I was fine, though I felt far from it.

"I think Ludek is waiting for me," I told Basz.

He looked at me skeptically, yet offered his arm, leading me away from the hall of history.

Ludek was in the library with his mother. I swallowed, steeling myself for her thorny remarks.

"My Queen," Basz greeted her with a bow.

"The young heir. I hear you have been playing in dirt and stirring up trouble."

And here we go.

"Mother," Ludek warned.

She waved him off and stood in front of me.

"Sshh, *allaine balaiche*," she said to him. "I want to hear from the princess why she thinks it was acceptable to hold a knife to your brother's throat."

"They were sparring, Mother," he said with impatience.

"My mother used to call my brother her beautiful boy as well." I met her eyes. "When Ewan and I were reunited, I remembered that. She was always smoothing his hair, and I remember thinking, as a child, that the stars shone in her eyes when she looked at him." I was speaking familiarly yet felt nearly entranced. "So many years had separated us. I can't imagine what she went through losing us all. The loss I felt was nothing compared to hers." I covered my heart with my hands. "Your loss is greater than I want to imagine. I am more than sorry for it, and I intend to help prevent any further pain for your family."

The room had fallen silent.

It was Ludek who whispered, "Your family too, Neysa. We are all one. My sister was a warrior heart like you. We are all family, even though I may not be your blood."

"Family is more than blood," I said. "Family is in the small moments. The ties that bind us. Threads that connect. Family is in the intention to protect."

Tears streamed down the queen's round, sun-kissed face. She looked at me once more and rushed from the library.

Ludek had a shine in his eyes. His mate stood beside him, a hand at his back. How handsome they looked together. Needing a show of strength, I pushed back thoughts of my mate who wouldn't touch me. How much easier his life would have been had he found a normal mate or even just a wife. Not some monster bound to both him and his cousin. A monster incapable of harnessing her powers alone.

On the wall was a map of Heilig. Ludek explained the different lands within it. He pointed out Sot, far to the southeast. A land of black sand beaches and plants which made their own water. The land from which we entered was Manu. It was the largest seaport, yet largely unpopulated beyond the port, as the jungles and forest converged there, making it difficult to maintain a settlement. Along the coast was a long land known as Biancos. The land was heavily populated, as many small cities were there, and it stretched inland for hundreds of miles, where it met with Ech, the central land in Heilig, largest of all. The palace sat in the very center, in a place known as Kutja. Kutja meant 'box,' he explained. It was said that the secrets to the heart of Heilig were here. The only land left to show me was Annos in the north. That was where much of the turmoil was happening—where his sister had been killed.

"Am I correct in thinking that you and I will be working together to figure out the course of action to take?" I asked Ludek.

"I believe I may be of use, yes. Arik likes to take action before it is wise to do so. I would feel more comfortable laying out the scene before any of you leave here." As he spoke, he walked around, tidying up things he had left in different places. Against the far wall, a curtain shielding it from the sunny window, was a book encased in glass. I walked to it and looked in. Symbols were drawn on the open pages.

"This is the book," I said, tapping my chin. "The Heilig queen's."

Ludek strode to me, his long legs crossing the distance in a flash.

"It is. Basz told you the story then."

"May I look through it at some point?"

He tipped his head side to side. "I don't see why not. We need all the assistance we can get. I can have it taken out tomorrow morning if that suits you?"

I nodded, wondering whether I could interpret anything in it.

"They are mostly elemental symbols," Ludek answered. "Those for things like water, silver, and such."

"Tell me honestly. Will I hate this party tonight?"

Both Basz and Ludek, huffed.

"It really just depends. Some like it because it is an opportunity to let go and just . . . be. Basz is not a fan. I don't mind it much, so he puts up with it."

I blew out a breath and touched Ludek's shoulder in thanks. A snapshot of him as a child flashed. He was standing with his sister, both identical in their dark olive skin and molten chocolate eyes. I looked up at the grown version of that boy.

"Pavla was beautiful. She looked just like you. I am so sorry for your loss."

He leaned over and kissed my cheek. "Thank you. And I am sorry for all that you have endured as well. It is never easy."

"Nothing worth fighting for is."

Cadeyrn said that to me so very long ago on that terrace at the Elder Palace. My heart ached for him, but I knew he needed time. Perhaps we all did. Tomorrow I would work on this new puzzle. It might take more of me than I had anticipated.

Reynard was lounging atop a curved stone railing on the furthest edge of the formal gardens. As his head was tilted back, allowing his creamed honey hair to brush the railing, I saw his eyes were closed, letting the sun warm his face. I jumped up onto the railing myself and leaned against the opposite curve. From the pocket on my jacket, I pulled a small journal and pen and wrote down the visions I'd had today. Something about the box I saw piqued my curiosity. I knew that whatever happened, I had to save Silas. The crown wasn't Ewan's, and, though that gave me a sense of peace, the fact was that I saw Silas dead and Cadeyrn distraught. That was a fate with which I simply refused to comply.

"Whatever you're planning, Little Mouse, count me in."

"Not planning anything, Reynard. Yet. But I shall let you know. Do I really look like war and death?"

"Not war and death. The goddess of such. Your lips have faded and the murderous scowl with them. But let's just say that had you looked like that when we first met, I may have thought twice."

"About biting me?"

"Mmm. Maybe."

I chuckled. He hopped from the railing and was gone. Good gods, he was fast.

The gardens were peaceful. Where I sat was hidden in ferns and summer blooms, and the only sounds were that of birdsong and trickling water from the fountain that ran the length of the garden itself.

Who was behind the blight here? Was it a Veil issue again? Regardless of that, someone had to physically control the phantomes. Who was it? Whoever had taken up Analisse's mantel was who we needed to find. Reluctantly, I made my way back through the gardens, enjoying the late afternoon golden hour of sunshine. I had planned to wear the black gown I purchased in the seaside village in Maesarra, yet Reynard's warning to 'tone it down' rang in my head. Ahead of me, sharpening her knife on a fountain side bench, was Saski.

"Hello, cousin," she purred.

Keep it together, Neysa.

"Saski. I meant to tell you I like those leathers. Might I be able to order myself some before I leave?" There. I complimented her. She smirked at me.

"Of course. On the subject of clothes, I've left you a present. I guessed that perhaps you mightn't have anything suitable with you, so I left a gown for you in your chamber." I wasn't sure how I felt about that, but I thanked her anyway. "If it's not right or doesn't fit, feel free to send it back with your handmaiden. She will find a replacement."

"I'm sure it will be perfect. I look forward to tonight."

A creeping, wicked smile appeared on her face that sent chills up my spine.

CHAPTER 19

NEYSA

Gertie, my handmaiden, was a chatterbox and gossiped until I had forgotten the fact that Cadeyrn had not returned to our chamber. What was more, his clothes had been moved. How I was going to get through this party without losing my shit was starting to worry me. Gertie made me look in the mirror on my way out the door. The cut lines of my shoulder muscles and thighs were back. I had regained some of the weight I'd lost. Once upon a time, I may have felt too prudish to wear this dress. I could bet money that Saski picked it just to see if it rankled me. Gertie curled and glossed my hair, pulling the voluminous barrel curls forward so they framed my face and spilled over my shimmering, oiled shoulders. The dress tied behind the neck with thin straps, which led to a skintight sheer black panel embroidered with copper and rose gold flowering vines that strategically covered my breasts. Well, part of them. The sheer panel stopped in a vee below my navel and became the flowering vines again as they fell in hundreds of swishing rose gold blooms, bracketed by the softest black silk which split at midthigh, putting my legs on display as I walked in four-inch copper heels that laced up the legs. Gold climbing vines started at the top of my ears, down through my lobes where they dropped to shoulder-skimming chandeliers. She pinched my cheeks until I threatened her, and while my skin smarted, she applied a gooey blush and gold shimmer powder before making my eyes smoky and dark. I applied a soft lip balm to my lips in lieu of lip color and thanked her for her help. Here we go.

Potted plants marked the entrance to the ballroom. They towered above, creating canopies within the room, small lights twinkling amongst the leaves. Cushions were all along the floors, small tables set amongst them. Servants meandered, pouring drinks and passing food. What I assumed would be a small party for the family alone was, in fact, a large to-do filled with fae. Many stopped to watch as I walked in. Alone. Without my mate.

Why do we bother? I remembered him saying. Stop it, Neysa. Shut it down. I needed to remember that I was here to fulfill a request for aid. A job to do. Still, it would have been nice to walk in with someone. An arm linked through mine.

"My sister sent the dress, didn't she?" Arik asked.

I nodded, still a bit too nervous to speak.

"Say what you want about her, but she definitely has good taste. You look lovely, cousin." Everyone did. There was not an unattractive face in the room. "I'll get you a drink and you can relax. I'm sure it's a bit much." He steered us toward a servant and pulled a crystal goblet from the tray for each of us. Arik released my arm and turned to face me while I sipped. "You really are nervous. I'm sorry. I should have told you it would be like this."

"It's okay. I just take a while to warm up at parties. Plus, the last few I've been to ended in full-scale battle."

He howled a laugh and drank his wine to the dregs. I took a few more sips as well, wondering where everyone else was.

"Well, not to worry tonight. I promise you it is just a party. Perhaps wild. But just a party. And you are certainly dressed for it."

"Don't you look the part?" Saski said, coming up behind her brother, Silas and Cadeyrn on either arm. They were both impeccably suited in black on black. I wanted to reach for Cadeyrn and tell him how good he looked. Saski angled herself in front of him. She wore a one-shouldered fiery red gown that barely covered her chest and, like mine, opened mid-thigh to show her legs. It was obviously a favorite style of hers. She looked incredible.

"What part might that be?"

"The heir of darkness."

Ah, so that's what this was about. Making me feel off balance in front of people.

"I shall take that as a compliment, then."

I knew full well it was not meant to be, but the wine loosened my tongue. She giggled slightly. Cadeyrn and Silas must have been drinking already, as they were swaying slightly.

In that moment, I recalled a question I had for Ludek, and I suspected I would be in no state to ask later, so I walked to him and Basz where they lay against cushions, chatting with a few other fae. They all looked up at my approach. This was an odd seating arrangement for formal wear, yet I squatted down to speak to them. Ludek introduced me to their friends. One female began playing with a vine on my skirt. She smiled sleepily at me. This would be a long night. I explained that I had a question for Ludek, and Basz threw up a shield around the three of us without so much as taking his hand from his mate's chest. He nodded at me, eyes much clearer than anyone else around us.

"I was told I am the Heir to the Goddess Heícate. I really don't know what that will mean for me, but I was wondering . . ." The same female had two vines twirling in her grasp, and her fingers found their way into the folds of my skirts, moving upward. I gently removed them and kept talking, Basz and Ludek softly laughing. "Could that mean anything in regard to the story you told me today, Basz?"

It was Ludek who answered.

"The thought did cross my mind. All the pieces seem to have come together at the same time. Whether you have a connection to only the lands or their intrinsic powers, we will have to see."

"What is your gift, Ludek?" I asked.

Basz smiled and kissed his mate's earlobe, making Ludek blush fiercely. "I am able to . . . understand things. That which others will not or cannot. And I am an oraculois. That gift runs in both our bloodlines."

"That sounds like a beautiful gift," I said, finishing my wine. A servant appeared, replacing it. "I find it hard to read people. Silas's sister, Corraidhín, sees intent. It seems similar. I feel I am always adrift." Oh, I must have been a bit drunk to have admitted that.

"I know you do. You're doing well, cousin." He turned to his mate, who caught his mouth in a gut-twisting kiss. I had to look away. Cadeyrn sat maybe ten feet away, sprawled like my companions, on rugs and cushions. Saski, Silas, and Konstantín sat with him. He didn't catch my eye, so I searched the room for Reynard. In the far corner, speaking with a small group, he raised his glass to me. I hated parties. Konstantín called me over.

"Niece, how lovely you look this evening."

I didn't like admitting that something in his voice made my skin crawl. Though he looked much like Saskeia, I did not find that warmth and sincerity my mother possessed. His hand crushing Marja's flashed in my mind.

"I heard you gave Arik a beating this morning," Konstantín continued. "I would have paid good money to see that. Please. Sit. I will be leaving the young to the festivities shortly. These parties get a bit wilder than an old man such as I can abide." He winked at me, looking no older than myself. I suddenly missed my mother.

"Was Saski named after my mother?" I had been meaning to ask, but it never felt right.

"Oh, yes. My beloved daughter to carry on the name of my beloved sister."

I hung my head a bit, sipping my wine. Konstantín left us with a hearty good night and signaled for more wine to be brought over. Looking around, I had the feeling that it was not ordinary wine we were drinking. Everyone was in some state of being atop one another, dancing, kissing, or leaving semi-attached. It wasn't offensive or crude, only very open. Saski toed at my heeled foot, and I looked up at where she sat between my mate and Silas. None of us had regarded each other, causing the ever-lurking hollowness in my chest to claw and throttle me.

"You seem to be having no"—she poked my foot— "fun." She poked it again and draped an exposed leg over my mate's. "At." Her hand was on Silas's thigh. I was seeing red. I met Cadeyrn's eyes, imploring him. This was more than enough of this bullshit. "All."

Her other leg crossed over Cadeyrn, and she turned into Silas's face, nuzzling him. He was fully drunk, eyes clouded and lust addled. I couldn't tell if Cadeyrn was so drunk on this drugged wine that he didn't care or notice the female's attention, or if he was challenging me. She reached back and touched his stomach. Had I not been drunk and trying to prevent another palace battle, I would have ripped her hand off with my teeth. She inched her legs further up his lap, and I saw his breathing hitch. Everything in the room deadened to the sound of his heartbeat in my ears. As she wiggled her legs atop my mate, her hands were on Silas's chest and face, and she began kissing him. His hands went into her hair and down her back. Tears were pricking behind my eyes, but I would be godsdamned if I allowed them to fall. Arik came behind me laughing and lifted me up.

"Princess Neysa," he introduced me to a male dressed in fighting leathers, though otherwise polished. "This is my very best friend, Lord Eamon of Kutja." He bowed to me, ebony skin glowing in the low lighting.

"Pleasure, Lord Eamon."

Arik brought us to a low sofa away from the males I loved.

"I'm saving you from my sister. She really knows how to provoke, does she not?"

"She's fondling my mate and my—" Shit, Neysa. "Silas."

He made a dismissive gesture. Eamon turned to me.

"Will you be training tomorrow?" he asked me. "I would be honored to spar with you. I don't know how you beat Arik, but I'd like to find out. I've been trying to for years."

I grinned at him and agreed to meet him before breakfast.

"You certainly have the shoulders of a fighter." He ran a finger along my collarbone and down my shoulder muscle and bicep. I shivered and swallowed.

"And what is your weapon of choice, Lord Eamon?" He raised an eyebrow at me, and I laughed. Cadeyrn was watching with sleepy eyes, Saski's bare legs pushing into his lap, her chest and lips all over Silas. What made me feel even more sick was that she looked like me. Eamon leaned into me as Saski looked over.

"You are more than welcome to join me in my rooms." Eamon's mouth met the shell of my ear.

"I think not." I laughed and gently pushed him away with an eyeroll.

Saski looked over, I opened my legs wide enough to show off the dagger I had strapped high on my upper thigh. With a feeling like a knock to my chest, I saw Cadeyrn's hand come down onto her legs and stay there. I excused myself from Arik and his playboy friend, making for the garden doors. Reynard caught up to me.

"Mousey."

"Go enjoy yourself, Reynard."

"Oh, I will. I'm just worried about you."

"I'll be fine. My cousin seems to be making headway with both Silas and my husband, so I refuse to sit around and watch."

The entire party was lost in a daze of partnering up. I did not like parties full stop and with this string of events, I was not happy. I didn't know where to go either. Back to my chamber to be drunk and alone with my thoughts? Even if I could scream at Cadeyrn at the top of my lungs, I wouldn't do that here. That old, sour question came back again. Where did I go? Where did I belong? If I didn't need to see the book in the library, I would have left this very evening to check on the Veil in the north.

Oh, Ewan, I wish you were here. I knew he couldn't hear me. In a blinding moment, I thought of what needed to be done. I would send a hawk to Corra tonight and look through the book tomorrow morning, then leave by nightfall. I couldn't spend another night here with Saski and even Arik, who was sweet, if not a little on the arrogant side. My hawk waited patiently outside my chamber door. I sent her off with a note to Corra and Ewan, then made for the garden again.

The serenity of the place in the day turned to a ghostly calm at night. Leaves blew in swirls; roses scraped their thorns against the stone walls, like nails along a hallway. The very rear of the garden, where I sat earlier, had stone benches and gazebos. I made for one, thinking I could even fall asleep in there. Turning the corner, I saw movement and was about to turn around but caught sight of a swath of red fabric. Grunts and moans carried on the breeze. Like a train wreck, I couldn't look away. Heart hammering in my chest, I walked closer. Silas had Saski backed against the lip of a large planter, her skirts open, both of them moving together. Quietly, I backed away.

God, I fucking hate parties, I said to myself. The sound of a grunt and female swear sounded behind me, and feet began to hurry in my direction. I ducked behind a hedge and tried to make my way back without being seen. *Oh, bloody great, I'm in a maze. Of bloody course.* Drunk, drugged, mind on everything it shouldn't be, in four-inch heels, on the verge of tears, and stuck in a fucking maze. *Think, Neysa.* Where was my beastie when I needed her? Turn right. Keep turning right. How did I get through the one at Hampton Court? I tripped over a bramble and stumbled, catching myself before going headfirst into the juniper. Turning right again, I was face to face with Silas, whose trousers weren't even done up all the way. I pushed past him and kept storming off but ended up in the same spot. I growled, lower and more viciously than an angry dog.

"*Trubaíste,* wait." Okay, so maybe the right turn thing wasn't working out for me. "Please." I heard him stumble. I couldn't stand the smell of him. Of her on him. It was too close to me.

"Back off," I snarled.

"Or what?" he snarled back, turning me.

"No. You don't get to dictate this scene. I am trying to walk away. From you."

"Just me?"

"Stop it!" I yelled in his face. I pulled the dagger from my thigh, which made his eyes widen in shock. Two quick slices through the laces on my shoes allowed me to kick them off and keep walking. Godsdamned heels.

"Why are you running?"

"I'm walking. You left your plaything back there. Go

play." I looked up and spotted a lowish branch, so I jumped and swung over the hedgerow into the center of the maze.

"Fucking *paitherre moinchai*," he swore and followed, dropping like a cat in front of me.

"I will say this once more, before it becomes a real problem between us. You know I don't play nice when I'm cornered. Leave me alone."

"I know it bothers you. I know this night was a fucking disaster."

"I am a fucking disaster, Silas! I am! Don't you see that? Run away from me! That little bitch knows it and couldn't wait to get her hands on you both." I was screaming now. With fae hearing, I was sure everyone could hear us. Though most were likely too drunk to care. "When we left Aoifsing, I needed to sleep for a month and take a vacation. Not deal with this shit! Go, have fun. The last thing I want is to stop you. I'm a horrible, selfish, stupid asshole whose mate won't even touch her now. Why would I wish anyone else to be as miserable as I am? Especially someone I love as much as I love you. Just leave me alone." I wasn't even crying. I was raging. Why were mazes a thing? Who enjoyed this shit?

I stalked off, leaving him in the center alone. Basz was waiting at the end, Ludek by his side.

"If you're going to leave, you will need an escort. And a shield," Ludek said. I stared at them. "Reynard was worried and thought you were leaving."

Great. I probably ruined his night too.

"Please don't say anything to anyone else. Is there another chamber I could use tonight?"

Chapter 20

Cadeyrn

I must have walked the halls of this godsdamned palace for hours trying to find her. I hadn't meant to be so harsh, but I couldn't in good conscience take her to bed when I knew my cousin had gotten her worked up. I just couldn't. I didn't understand what it was between my mate and my cousin. I didn't and I hated it. It might be the death of me.

So, I stayed away, even though I had wanted to be with her at the party. Saski intercepted Silas and me on our way, saying Neysa had been in the library with Ludek for hours and was running late getting dressed. I should have known. When I saw her walk in looking terrified, it clicked. At that point the wine, or whatever was in that wine, had my mind lusty and fucked. Even the movement of my hands lifting my glass caused color trails, which were mesmerizing. I had tried to ask Silas if he felt just as strange, and he gave me some stupid look and a gorilla-like chuckle. I guessed that was a yes, but his chuckle sent me into a giggle, holding onto Saski's arm like she was the last column of reality. Neysa sat watching Saski fondle Silas, and her expression was murderous. I was back where I was earlier, not giving in, and letting the viper wiggle her legs on me. The sick part was that Saski looked so much like Neysa it was bizarre. Somewhere on the fourth floor of this monstrously large castle, I picked up on her scent, mixed with that of Basz. I would bet she had them find her quarters for the night. I opened my mind to her, but she had shut hers down completely. Each time I tried to say something, I couldn't make it come out. I was still pissed. She was still pissed. We were still in this impossible situation, and, once again, I'd made Neysa feel like I didn't want her. If I could bury myself in her and stay there forever, I would. If only I could find her.

A NOTE LAID atop the table in our chamber the next morning, weighed down with a rock. Somehow seeing it had my legs feeling as though they were about to give out.

Cadeyrn,

I sent a hawk to Corra and Ewan last night explaining things. I can understand why you won't touch me. I don't know what to do about it because I love you and it hurts to be near you if you won't touch me. Regardless, there was a tale in the histories here that I felt held a key. Ludek and I spent the morning perusing a book that could help, and I think I know a way to fix the Veil. I am armed and prepared. Basz and Reynard are with me. I will try to be back in three months' time. It's some-thing I must do and it's not worth causing you and Silas more pain. I know I am a monster. What did Bestía say? "Who would want that crown of darkness?"

I love you more than life itself. Please don't blame
Ludek.
Neysa

I quite literally couldn't breathe.

"Silas," I wheezed, trying to be louder but not finding the air. "Silas." The door opened and he came in angry. I thrust the letter at him. Muscles ticked over and over in his jaw as he read. Our eyes met.

"Go," he rasped. "Go, you fucking twat! Or I will go."

"Find Ludek." I needed to see the only member of this household I trusted before I set the place aflame in fury.

"You stupid bastard." He had my shirt in his hands, face inches from mine. "She's out of her fucking head. Either you go or I will. Choose, brother."

Ludek appeared in the doorway. I didn't know who summoned him or if his gift alone had him come to us.

"I was sworn to secrecy. I'm sorry. Know that my mate will protect her with his life."

"What was the story?" I asked him. He looked repentant. "What. Was. It? Was it a prophecy? If you have sent her there to die, there will be more hell unleashed on this fucking land than you have ever seen." My quiet seething had heat building in the room. A storm was mounting outside, rain lashing at the windows. The rest of the family members gathered, no doubt drawn by our shouts.

"It was the story of the namesake of Heilig," the queen said. "The heart of our land. I saw in your mate's mind that she believed there was a way to close the Veil. She believes it is a Veil between the realm of the living and dead. I watched her walk out of the palace."

There was at least truth in her story, and for that reason alone, I heeded her. I briefly wondered about the dynamic between her and the king. A tangent of disassociation in my rage.

Silas swore, thunder echoing it.

"Did you see how she planned to close the Veil?" I asked, dangerously soft.

She shook her head and said something about elements.

"My mate and her brother closed the Veil between the human realm and Aoifsing. Do you know how she did it?" I could see the royal family take a collective breath. "She sacrificed herself. Did you know that? She crossed over and used human magic to close the Veil. The only reason . . ." I snarled and pinched my nose. "The only reason she didn't die was because your sister"—I pointed to Konstantín— "had a vision and gave every single drop of her power to her children so they didn't combust in the explosion. Did you know that, Your Majesty? Saskeia was murdered because she had nothing left. And you." I pointed to Saski. "You thought it would be funny to play with a female who had been beaten and torn apart."

"I'm sorry," Saski said.

"I don't care if you're sorry." I looked around the room, noting what Neysa took. "I need a fucking hawk. I want to know every single thing you know about this mess. I want a guide, a scout."

Everyone scrambled. Silas stood with arms crossed.

"Cadeyrn, I had meant to be there for her, and the night . . . went differently."

"Don't you think I know that? Why do you think I wasn't there? Do you think I gave a shit about what happened this morning? I fail her time and again, and she thinks *she's* the monster." I laughed, dark and sick. "I'm a worthless piece of shit. And she is willing to die for all of us. You know as well as I do that if there is something in that bullshit story they fed her about giving yourself over to the elements or some shit, she will do it. Neither Basz nor Reynard will be able to stop her." I was shaking.

"So when do we go?"

"Now."

He nodded and left the chamber.

Saski spoke to Silas in the hall. "I truly did not mean to cause such a stir."

"Of course you did. But this is not about you. You would like to think so, though. You want help getting rid of those ghostly bastards? Find my cousin's mate. Otherwise, when we do, we will get the hell out of here and let you lot rot. The only reason I fucked you is because you look enough like her and I was drugged with that swill you had at the party."

His bootsteps stomped away. I stood momentarily staring at the dress Neysa wore last night, draped across the chair. The dress had looked beautiful, but it wasn't at all her.

Neysa. Everything in my head is empty.

Chapter 21

NEYSA

The beauty of Heilig was wearing off. The ground was sodden, and leaves dripped on me all day and night. On a scale of stupidity, I was quite sure this adventure tipped the scale to monumentally asinine. So here I was without either Silas or Cadeyrn. Without Silas, I didn't know if my powers would behave. Without Cadeyrn, my soul was brittle. My mate and his wealth of gifts could have warmed my frozen feet by now and healed the massive cut I got from a thorn. That was, if he weren't still pissed at me.

The fire was low and comfortable, given the night wasn't terribly cold yet. According to Basz, as soon as we crossed the gorge the next day, we would be in Annos. I stared into the glow, getting lost in the dancing flames.

"I know I always tease you about it, Mousey, but help me understand the dynamic between you and both males."

I hung my head.

"Silas and I had a thing before Cadeyrn would even look at me. I was attracted to him. I mean, who wouldn't be?" Both males around the fire snorted. "Silas and I get along well. It's easy with him, and I didn't know he loved me. Until Bania. I fell in love with Cadeyrn slowly, and I am . . . quite stubborn. So is he. I thought I could never be loved like that. To love like that. The feeling of him being in a room with me makes me crazed." I looked at Basz, who gave me a small, understanding smile. "We want a life together. Without all this bullshit." I swiped at my face where tears were falling. "There is something between Silas and me, though. None of us understand it. There's an emotive drive that links us. The mystics gifted me this thread of love, and it wound into the skin of the three of us. I don't know what that means. I only know that it causes pain. I don't want Silas to be alone and unhappy, but when I see him with a female, I want to rip her heart out like I would for my mate. It makes no sense. I feel that I must be some sort of monster. To do this to them."

Surprising me, Reynard took my hand. The males were quiet, giving me room to finish my story while a chittering of insects harmonized with the crimped edges of my breathing.

"I could have killed Saski last night. I very nearly did. I could have dealt with her being all over Silas. But when she was writhing on Cadeyrn . . . and she touched his stomach."

"By the gods," Reynard gasped. "I've watched what that does to him when you touch his stomach. Even when he was spelled by Bestía."

I laughed a little and squeezed his hand.

"There was very nearly a diplomatic incident in that party," I said.

Basz kept sharpening his sword. "I believe, Your Highness, that the entire party was a diplomatic incident. You two get some sleep. I'll keep watch."

THE SCENT of rotting flesh permeated the air as soon as we crossed the gorge. An entire village had been overrun by phantomes. Children laid dead on the streets, parents half draped over their small bodies. Fires smoldered in cottages. There was a silence like the atmosphere itself refused to allow for breath. We three were shaking. No one escaped, it seemed. I understood then, soldiers coming home from wars where they witnessed atrocities. I understood the trauma and stress that could follow. The shapes of fae who were murdered in that village would haunt me forever.

I felt for a link. A tug. Something to tell me where the Veil was. I pulled on my magic, regardless of the distance. Something to make this senseless violence stop. According to the map, Annos wasn't a very large area of land. As we walked through the village, a desperate feeling of hopelessness overcame me. What if, in leaving, I caused Silas to die?

We walked for hours until I suggested we make camp. I offered to take watch as they slept, and, in the silence, I tried to scry in the flames. From the bag of gifts, I pulled a chunk of pyrite. It was a stone with a fire element. Holding it in my hands, I focused on the flames. After a time, images flickered in the orange. *Ewan with his head hung low, eyes sunken. Cadeyrn, battle ready, standing off with Konstantin and Arik. The prince had thick brows pinched together, eyes remorseful. The king's face was awash with little emotion. In my head I heard Cadeyrn yelling. He very rarely raised his voice. I listened closely.*

"Did you set her up? It's not even there, is it? Where is my wife?"

I was breathing hard, losing my grasp on the images.

A land of turquoise waters and white sand. Sea grass and dunes met the water and slunk back into cities and towns. A wobble in the atmosphere near a hidden cove.

My eyes sprung open. There was movement around us.

"Basz," I whispered. He was instantly alert. "Movement."

I felt his shield go up. Reynard moved quickly to smother the fire so we weren't night blind. Basz was to my left. I walked to him in a crouch; the three of us stood with our backs touching.

As though a curtain were lifted, phantomes spilled from the woods around us. Gods above. Reynard hopped to the highest branch and began picking them off with arrows while Basz and I used blades, cutting off heads. I unleashed my electricity, and it went straight through them as though they were nothing. Think. Pyrite, tourmaline, amethyst, rose quartz, and clear quartz. I had major protection stones. Yanking the necklaces from my neck, I held all the stones together and willed my energy into them. The air took a great pause, and, like a light switch, the phantomes blinked out. We collapsed. That was a lucky break. Had there been more, I am quite certain my stones would not have been enough. More movement came from the direction we had come from. Basz and I readied, and Reynard was still in his perch. A figure dove forward and rolled. An arrow went through her hand and she screamed. Reynard dropped down and aimed at her heart.

"Saski?" Basz asked, trying to remove the arrow.

My twin swords were trained on her. "Give me one reason to not kill you. It better be fucking good because you are at the top of my list."

"You're going the wrong way."

"I figured that out, thanks. Not good enough."

"Which hand touched his stomach, Mousey? I could take the other as well."

She snarled at him.

"I brought you a set of leathers," she offered. Hmm. Maybe.

"Why did you follow us?"

"I owe it to you. I was childish."

"On the contrary. There was nothing at all childish about how you acted. By every law, I could have your head for laying your hands on my mate."

She was sweating, and Basz was trying to staunch the bleeding. He looked at me, a plea in his eyes. His mate's other sister. Fine.

"I left as soon as I heard. I thought I could track you here best. I figured," she started and cleared her throat. "You may not want me telling the others where you are."

"Yet you thought she would want to see *you*?" Reynard sneered.

Saski gave him a look which could have burned through steel. She was right, though. I had needed out.

I told them that I had seen the Veil. It looked as though it were in Biancos, along the western shores of Heilig. It would be a week's trek into Biancos. From there, as the land was vast, who knows how long it would take to find the Veil. The bag of gifts pulsed as if in answer. We would head southwest in the morning.

As I fell asleep, I opened my mind slightly. The silence had been torture.

Are you okay? His tone was clipped and far away.

The Veil isn't in the north. It's in Biancos. We head out in the morning. Saski found us. I didn't kill her.

See. You're not a monster.

I am, though. And I'm sorry. For everything.

If you're a monster, he said, *then I am, too.* Tears were running freely now. *I don't care what it asks for. I don't want to lose you. Do not make that call, Neysa.*

You can't ask me not to.

I just did. I would rather see the world burn than lose you.

What would that make us?

Monsters in love? he said, and I could hear a slight smile in his voice. I could picture the twinkle in his eyes and his dimple gracing the world.

You realize you just gave me an image of two colorful furry things running toward each other on a beach, right?

Yes, that's clearly what I meant.

Good night, Cadeyrn.

Good night, Caráed.

SASKI WAS STILL HORRIBLE. Perhaps it was a defense mechanism. I knew how those could backfire. But she was awful, and, despite having come to help us, she seemed thoroughly uncontrite over how she acted. Squatting by a stream to fill our water skeins, I washed a bit of grime from my engagement ring. One stone for each province in Aoifsing, a diamond from his mother, large and clear enough to see glinting color from the aquamarine set beneath it. Our birthstones, our birthrights. Squeaking leather moved next to me.

"You know, you could have had fun at that party."

I glared at Saski. The males were doing their thing further away to give us privacy in our conversation.

"How so? You made sure I arrived without my mate. You were all over both of them fairly quickly."

"It wasn't my fault you two were arguing before. Nor was it my fault that Silas was so worked up by you I could have taken him in that ballroom."

Don't hit her, Neysa. Don't be that girl.

"Perhaps not, but you certainly used every bit of opportunity to cause trouble."

"I like a challenge. Surely you can understand that. I have

little issue finding male attention. Yours are both so . . . desirable. I wanted to see how far I could push it."

The entire stream lit up with electricity. Shit. I sat back and stuck my hands in my armpits.

"I'd say you got your answer. You drugged them and had your legs all over my husband and, fairly soon after, had Silas in the garden. A win for you. Congratulations." I made to stand. Maybe I could sacrifice her at the Veil.

"Mm. Your mate threw my legs off him the minute you walked out. Silas dropped me on the ground when he heard you. I had pebbles in my bum." She shrugged. "You know what he told me?" I rolled my eyes and gathered my things to start back on the path. "He said he only fucked me because I look like you." Oh, Silas. "I really don't think it's fair you have both of them, though."

I laughed a little. "No. It's not. It's not fair to anyone."

"That's for damned sure," Reynard said, sidling up to me, bow over his shoulder. He really had gotten handsome. The first time I met him I thought he looked like a demon. Shades of white and cream with dull eyes. It never occurred to me he had lost his coloring from being tortured. "Ready to go, Mousey?"

I squeezed his shoulder.

Thankfully, we made it out of Annos within a day. Not that it wasn't lovely. I had expected it to look like Festaera, but it was craggy and green with cold streams and wildlife everywhere. However, the draw of Biancos and the sea pulled me away with little thought for the rugged landscape behind. A week passed. Mounting dread filled me the closer we came. Once in Biancos, our path took us along the coast, as I had seen the Veil in a seaside cove.

Nausea woke me the morning of the second week on the road. I ran to the edge of camp to empty my stomach. The vision of the pregnant belly came to mind. Quick calculations in my head had me relaxing a bit. Just terrified, it seemed. Everyone was up with my retching, pointedly not saying anything.

Tall reeds of seagrass swayed as we walked through them along the cliffs and dunes. Even breathing in the sea didn't lighten my heart. I knew Cadeyrn asked me to not give all, but if that's what it would take to close the Veil, then I would give it.

"I don't know why you liked my leathers when you have those," Saski said, pointing to my aphrim skins. "Whatever are they?" She reached over and touched my arm. My first instinct was to twist it back and knock her knees out. Yet I didn't.

"Aphrim skins. Reynard had them made for me."

"Aphrim are great scaly beasts used as disposable infantry. They make phenomenal clothing. Watertight, moveable, almost armor-like. Jealous?" Reynard asked her.

I smiled, though the thought of the drooling, scaled creatures made me shudder internally.

"Quite. They also make your ass look amazing."

I burst out laughing. Okay, it was a bit of a hysterical laugh as I was on the edge of a nervous breakdown.

"No wonder Corra was envious," I replied, wishing Corra were there with me.

Dusk was coming quickly, and though there was a definite pull—a confusion in the atmosphere—it would be risky to keep searching in the dark. We made camp in a small valley of dunes. I forced down the crab we cooked, knowing I needed my strength. I hadn't heard from Cadeyrn since the last night in Annos. It was distant enough that I knew between the wards on the castle, the stones I carried, and now the proximity to the Veil, it was as though we had a wall up between us.

Sea breezes tickled the small hairs that escaped my braid. It was beatific in this land, but then, I thought that of most places near the sea. Then the wind turned icy, and I whipped my head to the others sitting around the fire. A high-pitched keening wail sounded in the distance.

"Mousey, get your stones ready." Reynard ripped pieces of his handkerchief and wrapped them around the tips of his arrows, dousing them in a bit of liquor from a canteen. He was ready to set them aflame. From the south we saw a fog rolling toward us. Phantomes.

CHAPTER 22

CORRAIDHÍN

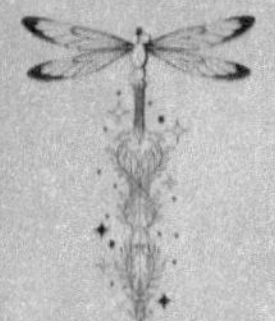

Oh, I was not at all surprised to receive a hawk from Neysa saying what she did. Ewan wasn't either. Knowing it might happen and receiving it, however, were vastly different.

We had been in meetings with representatives and merchants for weeks. Ewan was utterly exhausted, and these two hooligans in my belly were kicking all night. It never helped having to deal with Etienne and his cronies. That male made every hair on my arm stand on end. Although, admittedly, I hadn't much hair. Actually, I had none on my arms. I suppose that was a human phrase I became accustomed to using. Things were fairly calm here given the extremes we had not long ago. When the hawk came in, I was running along a path on the estate in Bistaír.

Corra,
I believe the Veil here is a separation between the realms
of the living and the dead. Someone has torn it open
and is commanding the phantomes. There is a story of a
queen from long ago, and a book she used to harness

elemental magic. I must go and see if I can close it. I have had visions of Silas dead. Cadeyrn refuses to touch me now, and I am a bit lost as you can imagine. Know that I will travel with Reynard and Basz and I will do my best to come home and kiss those babies. Should I not, please tell Ewan I love him, allaíne balaiche. Never let Cadeyrn doubt that I love him more than the stars could have ever known. Tell Silas he will always have my love. Thank you, Corra.
All my love,
Neysa

Poor sodding hawk. That was a long message. Ewan dismissed everyone from his office and put his face in his hands. I stacked the books he was always perusing on his desk. Aulde magic texts, dark magics, gateway realms, necromancing, all of the frightening things he had been reading lately in his little free time.

"I need to go," he said finally.

"Absolutely not."

"How can you tell me not to save my sister?" His eyes were red from lack of sleep.

"I can tell you that because these little beasties in me need you here. Alive. And if . . . if she saw Silas die, I cannot be alone, Ewan." I didn't cry, but I was close.

"Beastie." His head snapped up. "Corraidhín, her beastie. She needs her."

Neysa's little rat eater stayed hidden most of the time. She stayed on with us—we assumed to look after the babes once they were born—but she made herself pretty scarce for the most part. I went to the old barn, hoping she was there.

"Halloo, beastie, darling?" Couldn't Neysa have named her? Poor cow. There was a rustle in the moldy hay. Ewan stayed close by. "Neysa is in trouble, you see. She has gone off to deal with dead soldiers and ghosts and close another Veil."

At the mention of the Veil, the beastie's head snapped up and looked at Ewan.

"Do you remember when we closed the Veil the last time?" he asked her. She huffed and lay her great head near us. "It nearly killed us. You as well, my friend. Well, I am afraid my sister may be going to get herself killed too. And her mate and his *baethaache* are not with her."

Great wings spread wide. Oh, Neysa.

"Will you help her, darling?" I smoothed the scales on her snout. "You will have to fly across a great sea." She looked at me and closed her eyes. It almost looked as though she nodded. "Well then. Let's get you fed and on your way." She stood and followed me out. How does one prepare a *baethaache* for a long journey? Perhaps the same as I would prepare my brother?

Just as we climbed the steps to the house, another hawk landed.

Ewan,
You must have received a hawk from Neysa by now. I
have only just found out she left. I cannot hear her in my
mind. If you can, please . . . just tell her to come back. Or
wait for me. We are on our way. I'm sorry, Ewan. I
have failed you both.
Cadeyrn

Even if we sent a unit to her, it would take weeks to cross the sea. This was a waiting game now, and no one waited worse than I did. We stood and watched as Neysa's beast took flight and disappeared. I wondered if she would find her. And if it would do any good.

CHAPTER 23

CADEYRN

This was a mistake. Every intention we had in coming here was for the greater good, yet we all felt as though we had been led to slaughter. I was not questioning Neysa's aptitude for what she had embarked upon. I did question her ability to see reason in the face of the scale of what is happening. I might have lost mine as well. However, that was why we were all together here. To keep each other in check. And she left me.

Arik prepared horses and provisions for us to reach them in Biancos, a three-day ride west. He wanted to see his sister safely back and close the Veil. My only reason for keeping faith in him. Perhaps Saski's guilt rode her hard, and that's why she followed Neysa. I hoped so. Konstantín I did not trust. He was Neysa's uncle, and his lands were in peril, but I was under no illusion that he wasn't willing to sacrifice any of us in the process. Seeing as Neysa closed the Veil between Aoifsing and the human realm, he saw that success as his foothold. The only one I trusted—cautiously at that—was Ludek. Not only did he want his mate back safely, but he had spoken plainly to me, and to Neysa it seemed, since we arrived.

"I still don't see what this bullshit queen story has to do with Neysa," Silas said, pacing the floor. The only times I had seen him pacing like this was when our parents were killed and when Neysa was taken in Turkey.

"In her mind, she saw resemblance between her task and the queen's," I said, knowing how stupid it sounded.

"The queen found a fucking book and purified the ground water, then died. How does that relate to this ordeal?"

"The queen gave in to all her power and sacrificed it all to the land."

We were quiet.

"Why does she pull this shit, brother?"

I put my head in my hands and shook it. I didn't know.

"Don't start blaming yourself, either. She's a right pain in my arse. I don't care if she's your mate. Neysa refuses help, then lands herself in deeper shite than she started out in."

"We should have left already. What's taking Arik so long?" We were waiting outside the stables in the courtyard and, just as I asked, there was a commotion from inside. Arik stormed outside, Ludek on his heels.

"A faction has moved north from Manu," he told us, out of breath. "The port has been closed. They move to Biancos. Ships have moved to the coast."

"Where is your fleet?" Silas asked. Ludek looked murderous and fanned his hand to Arik as if to tell him to get on with it.

"It was mostly in Manu. We have a few ships off Sot, but that is too far for aid."

Neysa, we have a problem.

Having a problem of our own at the moment.

She screamed.

What's happening?

Phantomes.

Shit. A regiment is moving toward you. Enemy ships closed

the seaport in Manu and are off the coast of Biancos. Konstantín has no fleet available. If you can reach Ewan, tell him to send ships. We are heading out now.

Don't come.

Don't be stupid.

She screamed again, and I saw a flash of what was happening. My heart sank. They were overwhelmed. Four of them against a hundred. I pulled the horse to me.

"We ride. Bring hawks. They are under attack." I was shaking. Silas put his hand on my arm. "They are overrun, Silas. We're going to be too late."

"Like hell we are."

I mounted the horse and kicked it into movement. The sounds of others following behind became a matching beat to my heart.

Stay alive.

Trying. I can barely hear you.

Then she was gone.

ONCE WE REACHED the city limits, there were soldiers waiting to accompany us. I kept riding, noting the hawks launching into the skies. We scaled the bridge across the Matta River, and Silas disappeared. Bloody hell. He must have given himself over to his power and took the river to the sea. I refused to stop for the night, despite Arik and the others urging us to. It was dusk when we set off, and I saw well enough in the dark to keep going. Ludek, who I got the feeling wasn't much for warfare, agreed with me and kicked further forward. Exhaustion pulled at me after a full twenty-four hours of riding. No one would benefit if I couldn't muster my gifts when we arrived, so we camped only as long as necessary to recharge. Maybe Silas would get there. Maybe Ewan sent ships. The odds were against everything working out, and Neysa, bloody hell, I knew, had no intention of not seeing it all through to the end.

WHEN I WAS young and lived in the forest with my mother, we passed the days with her teaching me. She showed me how to hone my gifts. Even those which were foreign to her, like healing and particle transference—or 'that blinking thingy' as Neysa called it. She was proficient with the sword. Not a warrior, but her patience and control allowed her to give me a foundation for my skills. When I was three or four, we went to live with my aunt and uncle. The twins were a year younger and were not happy about the arrangement. I didn't let that bother me. I always wanted people to like me, and that included them. We three children began training together. Silas, though younger, had always tried to bully me. Until we began really training. Battle skills came so naturally to me that he struggled to keep up. I found him once, late at night, having snuck out of the house to practice. I watched him for hours and finally asked to join him. He was so pissed that I had been watching and nearly refused to let me join until I slunk off, half-defeated already. It was in Silas's nature to help, and when I turned away from him that night, he called me back. From then on, we both trained day and night, getting stronger and feeding off one another's strengths and weaknesses. Corraidhín found out about our nightly training by the time we were eleven. She was in a tip over it. She demanded we show her exactly how to be the best and threatened to tell her parents if we refused.

The three of us worked best together. It has been that way for almost three centuries. When Neysa came into the picture, it was Corraidhín who said she was our missing piece. Even before Neysa and Silas, and well before I pulled my head out of my ass and admitted I hadn't stopped thinking about her since the day we met. Now Corraidhín was half a world away, Neysa was quite literally at death's door, and Silas and I were at two separate points trying to get to her. Neysa was her own animal, and perhaps I was a fool to think she would not go off on her own. Perhaps part of who she was would have to need both my cousin and me for her to be satisfied.

When I was small, my mother soothed me when my cousins wouldn't play with me, telling me to always remember, 'Chanè à doinne aech mise fhìne'. I am no one's but my own. It seemed so apropos a phrase for Neysa's personality that I had that dagger made for her with the phrase etched upon it. Plus, the addition of 'my own beautiful disaster,' as Silas called her. I debated the dagger for weeks, thinking she would see straight through the gift and know I was out of my mind in love with her. Finally, I gave in. The relief I felt when she opened it—the total wash of heat when she stroked the blade and laid her head on my shoulder—I knew there was no turning back for me.

Years of learning to keep myself upright while riding was the only reason I didn't topple off the damned horse. My mate had been hit. I felt like I had been hit myself. Whether it was an arrow or a blade, I couldn't be sure, but I knew she was down. I whipped my head to Ludek, grabbing at my inner bicep. His eyes were wide, staring at me. We pushed on, and I felt another blow. This time to my stomach and another to my leg. It felt like a puncture. Dammit. I prayed to whatever gods watched over us that at least one of us made it to her in time, and that they both pulled through this. Arik called that we were getting closer. Only a few hours left, he said. We didn't have hours. I reached toward Ludek, willing him with my eyes to trust me. Hauling my powers from the deep well within me, I invoked my particle transference, and Ludek and I disappeared from our group of riders and landed in a roll amid a full-scale battle.

Before we could take in the whole scene, a blade came down toward Ludek, and I knocked it away. Perhaps Ludek shouldn't have come, but I wouldn't keep him from his mate. Phantomes were everywhere, confusing the scene. Who were they fighting? In the near distance, a roar sounded, and Ludek blanched. Basz came tearing through a group of the ghostly army, covered in his own blood, and limping.

"Where is she?" I yelled, hacking through the necks and torsos of the phantom soldiers. Ludek swung and used his shield to fend off the creatures. I threw a shield around him, knowing Basz had likely used too much of his already. I moved him to the outer rim of the fighting.

"She was close, and we lost her. She has her stones, but they weren't holding up."

"She's down, Basz. Where is the Veil?"

He pointed toward the sea. I ran, creating a tunnel of fire to burn through the demons.

Where are you? I'm here. Where are you?

A moan. Then the thumping beat of a set of wings. Within me, my *baethaache* pushed, trying to emerge. Neysa's beastie landed on a cluster of phantomes and roared. She charged toward a cove hidden behind a dune swarming with phantomes. Dammit. Where was she?

Arrows flew, tipped in fire, finding their marks far faster than anyone but Reynard could fire. I sent flares into the oncoming soldiers, and they fell. Beyond the horizon were twenty or so ships heading in. There were rowboats on shore and fae soldiers, both alive and dead, trudging through the sand. Any question I had as to whether they were friendly or not was answered when I saw Saski firing arrows, crouched in front of something. Reynard's shots were from the same direction. They were covering Neysa.

Fully encased in a shield of fire, I moved toward my mate. Anything near me incinerated as I made my way to that cove. I saw her crawling further to the cave mouth, blood trailing from her. I was swarmed by enemies, both corporeal and phantasmic, delaying my forward progress. I was screaming and slashing, arrows piercing, supporting my efforts. When the path had cleared again, she was gone.

Chapter 24

Neysa

Hearing that the phantomes weren't our only problem really put a damper on my plans. Basz and Saski wanted to know who the insurgents were. I told them that if a news brief containing the name and rank of their leader was sent to me, they'd be the first to know. Then I cut the head off a phantome and caused a whiteout around us. We held them off for a day and managed to keep a shield around us using crystals and the scraps of power the four of us could muster while we slept in shifts. Basz was limping from a blade that met his knee. Reynard tried a field patching of it, but his power was too gutted.

I didn't want Cadeyrn anywhere near this mess. If I tried to open communication with Ewan, not only would he send ships away from defending Aoifsing; if I knew my brother and Corra, there was a good chance that one or both of them would be on one. And I wasn't willing to risk them. We needed to hold out long enough to bring down the Veil.

The symbols in the book were quite basic, indicating there was a build-up of air and pressure, resulting in a continuous blast that kept the Veil seemingly closed to this realm. If I could get to it and destabilize the compression, the Veil could very well collapse from the force of it. If I were lucky, I could manage it from this side. If not, I might have to stand within. Either way, it had to close, and compared to the main Veil in Aoifsing, this task was elementary. That was, apart from the damned phantomes and insurgents.

Basz carried with him a sheet of paper on which we copied the symbols from the book in the order they were written. The first page of the text looked almost like the Periodic Table of the Elements, though far more simplistic. Elements in the human realm either did not exist here, or did not work the same. The knowledge I had used to close the Veil months ago was useless because, though my crystals worked in protection, their chemical makeup and mine were scrambled here. We had to rely on magic and strength alone. Kind of a letdown, really.

As I tried to sleep, I thought of my brother and the life he should have had. The love between him and Corra and the babies they waited on. My family. They were the reason this had to work. I drifted off, clutching the *adairch dorhdj*, and saw, amongst the ghostly fog of phantomes, my mother standing on the edge of the water. I tried to sit up, but she put her finger to her mouth and gestured to the sea behind her. Then she was gone. In her place was a vision of her brother, the king of Heilig, wreathed in darkness.

It was roughly eight hundred meters from where we rested to the Veil. If Basz could cover us while I made a run for it, Reynard covering from the high dunes and rock faces, then I might make it.

"I can use the wind," Saski said. We all looked at her, wondering why she hadn't said anything earlier. "To divert them. Blow them off course. With the sand, the fae would find it quite difficult to see as well."

"That was your escape?" I asked.

Basz shook his head, disappointed.

"Why not just go?" I spat. We had fought for two days straight. I was using my left arm only, as my right shoulder was shot, my grip nearly gone, and all of us were actively bleeding, our fae healing nullified. Yet she never indicated any particular powers.

"I considered it," she admitted. I scrubbed at my filthy, blood-caked face.

"Let's get ready, then." I checked my weapons and kissed the a*dairch dorhdj,* attempting to program it to help us out and maybe just for luck. I couldn't think about the fact that I had essentially said goodbye to my mate in a letter to Corra. Or that I may never see those babies, much less have my own. I couldn't think about the fact that I was sure Konstantín had willingly led us to slaughter here, unwilling to sacrifice himself. That he was a coward. Unlike my mother, his sister, who sacrificed all of herself for us. Unlike my father, who protected us all with his last dying breath. I had a job to do.

So, I ran. The weight of my weapons and the drain on my system from exhaustion and blood loss pulled me back, making me feel like I was running in a dream, never getting anywhere. Off the coast, a beast's roar sounded. My *baethaache* beat her wings furiously, knocking down sails and soldiers alike. She came ashore and tore through insurgents. I sobbed from relief and fear.

An arrow caught me in the soft spot between my neck and shoulder. I went down hard and was covered in phantomes immediately. Basz was yelling, trying to pull his shield up, but I felt him getting further away. Or perhaps I was being pulled. I couldn't tell. The beastie came closer and, siphoning off her link to my power—a storage unit of sorts that had sat, untapped, for a few months—I summoned electricity to blast the phantomes away. Clawing at the ground, sand running through my fingers, I managed to stand and bear crawl toward the cove. I felt heat from behind but couldn't turn to see. A swell of phantomes closed around my exit path. Not that I would use it. The throbbing aberration of the Veil loomed before me. I walked closer and heard two voices screaming for me. Silas and Cadeyrn both were trying to get to me. No, no. They weren't supposed to be there yet. My beastie beat her wings like a turbine, keeping everyone back. Almost there. Once the Veil was gone, the fae soldiers would be ripe for killing. It wouldn't be hard. Cadeyrn's power could wipe them out in one fell swoop. I hoped. The skies darkened. A sheet of charcoal smudged over the land. Thunder crackled and heat flared.

Walking into the Veil, there was an audible crack as I crossed into it, not quite crossing over. I was on the threshold of the living and the dead. A release of my white energy was the catalyst I needed to compress the air within the pocket of this in-between. I felt it rise and rise in me, then burst out like the colors that popped in the air while we were on the barge. The white energy pushed all around me, making this pocket of ether between life and death a pressurized capsule. Once I felt as though my head was near to bursting itself, I willed my electricity to come out. Cadeyrn's heat from outside as he neared the Veil pushed at the capsule I had built, causing the pressure to increase further. The dead swarmed against the threshold, mounting the invisible shield I had created. The pressure from Saski's wind, Silas's storm, and Cadeyrn's heat from the opposite side created a negative pressure, preventing them from entering. And me from getting out.

Every warning on an aerosol can or pressurized air canister cautioned against adding heat or pressure. They explode. That was how I intended to collapse this anomaly in the realm. The pressure from what my mate and the rest were doing outside created a negative pressure like a vacuum seal, keeping the explosion from harming them. Instead of the negative pressure keeping a biological eccentricity like a virus out, it was keeping out the magnitude of the particle explosion I was creating. Being in that moment meant I was past the point of being frightened. All I had left was my drive to end this plague, and a universe full of regret for the life I had started to build.

Once the Veil was fully swelled and pressurized, I felt an uncomfortable pop in my head. Objectively, as though looking from an outside standpoint, I registered that I had a small aneurism due to the effect of the compressed air filtering through my body. With that, I poured all my electricity out of me, releasing everything I had ever known.

Chapter 25

Silas

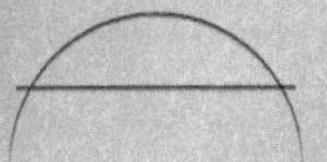

My entire head felt like it was going to blow apart. We all felt and heard the explosion, yet all that remained was a ringing in my ears. I had never been on a human battlefield with the weapons they used. Tanks, missiles, landmines. I knew from reading about it that, oftentimes, the eardrums of those who were nearby would blow. The profound silence around us where there had been noise and chaos a second ago was disorientating. Cadeyrn was kneeling, facedown, blood pouring from every orifice, screaming soundlessly. I looked beyond him, where he stared.

Neysa's beast lay sprawled in the sand, her mistress's arm flung away from her still form. I stumbled toward him, feeling an emptiness in my chest. My first thought was that we needed to keep Cadeyrn calm. I honestly debated knocking him out just to buy us time. The foreseeable problem was that the strongest fae warrior in Aoifsing just lost his mate. If we didn't think of a way to calm Cadeyrn, this world was going to burn to cinders, us along with it.

Basz nodded to me as though he followed my train of thought. He wasn't looking so good himself. I risked my ass and walked over to Caderyn. He looked up at me, blood running from his eyes, nose, and ears. Complete defeat shone on his face. His body swayed. I knelt in front of him, hoping he wouldn't stick his dagger through my gut, and placed my hands on his shoulders. If I could get him to listen long enough . . .

"Cadeyrn, listen to me." But I didn't finish because something slammed into my back and I went down. Hard. Cadeyrn incinerated the attacker, then yanked a sword out of me with a bellow that shook sand from the dunes and covered the wound with his hand. It still bled, so something in me knew I was still alive. Cadeyrn held himself over me, attempting to heal me. He hadn't even made a move to walk to *Trubaíste*. He knew she was dead.

"There might be a way to fix it," said a soft voice. Ludek, perhaps.

"If my cousin weren't pregnant," Cadeyrn began in a voice more smoke than male. "This world would already be gone."

He spoke with such unnerving quiet, I shivered. I took in a shallow breath. Another healer moved forward to take over for Cadeyrn, but he growled and waved them off.

"In the story of the queen, her mate finds her. He is a necromancer," Ludek said, but my vision was fading.

I watched as Reynard walked to where Neysa's body lay, still and battered. Her cousins stood around on one knee. I wanted to kill them. Her beastie lay just as still, a wing lying atop Neysa's chest. She was burned and bloody, her arms at odd angles. Cadeyrn kneeled, catatonic to everything around him. Reynard lifted her without a thought for permission from any of her family, and somewhere in my consciousness, I applauded the weasel. Neysa had been his friend when no one else had bothered.

Across the beach, to a waiting rowboat, he carried her body. Cadeyrn draped me across his shoulder and carried me as well. As he laid me in the boat next to *Trubaíste*, from her bag of gifts fell a wand of selenite. Reynard set it atop her, and it glowed. Other small craft moved onto the beach, and I saw Cyrranus step out with Turuin. They took in the scene. Cyrranus lunged for Neysa. He placed both her hands on the selenite, making it glow further. Cadeyrn was trying not to look at her face. Trying and failing. Her beautiful face, blue and bloody. I tried to reach out to him but found I couldn't fucking move. I knew pain in its most basic sense. I'd been cut and stabbed and shot with arrows more times than I cared to admit. Seeing *Trubaíste* like that—all but removed from this world—broke something in me I never knew existed. I didn't know whether I hated her for it. All I knew, as I lay dying, was that nothing in me would ever be the same without her.

"We need a necromancer," Reynard rasped.

The others from Aoifsing looked at him like he was stark fucking mad. He repeated himself.

"There was a prophecy. We need a necromancer!" he screamed hysterically, over and over. Cadeyrn joined my hands with Neysa's. An impossible situation. Others came up behind us.

"Where are your mystics?" Cadeyrn asked Arik or Ludek, I couldn't be sure.

"Likely with our father," Arik answered. My cousin nodded absently.

"One day he will burn for this."

"I know," Ludek whispered. His brown eyes went wide. "There is a spark left in her." He stepped forward. "Here." He touched her abdomen. "Where her *baethaache* was. There is a spark. We can keep the spark alive until we find a necromancer."

Cadeyrn scrambled into the boat and placed his hands on her face, her chest, her stomach. His tears mixed with her blood, running along the cold sides of her still lovely face. His body was rumbling, the very ground beneath us responding to his anguish. If it didn't stop, I sensed we might have an issue with the reverberations causing a tidal wave.

"If we can get them to Aoifsing, we can get someone to help," Reynard said, looking at Cyrranus for some reason. I was too fucked to figure out why.

"It's not as far as we assumed," Turuin said. "Take them to the ship. We can be in Saarlaiche within a week."

"I will come. Once I rest, I can force the winds to push us faster. Let me help," Saski pleaded. Her eyes focused on me with a mix of shame and horror, very little of the vixen I knew her to be.

"I will as well. I am not as strong as Saski, but I can keep her power going." Arik placed his sword in front of Cadeyrn. A token of deference.

"Then we go," Cadeyrn said, barely above a whisper. He looked up at us all. Flames burned in his eyes, and I knew that if she didn't come back, this world was in for an unleashing of hell.

"MOUSEY."

I woke to Reynard's voice.

"We are headed home," he said to *Trubaíste*. "You will be in Saarlaiche in a few days."

I had a sleep clogged memory of him coming in to tell Cadeyrn to go eat. I'd been in and out of consciousness for two days, and Cadeyrn had been crouched next to his mate's body the whole time. No one needed him sputtering out too. Reynard climbed on the desk in the ship's cabin and spoke to *Trubaíste*, though she was still not of this world.

"I told your mate to eat," he said. "Between you and me, I hope he bathes too. As it stands, you are dead and look better than he does." He touched her hair. "You fought for me. When no one else would. I don't even know why I call you a little mouse. You've never been a mouse. You were like a raging cat, and I thought, no wonder those two male specimens love you. So, hold on. Okay, Kitten?"

"*Paitherre moinchai*," I rasped from next to Neysa. "She is a *paitherre moinchai*." A panther monkey.

"So she is. And you, God of the Forest? Feeling alive?"

"No, but apparently I am, Weasel. My cousin?"

"Eating and bathing, I hope. Silas, if this goes poorly and she doesn't make it, Cadeyrn . . ." He trailed off, and I nodded shallowly. "Keep reminding him that there is good in this world."

I rolled with a grunt and laid both hands on her. The selenite glowed brighter than it had yet. After a time, the selenite glowing brighter and brighter, Cadeyrn walked in. He placed his hands atop mine. A white glow swelled in the cabin. The ship seemed to pick up speed. We were moving like arrows across the sea. Saski and Arik were working tirelessly to move the winds, but it seemed the tides were being pulled as well. I had to hope that between all of us and the company we kept, we could bring her back. Reynard whispered that he was sorry for all he put her through, and all she had endured. That she deserved more. She bloody well did. She always had.

CHAPTER 26

NEYSA

Sounds that I knew should be familiar were foreign. If I stayed completely still, the sounds might go away until I figured out where I was. Who I was. Scuttling and humming. In my mind, the sounds were close and invasive. To have gone from complete unconscious existence to heightened senses was frightening. Flowing sounds stopped and started, whistling, more scuttling. Thumping. Thumping from within me. Rationally, I was aware the thumping was my heartbeat. If there was another thumping sound, further away, it must be someone else's heartbeat. Who? I couldn't recall anything before this moment. The flowing sound became louder, and the scuttling faded away.

I opened my eyes to a box. Closed in. Not a box. A room. Baskets hung from rafters. My mind said the rafters held the ceiling up. Plants spilled from the baskets. There was heat. I looked to the wall, where a fire burned and a kettle hung. I knew heat. I . . . needed heat. There was little light, yet I could see. Memories came on in a rush. I was in bed and a man—my father—told me stories to drive away the darkness. In my mind, a boy sat next to me, looking out. Looking at the sea. I could breathe while thinking of the sea. If I concentrated hard enough, I could hear the sea from this room.

There were warm things on my body. I touched them. Stones? They lined along my midsection, covering my heart, my legs. One laid on my forehead. It slid off as I touched it and clattered to the ground. The flowing stopped, and the scuttling drew close again.

"Ah, *allaíne aoín*," a female voice said. "I wondered when you would wake." I shook and shivered. "Slowly, *caráed*. It is a transformation."

She removed the stones one at a time and wrapped me in something soft. My brain noted it was fuzzy and familiar. The only familiar thing, apart from the sound of the sea. There was a scent in it that seemed to merge with my own. Something like the sea, but softer. I closed my eyes again. The fae female, round-faced and dark-skinned, lifted me easily, moving me to a chair near the fire. She placed a stone in my hand to hold, and stones around my neck.

Memories came of placing stones around me and fighting. Swinging a sword. I winced, and there was an explosion in my mind. I cried out. Something was pressed to my lips. I drank, and it soothed me, reminding me of quiet nights with dogs. Then a memory of drinking by the sea with another fae. A male. His watery eyes were looking at me. I felt warmth on my face, eyes blurring. The female with me began brushing out my hair and singing. I didn't recognize the tune or words, but it wound around my soul. She stopped singing as she smoothed a sweet-smelling oil into my hair.

"Pl—" I stopped, choking on getting the sound out. "Please," I wheezed. I touched my throat. "Sing."

She smiled at me and patted my shoulder, then began singing anew.

"If I loved you more than life itself

If I brought you brightness to your day
Would you tell me you would light the skies?
Would you tell me I could stay?
If I stayed with you and made you mine
If I could braid my soul inside of thine
Could we stay forever thus entwined?
Could we never see the end of time?"

I squeezed my eyes closed, trying to reach for a thread that seemed to dangle tauntingly from that song. The female rubbed the oil on my arms, kneading the flesh and muscle. Dim light caught on a thin band of gold. I touched it, and faces appeared in my mind. Two sets of nearly translucent green eyes and faces so close to the surface of recollection. She continued her ministrations on my arms.

"Trying to get the blood flowing again. You've been through a trial, love." She moved to my hands, pulling the fingers one at time and wiggling them. Atop one hand was a collection of freckles. I knew those. They had always been there. I smoothed the skin over them. A picture formed of the night sky and the same arrangement of stars and the freckles on my hand. Then another picture of a broad, beautiful back with yet again the same constellation of markings. I took a sharp intake of breath as a pang went through me. She smiled.

Once done, a dressing gown was brought over and she helped me into it, then made to take the fuzzy wrapping from me. I protested, keeping it with me. The scent kept me from wanting to run. My legs felt the urge to sprint. I didn't even know where I would run and that scared me more. There was a shuffle from beyond a door, then a tapping.

"Rhia, It's Ewan."

I knew that name. The picture of the boy flashed before me again.

"Come then, *balaíche*." The door opened, a waft of sea air

following the man inside. Something cracked in my chest, and I squeaked.

"Hallo, *áoín baege.*" Little one, I knew it meant. "I've missed you." He sat on a stool facing me and took my hands.

"She's only just awoken. Have a care. Everything is new again." I looked into his eyes, a deep, warm, brownish green, and knew he was my brother.

"Yes, madam. Do you know me, Neyssie?" I nodded and squeezed his hands. Tears slipped from his eyes. "I knew you would. Corraidhín warned that you might not. I told her we would always know each other." That name he said sounded so . . . right.

"Corra?" I managed to get out.

"Yes. Corra. My wife and your friend. She is with children, do you remember? You promised to come back and kiss them. And here you are. Rhia tells me it may be quite some time to be back to yourself, but she doesn't know you, does she?" I didn't know me either. "Can I give you something?" I nodded. My voice was so harsh, and I didn't want to keep barking at him.

I don't mind you barking. I've missed having a dog. My mouth dropped open hearing him speak to my mind.

I had a dog. Two. Bixs—Bixby. And Cuthbert.

He wiped his eyes with the back of his hand and reached into the pocket of his jacket.

"This is yours. You may not remember it yet, so he asked me to give it to you. He said to take your time, and when you remember, he will be here. May I?" He slipped a ring onto my finger. I knew this ring. It had stones hammered into a white gold band, a large diamond shining from the top. It slid onto my finger, and a name came to mind.

Cadeyrn.

Yes. Cadeyrn gave this to you.

I could see his face in my mind, and touching the ring

made my stomach flutter. I knew it was his scent that covered the fuzzy wrap around me, and I knew I wanted him near, but he said to wait until I remembered him. And I didn't. Not really.

"It will take time. Do you recall when we were reunited at the Elder Palace?" I did. "Cadeyrn was there. He freed me from them. I knew when I saw you two together that he loved you. I don't even think you knew. He looked at you like you could make it rain sausages and it would be fine by him."

I coughed.

"So, think on it. And when you remember, call upon me. Or him. I must go, but I shall be back soon. I love you, Neyssie. Thank you for coming back."

I was so tired that I closed my eyes as he kissed my forehead. When I woke, there were two cold things pushed up against either of my bare calves. I moved my legs, and the cold things were replaced by wetness. Dogs. I sat forward and hugged them, sobbing. They stayed by me the rest of the night as I slept. When I awoke, Rhia was there making a ruckus with cooking and changing this and that. I stood and walked around, legs as shaky as a newborn fawn.

"Good morning. This was left for you." On the counter where she cooked was a slice of cake. It was yellow and spongy with a ribbon of red in the middle, and what looked like cream on top. On the plate next to it lay an amethyst. I touched it and recalled it floating from my hand. Then felt the memory of hands on me—in my hair and on my arms. I turned from Rhia, who had smothered a cough, and started in on the cake.

The dogs and I walked along the sea, and through a grove of gold and silver trees. The leaves caught the light, and I remembered walking through these with both males whose faces appeared in my mind. There was a wall at the end of the grove. I sat on it, the stone giving me visions of sitting there, my legs atop Caderyn's, my head on his shoulder. Suddenly it was hard to breathe. I panicked. I knew him. I knew all of him, and maybe I didn't know how to love him, but I knew my soul knew him. Yet I couldn't breathe. The dogs pawed at me with concern on their shaggy faces.

I know you, I said, hoping he could hear me. *I remember you.*

Would you be okay if I came to see you?

Please. Do. A feeling of relief came through. I swear it was less than a few minutes when a figure came through the grove. His head was hung, night-dark hair crested up like the wing of a great bird. I stood and smoothed down the light dress I wore. My stomach clenched, and my body felt like it was on fire from within. I didn't know where to look. Surely, he could sense how I felt. I was nervous. Finally, his eyes met mine, and his hands reached out to touch mine, asking a question with his fingers. I closed my fingers around his and held them against me.

"I don't remember everything. But I know you."

"It's okay. We can take it slow. These two," he said, scratching the ears closest to his feet, "were convinced I was keeping you hidden. I guess their assumptions were correct and they shall never trust me again."

I smiled at him. The first smile. His neutral expression broke, and a look like he lost something crossed his face. I touched it, unable to keep my hands from him. His eyes closed, and his hand went around my back. I had flashes of memory. Kissing on a balcony in a cave. Fighting in a palace. Laying on a bed of ferns near here. The visions faded, but I wanted more of them. I wanted more of him. I let myself fall against his body, looking up into his face. With one hand I traced the lines of cheekbones and jaw. With the other, I touched his stomach over the fabric of his shirt. His head turned down and he bent, slowly, a question in his eyes, and touched his lips to my cheek. Then my eyelids. My hand went around the back of his neck and stroked his hair. His lips moved along my jaw and finally found my lips, where they kissed me so hesitantly. I shuddered and clenched my hand on his stomach. His hand shot into my hair, and he kissed me more thoroughly. I couldn't get enough. The dogs started whining, and we pulled away at the sound of others approaching.

"So that's where you ran off to," Rhia called. "I suppose things are getting clearer, then? Majesty," she intoned to Cadeyrn and bowed. He bowed in return.

"Thank you, Rhia." Tears were streaming from his eyes.

I nearly looked away; the pain from those tears was almost unbearable. Behind her, my brother stood, shifting from foot to foot. I stepped forward and hugged him. With a force like rushing water, our lives together as children came back to me, then my life as a child without him. Memories of fighting alongside one another. The death of our mother. The death of our father. I hugged him tighter, and he wrapped his arms around me. It wasn't everything yet, but this—my brother— was the foundation for my memories. My life.

The circumstances surrounding what had happened to me were just out of reach, but I could grasp the feeling behind both Ewan's and Cadeyrn's mannerisms and Rhia's ministrations, and it all pointed toward my having died. Flashes of another female who should have been dead came before my eyes. Platinum hair and her hands on my mate. I tried to shake the images out. Memories of hitting her. Of feeling a fault line in my soul rip open from not having my mate. Of fighting him and loving him. Of a necromancer unravelling the threads that bound the female to reanimation. I looked at Cadeyrn, who I knew had seen the images in my head. I couldn't control them yet. Then I turned to Rhia.

"You are a necromancer? And you brought me back?"

"I am, and the answer to the second question is a bit more

complicated, *allaine colleine*." I implored her with my eyes and turned to the two males with me. "Perhaps you would like to hear your tale in your home? Your mate can tell it better. I must get to cleaning my cottage." She stroked my hair and tucked it behind my ear, then made a symbolic sweep of her thumbs across my forehead and chest. "Remember, it is not our memories alone that indicate our happiness. It is the emotion behind them. Some things may have lost their clarity, but nothing stands between the notion of two souls entwined. Good day."

Flagstones with tiny fossils made up the extended patio at the back of the manse. Home, Rhia called it. I knew it here. As soon as I touched the stone walls I remembered being here. Perhaps the happiest I remembered being. Cadeyrn suggested we sit out back where we could see the horizon over the sea. A low wall had chairs atop and cushions on the ground beneath that looked far more comfortable. My legs still ached enough that I chose to stretch out on them. He sat next to me and held out a glass of wine.

"Where shall I begin?" he asked, taking a sip. I was back on that cave balcony again, and the emotion behind that memory was a wave of granite against my mind. Without thinking, I turned and kissed him, needing that emotion to have a buoy to hang on to. Pulling back, he looked at me with heavily lidded eyes and a dumbfounded expression.

"I died?"

He stared out at the vastness of open water. It was still warm enough to sit outside in the gilded light of early evening, though a chill went straight through me.

"We were in Heilig." He touched my arm and showed me images of being there. Even that of a party. Through his eyes, I saw me looking uncomfortable and angry. I could remember feeling destroyed. "You heard a story of a queen who was able to save her kingdom and its lands, and it gave you the idea that you could do it too. But you had been given only half the story. The lands in the story were not plagued. They were cursed. It required a sacrifice to lift the curse. The legend was a prophecy doctored over centuries, and you arrived and fit the requirements of the prophecy." I heard a soft voice in my head retelling the tale, notes of regret in his voice. "You and I, we were at odds that day. You figured out what needed to be done to close the Veil between the living and the dead, and you left."

He yanked at the back of his neck and shot a hand through his hair, making it stand up. I touched it. He smiled at me, small and sad.

"I knew what you would do. You willful, beautiful creature. I guess you realized I would have done anything to stop you. I got there too late. You closed the Veil, but it exploded and stopped your heart and burst your brain." He tripped over his words, a sob coming out. "You were dead. I felt . . . nothing. There was nothing. You were gone, and Silas nearly died. A sword was in his back. I don't know how anyone was able to get that close to him. Ludek realized there was a spark left in you. Between Silas and me, we kept the spark alive until we got here. Your brother pulled the tides to get our ship here faster. He has so much power, Neysa, and it's all good in him. I've never seen someone so powerful and yet uncompromised."

"You," I breathed. "You are the same."

"No," he laughed. "I have done terrible things in the name of what I think is right. I nearly . . ." He drank the rest of his glass. "I nearly set the world aflame. When you were gone. Out of spite. Only the fact that Corraidhín is pregnant kept it intact. So, no. I am far worse."

"How long was I . . . gone?"

"A week? I think. It has been another three that Rhia kept you asleep to recover. Had you awoken when you were first brought back, things wouldn't have gone so well."

"Did you come to see me?" He nodded and fiddled with the fabric of my dress. It was an ugly dress. I must have sent that thought along because he chuckled.

"Hmm."

"What?"

"It's humiliating. I must have looked a sight laying there all . . ." I made an eyes rolled back, tongue out face. He laughed.

The three siblings from Heilig and Basz were staying in Laichmonde, under watch from Turuin's soldiers. They were welcome dignitaries, and it was because of them that I was here. I knew Saski came to my aid. I knew she pulled me out from under phantomes. I knew she pushed the winds to get the ship to move faster. I knew it all, and my head forgave her. However, she had taken advantage of me and Cadeyrn.

"Should I stay here?" I asked, sipping from my glass, keeping my eyes down. He looked at me, and I could see from my peripheral wetness on his cheeks.

"I would very much like that. This." He swiped at his eyes. "This is your home. I know you don't remember everything. I understand. But do you remember being my wife? My mate?"

I set the glass aside and took his away. Making to touch him, I didn't know where to start. Clumsy hands scrunched the fabric of his shirt and tried pulling him closer. He watched me and drew a thumb across my lips where they parted for him.

"Help me remember everything. I know that you belong inside me." My face instantly heated. "I meant, my heart, like . . ."

He laughed and crushed his mouth to mine, then laid me down on the cushions. As he hovered above me, his hair fell forward, tickling my chest, and I arched up into him. Behind his ribs a fluttering had him growling and sweeping across my mouth with his tongue. I raked my nails up under his shirt and down his rippled back.

"I take it back. I meant inside me."

Chuckling against my mouth, he teased his fingers along the neckline of my dress. I pulled his shirt over his head and stopped to stare at his chest before fastening my mouth to it. His hands dove in my hair and moved down my sides before lifting my ugly dress overhead. The breeze blew in and had us moan from the feeling of a thousand fingers tickling our heated skin. His mouth moved down my stomach, stopped by my navel and circled it with his tongue as his fingers leisurely slipped along my body. I pulled my feet high up and pushed at his trousers with them until he was as bare to me as I was to him. He looked at me with eyes that were nearly in an alternate plane of existence. My hips rolled back and forth over him, his hands making their way up to my breasts and pushing them together. I arched into the touch. He sat up, his full lips on my chest, as I kept rolling over him. I moved back incrementally and pushed further. He swore and scraped his fingers through my hair. With him holding my back, pressing my chest to his, I kept moving until I was gasping for air.

We laid there, the night falling around us, chilling our overheated skin, still joined.

"Don't even think about moving," I said, so tired yet content.

"Not for the world." He kissed my temple and ran his hands along my arms and back.

"I feel like I remember everything. I know I remember loving you. Feeling like I could die from wanting you or being apart."

His hands stilled on me.

"I lost you. It was bloody great luck that had you back with us. I keep thinking. If the same thing had happened the way you thought it might, when you and Ewan collapsed the

Veil in Aoifsing, there would not have been a way to save you in the human realm. I wake up from nightmares screaming sometimes. I'm sorry. I am not sure I was myself at all when you were gone. If I'm different—if you find me unappealing, I will understand."

I pulled my head back to look at him, my hair falling over my shoulder onto his.

"You told me once that the only thing about me that was unsavory to you was my lack of self-preservation," I began, and he snorted. Okay, he had a point. Or two. I was a train wreck in that department. I must have been remembering everything, because a pain akin to a wave slamming my face into a rock came back.

"You have, historically speaking, because I am perhaps still waking up, you see . . ." I chattered nervously, and he rumbled a laugh into my hair. "—pissed me off when you try too hard to keep me from doing reckless things. And when you pull the overbearing male thing. Unappealing, though, is a word that could never be used about you." I pursed my lips and stared at his face with those cheekbones and full lips, the strong brow and green eyes that had little lines at the corners which deepened when he smiled. I cocked my head to the side and touched the hair above his forehead. There was a tiny sliver of a silver streak in his dark locks.

"Corra told me I would give her grey hair," I said.

"It seems as though your death took its toll on me as well." A lopsided smile.

"It just makes you more ravishing," I told him, smoothing the hair with my thumb. "I love you. I was hurt. I know you were too. I'm sorry. I just wanted you. Know that I came to you, wanting you. That party. I hate parties." He snickered. "She was very lucky. I was going over the laws of Aoifsing in my head while I sat there staring at her legs on you. I knew I had license to kill her for touching either of you."

"I know. We were so drugged, but you sent those thoughts to me. I also seem to remember thoughts about you knocking her out of the way and taking up Reynard's persistent suggestion."

Er, well . . . "No comment."

THE DOGS WOKE me after dawn. Cadeyrn threw a pillow at them and hid us under the covers. I wanted to start training again, so I tried to push out of the duvet. Strong hands pulled me back and asked me to wait a little while longer. I gave in but made him promise to properly spar with me after breakfast. After breakfast, we were still wrapped in blankets, lounging on the couch, when someone came up the steps to the front door. I tried to sneak off to get clothes on, but Reynard appeared in the living room before I made it off the couch.

"Really? No clothes again, Kitten?" he said with a half-smile.

"I only dress up when things are scheduled to go to hell."

He fidgeted. I tucked the sheet under my arms and moved to hug him.

"What have you been doing with yourself, Reynard? Surely things are slow when you're not sweeping up my messes."

"Dreadfully. Have you got any famine or floods with which to contend?"

Cadeyrn returned with tea and a dressing gown I could slip around myself.

"No one was sure you would remember any of us. Apart

from this beautiful beast." He gestured to my mate, who rolled his eyes.

"Apparently I am too stubborn to abide by the rules of nature. Some things are foggy, but we've been . . . clearing the cobwebs."

"Yes, it certainly seems so," he teased. "Not to spoil your homecoming, but I've been to see my parents." We all groaned. "Your cousin joined me on his way to Bistaír."

"Silas is in Bistaír?" I asked.

Cadeyrn nodded. Disappointment pierced through me.

"My father is vying for the position of a representative of Maesarra. He has been campaigning."

"Why am I not surprised?" Cadeyrn said, handing us all plates for the pastries he set down. I smirked at him, and he rolled his eyes at me.

"Where is your apron?" I asked. He reached over and flicked my nose.

"Apron?" Reynard asked.

"Mm. Yes, it's pink and green with little flowers. I gave it to him for Yule."

"I would pay to see that on him."

"I don't share, unfortunately."

"We know. So, I asked for a rundown of what my lovely father would like to accomplish as a representative, and it's quite a list. First and foremost, he wants to allow the establishment of personal militia. Followed by a class-based system of government. That's the start of the fun. He has some support, Cadeyrn."

"No doubt. Money is power. Has there been any word from Naenire or Prinaer since the uprising?"

"Ainsley Mads would like to speak with you and Ewan." I didn't know if he was referring to Cadeyrn or me. "She has taken over the family mines since her father and brother were killed in the battle of Prinaer. She has ideas for a unified territory of both Naenire and Prinaer, as they have worked in tandem for a millennium."

"I knew of her family. They fought alongside us. Has she elaborated on her ideas?"

"She wished to speak with you lot. I'm just the messenger."

"I've no desire to travel yet. Either we wait, or she can come here once Neysa is ready."

"If we need to go, or you need to go, I can be ready," I said.

He stood and knelt in front of me, putting a hand on my face.

"I know you would be, *caráed*, but I am pulling the overbearing fae male card now. I am sick of running around the world to do others' bidding. Right now, we stay here. I would assume we would both like to be in Bistaír when the babies are born, so let that be the time frame we plan to leave here. If anyone wishes to speak to us, they can come to Saarlaiche. I am quite sure the reason we have is sufficient."

Reynard was looking away.

"I don't want to seem weak," I told Cadeyrn. "I don't want you to look like you would put me before what needs to get done."

"I will put you before anything. It's not weakness. You come first."

"No one would think you weak, Kitten. Not you." Reynard put his hand on my arm, and I was struck with a vision so clear it was as though I were standing in the scene.

The male next to me, fine and golden as he is now, holding another male who had tanned skin and brown hair. They were speaking quietly and laughing with playfulness glinting in their eyes. Solange, Reynard's long dead sister and Cadeyrn's long dead wife, walking into the room and seeing them together. She smiles and leaves. The piazza at The Elder Palace, Solange speaking to the Elders. Reynard's partner standing between

Elder Guards. Nanua, the former Elder of the Twin Provinces and lupinus Alpha, had eyes glowing, and Reynard screaming and fighting to get to the male.

With a lurch of nausea, I was thrust from the vision.

"He was taken from you. She had him taken from you," I said to him.

Horror showed in Reynard's eyes. He snatched his hand back.

"He was my world. That is why I couldn't let either of you lose each other. Love is drowning, and it is pleasure spiked with pain. Loss of a love like yours is drowning for eternity. There is no breath that doesn't burn. No night short enough to lessen the crushing weight."

I left the room and came back, dropping a crystal into my friend's hand. He looked at the rose quartz and gave me a quizzical look.

"It is the stone of love. Maybe that part is far-fetched, but Ama gave me the necklace when she healed me, and she dropped one—this one—in Cadeyrn's pocket when he wasn't looking. What I want is for you to know love again. Perhaps not the same, but something wonderful. Then we can drink wine and chat about boys." I winked at him. He sniffed a laugh.

So, Reynard would dispatch messages to all the candidates for representatives, stating that they could meet in Saarlaiche in a month's time if it was their desire to help lead Aoifsing. No large summit. No palace ordeal. Small meetings.

Corra was due in three months, putting us all together at Bistaír for Yule. It seemed so long ago. So distant a place when we celebrated Yule together in that manor in Barlow Combe. It was one of the most wonderful nights I had spent. I was so in love with Cadeyrn and terrified to be going to Bulgaria with him. What a turn of events.

I touched the gauntlet on my right arm which hid the

forearm holster for my dagger. The words etched on it seemed to glow through the gauntlet. It felt good to be putting weapons on. After clicking the eyes of my training jacket, I braided my hair before a large mirror in our bedroom. I needed to see Silas. I needed him to know I was never angry with him. I just needed to see him. And that made me horrible.

You can't speak back to me, and maybe you can't hear me anymore either. Since, you know, I was dead and all that nonsense. But I was wondering if I really had to wait until Yule to see you. It's okay if that's the case. But I miss you. Did I mention the thing about me having been dead? Because that's a pretty big deal, and sometimes that trumps other bullshit. If you do hear this, give Corra a kiss for me. There was a quick feeling, like touching hands through a glass window, then it fled.

Chapter 27

Silas

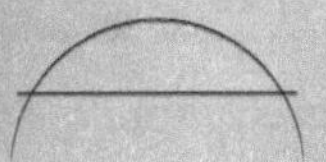

This was a shithole. The entire town stunk of piss and ale, and somehow this was where I chose to be for a week. When Corraidhín asked me to dispatch messages, I took leave of the estate and all the feel-good coziness she and Ewan put off and found the worst cesspool in Maesarra. Comparatively, it was still not quite as bad as the Ukrainian tavern where I found my cousin after he slaughtered hundreds of human slave runners. That was worse. There was ice on every surface of that tavern, and not the kind in the ice bars in Scandinavia where there are blond gods and goddesses walking around in knickers and fur. No, this was puke and piss iced over on the floor. I knew Cadeyrn had gone off on a rage bender when we hadn't heard from him for a couple of months. A search for the crystals turned into vigilantism. I would have done the same, sure. But it was hell to clean up.

This piss shed in the north of Maesarra seemed like a good idea at the time. The messenger I was waiting on staggered through the door and nervously handed me a slip of paper. I dropped a coin in his palm, one on the filthy table, and left. It was all but five minutes of being inside the home of the wealthiest merchant in the area before I had his daughter—or was it his wife—spread across the bed, begging me for more. She had found me the day before and offered information on. . . oh, it was on her husband. Shite, I must need sleep. Anyway, she said he wanted to assist Etienne, Reynard's bastard of a father, in becoming a representative. I asked her price and there we were.

Sad part was, I didn't care. She was pretty enough, and I was bored. So it went pretty much everywhere I heard a buzz of who wanted to fund, support, arm, whatever, any particular male or female. My sister must know this was how I was sending back so much intelligence. I'd hardly been in the state to be sweet-talking my way through things.

This particular day, there was a noise as I slid off the female I was whoring myself to get information from. A door clicked quietly downstairs. Fuck it all to never. She pointed to the window. I grabbed the ledger she pulled for me and slid out, jumping down at least five godsdamned meters. My legs were burning as I ran full-speed three or four towns away, until I found a stream to dissolve into. Thank the fucking gods for this power. It was the only time I had any peace of mind.

As I started to pull back into my corporeal self near Bistaír, Neysa's voice sounded in my head. She always had a way that made me crazed. If she weren't mated to my cousin, I would have sworn she was my mate. I didn't understand it. So, she wanted to see me before Yule. I pinched the bridge of my nose and kicked the root of a big fucking tree. Thunder rumbled overhead. I yanked my boots off as I stormed into the main house of the estate. I didn't know where my sister was and, at the moment, she would see right through me.

"How many was it this trip, brother?"

I tossed the ledger, files, notes, and sworn statements.

"You don't have to do this anymore. I know why you are

doing it," My sister said, turning my annoyance into a full-on thorn in my arse.

"Not now, Corraidhín," I said, the pull of a bath and clean bed too strong.

"Silas," she said. Her hand was always on her belly. I wondered when Neysa would be with children. "Go see her."

"No."

"You're destroying yourself."

"She destroyed me."

"Then get your shit together and saddle that horse. Or whatever the saying is. Listen, brother. This will get you killed, and I can't have that."

"Cadeyrn threatens to burn the realm to ash without an intervention, but I fuck a few bastards for information about their sorry ass lives and I'm the greater threat?"

"Do you remember the story our aunt used to tell us?"

I was impatient with her now. I had been on my feet for two full days and nights.

"The brothers who shared the apple tree?" she prodded.

I scrubbed my face. "Say whatever you want to say, Corraidhín, and let me leave."

"The brothers grew up dreaming of having the apple tree to share between their families for their whole lives. Then as they got older, the one brother gave apples to friends and neighbors, blossoms to pretty females, and built a house that looked upon the tree. He grew up to have a wife and children, and they played around the tree and climbed the branches. The other brother took his apples to the next town and sold them. He built a house that looked away from the tree and would sneak the apples from his brother's side in the middle of the night so he could sell more. Eventually, the tree stopped producing. There was one apple that grew slowly at the top of the tree. They all watched it for weeks and weeks. Then one night the family-minded brother was out walking, and he spotted his brother climbing the tree, taking the last apple. He realized then where all the fruit had gone. All he said to his brother as he looked upon their beloved tree, as it withered away, was, 'I would have given you my apples if you had asked.'"

"That has nothing at all to do with me, Corraidhín." I was out of patience.

"Oh. Perhaps not then. I thought it did—wait! No, it does. Sorry, darling, these babies are making my mind flaky. I am not saying you don't share well. However, Cadeyrn understands there is something between you and Neysa that is not ordinary. Perhaps just ask him."

"That was a fucking long way to get to that point, sister. Good night." I kissed her cheek. Like *Trubaíste* had asked me to. I could do that for her.

CHAPTER 28

NEYSA

Admittedly, I was running myself into the ground. I took the afternoon to work on sprints. Estimating distances, I laid rocks at different points and would sprint between them, practicing turning and rolling from the run. Eventually that got boring, so I would sprint and run up a tree to back flip. Really, it was impressive that I could still do these things. There was an excellent tree for pull ups and hauling myself between branches to work on balance and coordination while I slashed with my sword. I hung upside down from a high branch and began sit ups from the hang, using my sword to reach up each time and touch a higher branch.

"For someone who was just dead, you seem to be fairly energized," a female voice called from below.

I flung my sword down and it pierced the ground about a foot from her, then I flipped from branch to branch until I was on the grassy ground, facing Saski.

"More energy than ever," I responded.

"Want to play?" She smirked.

I still wanted to rip her to shreds. So, I bowed in invitation. She unsheathed her curved blade with the bird hilt and tapped from side to side. I moved in a semi-circle around her, then lashed and ducked. She easily avoided it and slashed her own blade, which I met with a ringing of steel. We both pushed at the position, grunting.

"Thank you for helping me," I said to Saski. "I still want to put depilatory cream in your shampoo for touching my mates but thank you."

"I don't know what that is."

"It makes your hair fall out."

Her face blanched, and I laughed.

"Your mates?"

Oh, shit. I did say that. I didn't even know why I said it. My tongue was certainly forked these days. My eyes darted around, making sure no one else heard. She used my distraction and swiped my blade out of my hand. I released my arm dagger and pulled a short sword from my thigh, jabbing and slashing.

"Saski, I am going to ask you, as a female. As a family member. As a decent individual. Do not repeat what I said. It was an accident. Truly. I'm still figuring things out, and I don't remember half of my life." That wasn't exactly the truth.

"I won't. But I think it's true. That was one reason I tried so hard to push you."

"Then you thought it would be funny to bed someone you thought was my mate?" I scream-whispered at her.

"Good point. However, if you would stop trying to take my head off, perhaps we could have a real conversation? Ludek would like to speak to you as well." Saski's hands were planted on her hips as she spoke to me. I stopped launching at her and stared, nostrils flaring. "I think that maybe we could help." Saski said. I snorted. "I apologize. It was reckless. Just please, speak with us. Cadeyrn can be there too. Please."

Cadeyrn entered the clearing then with Ludek and Arik in tow. I nodded.

A hawk landed next to my mate. He pulled a note from its underbelly and looked at me.

Silas asked to come see you.

And?

Is that okay with you?

Of course. Why wouldn't it be?

I heard you had words. Before you left.

Tell him to come, I snapped, and he looked stung. I took off at a sprint again and flung myself higher into the tree, landing on one foot. Arik swore.

"I brought your leathers and wine. See you at the house," Saski called. Though it must have looked like a circus act, I couldn't come down. Not from the tree, nor my own manic behavior. What I realized was that I felt like I was on a constant battle high. I couldn't release enough. Personally speaking, that was never a good thing.

Silas. I am going to assume you can hear me because otherwise I'm the once-dead girl who talks to herself. That's weird even for me. I told Cadeyrn I wanted you to come. So, get up here. Please.

Ludek began by explaining they wanted to talk about our families. Konstantín manipulated us into coming and beguiled me into willingly sacrificing myself for his lands. I was past the point of being able to forgive that. What they brought up additionally was the subject of their mother. She birthed two sets of twins. I had wondered about that.

I did as well. I've never heard of that in this realm.

She married Ludek and Pavla's father when she was young. The children were born a few decades into their marriage. Konstantín met her while on a campaign around the lands. They recognized each other and mated, immediately impregnating her with Saski and Arik. The sets of twins were merely five years apart. Ludek's father killed himself from the grief of losing his mate. I sat back abruptly. Cadeyrn leaned forward and pinched his nose. There was an awful, festering silence.

"Is that possible?" I asked. Cadeyrn looked at me, eyes pleading.

"It seems so. Our parents say it was," Ludek told us. "Our mother never got over her mate dying. She loved him. Then when Pavla was killed, she became inconsolable."

I was trying to stay normal. I sat closer to Cadeyrn. He flinched, which made me want to scream, but then he picked up my hand and kissed it.

"We will deal with it."

"How?" I asked. He shrugged.

Saski's sword glinted in the light streaming from the windows.

"I've seen those birds," I said. "They were all over the palace in Bania."

"This was a gift from Analisse when she visited."

In the interest of being honest with myself, I was aware that it wasn't normal to have made the hasty exit I did when Saski explained that her sword and many others had come from Analisse. As a gift to Heilig, Analisse brought an armory's worth of Festaeran steel welded and etched with the emblems, stories, and symbolism of Veruni. Perhaps I had become like the pockets of energy in Heilig that couldn't contain anything else, so they burst. I needed to release my energy.

One moment Saski and Ludek were explaining the steel, the next I was in the forest, running at full speed. Wind ripped strands of my hair from my braid, causing them to whip into my eyes. The afternoon turned chilly, and it seemed an early autumn storm may be moving in. Yet still, I ran.

Every day in my human life I ran like this. Absolutely given over to the need to be out of my head. It seemed since waking this morning I had been unable to stop moving. Whether losing myself in Cadeyrn or flipping around like a circus monkey in the tree, I needed to move or release magic. As a child, I read the story of the princesses who snuck out night after night to dance until dawn, and literally danced themselves to death. What if I was doing the same? What if how I was brought back was all stored in a well within me, creating a finite sum of life, and I was acting like an immune response and attacking the life force? What if I were dancing myself to death?

The panic and thoughts fired in like a barrage of bullets, yet I ran. The pressure of the oncoming storm built, and I was sweating from the humidity and expenditure. I knew I was far from the coast at this point and wondered how far I had run. The soles of my boots were flapping, my heart pounding. If I stopped suddenly, it would likely cause a heart attack. So, I slowed to a jog, albeit a fast jog, then after perhaps twenty minutes, I stopped. Where. The. Hell. Was. I?

I had no watch to tell me how long since I left. It was evening. Birdsong had quieted and the lazy chatter of things snuffling about had replaced them. There was a stream nearby I could hear, and gods was I thirsty. I sat and drank my fill, thinking about what a stupid idiot I was to have left like that. But I didn't actually decide. My body just took off. I quickly opened to Cadeyrn and told him what happened. My ego kept me from telling him that I had no idea where I was, so I said I'd be fine and head back soon. Stupid, Neysa. So I sat on my ass in the middle of Saarlaiche, likely a hundred miles from home, with soleless boots. What an asshole. Too bad I didn't have my beastie. I couldn't pull that thread. I couldn't seem to remember where she was—was she still with Ewan?

Where is she? I said to anyone in my head. I was feeling hysterical and didn't know who I was asking. Ewan. Ewan would know.

Who? Ewan answered.

My beastie. Where is she? I can't remember.

Oh, little one. She didn't make it.

No. I cried. No. She . . . how?

I wasn't there. I don't know. I pressed my hands into the soft, damp earth next to the stream and tried drawing deep breaths to calm myself. There was a trick I used to do with my breathing, but I couldn't seem to remember. Electricity crackled in my hands, lighting up the stream. Fish and frogs floated to the surface. I vomited, seeing what I'd done, yet the crackling commenced. The storm came in closer, and the sky lit up. I was suddenly wet and shaking on the ground. I jumped and spun in circles, looking around. My heart was racing, and my head urged me to run again, but I wasn't sure what direction. Shit, I could end up in Festaera for all I knew. Had I run north? The only thing I did know was that I didn't come east because the coast was far away. Something was there. I was wet and cold and there was another presence. How did I access my power? Oh, Gods. I was like a child. I couldn't remember. Couldn't make myself be rational. Run. Just as I set off, there was a voice.

"*Trubaíste*, wait."

A smudge along the bank of the stream showed me where

he was. That was why I was soaked. I couldn't move. Slowly he gained his body, and I just stood there.

"What in the bloody hell realms are you doing here? Do you have any idea where you are?"

Still, I stood there.

"Are you hurt?"

I stared at Silas. *Christ, Neysa, say something to him.*

"I can't control it," I blurted.

"What?"

"Anything. I can't stop moving."

"You've stopped now. You haven't moved at all."

I yanked on my jacket, frustrated. "I've been running. I was at home. She said something about Analisse and I ran and couldn't stop."

He stood where he was, as if afraid to come closer.

"You woke yesterday?"

I nodded.

"I felt it," he said. Interesting. "Did it start then?"

"This morning. I woke up needing to move." My cheeks heated thinking about this morning, and he snorted.

"Let's get you home." He brushed past me, not stopping. I stood stock still, looking at my hands and my boots.

"For someone who says she can't stop moving, you haven't even breathed much. Come."

I pulled the length of leather string from my hair, broke it in two and used each piece to wrap around my boots, attempting to hold the soles together for a short time. Silas watched me, though he said nothing. Once done, I began walking. Run. Move. My body urged me. My heart beat faster and faster, but I kept walking, thinking maybe, just maybe, he would speak to me. Hours we walked in silence. I knew I'd run in a straight line. If we had been walking in this direction for a couple of hours, then surely, if we kept going the same way, we would be back in Aemes. Run. So, I did. The leather soles ripped off my boots. He swore and ran after me.

"Neysa, stop."

I couldn't. Especially not now. With everything that had happened and my needing to see him, I couldn't contain what was inside me. Magic built within me, an inflammation of strength and plyometrics as though I were filled with helium, and I jumped to a branch, then ran along it and flipped to another tree. Logically, I knew this was ridiculous. Physically, I needed to keep moving. Tree after stupid tree. Finally, I dropped to a crouch and geared to run again when there were arms around me.

"Stop," he growled, face in my hair. I growled back, trying to move. "You can't keep this up. It will kill you."

"I know." The arms dropped, but I had been pushing so hard to get away that I fell face-first into a root, splitting my lip.

"Shite," he swore.

I waved him off, pressing my hand to my mouth, smearing blood across my face. Silas shuddered and turned away.

"Keep moving, then. Go. Just don't run." He was still looking to the side.

"I'm going to stop and rest. You can go. I'm fine on my own. Goodbye, Silas."

"You're good at that, eh?"

"What is that supposed to mean?" Rain started then, sheets of it, slipping into my collar and waistband, filling my mouth with water and blood. At least it covered my tears. No need for him to see those.

"It means you're a selfish *colleíene, doinne áech mas, á miss, á trubaíste, áech nooooo. Tus á bás á misse, aech misse cumachnd aimserre.*" He was rambling, shucking weapons down and tearing off his jacket.

"I have no idea what the hell you just said." I walked off

and threw up, shaking and cold. The adrenaline was ebbing away. Who knew when it would spike again.

Don't say you're okay. I can feel it's a lie. Where are you? my husband implored me.

I ran. A long way. I'm in the forest. I accidentally killed a bunch of frogs and fish in a stream. I started sobbing. *Silas found me.*

Of course, he did. Bitterness filled his tone.

Don't you start. I don't need both of you being assholes to me.

I suppose I shall see you when you get here, as I'm sure you will tell me to not come to you. I started throwing up again. Great. Now I was totally empty. *It's the adrenaline. I can see if I can help with the energy thing when you get back. Be careful, caráed.*

I had nothing to say. Like a switch being flipped, my former energy bottomed out. Emotionally and physically, I was just so tired.

"What did Cadeyrn have to say?" Silas asked with a snarky tone. I wiped my mouth and glared at him.

"You obviously don't give a shit, so don't worry about it." My eyes closed wanting to cry, but not having the energy.

"Yeah, clearly I don't give a shit." He turned his back to me.

I fell asleep against the trunk of an overturned tree and didn't wake until the early birdsong of the forest canopy came alive.

Silas handed me his water skein and told me to finish it. We didn't speak; we only walked. I lagged behind, shooting daggers at his back with my eyes. It was midmorning when we passed a stream, and I stopped to drink and wash my face and sweaty body.

"Silas, you don't have to see me back. I am fine on my own. You clearly do not want to be around me. Go back to whatever or whoever you had been doing in Bistaír." Maybe that was the wrong footnote to add. His eyes were like wild-fire. His lips pulled back in a feral snarl. I stepped back, darkness rising in me.

"Would you like that? If I said I had someone to go back to? Would that make your life easier? You wouldn't have to ask me to stay with you. 'Please stay,'" he mimicked my voice.

"I begged you to stay because I saw a vision of you lying dead!"

"Did you see one of you dead? Did you know and not tell us? You fucked off out of that palace and went on a suicide mission."

"I did what had to be done."

He snorted and made a motion with his hand that had mist covering the area.

"You always say that. Whether it gets you killed or my sister shot. Doesn't matter to you. You don't care what it does to us. You just go. You're a fucking disaster!"

"Don't you think I know that?" I yelled. "Don't you think I hate myself for it? I said that on that beach in Laorinaghe. I ruin everyone. Then on top of it, I came back wrong. I am an abomination." I walked away. I couldn't keep doing this. I should be dead. They should have let me die.

"Maybe you are."

"Thank you, friend. It's good to see you too."

"We've never been friends, Neysa."

The darkness rising wrapped around me like a noose, pulling at my throat.

I had to get away. I wished for my beastie. Her missing piece doubled me over with pain. I screamed at the wind for her. Screamed for my parents. For the mess with my mate and Silas. Screamed for Reynard and all he endured. Darkness wound around me in sparking clouds.

"Fucking hell." Why did he follow me? "When did that start?"

"It started last night. You aren't helping, you asshole. Just go."

"I can't."

"You can. You turn your nice, intact boots around and walk away. I don't hold you to anything. As you say, we aren't friends. Leave."

And let me mourn, I said to myself. *Let me let her go.*

"I'm sorry she died. She saved you. Her spark within you allowed us to bring you back."

Oh. I couldn't breathe. One more life to add to the list of those I'd ruined. I laid on the ground and pushed my fingers into the dirt, curling my legs into my stomach.

"You're probably blaming yourself for that too. I guess you'd be right."

Instantly, I was standing and pushing him. He flew back several meters.

"I don't need this. Not from you."

"Why, because I coddle you and save your ass every time you do something stupid?"

"Because I have nothing left in me! So why keep kicking me down? I'm down. I'm there." I shoved him again.

"You're a right pain in the ass."

"What are you trying to do? Say everything, every word you have been afraid to say to me? I know I'm a pain in the ass. Go on then. Send that hate mail my way."

"If I wanted to say everything, we'd be here for years. I hate you." He leaned in close to my face. My stomach flipped over. It was fair. I knew it was fair. Still.

"I hate what you've done to me," Silas said. "I spent the past month gathering the largest compilation of intelligence for your brother. I whored myself for it." I was going to be sick again. The water I'd drunk was sloshing in my guts. "I didn't care."

"Why?" I asked quietly.

"Because you left. You left us and you died." He pressed his lips together and widened his eyes, shaking his head. "And nothing else mattered. I hate you."

I nodded absently like a bobblehead doll.

"I'm sorry. I wanted to say that to you. Doesn't matter, I'm sure. But I'm sorry." I walked the rest of the way home on my own. I knew he was close. But I was alone. *I hate you.* I hated me too. I walked all day and night and arrived back sometime after dawn the next day and went straight to Rhia's cottage.

RHIA HAD PORRIDGE ON, which she loaded with honey and Araíran-aoír nuts. She thrust tea, ladened with cream, into my hand.

"I think I came back wrong," I admitted to her. Cadeyrn knew I was there. She sent word as soon as she saw me on her doorstep. The dogs were with me, snoring on the ground.

"Why ever do you think that?" She fussed about, feeling my head and glands, lifting my shirt to check on healed wounds. I explained about the need to move. The need to release. The loss of my *baethaache*. Silas. Cadeyrn.

"Ah. You are the heir to the Goddess Heícate. You make your own magic. You can transform that need to move to anything. But, like the Goddess, you have two mates."

"I cannot," I cried, sobbing into my hands.

"Do you not love them?"

"I do. I will destroy them. Silas hates me already, and I won't hurt Cadeyrn that way."

"Ah, you see it differently. In magic there is balance. Strength and weakness, dark and light. To be imbued with such gifts—magic, darkness—one needs support. Even a goddess cannot shoulder it all, and one mate would carry a great burden. Yours carries his own birthright and will need" —Oh please don't say he has another mate. I would die right here— "you to be grounded."

Phew. She explained that the Goddess had her mates not only for her own needs, but to be a part of the realm. The strength of all three together carried the instrument for all magic. She had children by only one.

"Is it mere coincidence that you coupled with He of the Forest on Mabyn, the autumnal equinox? Did you not exchange gifts of the heart and admit to yourself your love for the Battle King on Yule, the Winter Solstice? Did you not officially solidify the *Cuiraíbh Enaíde* over the celebration of Imbolc? I see much, my lady. You did not come back wrong. You are blessed and perhaps a bit cursed." She winked at me. "It is a burden to carry. For all of you. However, you came back to them. To us all. Live." She made her markings on my forehead again and fussed at me to eat my porridge.

CHAPTER 29

NEYSA

There were things I could do. I knew that. Rather than dancing through my slippers, I could make myself useful. I checked on the grinder for the Araíran-aoír nuts. The tinkerer was excited to show me the beta unit. I sat at the stool in his warm shop and pumped the foot pedal, cranking the handle and grinding them into a thick nut butter. It wasn't completely smooth—crunchy Araíran-aoír nut butter—but it would have to do for now. It was a positive in a mind-numbingly dark time within the confines of my head. If I could contribute something to this realm, why not contribute a substitute for peanut butter cookies?

Warmth spread through my stomach when I thought of Cadeyrn. His shy smile that lit up a room and the way his head tilted a smidgen when I spoke to him, like every facet of him wanted to focus on me. When we were alone, the world could fade to black, and I might not notice. I wanted only him. I was happy to have only him. I loved Silas, and I knew I always had, but to have them both forced into this seemed torturous. Silas, who held us all together. Every godsdamned time I fell. Silas who never let me doubt Cadeyrn's love for me.

My foot came off the pedal as a surge of adrenaline raced through me, demanding I release energy. I thanked the tinkerer and paid him for the unit. Back at the house I sequestered myself in the kitchen and made batch after batch of Araíran-aoír nut butter cookies. I ran. I practiced on my bow. I avoided the males I needed so desperately.

"Have I done something wrong?" Cadeyrn asked, standing at the edge of the grove where I was walking toward the sea. My heart broke.

"No. Not at all." I walked to him and finally let myself hold him.

"I saw Rhia," he said softly. I tightened my arms on him. "I suppose I knew. We will figure it out." He kissed my nose.

"I can't see how. If you had another mate, we wouldn't be figuring it out. It would be a death match. Even if she were my cousin. *Especially* if she were my cousin."

He chuckled. "I'm quite sure it would be. If we need to take time apart I can—"

"No. I don't want time away from you."

"Then we deal."

"It was a catastrophe. Silas finding me. I've never heard him speak that way. To anyone."

"He is not himself at the moment." No. He was not.

I RODE to Laichmonde to see Reynard, who still rented Silas's flat. When I walked in, he was sitting at a low table sorting piles of correspondence and notes written in my brother's hand. I sat and handed him papers, working in silence for a time. I hadn't been there before. It was sleek and simple with clean lined furniture in shades of grey and beige with ebony stained wood floors. Every breath I took sent me spinning, as it filled me with Silas's woodsmoke and cedar scent. A mate I didn't realize I had. Another victim in my massacre.

"Breathe, Kitten. Passing out won't help anything." Reynard explained the different candidates for the positions and who their rivals and supporters were.

"Why can't you hold a position?" I asked.

He giggled maniacally. "No one would want me."

"I would. I will give you my vote right now."

He gave me a sheepish smile, stacking piles of paper.

"You would be in a great minority, darling." His head popped up as the door clicked. "Shite. I forgot."

"Weasel. I have the latest from Festaera to add to that bloody great—oh." Silas came through the doors to the living area, and his face went from surprise to disgust in a millisecond. "Shall I come back?"

"I can go," I said softly, beginning to stand.

"Speaking of Festaera," Reynard said. "Neysa was about to tell me her concerns over some gifted Festaeran steel."

"No one is buying it since word got out that it was spelled, so it's likely an ill concern," Silas countered before hearing me out.

"Analisse gifted the royal family and its guard an entire shipment of Festaeran steel when she was last there. Ten years ago. I recognized the birds on Saski's blade."

"Ah. That could be a problem." The least hostile thing he'd said to me. I pulled out a rough sketch of Saski's blade and smoothed it on the table. The two males looked at it. "I don't need to see it. It is either spelled steel or it isn't. You wasted your time sketching this." Silas's vitriol crawled under my skin like heated barbs.

"There is no reason to speak to her that way," Reynard said in my defense, standing as I was. I touched his arm in thanks.

"Perhaps it was a waste of time, but it gave me a way to focus my thoughts. Things are scrambled most days since I came back," I admitted, not liking that I felt I needed to justify any of my actions. "It let me think more clearly. Plus, when I touched the drawing, I had a vision."

Silas plunked himself on a sofa, stretching his long legs and crossing them at the ankles. He was lying back in a guise of relaxation, but I knew him, and the stiff set of his shoulders told me he was anything but relaxed. He made an obnoxious 'get on with it' motion with his hand. I rolled my eyes, then turned to Reynard and told him.

Pavla, Ludek's sister, had her Festaeran steel blade, and it did nothing against the phantomes and the insurgents, allowing her to be killed. The wards around the palace in Heilig were useless due to the presence of the spelled steel. The metal itself was cursed with a kind of reverse *draichnhud aemdifnaid*. A reverse magical shield. A dismantler. They both swore. We would have to put out the word to have all allies remove the questionable weaponry from their cache.

"Perhaps," I began, "be on your guard during the meetings ahead. All it would take is one spelled blade."

Silas scoffed and said something along the lines of what a brilliant idea and he wished he had thought of that.

"Did you then? Think of it? You can hate me all you want, but I am a part of putting this place back together. We are working together. All of us. The least you can do is show me some respect. I won't take your shit anymore than I would take anyone else's. You want to pick a fight again? We can do it elsewhere. Not when the issues here are this serious."

That shut him up. I was beginning to dislike the male lately, and that scared the shit out of me. He had always been my closest friend. My staunchest ally. I said Cadeyrn and I could go to the Festaeran mines and see if there was a way we could find the catalyst for the spell. Reynard made a face like I was crazy.

"That is a spectacularly stupid idea. With respect, *Princess*," Silas said to me with a sneer. "It's a death trap. Though that seems to be your method of operations."

I was off the ground and out the door in a blink. Slamming the damned door so hard it rattled the building, I tromped down the steps onto the street. His flat was the opposite side of town from Cadeyrn's, so I made my way across the vast park, seething as I went. It was quite chilly for early autumn, and I wrapped my black riding jacket tighter around me. I had to stop at Cadeyrn's to retrieve a book he told me was there. I hurried so I could be in and out before I ran into Lina, who lived on that side of town. That was all I needed today: dealing with her. I liked the apothecarist, but she really disliked me. And really liked Silas. Though I wondered if she would still with the new brand of asshole he wore like a bad cologne.

Letting myself in, I wiped my boots and was about to go up the stairs when movement had me pulling my dagger.

"Did you know I was staying here?" Silas asked, casually leaning against the door frame into the sitting room. How did he get here before me? "There's a quicker way than through the park."

I backed up. I didn't need the book that bad. "I just came for a book Cadeyrn had on aulde spells and warfare. It's not important." And I couldn't stand another verbal assault.

"Just find the damned book."

"No, thank you." I turned, trying not to sprint, but he was there blocking my way.

"What book is it?"

Breathe, Neysa. I started to duck under his arm.

"I'll go find it for you." His tone was softer. I told him the title and waited in the sitting room. He brought it back and handed it to me. My hands were shaking when I took it; our fingers met. There was a jolt of the electricity we both carried, and I started.

"Apologies, *Trubaiste*," he said, and it felt like a segue to a letdown.

I nodded and started to turn, but he grabbed my hand.

"You've been horrible," I said quietly. "I've never been spoken to that way by anyone." Well, I had a professor in my junior year at university who really didn't think highly of me. He was a patronizing, chauvinistic bastard. "Hate me, but have the decency to at least be respectful."

"I do hate you."

"Yes, you have made that abundantly clear. And I'm sorry for eliciting such vehemence. I should go." My chest started to cave. Then I thought of something. "What did you say to me the other night when you rambled on in the aulde language?"

"A load of rubbish and that you're the death of me and I have no power to stop it."

I walked to the door and put my head against it. I kind of felt put out because everyone was pissed at me, saying that I'd be the death of them for going off and dying. Yet no one was addressing the fact that I quite literally died for them. The gratitude was astounding.

I miss you. I could hear the rain outside. It would be a miserable ride home. *I miss my friend.* I reached for the door handle, and his hand closed over mine, interlacing our fingers. I felt him step toward me, and I leaned back into him, breathing him in. I wanted to tell him everything Rhia had told me. But it wasn't fair to do it yet when I had not sorted out how I would deal with it all. So, I turned and let myself lay against his solid chest. He stroked my hair and my cheek, feeling the wetness there.

"Och, *Trubaiste*. Don't cry for me. Cry for the poor dead frogs you electrocuted."

He laughed, and I whacked his arm, but he pulled my face in and kissed me. A slow, tentative exploration of my lips. I held my hand over his as it rested on my face and had my other wrapped around his shoulders. Something manic and jittering settled in me as we stood, suspending time in our kiss.

"Is that what you wanted?" he said with a cruel tilt to his mouth. Confusion must have shown on my face. "A little bit more, maybe? That 'release' you spoke of. Want to use me?"

He pulled me closer. I started to squirm. I felt his heartbeat, his desire. Yet his tone was icy. I squeezed my eyes shut, trying to shake off what he was saying.

"Something you want to say to me, Your Highness?" He released me. I was fully shivering as though my body were in shock. I dropped the book.

"I have nothing left to say, Silas."

I didn't know Laichmonde very well, and it was dark and raining, so finding where I stabled my horse was an effort. Near Reynard's were the mews houses where the animals were kept, yet I couldn't find them, and I ended up back at Reynard's soaking wet and hysterical. He led me back to the mews and helped me saddle up the lovely beast to get me home.

"I'll see you in a few days for the first meeting. Chin up, Kitten. Remember who you are. Go home and let your husband take his time with you. I know that would work for me." He winked and watched as I mounted the horse and set off for home.

My husband was waiting up in bed, reading a book. The lights in the house were all out, bar the low lamp he had near the bed. It seemed almost too low to read, but I guess I hadn't read in bed since allowing my fae abilities to manifest. Every inch of me was soggy and wrinkled from the rain. I stripped down and pulled on pajamas from a drawer, then crawled under the covers. Wrapping my body around Cadeyrn, I buried my face into his chest and cried. He set the book aside and pulled me tighter against him. All I wanted was Cadeyrn. I didn't want to want Silas. I didn't want to need him. I loved and adored him, of course. There used to be an easiness with Silas I never had with anyone. More playful and effortless than even Cadeyrn and me. But to be mated to him? To need both of them seemed cruel and cheap. I didn't ask to be linked to the Goddess.

"I know I've said this before, but we don't always want the lot we are given," Cadeyrn stated.

"How are you so calm about this?"

"I'm not. I'm angry. I'm jealous and trying so hard to control myself. But I know it's not your choice. I know it's not his choice—well, not entirely. I suppose I realized that acting upon my contempt would do nothing but make it worse." At least one of us was rational. "I'm sick of dealing with every-one's endless self-important bullshit when all I can think about is you. Us. Me, burying myself inside you."

I tightened my legs around him.

"Well, get on with it then," I said, still sniffling but feeling heat rise between us. I met his heat with a silken darkness that swept over us, removing clothing and thoughts of anything other than the two of us together.

"New trick?" he asked, lying atop me.

"Learning new things every day."

CHAPTER 30

NEYSA

Generally speaking, everyone was impressed at Reynard's quick execution of getting meetings set up for all the potential candidates. Cadeyrn's flat in Laichmonde was the center of activity. Since Lorelei's death, there were many who were confused about the closing of the Sacred City, and many who questioned the legitimacy of our involvement in her death. Her personal guard and most of the City's defense unit saw what had happened. It was a sad circumstance.

There were a handful of candidates who came forward, Yva being one. She walked in, serious faced, wearing a freshly pressed captain's livery. When our eyes met, hers twinkled and she bowed, golden brown hair shining from its neatly twisted bun. I grasped elbows with her and the three others who came forward. We had met with those from Dunstanaich first. Soren wished to keep his position, opposed only by a male whose platform was solely based on his being as old as dirt. The session went fairly quick, Reynard making notes and trying not to smirk. I saw as they walked out that he was drawing a small flip book of sheep chasing the old fellow. I burst out laughing. Cadeyrn and Silas snapped attention to us. Quickly smothering the laughs with the back of my hand, I cleared my throat. That was when Yva and her contenders entered. Before they had a chance to sit down, the door opened again, and I was immediately there, throwing my arms around Corra.

"Well, halloo, you," she greeted me. I pulled her out onto the porch and hugged her again. She shooed me off, and I looked at her enormous belly. "I'm quite sure you've heard it all from all the males in your life, so I will spare you my verbal lashing. But I don't want a message again like the one you sent. Are we clear?"

I squeaked in response.

"Good, because the poor hawk was limping from the weight of it."

I sobbed a laugh. "I kept my promise, though," I said, wiping my nose. She straightened my necklace and wound one of my dark waves around her finger.

"My brother? Has he been himself?" she asked in a whisper. My silence must have answered enough. "Have you told him yet?"

She always knew. I shook my head, and she tsked. I bristled.

"Perhaps when there is a break between his verbal abuse. In the meantime, he can kiss my ass." Of course, as soon as I said that, Silas came out to fetch us. I groaned, and Corra laughed, patting her brother's cheek. He shot me a look I couldn't decipher as we walked in.

Two of the Laorinaghan candidates seemed to be on the same page for their vision for the prosperity of the province and seemed interested in what Yva had to say.

"I believe," Yva began, "that we should be more transparent in our leadership, whether I am a representative for my home province or not. It is an age in which we should be able to be open and accept the criticism and suggestions of the folk. Should I not be chosen to help lead, I would like to be considered for a position to advise or even negotiate between the leadership and the folk." One of the other three was more of the arcane frame of mind and rolled his eyes at her so-called idealism. The other two listened intently. One spoke up. He was Arturus, the main intelligencer for Lorelei.

"I have found in the years I held position with her ladyship that with whom we work is more the guarantor of success. Lady Lorelei had always been transparent, as Yva—Captain Sonnos calls it, and worked with us closely to maintain the peace and prosperity within the province. It was uncharacteristic of her to close us off when she shut the city down. However, because of the system in place, her rule was solid. We had little recourse. Perhaps we could govern jointly in Laorinaghe, thereby keeping the power dispersed. Would that be an option to consider?" he asked.

"From what I have seen in both ours and the human realm," Silas began, "when a system of government has multiple heads of state, or at the very least more stringent limitations of power on a single head, the system runs better. I think, Arturus, it is a fine idea."

"I agree with Silas," I added. He looked at me sidelong, and I felt the weight of his eyes. "There may be more bumps in terms of decision-making, but to have a system where there are more than one of you focused on creating a fairer and more prosperous province, historically, should be better."

He tipped his head to me in thanks.

"Would you be willing to share the job with those present?" Cadeyrn asked. "And would you, candidates, be in favor of such a system?"

Yva, Arturus, and Farus, three out of four of the candidates for Laorinaghe, responded positively. The fourth candidate shook his head and gave a definite no. Within our council, we wrote a decree to instill the three in agreement as representatives for Laorinaghe.

"Yva," Silas said, inclining his head. "Congratulations. May you enjoy your leadership." She bowed to him and smirked, turning to me.

"Are you free this evening, Neysa? I've brought a bottle of Laorinaghan wine and fresh dates. Perhaps we can partake without you losing your trousers and stabbing Lord Silas."

I laughed and muttered that I may stab Silas anyway.

"How did I miss out on that fun?" Reynard asked, introducing himself to Yva. Cadeyrn came up behind me and slipped his arm through mine. In my peripheral I noticed the amused half-smile playing at his lips. I reached up and ran my fingertips over his night dark hair.

"I can tell you, Lady, you were the topic of tavern chatter for months after," Yva said with a hint of amusement. Reynard looked affronted. I giggled and told him I would tell the tale later.

"Make sure you don't leave out the part about you losing your shit and your weapons like a child," Silas added.

The room fell silent. Cords of muscles in Cadeyrn's arm went taught as he tensed. Ewan began walking over, looking like death incarnate, but Corra put a hand on him. Instead, she faced her brother and punched him square in the jaw. He saw it coming and took it, rubbing the spot where a huge bruise bloomed. Fae healing had the blood rushing to the surface quickly. I knew by morning it would be gone. Cadeyrn's nostrils flared, and he told him to go find another healer.

Yva was staying in the city, and though we had planned to go back to Aemes for the night, I told Cadeyrn I'd stay with Reynard so I could spend time with Yva and Corra.

If I kiss you goodbye here, do I have to be chaste? Cadeyrn asked me, his long fingers twisting under the hem of my jacket.

If I pushed you against a building and marked your neck with my teeth, would you object? I answered. He swallowed and turned pink. Ha. Score one for me. He put his hands into my unbound hair and gave me that unchaste kiss, so I returned the favor and pushed him against the building, but stopped short of the marking.

We parted ways, and I headed off to enjoy Laorinaghan wine. On a large terrace overlooking a private back garden, Yva laid out the dates and cheese to stuff inside. Reynard howled at the tale of us drinking on the beach and said the realm needed more leaders like us.

"Help me, Yva. I believe Reynard would be a fine candidate for Maesarra."

Corra looked surprised but agreed.

"Thank you, Kitten, but truthfully, I would rather not go up against my father. I would be happier serving in a different capacity."

Fair enough.

"Would you be our intelligencer? In an official capacity?" Corra asked him.

He looked down, and I knew he was shocked. I put a hand on his back.

"It would be my honor, Lady," he said.

I filled our glasses (apart from Corra, though she insisted that fae metabolized alcohol differently so it was not forbidden whilst pregnant) and toasted to his new position. We turned our heads to the sound of boots coming up the stairs in the house. Corra smiled at my brother when he came through the double doors to the terrace, Silas behind him. It was late and time that everyone made their way out. Yva pulled another bottle from her satchel and left it for me with a wink.

"Until next time," she said to me. She walked out with Ewan and Corra. Silas was speaking to Reynard, relaying some information Ewan gave him regarding the Festaeran steel. Normally I would not hesitate to include myself in the conversation, but I was so out of sorts with Silas's attitude, I hung back awkwardly and poured myself another glass of wine, topping off Reynard's.

"Wine, Silas?" I asked. He paused, mid-sentence, and took the offered glass. It was my own as there wasn't an extra goblet. He sipped at it and kept speaking. I sat back in the cushioned chair and propped my feet on a massive planter that held a tree of some sort. Not caring much in the present company, I toed off my flat slippers, stretching out my feet. It was quite chilly, but with drinking the rich red wine, and my cashmere wrap around my shoulders, I was comfortable. This city felt at once urban and country. Not for the first time did I think it reminded me of Corra—and a bit of Cadeyrn. Silas must have noted that he drank from my glass, because he handed it back to me after refilling it and went back to his discussion with my friend.

I pondered to myself the issue of the enchanted steel. Wouldn't someone need to be extraordinarily powerful to spell all the steel in a province? Wouldn't that technically be averse to the laws of nature, even here? Shields, whether inherent to an individual like Silas or Basz, or a manufactured one, like the tonic Lina made us, had to have a degree of maintenance. The tonic ran its course. The inherent shield dropped when the magic wielder was burned out. Magic and power were not depthless. They needed rest and replenishment like physical strength did. How would weaponry that had been distributed be able to maintain its spell? I sat up slowly and opened my mind to the thoughts. The inspections Paschale had inflicted on his people. On Reynard. Silas turned his head to me in stunned acknowledgement. His rugged features went slack at my projected realization.

"Care to let me in on what you just figured out, Kitten?"

"Why have you switched from calling me Mousey to Kitten?" I asked, a bit drunk.

"You're no one's prey, gorgeous, and I've seen those claws when you're ready to use them. So, tell me what I'm missing."

I patted the seat next to me.

"Can you tell me anything about the so-called inspections Paschale ran?"

He paled, and I could feel rage and distress seeping through Silas's pores. The memory of his telling me about what he'd endured with Analisse came back to me, and I realized I'd left my mind open to him. He took the glass from my hand and downed it.

"They wanted to see how much of my power they could extract, and whether it could be replaced with something else. Using me like a vessel."

Oh Gods. I grabbed his hand.

"I was there for a month—months—I don't know. After the initial three days of pure torture, they realized I could erect a wall within me that kept the vessel from being filled. Once it seemed impossible, they tried to wipe my memory of the time I spent there. They couldn't kill me like so many others, you see, because, weel, at the end of the day, my parents knew I was up there. While they don't love me, it would look bad if they let me die. Especially right before their daughter was married."

Oh my God.

Silas, oh my God.

Reynard chewed at his lip, staring at the tiles.

"So we know that for over 150 years they have been doing this. Who knows how many 'vessels' they have managed to fill." Just saying that out loud made me sick to my stomach.

I kissed Reynard's icy hands. How could his parents be so callous? Why favor one child over another and be so caustic to him even now?

"You're exceptional, Reynard. I am proud to call you my friend."

He smiled at me, and I was struck again by how dapper he was.

"I think it's time for me to be off to bed." Exhaustion pulled at his every word, as though admitting what had happened cost him. He leaned down, kissed my cheek, and walked off.

"Does anyone else know or suspect, Reynard?" Silas asked, voice rough. Reynard turned to us from the doorway.

"Cyrranus does. I'm sure many others do, though no one wanted to come forward." He ducked through the doors and into the house.

Silas sat hard on the chair that Reynard had vacated. I filled the glass we shared and handed it to him.

"Tomorrow should be fun," I said with absolutely no humor. He blew out a breath and took a sip, then passed it to me. I didn't need to be drinking any more tonight, but I wouldn't sleep with all of this on my mind. "I kept thinking that maybe there was someone with more power than most of us who was controlling the spell. It requires too much power. Even Paschale didn't have that. But really, all it took was someone clever enough to forge a plan to contain that kind of power. Over time. I wonder when it really started." I took a sip and passed the wine back. Paschale had torn my arm open and seen just how much power I could contain. I shivered.

"I would have found you," Silas said, after being quiet for so long. "If Reynard hadn't managed to get you out. I would have found you."

I shrugged.

So, we would have to convene in the morning and let

everyone know what we figured out before meeting with the Festaerans and Maesarrans. It was going to be an awful day.

"This is good wine," he said, looking at the half-empty bottle. "Is this what you two were drinking on that beach?"

I was trying not to gape at the attempt at friendly conversation. Tried not to suspect he was leading me to another round of humiliation.

"I really have no idea what we drank. It was in a jug, so perhaps not the best quality?"

He chuckled and gave me a half smile.

"Well, perhaps the ill quality attracted the shark," he joked. I rolled my eyes and flicked a piece of cork at him. He caught it and flicked it back. "I shouldn't have said what I said."

If we were going to go there, then I wouldn't be lying down for it.

"Which time?"

He still had a nasty bruise on his jaw from Corra's fist. He was lucky it wasn't Ewan, as I didn't think my brother would have pulled the punch as Corra did. His eyes slid to mine, narrowed in their glassy depths.

"I divulged a confidence we had between us, and it was unsavory of me."

"Unsavory is when something reflects poorly on your own character. Are you apologizing because it made you look like a dick, or because you realize you were one, and that every fucking thing you have said to me since we have seen each other again has been brutal?" He just sat there. "You could have just said, 'Hey Neysa. Look, I hate you and it would be fantastic if I never had to see your stupid face again,' then left it at that. Not this peeling away of everything I know and feel about myself. Then kissing me? Is that part of this apology?"

"Yes."

I sat back hard enough that it almost knocked the wind out of me.

"Everything. I apologize for everything."

"But you meant it all," I whispered. "It's all true."

"It's not," he barked. "Fuck it all to never."

I was so cold my teeth were chattering. I gave a half smile that was anything but happy and nodded.

"Do you know?" I guessed it was time to ask. My shoulders were rocking from cold and apprehension.

"What?" He sat forward, arms braced on his knees. I tucked my feet under my legs and took a deep breath. "Do I know what, *Trubaiste*?"

I nearly threw up from the nerves. Something in his face I recognized but couldn't read.

"You're . . ." I choked on the word. "We're . . ." Ugh. Dammit, Neysa.

"Mates?" he asked. I covered my face with my hands and asked him how long he had known. "I could have sworn it forever, but you're mated to my cousin. It just kept getting stronger." He scrubbed his face. "How I feel."

"How you hate me?"

"Yes, that too," he laughed. I didn't. "The night you left. When you died. Still, it didn't make sense. You don't want me, though. Not really. You want your life with Cadeyrn. I knew that. I know that. You married him. You love him."

"I love you too," I said tacitly. "I hate myself more than you ever could because I love you both. Rhia said . . ."

"I went to see her yesterday. It's some woo woo goddess shite. Yeah, I know. Apparently, you and I enacted something on Mabyn last year."

He waggled his eyebrows, and I laughed.

"It's been a year," I breathed. "Tonight is Mabyn. So much has happened in a year."

"Och, yeah. Something about time changing everything,

yet nothing, and shattered remains, or some such depressing words in the songs you sing."

"Something like that," I answered with a smile. In my head I heard the song Rhia had sung me.

> *If I loved you more than life itself*
> *If I brought you brightness to your day*
> *Would you tell me you would light the skies*
> *Would you tell me I could stay?*
> *If I stayed with you and made you mine*
> *If I could braid my soul inside of thine*
> *Could we stay forever thus entwined?*
> *Could we never see the end of time?*

He looked a bit pale.

Is that better? I asked, half kidding.

He cleared his throat and said, roughly, "I don't know." He held his hands out, and I took them, feeling the rough callouses and the warmth. "Come here, *Trubaíste*, and let me say hello properly."

Pulling my feet from under me, I scooted myself off the chair, and he gathered me up in an embrace. I pushed my face into his neck and breathed him in, calming. It seemed like ages that we sat there. His hands made circles on my back and pulled through my hair. I threaded my own through his hair and held his face against mine. His body shuddered against me, and I pressed closer, kissing under his ear. Hands stilled, then moved to pull my arms down, holding me just in front of him.

"So, you're a goddess now?" he asked. Wow, that sounded so dumb.

"Heir. Heir to the Goddess. How, I don't know. But like the Goddess, I need you both, it seems."

"Because you're sooooo special and powerful?" I punched

his shoulder lightly. "What is it you need from me, *Trubaiste*?" He put his mouth on the base of my throat and moved up toward my chin. "A friend?" His mouth moved to the corner of mine as he spoke. "A bodyguard?" He pulled my hips further onto him as his mouth travelled along my cheekbone.

I had drawn equal parts darkness and light down, casting the atmosphere around the terrace in odd shadow play. His mouth moved to my ear and touched with his tongue the same spot where I had kissed him. Shaking, I drew my fingers along the muscles of his arms, feeling the strength in them. The command of them that moved his sword and bow, that had held me, and had hidden me. While I stroked languorous fingers along his arms and sides, he slid his under my waistband in the back and pushed me even further against him. I made a small sound and felt him smile against my ear.

"What do you need? From me."

I don't know. Because I didn't understand why any Goddess would put us in this position. I just didn't know, and it made me want to cry.

His mouth teased at my neck, teeth scraping down along the soft part of my neck where I was hit with an arrow. His tongue circled the scar and moved over my shoulder, down my arm where a sword had slashed, and the explosion broke it. He kissed the faint scars there. I stared into his sea glass green eyes and felt my world sliding into place.

My hand touched his shoulder blade, which struck me with a vision of him being run through with a sword. I gasped. I hadn't known how close he'd come on that battlefield. We both made it back. I loved him. Yet, even mated to both, I couldn't bring myself to take the next step and do that to Cadeyrn. To us. I didn't want it. Silas had loved me like no one else, and yet I couldn't give all of myself to him. I took his face in my hands, kissed him, and said to him in my mind that I will love him forever, but I could not make love to him. He kissed me back, desperately. For ages. I drew him inside, to the room I was staying in, and had him lie with me. I entangled myself with him and faced him, stroking his arms and back, feeling him against me. He drew hands over my skin and never pressed for more than I was giving.

After a time, we slept. I woke and found his eyes on me, and I lost myself for a moment in the clear depths, wondering how I could be so blessed and cursed at the same time. Wondering how I could not give him my all. Wondering how I could stomach breaking his heart as I kept doing. Breaking both their hearts.

"I promised to always see who you are," he said, voice scratchy from sleep. "So, I know. I know what troubles you. I won't ruin you and him."

You deserve more.

"I've had centuries of mindless sex, *Trubaíste*. I would rather wake like this once in a while than destroy what you have. Mates or no."

I traced the tattoo on his arm and kissed it. "I'd like to get one as well."

He swallowed and kissed the same spot on my arm.

"I could even add a little tree and woodland animals that embody the whole He of the Forest thing," I snickered. He pushed on top of me, his hair tumbling over his eyes.

"Terribly cruel to me. Maybe I'll add a *paitherre moinchaí* to represent you. Forked tongue and all." Hmph. "Are you ready to see everyone?"

I took a deep breath and said I was. I needed a few moments to talk to my husband before we all met.

CHAPTER 31

CADEYRN

efore Corraidhín became a connoisseur of documentaries on television in the human realm, she made me watch some science fiction show with her. In the episode I suffered through, the characters stumbled into a wormhole in the space-time continuum, and it triggered a time loop. They constantly revisited the same events in the same day, time and again. By the end of the show, I was pacing and wanting to throw axes at things. Somehow the events we had all endured in the past year felt like that. A loop of death and separation, misunderstandings, and chaos.

So, my mate had her own birthright to contend with. One that included having another mate. How was I supposed to feel about that? The thought of someone else touching her in that way lended a homicidal rage to my demeanor. Neysa told me she did not take the final step. That she wouldn't, because she loved us. Our life. She chose us. Sometimes, though, choices were made for us. It would only be a matter of time. I knew Silas, and he wouldn't push her, though he must have known since they coupled last year. Neysa, by the gods, was so stubborn. She bit back at the laws of nature. And I was totally bloody smitten by her.

Festaeran steel being spelled by using gods knew how many helpless fae bodies as power vessels was brilliant in its vileness. I looked forward to dismantling it and freeing those poor souls once we got through the meetings today. It felt prudent to bring the Heilig contingent along as they had been victimized as well. When I explained Neysa's theory to Ludek, he became silent, and I could scent a rising rage in him that I would put money on being a rare occurrence indeed. His gift saw and understood what laid beneath the surface of an individual. I could kick myself for not thinking to have him sit in on the meetings from the beginning. I supposed my mind had been elsewhere.

Neysa sat on the steps to my flat when we arrived. The others went in ahead of us, and she asked me to walk with her. We stood near the mews, fumbling around for something to say. She asked if I'd eaten breakfast because I got cranky when I didn't. That was it. I had us in the hay, getting thoroughly rumpled, and she made good on her promise from yesterday and tore her teeth down my neck. It was ghastly, and if there hadn't been centuries of innocent fae being tortured in Festaera, I would have called off the meeting and given the horses more of a show. Especially since it would have pissed off Etienne.

As we entered the flat, hoping to have more time to discuss amongst our family the course of action for today, I pulled stray bits of grass and hay from Neysa's hair and clothing. She turned and smiled in thanks, picking some off my jacket. Etienne had arrived early. As had—and truly, I could throttle myself for not thinking of this—Bestía's brother and mother. They shouldn't have all been here at the same time, so alarm bells began ringing in my head. Silas nodded to me. He grabbed Arik and Saski, then they fanned out, checking wards and defenses. We greeted them tersely, saying we needed a moment. It wasn't surprising to hear coughing and snide remarks as Neysa and I ducked into the kitchen to clean up my neck. She looked at me and burst out laughing while she wiped the blood from my neck. I rolled my eyes at her and wiped a bit of blood from the corner of her mouth, catching her lips in mine.

"When did you two find the time for that?" Silas slammed into the kitchen. "Stinking up the place and looking like something from the other realm. We do have serious matters here to deal with." His tone was light and joking as always, but I felt the pain underneath. And I hated it.

The wards were intact, and Silas had Magnus pull his men from around the city to stand guard. I wasn't going take any chances this time. While they were all there at once, I pulled files on each of them, sliding them across the table between us all, and took a moment to allow everyone to settle. Etienne initially paled at seeing the intelligence we had on him and his supporters but reorganized his features and had the nerve to look into my eyes and sneer while casting a glance at Neysa.

"So, the bastard son-in-law acquires a mate who has another mate. That must make you feel insufficient." Before any of us could react, Reynard had his knife at his father's throat, pulling him to his feet.

"Unless you would like us to give you to the Festaerans to see if they have more luck with you than they had with me, I would suggest keeping your misinformed assumptions to yourself."

Etienne had the gall to smirk. I reached out with my powers and used particle distribution, then reversed my healing gift to release his urine from his body, making it seem as though he pissed himself.

Did you do that? Neysa asked, surprised.

I am not proud of it. She squeezed my knee under the table.

Okay, perhaps a bit proud. I knew I had let just enough out to show through his trousers, but my cousins must have thought it great fun, as the poor old bastard kept wetting himself. *I believe your other mate is having a go at him as well.* She smothered a laugh and put her hand on Silas.

Three candidates were here from Maesarra, including Etienne and, after encouragement from Corraidhín, Cyrranus. He would have a tough run against the others as they had money to influence people. All we could hope to do was release the dirt we had gleaned. Deep down, I knew Silas must have been debasing himself to gather the intelligence amassed, but I hadn't paid much attention. We weren't speaking after Neysa's death. Neither of us could bear the conversation. Neither of us could come to terms with losing her, and, ultimately, sharing her.

Cyrranus spoke of leading and protecting a province of people who were kind and hardworking. He was a good male. The other candidate, Arneau, piqued my suspicions. He countered each and every thing Etienne said, from personal militia to class-based rule to slavery. I pulled a file and held it up, pointing to particulars written, and asked Neysa, mind to mind, to confirm with Silas through their connection whether this was the last male he had investigated. She paused and looked at Silas, who turned his head to hers. Sometimes I forgot he could not answer. It only happened between Neysa and myself after the *Cuiraíbh Enaíde* clicked into place. So, she had his lips next to her ear, and she touched the file and his hand at the same time. Clever girl. Saski groaned from the charged air.

"Don't pout, cousin," Neysa said to her. Then to me she sent images of Silas bedding a female against a wall and finding ledgers and files sitting, waiting for him. Then he jumped from a window and ran. Holy bloody Mother Aoifsing.

"While I'm glad to hear you disagreeing with Etienne on

these matters which we in the bulk of Aoifsing abhor, I have a few questions."

"Of course, my lord," Arneau answered mildly.

"We have taken the liberty of running checks and intelligence on all candidates. After all, the goal here is for an Aoifsing that prospers. In this file, we have sworn statements from former servants, fellow merchants, bank managers, and blacksmiths, all saying you regularly involve yourself in each activity and institution you opposed within Etienne's platform."

"With respect, Cadeyrn," he said nervously. "Surely the word of a former servant—likely one whom I fired for theft—"

"She was fired after you beat her," Silas interjected.

"Lies. Regardless, it is not an indication of collusion. Whatever a blacksmith has to say seems amusing at best."

"One," Neysa began. I smiled slightly, knowing it was about to get lively. "It is an indication of your character which clearly is lacking in integrity, if not a basic sense of right and wrong."

"Says the female with two mates," Etienne spat.

"Excuse me, my love," I interrupted. "Speak to my mate like that again and you will be shitting your pants as well as wetting them. Continue, *Caráed*."

She kissed my cheek.

"Two," she kept ticking off her fingers, "the amusing thing about blacksmiths and swordsmiths is that they make weapons. So, when a small-time merchant such as yourself orders the production of a thousand swords with your household insignia on them, plus two ballistae to sit on your sad little roof, it raises suspicion."

"This is a set up. You have no proof of any of this." Arneau's voice rose.

I plunked the ledger down in front of him and flicked through to the past three months.

"As we can see, all of these expenses are listed in this household ledger."

"You broke into my home?" he asked, incredulous.

"Your wife invited me for tea," Silas said.

Saski choked and cleared her throat. Arneau turned red, and anger had him cracking the arms of his chair.

"While we can safely say your bid for candidacy is rejected, I'd like to point out what the situation seems like to me," I said. "Etienne was aware of our reluctance to have him lead a province, given his previous involvement in supporting the massacre of our soldiers. Plus, I truly do not care for him. As such, he reached out to you, knowing you share a similar desire for corruption and domination. If you were to make a plea to lead Maesarra from a platform in opposition to Etienne's, we would support your candidacy. Once established, you would be a puppet for Etienne. Have I missed anything?"

"So, who will lead Maesarra?" Etienne seethed.

"Cyrranus," I announced. Surprise, shock, and disgust limned the features of the three males sitting across from us. Two of them stood abruptly, sending chairs flying.

"Etienne," I said, dangerously quiet. "You're a sneaky bastard. Don't give us any more reasons to fertilize the fields with your ashes. For what you allowed to happen to your son, I could have you imprisoned or killed. Tread carefully."

He spat and left the room with Arneau.

We all collapsed back, steeling ourselves for the Festaerans who were waiting in the next room. Neysa left the room, a trail of darkness like a dust cloud behind her. I turned to the others and saw Silas looking down, fiddling with his hands. I pinched my nose and elbowed him, mouthing for him to go after her. He slowly rose from the seat and made his way out of the room.

"Don't, Corraidhín," I said to her, feeling her keen eyes on me. "Not now. Please."

"I was just going to say you should count your blessings that she wasn't mated to all three of us. I wouldn't share nearly as well as either of you."

I thumped my head on the table as the rest of the room gave in to laughter they were trying to hide.

"I can share," Saski said, ruffling my hair. "If you ever need to get away." She winked at me. Ludek growled.

CHAPTER 32

NEYSA

I made my way toward the back stairs to sit in the quiet of the bedroom and think for a few moments before the shit hit the fan with the next lot. Wine in such generous amounts still left my head sore in the morning. I heard Reynard's voice. He followed the Maesarrans out, and as I came closer, I saw Cyrranus stroking his face and speaking intimately close. In the same instant I saw them, they knew I was there, and I felt like an intruder. I made a show of covering my eyes with my hands as I turned to go up the stairs. Well, I didn't see that one coming. Cyrranus said a hasty goodbye to my friend, and the back door shut. Closing the bedroom door behind me, I plunked down on the bed.

It was the vision of Silas and that lonely woman that sent me over. Gods, my head was pounding. I know he told me he whored himself. It was just seeing the amount of intelligence he gathered from those trysts seemed staggering. Bootsteps came down the hall. A quick knock preceded Silas slipping into the room. I patted the bed beside me, lying back, my hand over my head. He laid next to me and rested his hand on mine.

"How many?" I asked him.

He shrugged.

"Why?"

"I was being useful."

I pressed my hands into my eyes, no doubt smearing my makeup. After Analisse, I thought he wouldn't put himself into that position. I went to the adjacent bathing chamber and used a flannel to put cool water on my head.

"You took a stranger to bed last night?" he asked, a smile in his voice. Standing by me and taking the cloth from my hands, he wiped my brow as I had done for him.

"You're not a stranger. You're mine." I put my arms around him and held tight. "No matter what. Even if you hate me. Even when the next realm claims us."

"Weeeell, you disposed of the gateway to that realm, so fuck knows what's going to happen now."

I looked up at him, trying not to think of how the male felt his worth was best placed in whoring himself. He hadn't shaved, the shadowy scruff on his face lending him a darker quality which suited him. Within that brooding handsome face were the eyes that looked just like Cadeyrn's. They stared down at me with a world of intensity. It was time to get back down there. I was sure there would be snide remarks and inferences, and if I were to let those get to me, the flat would be abuzz with electricity.

JUST THE SIGHT of Bestía's kin sitting there, facing Cadeyrn, had my powers rising. It was as though my whole body filled with a roadmap of options to vanquish the two fae before me. Every ounce of focus in my being zeroed in on them. I shook off the hand Silas had at my back as I walked to the two. There was nothing at all to say to them, so I stared them down like an angry dog.

Hey, I'm here, Cadeyrn said. *She's gone. Come sit, Caráed.*

I shook my head. He was right. Starting out like this would do nothing for us. Sometimes I wished I could kill her over and over again. I wished I could have been the necromancer who stripped away that which kept her alive, if only to see her wither away slowly. In the back of my mind, there was a whisper telling me I could have been. I had that power. That darkness. Cadeyrn was looking at me, and in his eyes, I knew he understood.

I may not be colorful and furry, but I guarantee you I am monster enough to remove their every last breath if you wish it. Say the word, he said to me, squeezing my hand.

Then we'd be just as bad as they all are. We would need to go live in some tall tower covered in thorns where the sun doesn't shine, and the food probably sucks.

It's always about the food with you, isn't it?

I have very basic needs. He projected a quick snapshot of our morning tussle in the hay, and exactly what needs were met when I marked his neck. Just as quick, he brought the meeting to order and there was the slightest, self-satisfied male lilt to his voice which I quite liked to hear.

None of us beat about the bush. We were aware of the depth and magnitude of what had been happening in Festaera for many years. Alongside Bestía's brother, Olek, and her mother, Kíra, there were three there from the province. A set of twins, Tuso and Petyr, and a male whose skin was at once dark and light, as though perhaps a deep brown that had been drained of color. Like Reynard. He introduced himself as Sergo.

Slight pressure on my aching head gave me pause. Ludek lifted a single finger, as if to signal it was his doing. I allowed the pressure again, and he spoke to me through an oraculoís connection.

Though it may be obvious even to the rest of you, the ill intent of a few of those fae is staggering. I see Sergo's need for rectification and healing. He hoped that in coming here your mate would be able to heal him, but he has been kept by Tuso for decades. He is younger than most. Perhaps as young as you and Ewan. There is uncompromised hatred for you and Cadeyrn tainting Olek and Kíra. They weren't always this way, but they seek revenge.

So, just a normal day then. Gods, my head was killing me. Ludek's hand went on Basz's arm, and instantly a shield went up around them and Saski, Silas's covering the rest of us. Spears of power pricked toward us, taunting, but not penetrating the shield.

"I've invited you into my home and given you a chance to speak on behalf of your candidacy, and this is how you want to present yourself?" Cadeyrn asked, his tone tepid.

As they were for the last meeting, files and ledgers were spread across the table. The thought of Silas in Festaera doing what he had in Maesarra terrified me. I should have asked to look through the files before today. I was so wrapped up in my own stupid issues that it didn't really occur to me to do so. *Stupid, Neysa.*

"Festaera spent little to no coin in the past fifty years. How is that possible? Yours is a large province," Cadeyrn said.

"I would say to ask its Elder, but he and his mate, alas, are gone," Olek answered.

"Yes, but its treasurer sits before us. Tuso, explain the findings. Also, I was under the impression that Somoían would be here. Admittedly, he is not my favorite, but his absence is noted. He was head of trade."

I touched the ledger, hoping that it would explain something, but there was nothing. It was spelled.

"We are a self-sufficient province, Cadeyrn. You may have influenced my sister's loyalties and mind, but we are not so easily led." Olek spoke with unmasked hatred. Heat flared, and I didn't know which of us was going to lose it first. Cadeyrn stared him down.

"Your sister was a witch," Corra said. "Not only that, but she allied herself with dark-powered individuals who sought to destroy my cousin and his mate."

"From what I hear, she merely was brought back from the other realm and happened upon a lonely male in his time of need."

Something changed in Cadeyrn's face. Where his hand rested next to my arm, I felt a tremor go through him as though vast amounts of power were being expended. Olek flinched, but nothing else seemed amiss.

"Yes, well, if by time of need, you mean when we needed an army to fight phantomes and invading forces, then you would be correct," Cadeyrn said, as though nothing had just happened. Ludek was looking at us.

"The initial matter at hand today," Ewan began, sensing a downward turn this early in the assemblage, "is who will represent Festaera. It is the opinion of my position that both Olek and Kíra have a conflict of interest. Thus, I shall speak plainly in saying that I do not condone either of you as representatives."

Olek slammed his fist on the table, and ice erupted along the top. The room warmed uncomfortably, and Cadeyrn twitched his lips in a half smile.

Ewan told Tuso and Petyr he would hear their platforms. Petyr began to speak, but his sister turned to me.

"I wonder," she said, cool and collected, a cruel uptilt to her mouth, "how did your mate retrieve all this information? This ledger from my office? Have you asked?"

Though I had no idea, I merely smiled, internally wishing

we had delayed the meeting to gather our wits regarding the vessels. She let Petyr speak, though I felt her eyes on me while I flipped through the nearly empty ledger and some of the files.

"You will excuse me while I review this," I said, eyes on the book. "I wasn't available of late to do so."

"A getaway with your other mate?"

Okay, the two mates barbs were getting really old.

"I was dead," I said sweetly, reading through the information. "Look here. Under the sales heading for Festaeran steel, it lists sales and distribution to swordsmiths throughout the realm. Under some of the entries, there is a small marking." I turned to show the twins. Cadeyrn and Silas peered over my shoulders. "The first one is dated perhaps 200 years ago, with a footnote. Now, I am not yet fully versed in the aulde language, but *draíchnhud llong* means, what, my love? Magical ship? Boat?"

"Vessel," Sergo said. He flinched, his eyes sliding to the twins.

"Do refrain from threatening or hurting any of my guests," Cadeyrn said to Tuso. She inclined her head.

"Under these entries there is no coin recorded. Care to explain, treasurer?" Silas asked. I passed the ledger and files down to Ewan. "Majesty," Silas said to my brother. "We have seen similar markings and entries from other provinces in the reverse, have we not?"

Indications of slave trade. Ewan confirmed what Silas was asking and explained that many of the provinces seemed to have been trading their citizens for Festaeran steel. At first glance, it appeared to be standard, abhorrent slavery. It needed immediate eradication. However, what it showed us here now was that these slaves were being used as vessels to contain the spells cast upon the steel being purchased. Every item made of Festaeran steel was a risk to its bearer.

"So, what, exactly, are you accusing us of?" Petyr asked.

"Slavery, for one. Trafficking of fae. Molestation. Conspiracy both of murder in the general public sector and conspiracy to the Crown," my brother listed.

I looked to Ludek, who nodded in agreement.

This sounds really bloody familiar, I said to both Cadeyrn and Silas.

"I'm holding you both in contempt." Ewan then addressed my mate. "Cadeyrn, is there anything we need to hear from them at the moment?" Cadeyrn made a dismissive gesture and told him they were all his. "And Kíra and Olek?"

"I would say they are free to go. Sergo, would you mind staying on? We have yet to hear your bid."

"You have no idea what you are disrupting," Tuso spat. She flicked her fingers, and Sergo grabbed his head. At once, Tuso began choking and gagging. Corra sat, rubbing her belly and grinning like a cat. Guards entered and dragged the twins out. Kíra looked us dead in the eyes.

"We shall meet again."

Oh, for the love of all that's holy. What a load of overused rubbish.

"Quite sure," Cadeyrn said, looping his arm around me.

CHAPTER 33

NEYSA

Had the circumstances been different, it would have been a party. All of my family and friends in one place again with wine and food. Except that the aftermath of the meeting left us drained, Cadeyrn especially. He spoke with Sergo privately regarding what the male had endured, and he began the slow process of healing that he had provided Reynard. Sergo had almost no desire for the position he was now heading into. His initial reason for putting himself in that position, heedless of what Tuso would try to do, was to tell us what was going on up there. Sergo was escorted to an inn, guards stationed outside his door.

Someone passed me a glass of wine, which I refused, stuffing my face with bread and crackers. I quite literally could not see straight. There were blinking lights and a dull throb behind my left eye.

"What's wrong with you?" Corra asked when my males were otherwise occupied.

"My head is killing me."

She narrowed her eyes, making her seem like a dragon in waiting.

"I miss you, Corra."

She handed me another piece of bread. "I do too, darling."

Reynard brought over a cold glass of water and handed it to me with a wink. I gave him a knowing smile.

"Don't start, Kitten."

"Oh no. You are so in for it later."

He laughed at my threat. "Touché. Perhaps over a bottle of wine."

Oh, Gods. I might throw up from the mention of it.

"Yes. Just, not anytime soon. Excuse me." I ran full speed for the bathing chamber and emptied my stomach. Great. Now I'd need more bread. Shutting the door, I sat on the floor with my face pressed to the cool wall. I knew there were two males waiting outside the door.

"Her head is troubling her from the wine," Silas said quietly.

"Why didn't she say anything?" Cadeyrn asked.

Because you're drained. I can see it.

Neysa.

How did you get the ledgers?

The sound of Silas growling and walking off filled the pregnant pause. Warmth came through the door, and I backed away, allowing Cadeyrn in. He squatted down, hiking his trousers up to get down to my level. The chamber was by no means small, but he seemed to take up so much of it. Warm fingers touched my face and stroked it like I was an instrument. One hand held the base of my skull where a thick throbbing ache had centered itself from the migraine; the other hand covered my left eye. After a time, the pain subsided, and I sagged against him. To my mind, he showed me how the ledgers were retrieved.

Silas had gone south. He was in and out of the twin provinces, Maesarra, and Laorinaghe. Cadeyrn was waiting for me to wake, feeling useless. He knew where to look in the palace in Laorinaghe, and though Silas was sorting through those who would be allies and who would be foe, it seemed we needed to get a hold of the ledgers. All the files from Lorelei's cabinet, so to speak. He let his rage take over, and he became his *baethaache* form and went to Laorinaghe. It was a successful mission, apart from him and Silas having a throw down in the forest outside of the Sacred City. Cadeyrn used his *baethaache* form to go straight to Festaera and do the same thing. He knew Sergo was being held by Tuso and Petyr and slipped into her office.

Shouting and snarling erupted from the other room. We looked at one another and stood. Saski was in Silas's face, her finger pointing at his chest. Arik threw his hands up when we came in and downed a shot of liquor.

"You knew something was going on up there. What were you lot doing here the past hundred years?" she yelled.

"Sorry, am I being questioned by someone who has sat on her pretty ass her whole life? You don't know what you're on about," Silas responded, attempting to remove her finger from his chest. She pushed forward and backed him against the wall.

Basz sidled up to us. I raised my eyebrow.

"You lot work in a devious manner," Saski continued. "I don't appreciate having to sit in there not knowing what we are going to be facing."

"What part of our telling you they had phantomes don't you understand? They brought an ex lover of my cousin's back from the fucking dead to take him away from Neysa. They experimented on Reynard. What more did you want to hear about? Sorry about your favorite toy, Your Highness. We've all lost something lately."

"You fucked your way through three provinces to get answers! Who does that?" she screamed. I wondered why that bothered her, and in my mind, seeing her legs wrapped around him gave me pause. Silas was wide-eyed looking at her, his back to the wall, Saski in his face.

"You were the impetus that had Neysa going off to her death. It was you. Your bastard of a father too. But if we are slinging shite at each other, lovely, I blame you. You are provocative, deceitful, and dangerous." He said it with an undertone of thunder.

She breathed heavily but pulled her finger from his chest.

"I do not trust you. Your brothers, maybe. You? No," Silas told her.

"You were more than happy to be between my legs," she said. The room went white. I lost it.

"Saski," Arik warned. "That's enough."

The door slammed, and I knew Silas had left, though there was nothing visible in the room itself. Two sets of hands were on me. Ewan and Cadeyrn. My headache was back. I leaned against the back of the sofa as I gradually brought the room back to normal.

"'People never lie so much as after a hunt, during a war, or before an election.'" I quoted Otto Von Bismark. Everyone's eyes were on me, though mine were closed, trying not to move much. "Saski, you are full of shit. You lied to get my mates in bed. You all lied to get us to Heilig. Though perhaps not transparent, we never deceived you about anything here. What we do know is that we need to shut down the operation going on up there."

I groaned and grabbed my head. Ewan put his hand on my face and sat beside me. Cadeyrn was using his gift, fishing around, trying to figure out why the headache came back. The niggling memory of Bestía and Analisse removing my magic and my link to Cadeyrn had a seed of panic forming in my gut. Forcing myself to open my eyes, I stared between the two males with me.

"It's her gifts," Ludek said, his voice like the wind through an open window. "She needs to master them. She needs to release vitality and embrace the darkness in her. She fights it."

Because I don't want to be a monster, I said to Ludek.

"Darkness is not contemptible. It is necessary for balance. If you do not balance yourself, Neysa—"

"How do I do it?" I felt like throwing up again. *Cadeyrn.* He blew lightly in my face, and the nausea eased.

"I can only see so much," Ludek explained to me. His tone was gentle. "Perhaps it will become more obvious to me in the coming days."

I needed this migraine gone. One minute I was on the sofa, the next I was in a bed. I curled into a ball, pulling at my hair.

"May I make a suggestion?" Cadeyrn asked in a whisper, allowing a cool mist to cover me. I grumbled something that he was going to anyway. He ran a hand along my hip and the outside of my thigh. "Perhaps you must . . . finish the mating with Silas." I pulled the pillow over my head. "If you are coming into so much power that you need two mates, then it's not like you can give half effort." Like a snail up a hill, I turned to him.

"Half effort?" I glared through one eye as the other was closed in excruciating pain. "Is that what you think?"

"You are acting like I am your only mate, when unfortunately—for me that is—it just isn't true. If you aren't fulfilling the mating requirement, perhaps your balance is off."

"Ugh. Typical male. It's always all about sex."

He laughed.

"I love Silas. As you know. I'm sorry I'm telling you this." I bit my lip. "He and I. It's always been easy between us."

"Yeah," Cadeyrn breathed. His eyes were on the duvet. "And you and I seem to always stagger around a bit, don't we?"

"What I mean is that it would be so easy to let go and have him. I mean, it's expected." I moved my hand, and the low lamp that was lit dropped to darkness. That was a new one.

"But I chose you. Not between the two of you. I chose us. I love you more than anything in any realm. Because I don't care how much we stumble or bite each other's heads off. I want you."

"You may not be at liberty to make that choice." He pulled at a stray thread on the blanket. "Believe me, Neysa. If it could be just the two of us forever, that's all—all I've ever wanted. But we are a part of something bigger, and I won't have you burn out or die because you refuse to hurt me."

"Damn it all," I said through a sniffle. "Just a horrible monster."

"I killed Olek." Pardon? "It wasn't going to end, and I lost my grip. I released a blood clot in his brain. It may have killed him eventually anyway, but I did it. He will likely be dead before they get home. So, you see, if either of us is a monster, my love, it's me."

"Shit."

"Precisely."

I sat up, and though my head felt like there was a team of horses inside it, I crawled onto his lap and took his face in my hands.

"But you're my monster." I kissed him.

CHAPTER 34

SILAS

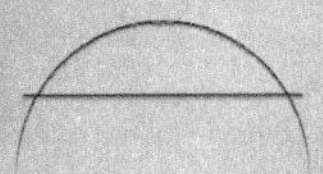

While the others were shocked and feigned disgust at what Cadeyrn had done, I wasn't. I wished I'd done the same damn thing. In fact, I may have taken out Kíra as well. However, the fact of the matter was that whether Olek died today or a week from now, we would get blamed. Funny how, in the human realm, they would have blamed it on something else. A blow to the head. An accident. Here, they would know. And they would hunt us for it. Problem was that my cousin was already on the hunt. The minute we started in on him for it, he walked out. We heard the whip of wings and the flight.

Neysa's head was still pounding, and she grabbed it while we went over our defenses and how to instill Sergo as represen tative without getting him killed. A coupe. They would say we caused a coupe. I guess we did. Arik suggested he go to Laorinaghe and speak to Yva and her group regarding their take on the matter, then meet back with Ewan and my sister in Maesarra. Saski had blood lust written on her face. She seemed to need a task. Like me. Working dogs. That was what my mother would have said.

"In 1914," *Trubaíste* spoke up, "in the human realm, an archduke was shot and killed. He was a figurehead of a corroding monarchy and was killed by an idealistic young student, who was a part of an assassination group." Neysa started talking, and everyone quieted down. She spoke to us with her head still in her hands. I was pissed off she was in pain.

"It happens all the time. Figureheads being killed. I could list hundreds in the mortal realm if you want, though I'm sure it's unnecessary." Saski snorted, and I flicked her shoulder. She air kissed me. "The problem with this one wasn't that it was the death of a monarch," Neysa said. "It was the pressure point on a world that was ready to change. The event is known as 'The Shot Heard 'Round the World' because it was what spearheaded World War One. The empire the archduke was heir to fell. The opposing empire fell. Two great empires ended, and it was the birth of the modern world through the blood and politics that followed. The countries who fought and died during that Great War had little to do with the empires that collapsed. It was merely a stone that was set in a downhill motion."

"Blood and politics always follow blood. What is your point here, Neysa?" Saski asked.

Neysa was so fucked with pain, she didn't take the bait.

"I believe," Ludek joined in, "her point falls somewhere along the lines of it not taking much to start a revolt. Cadeyrn's killing Olek could lead to revolt. So could our being here. We could be seen as usurpers. Anything could start it."

Neysa nodded her head in agreement, then stopped, squinting with the pain. I went to get her a flannel with peppermint as she had done for me on the barge. She looked up at me gratefully. I placed it on her neck.

"So, do we wait?" Arik asked.

"We move," Saski said. Fucking gods, she was just like me.

"We work immediately to put things in place to prevent any retaliation from spreading throughout Aoifsing," Ludek announced. "The uprising in Heilig ceased upon our leave, though one might assume it is in conjunction with the Veil being down. Basz and I can leave to be with Father to organize our own defenses."

"I will leave for the Sacred City in the morning," Arik added.

"Someone has to stay with you lot and shed a little blood," Saski said with a shrug.

Reynard walked in with the layout of the keep in Festaera. He had been mostly absent this evening and, coming in with a scaled sketch of the layout, I could now see why.

"I need air," Neysa said, pushing her way to the door. She wasn't dressed for the cold outside, but I wasn't about to say anything.

Messages went out to my scouts right away. I needed wraiths in and around the compound in Festaera. Eyes needed to be in every stinking shite hole up there to find where the vessels were kept. After an hour, Neysa wasn't back. It was Corraidhín who looked at me with anxious eyes and motioned to the door. I ran my hand through my hair and stood, strapping a sword across my back. A couple of years ago, I would never have walked in Laichmonde dressed for battle. So many changes in a year.

I wandered around, looking for her in the dark streets, catching her scent here and there. Bloody hell, even I was getting cold. It took me longer than it should have to realize I'd scented her in every elemental temple around the city. A right thickheaded twat I was. The last was the temple of weather on the outskirts of the city. I moved quicker, hoping to catch her, as it was a steep climb to the top, and would be very cold up there. Huddled in the corner, where we sent out ashes to find Cadeyrn early this year, was the female I was mated to. But not really. I rushed over like a stupid lad. She was blue and shaking.

"*Trubaiste*, you need to come with me. It's fucking cold up here. What were you doing?"

Her teeth were chattering.

My head feels better in the cold. She couldn't even speak out loud, her body was shaking so hard.

"Yeah, but the rest of you doesn't agree. Come on. Up you go." I took my jacket off and wrapped it around her.

My arm was around her as we walked, and she was leaning into me like she was happy to be there. I had a sinking feeling I knew what was making her head pound, but I wasn't about to make that suggestion. For a fuck tonne of reasons. However, I did hold my hand out, allowing a cyclone of wind to swirl over my palm. She reached for it like it was a gift, hovering her hand over and pulling up, even smiling slightly as she stretched the cyclone between her hand and mine. Midnight darkness showered from her hand, mingling into the mini tempest we shared. It built and we brought our hands together, but instead of it disappearing, our touch made it swirl around us, covering the two of us in a dark cloud.

"This is where a different male might say something about us making beautiful magic together or some shite," I teased her.

She pulled me to her and claimed my mouth. Bloody. Fucking. Hell. I gave it right back to her with the same enthusiasm. We were near my flat, and I was counting on Reynard still being at Cadeyrn's dealing with the children playing war. Part of me knew she was just trying to please that pressure in her head, and part of me knew she had a need of me beyond that. A year ago, I decided that I would give her whatever she wanted. Which made me an arse for so many reasons. Inside, her shivering started to go away but I could tell her head was worse. This whole thing was such a clusterfuck. I couldn't even take her to my bed, as that was what Reynard had been using, so I led us to the room we shared last night and shut the door.

When I turned around, she was looking at me with such determination, I already felt stripped bare. By the gods, I loved that face. That complete fucking destruction of a female. I didn't think I had ever told her that. She unstrapped my scabbard and laid my sword reverently on the floor. I watched every movement, thinking she would walk away.

"I love you," I said, and it came out so quiet, I wasn't sure she had heard me. I felt sick. I'd never told a female that. Her eyes met mine. Tears were streaming from them. "I know you know that."

She reached up and held my face. I leaned into it while she reached to pull my shirt off. Then I heard it. A catch in her breath. A whispered thought at the back of her mind.

I don't want this. Like a bucket of icy water was thrown on me. I wanted to be angry. I wanted to hit something. But I couldn't blame her. She wanted to be with my cousin. I was the piece of shite coming between them. Whatever was between us was a cruel wickedness. She was still touching me, and I took her hands.

"*Trubaíste*, don't." Confusion. Then she must have realized I heard her. "I understand. I do. We will find a way to sort this out without any . . ."

I made wiggly eyebrows at her. She made a play at reaching again, and I kissed her. Hard. My hands were on her face, and I wrapped a leg around hers, then told her I would always be here. But I wouldn't do this with her not wanting it. She sagged against me like a ragdoll.

The problem was her head was still a loaded canon that

needed firing. I knew how it felt. Perhaps if she and I were to combine our powers, utilizing them in a different fashion, the connection would still work the way it was supposed to. Almost like when she and Ewan formed that magnetic field. We could beat it another way.

We laid on the bed, completely wrapped in each other, much like last night. I wasn't lying when I said I was happy to be with her just like this. But I'd be a lying sack of shite if I didn't say that, more than anything in this world, I wanted her. All of her. So, when I held the little beast, it was the greatest effort of a lifetime not to seduce her. We laid there, and I tried something I had never done with anyone. I let my magic pour into her, bit by bit. She looked at me, startled.

"I can feel it trickling in." She closed her eyes and tipped her head back like there was some sort of relief. Then I felt her open up. "Can I try? To give you mine, I mean?"

I squeezed her back in answer. I didn't know why this made me as nervous as it did. I kept letting my gifts seep into her. When I concentrated, I saw it moving through her like blood in her veins, lighting her up. Pure magic. I tried not to swear when she released the flood gates on her power.

"Fucking hell." I tried and failed.

She glowed white, with night black surrounding us, energy crackling between us. It started tapping at me, looking for a way in. I let go, feeling that darkness slither in me, the light racing along the electricity within her. It mingled with my own, playing within me. I held her as she thrashed against me, distantly aware that my body was moving the same. Pressure built in the room. She cried out, then the storm started outside and she moaned, resting her head against mine, her magic still coursing from her into me. I pressed myself against her, vaguely aware that we were both here and not here. With a final burst, she released a wave of darkness into me, and by the gods, I couldn't stop myself from bellowing and shaking against her. She threw her head back, and a sound like the flight of a hundred birds came out of her. Her body dropped back onto mine, asleep. Gods above, I hoped that helped her head, because I had never experienced anything like what we just did. Ever.

CHAPTER 35

NEYSA

Arik was in Laorinaghe. The Heiligan prince and the Representative to the Province of Laorinaghe seemed to share a similar outlook on how the realm should run. Arik presented himself as the cocky prince. A laissez-faire attitude belied a determined and definite sense of how the world should be. While we hadn't recognized that determination straight away, it came to light when the situation demanded he show it to us.

Olek of Festaera died less than a week after leaving our meeting in Laichmonde. His mother blamed us, as we knew she would. Others were skeptical. A hawk was sent the following day.

"Your demise is my debt to my children," it read.

Cadeyrn grabbed at the back of his neck. He blamed himself. Well, I suppose it was his doing, even if I didn't fault him for it. He left that night and was gone for two days. I was hurt. Hurt that he never said goodbye. The pain I had in my head finally let up after Silas and I shared our magic. It was just as intimate as if we had ended it otherwise, but I felt it was less of a betrayal to my relationship with Cadeyrn. When my husband returned, something was different. He was cold and calculating.

Three days after he came back, we were readying for Prinaer to speak with the Mads family heir about running the twin provinces. Cadeyrn suggested I stay behind. I scoffed at him. He threw up his hands and tromped across the room, grabbing weaponry. We hadn't been together in bed since before everything happened. I felt the strain. He must have as well. I tried to corner him. Tried to force those eyes to look at me. Only briefly did they meet mine before looking across the room where a knock sounded at the door.

"We're leaving, Cadeyrn." Corra's voice. I wanted them to stay. I wanted to have them here. I didn't want to fall apart, because this time, I refused to let Silas pick me up. And I wasn't sure Cadeyrn was in better shape. He moved past me and opened the door. Corra's eyes shot to mine the moment the door opened.

"You okay, darling?" she asked me.

I forced a smile.

She walked to me and lifted her chin. "Don't let them get you down. You are the goddess, Neysa. You."

A jolt of pain lanced through me, and I honestly couldn't tell whether it came from Cadeyrn or me. I kissed her cheek and left the room to say goodbye to my brother. Whispers and the sound of something hitting a wall trailed behind me.

Only Cadeyrn, Reynard, and I went to see Ainsley Mads. It was three nights sleeping in a tent again. Sleeping next to him with not even a scent of desire. The last night, perhaps an hour or so before dawn, I reached over. I couldn't stand it anymore. I put my hand on his stomach. His eyes shot to mine.

Touch me, I begged. He turned, staring into my eyes, and

finally lifted a hand and stroked my hair behind my ear. I was dizzy already, needing him. I walked my fingers up his chest and touched the short hairs at the base of his neck.

Where are you lately?

"I'm right here." His voice was sleep-mussed. I pressed closer.

Prove it.

"Neysa," he growled out loud.

"No. Don't Neysa me. Prove to me you are here because I'm not buying it yet."

The quiet in the tent, in my head, in the mountains around us, was deafening. Finally, I dropped my eyes and pulled my hand away, trying not to shake. He reached between us and grabbed my hand, bringing it to his mouth to kiss. Our fingers interlaced, and his other hand began slowly proving to me he wanted to touch me.

AINSLEY WAS as formidable a female as I had ever met. She was taller than me, standing just under Cadeyrn, with jet black hair and russet skin. She had her hair in multiple braids pulled back from her face, leaving the stark countenance of her bare. As soon we walked into the hall of her family compound, she clasped elbows with each of us, her leather gauntlets rough against my skin. She had a gaggle of rather large males and females in the hall, eyes on us.

"Did you kill Olek?" she asked before introductions.

"I did," my mate answered matter-of-factly. No deceptions, no beating about the bush. He was owning up to his actions.

"Was it necessary?"

"It was a quick, hard call on an escalating situation. Necessary? Yes. He was threatening my family. His sister had caused enough damage. Once we address the situation in Festaera, we can revisit your question."

"Would you have made the same call?" She faced me, arms crossed.

"I would have," I said, standing a little taller. It was a rare day when another female made me feel short. She nodded and led us into the hall.

We all sat along benches at long tables, casually telling our tale. Ainsley explained the way in which she would organize and lead her provinces.

"It has been too long under the thumb of those two Elders and their brutal ways. We are at a time for change." She gestured around her. This place seemed least likely to change, with every fae here dressed for a raid like a Viking village. In the middle of the mountains.

"Are your ways not brutal?" I asked. Not implying. Simply asking. "Allow me to rephrase. You seem less inclined to bullshit and more inclined to plan, assess, contain, execute."

She laughed and drank from her ale.

"My wife has no inclination to bullshit either," Cadeyrn said with pride in his tone. "See it as a compliment."

I nearly kissed him. Instead, I ran a hand along his leg.

"It is a fair assessment of my nature," Ainsley admitted. "As you know, my father and brother died during the battle near here." I hadn't realized we were in such close proximity to the battlefield. "We mourn for a year and day, keeping the fires lit for them. I believe in the world you are trying to create. I believe in keeping power in check. One concern I have is the presence of royalty. I would like to keep the twin provinces sovereign from the rest of Aoifsing. And I beseech the dismantling of a monarchy."

Cadeyrn did not look phased at all, but I felt a tightening of the muscles in his leg. Reynard laughed and told her she had balls.

"That's quite a list of stipulations," my mate said. "I have no issue with your sovereignty. It really concerns me very little, so long as, as we have discussed, you keep power in check."

She pursed her lips and tilted her ahead in agreement. "Neysa, would you care to jump in?"

"From what I have seen and experienced here in Aoifsing, the monarchy is a suggestion. It's a safety net. My family was brought here to balance the magic of the lands and help keep it all running. According to the annals I have read, none of the monarchs who have been here, from my grandparents to my mother, and now, my brother, have enacted a singular rule. It had always been the Elders. Am I correct?"

"Yes," she said carefully. "However, it is the potential for that supremacy of which we are fearful."

"At the moment my brother is working in Maesarra from a position of keeping that province safe. In the bigger picture, we are all trying our damnedest to bring together those who might change the structure of how Aoifsing has been run historically. Giving the fae of this realm more of a say in the day to day of their lives. Had Ewan not stepped in after the murder of our mother, there very well could have been a massive downturn in Aoifsing."

"We shall stand behind your bid as representative," Cadeyrn said. "However, I need your word that you will not make a move against my family, nor will you disrupt the monarchy. In return, I will give you my word that apart from protecting the rights of your citizens, the monarchy will not interfere with your undertakings."

She sat back and looked at her flanking behemoths and considered. For long, uncomfortable minutes, she stared between the three of us, then agreed. We shared a meal and ale.

"Our enclave has self-sustained us for centuries," Ainsley began, the room falling to a lull. "Most would not be daft enough to disrupt our way of life." She looked to her right, where a female with scars crisscrossing her face and neck closed her eyes in what I took for concession. "Some time ago, Ursa —" she gestured to the scarred female, "—was running patrol on the border of Naenire with her two bairns. They were naught but sixteen at the time. Babes. Their unit ran across a pack of lupinus." She took a steadying breath, and I steeled myself for what I thought I knew was coming. Cadeyrn shifted next to me. "They stayed hidden. We are a forest fae, able to become one with the gullies and canopies. We have all seen lupinus train. I have been with Nanua in her selection ceremonies in times past. It is barbaric." Ursa scrubbed a hand over her face as Ainsley spoke. I looked around the hall, noticing the attention of every other large provincial present was focused on Ursa. All offered regret and sympathy.

"What Ursa and her bairns witnessed that day on the border," Ainsley continued, "was a pitting of children in a ring. Soldiers held lupinus and their lupine charges back until first blood was spilled between the children in the ring. Then they released the lupinus."

My stomach rolled and my hand shot to Cadeyrn's for comfort. For a link to whatever humanity was called in this realm.

"Who was in charge of this?" Cadeyrn asked, his voice tight.

"My lads begged me to go help the children. I knew we were outmatched and so I refused," Ursa told us. "We made camp that night and they snuck out. Always trying to right the world, they were." She swallowed. "Their heads were delivered to my tent before dawn." Ainsley grabbed her hand. "I took two of my warriors and went to the border. As you can see," she gestured to her face, "I was unsuccessful. And my lads were gone. You ask who was behind this? It was Etienne of Maesarra and a small group of fae with accents I could not distinguish. That is all I know. But I will fight."

As though her final words were a signal, the hall rose in chatter. In the late hours, Ainsley and her top behemoth brought us to a dark office. An ancient map was pulled from a bookshelf and spread atop the desk. Sconces threw amber light across the spread of hide; mountains and roads were inked. We peered closer. With a wave of her hand, markings on the map began to flow, revealing turns and corners that were hidden before. Tiny rivers moved along the map, dim light catching the caps of white water. It seemed as though they flowed . . .

"Central Prinaer to Festaera. A direct link through the mountains. The mines and caverns in the north can all be accessed from here."

Reynard whistled and clapped her on the back. She glared at him, narrowing her dark, almond-shaped eyes. Cadeyrn ran a finger along the flowing lines, making them glow with light. I reached out, not expecting much as the map was spelled, but images came to mind.

A clock, worn and perhaps broken. Seemingly endless streams of water. Caverns stacked with fae in suspended animation, drained of color. Light. A goddess, calling to me. Silas and another female, who was pregnant. Cadeyrn, walking away from me, smiling, though I was screaming. City lights. A river. A sunken meadow, damp with leaf rot, wind blowing. I had gotten better at managing the visions. As long as I didn't try to speak yet, I could act as if nothing had happened. A light hand on my back told me he knew.

"You give us permission to use these waterways to liberate the folk being held in Festaera?" Cadeyrn asked.

"And you will allow our return passage as well?" Reynard

added. "I was brought there through these. Nanua did it. I don't remember much, but I recall waterways through the mountains. I had thought it a dream as I was beaten."

Anger flared from me, darkness pooling around my feet. Ainsley looked down in interest.

"We will allow passage both directions. I will come as well." She pulled me aside. "We have a temple here. A lesser goddess who has protected us for millennia. She, like Heícate, dwells in both darkness and light. I believe she would be eager to be summoned by you. May I show you to her temple tomorrow?"

Bloody great. Another goddess to deal with. Maybe I would get a third mate, a hellhound, and an extra set of arms.

Let's not tempt that, shall we? Cadeyrn said seriously.

"Thank you," I told Ainsley. "I would like that." Bugger.

BENEATH A WOODEN PERGOLA was a set of stairs. Ainsley and my husband stood at the top, allowing me privacy. As though following a rope wrapped about my waist, I let it pull me deep into the temple. The walls were lined in gold, its reflection being the only light within. A dark pool was in the middle, clear as glass, daring a dip of fingers.

"Go on, child," came a seraphic voice, urging me to touch my hands to the surface. As the inky water lapped over my fingers and palm, I was pulled under.

Do not wish for me, for I may prove less a blessing, more a demand. Call upon me gently, praying in the night, for I am the will of the mother. Wrapping my arms about my children, allowing them to feed themselves with only what their soul truly wants. I see compassion, identity, love without bounds, love without death, love that transcends time and space. I will strip away your ego and allow you to embrace your darkness. So do not call for me should you wish to remain fixed to that which holds you back. Call for me only when you have need of holy wrath and your own beautiful destruction.

I could see her standing, many-limbed, swathed in glittering black, slicing at ties that bind others. Calling me. *Who are you?* I asked.

I am Kalíma, and I am in you, child. I am youth and age. The great dark womb of mother creation. I despise shackles and cages. I permit you to break free of any bind that sours your soul.

I tried to carefully keep my mind blank, not wishing anything. She laughed. At once I was out of the pool, coughing up water on the ground of the temple.

When I emerged from the stairs, soaked and shaken, both Ainsley and Cadeyrn gave me a look. I held up my hand, adjusted my sword belt, and walked off.

"Training ring. Now."

BIG, burly, dark Vikings. That was what this whole place seemed to be filled with. They wore horned helmets and fur boots. I was tossed a wooden training sword as soon as I stepped into the ring, sodden and utterly needing to release some energy. Thurton, Ainsley's second, paired me with a male who was relatively small compared to the rest of them. Meaning he was roughly the size of my mate, who could take me down in two moves. My blood heated as soon as I thought of being in a ring with him. As I spun my sword, I caught Cadeyrn's sparkling eyes.

You're next, Cadeyrn.

Oh, no. Not here. Maybe in private.

Promise? Silence. *Ah.*

Neysa.

I took off at a stupidly fast run and flipped over my opponent, knocking his elbow with my sword. He dropped his and swore heartily. There was cheering and clapping, ale mugs slapping together. Bunch of bloody Vikings. So, I would be the Valkyrie. With a pang, I missed my *baethaache.*

Igmar, my opponent, crouched and launched for me, reaching to grab my waist. I pitted and rolled over his back, landing in a half squat, then stood. We squared off, and he toed a line on the ground. I narrowed my eyes and scratched my own design in the dirt. He looked at it in question and laughed. It was a kissing-faced stick figure with a sword. I shrugged.

We knocked swords back and forth, but I was riled up by the goddess, from not having my mate. From needing to run so far I'd end up in Laorinaghe. Or Maesarra with Corra who would tell me to chin up and fuck them all. Bored and ready to let go, I dove between his legs and slammed both elbows backwards into the backs of his knees, bringing him down, where I sat on him.

"Yield, friend?" I asked.

"Aye." He took my offered hand before I bowed and told him good match.

In the hall, cups of ale were continuously brought to us. Apparently, it went a long way that I was willing to knock swords with one of their own. In a quiet moment, Cadeyrn whispered to me that he sent out hawks telling everyone where we needed to meet. In the meantime, he and I would stay here while Reynard went to Maesarra to stay with Corra. The ale was going to my head, and I felt full and bloated. I touched his lip with my thumb, listening to him talk, wishing we were alone. He stopped and kissed my cheek, walking off. Ah.

"Wait," I said, louder than I'd intended. The room fell silent as Cadeyrn turned around. I turned red and apologized to the hall. Cadeyrn walked back to me, and the room lit with chatter once again.

"I saw things. When I touched the map. A clock. I think perhaps the spell is linked to time. The Goddess. Kalíma, she is the destroyer of time and ego. She said many things. I saw so many things." He looked around and sat, knees against mine. I explained the look of the clock, the feel. The meadow and the lights. A look of terror washed over his face, and he muttered about finding Reynard, then left.

In our chamber, alone, I sat on the wooden floor, toying with a loose thread on the woven rug, then began to scry with a crystal pendulum. This one was made of tourmaline for protection. As I was asking my basic questions to find the direction it would move, the door flung open.

"What are you doing?" Cadeyrn barked. "Don't do that here." He grabbed the pendulum, breaking my connection.

"Dammit, Cade!"

"Oh, it's Cade, now?" His eyes flared. "There's too much at stake now. I don't want you opening any doors we cannot shut."

I snorted. "Too late for that." I stood, walking to the water ewer to drink a glass. Even though my belly felt full to bursting. I hated ale. "The clock," I started to say.

"Is a relic. It is on the mantel in Bistaír. I saw it once, long ago. Solange tried to take it as a wedding gift. It transforms when touched, showing the time left for he who holds it." I shivered. "So, if you think the spell in Festaera is linked to time, then this clock is probably a part of it. Reynard will bring it back."

I dropped the pendulum into a small velvet sack and tucked it in my satchel.

"Do you remember traveling with a suitcase and clean

clothes? Waking up in a hotel and not having to get up right away? Room service?"

"Do you miss it? The human realm?" He sat on the chair next to the window, his leather groaning as he stretched his legs. I wanted to climb on top of him. Have him hold me, do whatever I wanted to him, but I knew I couldn't. Again. The ale burned like acid, rising in my throat.

"Sometimes," I said honestly. "Some things, rather." I jumped to the side of the elevated bed and sat, staring at my hands. The constellation of freckles that matched his. "What I miss in either realm is us."

"How's your head been?" My eyes snapped to his. His mouth was pressed into a hard line like it always had been when I met him. I hadn't even known the softness of his mouth until I watched him sleep. He did not realize what happened between his cousin and me. He must have thought . . .

"I released my gifts," I told him. "We did it together. The darkness and light, everything I know how to control. I gave it to Silas and he gave me his. It was beautiful, and it worked."

"That's good."

"I thought so."

"What do you want me to say, Neysa?"

"I don't. You know what I want? What I always and singularly want? It's you. It's us."

"Us is a multi-leveled operation now. Us is a factor in a plan, a thread in a tapestry. It's not you and me." That he thought that made my body go numb.

I couldn't help the damned tears. "That isn't true. You know it's not true. It's always about you and me."

"We have to get this problem taken care of. Then maybe we can see about . . ." He started to say something I couldn't listen to. Darkness cocooned me.

Is this about Silas? Because it's a stupid point. There is you and me and a cast of supporting actors. That's. It. I'm going to bed. Feel free to come too.

He left the room.

CHAPTER 36

CADEYRN

The clock was going to alter time. It would distort our sense of what would happen, and it would ruin us. I saw in her vision the sequencing. I saw the city lights. I knew those, and they weren't in the fae realm. I knew that meadow. Maybe Neysa caught a glimpse of the past as she had done before, but something deep within me knew it was a future. A prospective future, at least. The walkway outside of our chamber had a wooden railing with stars carved into it. I traced the stars with my fingers, wishing I could go back in and run my fingers along Neysa's body. She would like that, but I was too afraid. For her. For me. Perhaps I was a cold bastard.

I tore apart fae I found doing despicable things when I went off last week. I found wretched folk and ripped them to shreds using talons, fangs, and a sword. Fae and creatures alike who were taking advantage of females. Ones who were beating their dogs. Anyone I could find and justify needing to be eliminated from existence. I killed them. I was not in the right. I knew that. I knew my soul would pay. Monster. If that was what I had become—if I couldn't be myself and separate my actions from that of the *baethaache*—who would I be?

I walked down the stairs to the main square of the grounds. Dogs were laying in huddles near a large tree. I squatted down and held my hand out to them. They walked over and let me pet them, attempting to calm myself by stroking their long ears. Bixby and Cuthbert would be a wreck when it all happened. However it happened. I was momentarily so glad they were safely home in Aemes with the groundskeeper. The night shifted, sounds approaching from behind.

"Your mate has strong gifts." Ainsley came up to me. "I have never seen Kalíma respond to anyone."

I shook my head. Fucking goddesses.

"She is strong across the board."

"This was given to me by a crone. I was barely out of childhood, so it meant nothing, yet I kept it." She held something out to me. It was a small brass arrow, razor thin. "I feel it prudent to give it to you both."

At the back of the arrow there was a hole. Turning it this way and that, it became obvious to me what it was. I went back to our room and sat on the bed, looking at the arrow, debating waking Neysa to tell her about it. About everything.

She was exhausted. I could see it in the smudges under her eyes. She had taken out her braid to sleep, and her hair fell in structured dark waves that I wanted to touch. I wanted to throw up a wall of fucking fire and keep us together in it forever to stay out of the mess that was building. But that would be a cage. And, ultimately, it would help nothing. The sheet was clutched in her hands in that way she does when she was trying not to cry. If I pried it away, there would be half-moon marks on her palms where her nails pierced the skin.

A breeze smelling of pine and oak blew through the window, and I watched the skin on her bare arm and shoulder rise in bumps. Just like that, I knew I'd lose her. I didn't know how or when, but I knew it was soon. I couldn't fathom how to process the loss. I didn't know how Silas did it—loved her and resigned himself to not having her. Her eyes fluttered open, and she looked over her shoulder at me, holding out her hand.

I placed the arrow in it, knowing that was not what she wanted. Monster. Pushing up on her elbows, the sheet barely covered her, and I was nearly blind with wanting her and holding myself back. I felt the same in that hotel in Bulgaria. Then again in Turkey. She set the arrow aside, not caring what it was, and sat up straighter, the sheet slipping completely.

Kneeling on the mattress, she pulled me to her. In her eyes I saw there was no way she would let me say no. She didn't understand what I could see. So, I let her pull me in and take my clothes off until we were both kneeling on that bed, bare to one another. My lips marked every freckle on her shoulder, every scar on her arms, her belly, every warm fold of her. Each place my mouth travelled caused her hands to knead my skin. She needed to know she was all that mattered. Even when I knew that somehow I was losing her to another realm. I lowered her down and sunk myself deep within her, hoping more than anything in this world and the next that I wasn't right.

Neysa

EVERYONE ASSEMBLED four days later. Ainsley prepared watercraft and chose two of her trusted males to come along, leaving Thurton behind to hold the fort. By the look in Ewan's eyes, I could see he was half crazed being away from Corra, and I questioned whether he should have come.

Saski was laughing as she and Silas emerged from the mountain road.

The clock was an odd shape. Silver, brass, and worn wood composed the piece itself, which looked like it would melt from one's hands. As though when Reynard passed it to Cadeyrn, it was a bag of water, awkwardly slumping. It was an illusion of course, as the materials that made up the clock were sturdy. Cadeyrn set it down and gently lifted the glass crystal from the face. He had tried to hand me the arm of the clock the other night. It was relevant, important, and might be the key to making this operation work. In that moment, I hadn't cared about anything other than my mate. He placed the arm on the pin through the tiny hole at the back of the arrow. Once the two hands were joined on the tapered pin at the center of the odd timepiece, they spun. A sickly feeling roiled around in my stomach, and by the looks of everyone else, they felt it too. Almost like a drop on a rollercoaster.

Cadeyrn had warned me that the clock altered senses. Instinct made me want to smash it to pieces right away, but knowing that hundreds, maybe thousands, of lives depended on our breaking the spell kept me from doing so.

Three smaller bezels on the clock face all stopped spinning at the same time as the main arms. I peered closely at them, trying to remember the parts on my chronograph watch. One was a countdown bezel, used for everything from racing to running. Another seemed to be a GMT, telling the time in another time zone. Before this moment I never considered there being different time zones in this realm, but it was so obvious now I could kick myself. Next to me, I must have projected that thought, because Cadeyrn sniffed a chuckle and ever so briefly touched my back. The last bezel looked to me like a telemeter.

"That's interesting," I mused. Saski stepped forward and

looked. "These aren't normally used on mantel clocks. It's more on certain chronograph watches."

"Meaning?" Saski asked. Watches. Not a thing here. I explained watches and chronographs.

"This bezel on a chronograph was originally designed to measure the distance of a sound or pressurized event for officers in wartime. It started during the First World War," I explained.

"Is that the one in which the archduke was shot?" Saski asked. I smiled at her, pleased she had actually listened to me.

"It is. Before then, pocket watches were commonly used, but the military found that wearing the watch on one's wrist gave it better protection and stability as magnetic fields changed, and the stability lent itself to water tightness."

Cadeyrn stood up, arms crossed with an amused expression.

What? I asked him.

Nothing, I just never knew you knew so much about watches.

I like military history. And anything that made money change hands during wartime was a specialty of mine. Plus, watches are lovely.

Would have made a good gift for you.

Still could, I said, scrunching my nose and giving him a half smile, but his faltered, a look of distress covering his face. He turned and asked me to keep going.

"So, what is it used for?" Silas asked. Ewan was studying the bezel, then looking around. His head tilted to the side, and he tapped the knob closest to the telemeter bezel, then waited, tapping it again.

"It measures distance of sound," Ewan said. Gods, I wished we could be around each other more. My brother figured that out without any other indication of its use. He was even more brilliant than our father.

"Correct. However, it measures both sound and light. So,

you could see a flash of lightning and set the chrono, as Ewan just did, and measure the time between the flash and the sound of the thunder that follows to calculate the distance between the two. So, Silas, we could finally figure out just how far reaching your temper tantrums can be," I teased him, and he chuckled, pinching me. "It can be used as the military used it, in measuring firing range. When gun flashes were seen, especially in the night, a soldier would measure the time between the flash and sound to determine how far the enemy fire was. Quite handy at the time."

I knew everyone was thinking as I was. How did this help us? This was not a human-made clock. It was fae-made and old, so all these bezels had functions that were of use here. So how would this chronograph fit into the dismantling of the Festaeran spell?

The passages into the caverns in Festaera were a straight shot, but we knew that once within the network of tunnels, we would be blind to which direction to take. There were hundreds of miles worth of tunnels and caverns in the Vascha Mountain Range in which the vessels could potentially be kept. Perhaps the telemeter would pick up the lights, sounds, or pressure of the magic in constant use to keep the spell going. I said as much. What about the other gauges? I tapped my foot impatiently, looking at the clock.

"The arrow I gave you, Cadeyrn," Ainsley said after a long while. "The crone said it was special because it was the Hand of the Goddess."

My husband excused himself, walked off behind a wooden structure, and threw up. I followed him, panicking about what had made him sick. Silas and Ewan were right behind me. Cadeyrn's arm was braced on the structure, his face pale. I placed a hand in the middle of his back and saw it. A blurry snapshot in the mountains. An abhorrent brace between realms.

"The countdown clock. Once we use it, which we have, it imprints itself onto our cause. It will count down the time we have left. It could be the time left to successfully complete what we must. It could be until the death of one of us. It could be . . .the end of everything." His eyes met mine and held them. I showed him the Veil in my vision. Then the blood and broken crown.

"So how do we know what it's counting down to?" Silas asked from behind me.

"We don't," Ewan answered. "It alters our sense of time and works differently for each of us. Cadeyrn?"

Cadeyrn nodded, glassy eyes still locked on mine. I moved closer to him. He knew. That was why he was so angry. He knew it was all borrowed time.

I'm sorry, Caráed.

"We can fight it. We aren't green youths who allow magic to break us," Silas insisted, pacing and kicking at the grass.

"This kind of magic buried my relationship with my mate. It took away all I knew of her and stripped her powers, Silas. We are as vulnerable as anyone."

"Then we make better choices," Saski added. No shit. "I mean it. I'm the first to act without thinking. We need to go in ready to calculate each and every move we make."

"It's already begun!" Cadeyrn yelled. His face turned bright red, and heat flared from him. "Don't you understand? It began when Neysa saw the clock in her vision. We started the continuum. As soon as we put the fucking hand on the clock, it started. At this point, we should all have a picture in our heads—a sense or feeling for what exactly we are chipping away. What we are losing," he concluded, not quite louder than the autumn breeze in the forest.

Ewan paled. The others fanned out, hands on their faces or in their hair, growling. Silas was looking between Cadeyrn and me and Saski, shaking his head, nostrils flaring.

Couldn't I refuse to go? Couldn't it be that simple? Choices. Saski had a point. These were all threads. Not scaffolding. Even in the mating bond. Sure, it would be easier to give in and take Silas and let the thread pull tight. But that would unravel what I had made with Cadeyrn, and there was nothing I would fight harder for. So, I refused to give in. I made that choice.

"What's the last bezel? The GMT?" Ewan asked.

"It's the time. In the human realm. In England," Cadeyrn told him, and their eyes locked.

"No," Silas said. "No. Just fucking no."

"We need to go," Ainsley said.

Yeah, we were running out of time. How poetic.

CHAPTER 37

NEYSA

It was early autumn in the mountains, and despite the stark threat ahead, the waterways were stunning. Clear and cold, bordered by moss-covered rock sheer, clear skies overhead. I tried to stay alert, but hours on the water had me laying back, my head against Cadeyrn's chest, drifting off. Daydreaming about the house in Aemes. The dogs. A beach house we would never have. City lights I never again wanted to see, with implications reaching further than I ever wanted to think about. My niece and nephew—or whatever they ended up being. The children I would never have. The pregnant female with Silas I would never see. Would I hate her if I knew? Would it matter?

I will make the right choice. I refuse to make the final call.

We don't always have the luxury of choice, Cadeyrn said to me, stroking my hair.

Well, I'm too stubborn to bend over and let fate make me its bitch.

Such an image, my love.

I turned around and looked at his glassy aquamarine eyes

and stark cheekbones. I would have liked to have said something poignant or clever. Romantic or anything. There was nothing. He knew it all. I knew it all. All there was left was to fight.

There was a howl. Nearby, wolves were on the prowl. I sat up.

WHERE ARE THEY? HELP US SAVE THEM, I commanded. The howling ensued, every five minutes on the clock. We followed the sound as it banked right, heading further west. Every five minutes for six hours. When more waterways and streams appeared, the howling indicated directions to guide us, until we reached the cavern entrance and the river mouth ended. We disembarked and continued on foot. Even the wolves wouldn't tread in these caverns. I glanced at the clock, the countdown like a sick vice I couldn't unsee. Time was rapidly decreasing. Flitting light like flares from an artificial torch bounced off the walls in the distance. I clicked the knob and waited. Moans followed. Kilometers. Perhaps fifty. The cavern walls would distort the movement of light, so I wasn't sure if the telemeter would be completely accurate, but we had a while of walking to go. In the dark, I saw a glow from Cadeyrn's eyes that made me shiver. He was becoming closer to his beast. I wish I knew what he had seen. I had a feeling, but he would not disclose the whole thing.

A trickle of water from a spring deep within these mountains moved along the ground with us. Silas started to dissolve, and I cried out.

"Not yet. Please."

He took my face in his hands.

"I know how to be careful. Remember, *Trubaíste*. I've sworn an oath."

Then he was mist and water. Saski bristled and snarled. I whipped my head to her, and she turned away. We sped up, making double the time we had initially. In the dark there was a clash of swords, and Ainsley was barking at her warriors. Cadeyrn moved me behind him and blocked the scythe of an advancing fae. A small contingent of colorless fae moved on us. Had they lived under the mountains their whole lives? Unlike the phantomes or beasts that Paschale had manufactured up here, these were sentient warriors, grunting, swearing, bleeding like the rest of us. They were just unexposed to sunlight.

I took a blade to the shoulder and fell against the slick rock wall, crying out. Cadeyrn swiveled to look at me and narrowly missed a scythe to the neck. I screamed and lunged at the offender, drawing my twin swords across his midsection, splitting the pale warrior in two. Moon white skin rolled into the stream, the warrior's head caught a rock and hung in an eternal grimace between the water and granite.

Reynard's arrows pierced the necks of two waxen fae who had made their way past Ainsley's warriors. Blood warmed my arms, most of it catching in my leathers, making my grip slick. We kept pushing forward. In the dark, Ainsley shrieked, and there was a thud as one of her males landed at our feet, head rolling. A loud, guttural roar sounded, and it took me a heartbeat to realize it was from my mate. He lashed out with his power, incinerating the remaining cadaverous enemy. Without pausing, we pressed forward.

Silas. Where are you? Please.

There was an electrical flash like a torchlight on water, and I hit the knob on the clock. Not far. I told them we could make it quickly. Nearly out of breath, we rounded a corner and were in the main section of what looked almost like an enormous incubator. Instead of maintaining life, it was keeping the life sustainably drained to contain the magic necessary to maintain the spell.

Not one of us could keep the disgust off our faces. We all spun in an awed circle, trying to process what we were seeing. We knew what we were coming to find. I had seen a picture in my head, but seeing it in person was sickening.

The countdown bezel was nearly up. We all looked to one another as lines of magic ran along the wall of the cavern, winding in and out of all the vessels as they hung in the air.

From the far side of the room, figures began to emerge. Cadeyrn snarled. Silas was being dragged by the neck. As they all got closer, Saski screamed with a rage that had the vessels trembling.

With an iron chain choking him, Silas was dragged towards us by Konstantín, with Kíra, Petyr, and Tuso beside them. I tugged on every tether we had between us to find a weak link so I could get him out of the damned chains. Cadeyrn became his beast, snarling and scratching at the floor, which, honestly, wasn't very helpful.

"Oh, come, daughter," Konstantín said to Saski. "It's strategy. Beat before being beaten." He addressed me. "Niece."

"Let go of my mate, you stupid prick."

There was a loud, ominous tick on the clock. We needed to break the spell and didn't have long.

"It's sovereignty. To be able to have control over the entire realm is quite a thing. Your mother never cared for such things. How about you, young king?"

Ewan was drawing up power. I felt it building in him. Cadeyrn's power speared from him to the nearest vessels, testing to see if he could heal them. As his magic touched them, the vessels turned to ash. Horror bled from Cadeyrn's emotions. I pulled on the darkness surrounding me, feeding me, and willed it all inside, trying to merge the dark magic with my darkness that was not vile. My mate sensed what I was doing and wrapped his power around mine. I tapped into

Ewan's, and the three of us began pulling the ties that bound the vessels, string by string. That was when Silas started screaming.

Sweat poured off him while Tuso had a viper-like grin on her face. Saski charged at her father, who held the chains, and attempted to drop into him, but Petyr slashed out with his broadsword. She turned in time and went for him instead, swinging her blades. Silas was hollering to keep doing what we were doing. Ainsley and Saski held out against the twins, and Tuso was finally distracted enough to drop the pain she had lancing through Silas's head. He slumped to the ground.

"Did you figure it out yet, Cadeyrn?" Kíra asked. "What it will take to break the spell?"

Bestía had said the same thing and I knew—I knew Kíra had been a part of bringing Bestía back. She smiled at him, showing all her teeth. His beast snarled. We kept pulling on the threads. Some of the vessels started moaning. Some turned to ash. Healing had the opposite effect on them. We had to unravel the darkness and merge it with our own.

Petyr had a dagger at Silas's neck. I met his eyes. He tried to tell me something, but I couldn't see beyond a flash of losing them both. I exploded with power and a bolt of lightning lanced from me, through Silas and into Petyr. He died instantly.

Tuso screeched and tried to run, but Saski separated Tuso's head from her body with one well-timed swipe. I had known that my lightning would never harm Silas. It was a part of us both.

From the shadows, Basz and Ludek emerged, a shield around them both. My heart sank, thinking they had betrayed us. Then Ludek gave me a look. *Trust me.*

Did I really have a choice?

"You could have had it all, Saski," Konstantín said to his

daughter. His first in line. He tsked, pulled the wind energy from his daughter, and sent it into Ewan, closing off his breath, keeping him entombed in a tunnel of hard, impenetrable wind. "I'm sorry, nephew. You must understand; you are in the way."

The final tick of the clock sounded, and we paused, horrified. With a last pull of darkness, the vessels awoke, slamming to the ground. Reynard shot an arrow that hit Basz, whose shield had been down in his shock at seeing the vessels, and I screamed. At that moment, Ludek was bellowing, and Konstantín and Reynard realized that I had reacted on behalf of Basz. I ran for the even-tempered guard and put my hands over his wound. Ripping my jacket off, I tore a piece of shirt to make a tourniquet. Ludek turned and stabbed his stepfather through the gut and kicked him to the ground next to where I was kneeling with Basz. Cadeyrn lunged for Ewan, who had been dropped from the wind, and Saski had thrown herself over Silas. My shoulder wound gushed blood, and I saw now how deep the gash had been. Bone shone through, wet and ivory, inches from my neck.

Child. A clear divine voice sounded in my head. *There is so much loss. For whom do you bleed?*

I was tying the fabric around Basz, getting Ludek to put pressure on it. Reynard stood, stunned, then looked at me, horrified. Whether horrified at my injuries or at his own misstep in shooting Basz, I didn't know. Light and darkness swirled.

For whom, child? The voice persisted.

For those I love. For those who were harmed. For love itself. I stepped back from Basz, looking for Cadeyrn. My blood hit the ground next to Konstantín, and there was a rip sounding in the atmosphere. The air rippled, and I heard Silas yell. Cadeyrn spun to me, his beast disappearing. Having cast herself in shadow, Kíra appeared before me, and thrust her narrow sword into me. Rather, it would have gone into me, had Cadeyrn not gotten in front of the blade, taking the length of sword through his abdomen, out his back, and pushing me away. Into the Veil.

Part Three

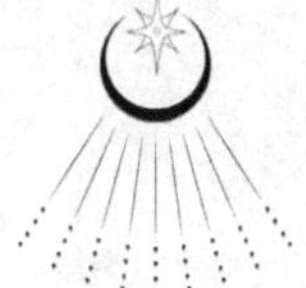

Chapter 38

Neysa

England, Nine Months Later

Six months ago, I stopped being angry. Or at least I stopped acting on it. If I were honest with myself, there had been signs. So many indications that it was primed to fail. Just because something was written in the stars didn't mean it was permanent. Everything was stardust. We saw stars all the time that had long since faded from existence. What was left was the lingering light, the hope of what was out there. Our stardust could only hold together for so long before a strong wind blew it apart, scattering us to the elements, and we became residual energy. Specters of galaxies long gone.

Residual energy was what I was now. An accumulation of all that made me who and what I was in a volatile package, ready to explode if the pressure wasn't released bit by bit. For six months, I let it build. Let the troposphere of my emotions build within me while I raged and thrashed and destroyed who I was. Then one day I walked away from it. I was still angry, but I finally felt a budding of myself. From that shoot of self came a little more power. Letting go of my rage as my power, I embraced that bud and tried to nurture it. I was not my anger, my darkness. I was a survivor. A warrior. Even if the battle was in me. Even if I had no real hope of walking off that battlefield.

The streets of London allowed me to be a face in the crowd. I wasn't an heir to a throne or a goddess, or someone who once had a great love and two mates, but just a pretty face who didn't look out of place in a city that held the past and future in the palm of its hand.

Once I started trading again, I was able to leave. I could afford to travel here and there, spending time amongst the people and histories of places I'd always dreamt about. Then I would come home to my flat in Richmond. It felt the most like Laichmonde, with the river and the parks. I made acquaintances and never spoke about my past. They knew I grew up toeing the line between the U.K. and California and knew as far as when I moved from Los Angeles. I couldn't say I was a part of anything bigger. That I'd had more than I ever could have wished for, and watched it leave. Watched him leave. Finally leave me. Because we were all stardust, and as careful as we were with each other, there was a final touch that dispersed what held us together. And so there I was in the mortal realm, an immortal with no real desire to see the years approaching.

He hadn't known when he pushed me through that Veil. We had been conflicted for weeks, trying to figure out how to live without one another, I think. He wouldn't have known there was another thread to pull. That there was a choice in that moment. Had he pulled the other thread, we might have held together. I saw it as I crossed. The possibility. And then it was gone. The visions. The connection. The power. All my power. Like my beastie, it was all gone. Even the Veil. Only memories remained like the light of long dead stars. Perhaps one day they would fade too. Perhaps, like stardust, I too would fade.

When I slept at night, those rare times when I didn't lie awake all night, I dreamt of Aoifsing. Sometimes I thought they were visions. Faces I knew and loved. Memories and visions of cities and events. There was blood too. Broken bodies and bird's eye views of things that had happened to me during our many battles. Memories would surface of being with him. Loving him. Of a bond so real and consuming it shook the skies when we let it. Then I would wake, unable to breathe, sweating, barely able to make it out of my flat to run. Run from the ache and the loss and run until I physically couldn't go any further. I was wrong here. Out of place like ghosts in daylight. I went out and drank and worked and trained, but I was wrong. A shell of what and who I was meant to be. And I wished it would kill me quicker than it was. Because as much as I tried, I couldn't fucking live like this.

JULY 15TH, on the train from Richmond to Oxford, I read the biography of the doctor presenting at the Ashmolean Museum. He had studied and worked in India, camped in the Himalayas, and embedded with tribes in remote Pakistan. The doctor taught anthropology at Durham University in England and was visiting Oxford to give a talk on lesser deities of India and the Middle East. I was bored, so when the notification popped up for the talk, I booked the train.

I loved Oxford as a city, and I hadn't fully admitted that to myself, but I came up half-heartedly looking in terms of moving. I had run out of excuses for not meeting with friends and colleagues in London and Richmond and needed to put some distance between myself and the cities. I hadn't been back to Barlowe Combe in the past year. Why bother? Why open that box when I could barely manage to compartmentalize that part of my life? It was pissing down rain when I arrived, and I tried to keep my laptop dry as I ran into the museum.

Dr. Dean Preston took to the podium with a nervous clearing of his throat. Did anyone ever check the height of microphones in relation to the speaker before the poor sods went up? I laughed to myself, thinking it was something Corra might say.

"The goddess Kali-Ma," he began. I jackknifed forward at the goddess's name. "She is feared and revered. Known as a cruel and fierce deity, culling those who are troublesome or unworthy of her children. We are all her children once we give up our dreaded egos. So, good luck." He paused, and a tremor of polite, academic laughter went through the crowd.

I marveled at the coincidence of this presentation being on the one goddess with whom I had most recently interacted.

"Like her Egyptian sister in crime, Sekhmet, the goddess of both war and healing, she instills balance to our world. Where would we be should we give up our ego? Would time itself allow us to hold what precious time we have? Kali was once said to hold the thread to all motherhood. In every culture, a personification of the mother, the womb, the fertile darkness, has come to have been penned. Who better to hold the reigns of time than the mother herself?

"What I would like to discuss with you today is the possibility that the holder of time, Kali-Ma, can play with time as we know it. If she were to hold the seed of time in her hand, could she hold infinite possibilities? Would each possibility sprout from the seed to form trunks, branches, and roots? To answer this, we must first delve into whether time is linear. We have always been led to believe that we are born, we live, we die in a linear fashion. Many fellow scholars agree that time is not linear, but in fact layered. If we strip the layers apart, the possibilities of different occurrences and existences is astounding."

People began to shuffle out. This wasn't the talk they were expecting. While it wasn't what I was planning to listen to, a rock-hard feeling in my gut had me glued to my seat. I stayed until his final word. In the end there was just me and two others sitting there, listening to Dr. Preston, who would likely never be invited back to Oxford. I thanked him for his talk, and he shyly inclined his head to me.

"May I ask you a question?" I spoke in a quiet rush, keeping my eye on the time so I would make my train back. It was tempting to book a room at the MacDonald Randolph Hotel across the street, but the last time I stayed there, I had a dream of Cadeyrn so vivid, I awoke breathless and needing him to the point of physical pain.

"Of course. I think we have cleared the room." He shuffled his papers, dropping them into a Tumi messenger bag. He was younger than I expected, with floppy blond hair and a twinkle in his eye that led me to think he couldn't care less that he had emptied the room at the Ashmolean.

"In theory, if Kali were to hold the potential for layered time and threads, would there be a chance . . ." Oh shit, Neysa, watch your phrasing.

He raised an eyebrow at me. "To earn back unrequited love?" His interruption was as patronizing as they came.

I gave him my best sardonic smile while handing my business card over.

"Never mind. Thanks for the talk."

"Wait. I apologize. I'm often not taken seriously in my research, and sometimes I get people who are off their rocker. You are a currency trader?"

"Yes, but my question had nothing to do with that. My father was an anthropologist, and I have been putting together some of his research."

"Ah. Interesting. May I buy you a drink? We can talk then."

I agreed, cursing myself for missing the train. We sat in the bar of a brasserie a couple of blocks away.

"If the spool of time, layers, knots, whatever, were held, would it be possible to revisit an option from a particular thread?"

"I am not a quantum physicist," he remarked with a smirk.

"I am not speaking of time travel." I took a notebook from my handbag and began scribbling, pushing my Pinot Nero out of knocking range. "Not reaching back in time, but rather plucking an option from a sheet of time. If these are the layers of time—" I began with a mess that looked like a ball of yarn, knocked about by an angry cat "—and we have taken one thread—" I drew a line from it "—if that thread was wrong . . . If it messed up the world or the space-time continuum . . ." I explained with a grin that I knew made men take pause. Usually, I'd internally roll my eyes, but I was too focused on this. His attention narrowed. "Could we somehow, whether it's calling upon Kali herself—" I grinned again to seem as though I was possibly, maybe, kind of, sort of, joking "—or simply finding a way back to the initial point of pulling the thread . . . Could we alter the thread taken? Without the potential for disaster, which we all know would occur with time travel." I winked and felt ill for doing so.

"You're assuming there is a tapestry woven. In your lovely diagram here, you have shown me chaos. In chaos we often pick the thread that leads us out. No matter the cost. It is chosen as an escape hatch. The way out can entangle things further." My heart clenched. "Sometimes we can exit and reestablish the tapestry. Sometimes, like a missing stitch or a catch in the stitch, pulling harder on it tangles the thread, creating greater chaos. Or it can even snap the stitch." Like a Veil opening and collapsing instantaneously.

"So, if we were to figure out how to back the stitch up, could we get back to the original tapestry?"

"Whatever is your story, love?" he asked me with a lopsided grin. I pointed to the ball of yarn sketch and said that was about the long and short of it. He laughed and signaled for another round. "I would say, that as time is nonlinear, we should be able to reach back and pluck the other thread. You must know where to look. I will warn, though, that Kali likes balance. If you are reweaving a tapestry out of self-importance or revenge, she will not be so accommodating." He winked.

"But how?" I asked aloud, meaning the question for me alone.

"While I am an academic, and perhaps not of the class of citizen generally regarded as dealing in the occult, I would, perhaps, advise you to try to connect yourself—your being— to the Goddess, and see where that takes you." He leaned in closer and said conspiratorially, "You could try scrying. Or something to that effect."

"Oh, I'm just asking for a friend," I said with a wry twist to my mouth. His eyes twinkled.

"Where are you staying?" he asked, sipping the last of his drink.

I muttered about missing my train and looking at the Randolph. The nicest hotel in town in my opinion. He whistled.

"You could stay with me."

The air went a bit stale.

It wasn't the first proposition I'd had since coming back. Far from it, unfortunately, but it felt more possible, which scared me. He was easy to talk to and cute to look at, but I was not a whole person. I was still in love with a ghost. So, I politely declined, and we parted ways on the street.

CHAPTER 39

CORRAIDHÍN

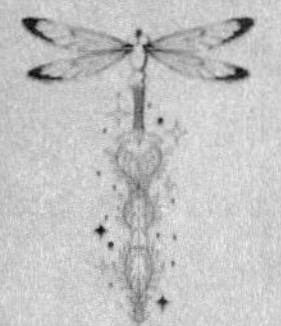

I supposed I understood that we all lost something that day. None of us escaped unscathed. It was nearly a week afterward that I was told all that had happened. All that we lost. I didn't think I had ever met someone who had fought as hard for everything and everyone the way that Neysa had. I surely hadn't. I would have given up. Had it been between losing my mate and saving the rest of us, I think, honestly, I would have said to hell with the rest. Yet, here we all were because that beautiful beast fought for us.

Ewan walked in and I knew. Well, I didn't really know, but, you see, I knew there was a problem. He kept saying, "She's gone. I've lost her." Over and over again. He spent weeks not wanting to speak to anyone. My own twin had been injured, but I knew he was safe and cared for, if not destroyed over Neysa. As I said, no one was unscathed. Cadeyrn was in Saarlaiche, being kept sedated. He was run through with a sword, which pierced his liver and spine. Rather than healing himself, he used the last of his gifts to blow Kíra into the nether realm. There was nothing tethering him to this world.

It had been three months since that day.

Silas came to see us, escorted by Saski and her brother. Sometimes I wondered about them. I shouldn't speculate. It was time to begin bringing our cousin back, as I would be godsdamned if he wasn't here to meet my little ones. I read once, in the human realm, a saying: When one door closes, a window opens—or something like that. Perhaps the losses we had endured would be softened by the new arrivals. Though, I would imagine that, for Cadeyrn, it would only serve to remind him of the mate he no longer had, and the children he would never father. I knew, as I knew my own mind, that he would never get over Neysa. I just wanted to try to keep him alive.

Chapter 40

Neysa

I f the phone would stop buzzing and let me enjoy the rest of this stupidly early morning, that would be fabulous. I groaned and rolled over to see who was calling before answering.

"Perhaps I was a bit forward last night. May I take you to breakfast?" Dean asked.

I rubbed my eyes and fell back on the pillow. I really didn't want to get out of this bed.

"Breakfast is low commitment. You can just order a coffee and lie to me that it's all you normally have, or you can do a full English and we can talk shop."

I smiled despite myself and agreed to meet him downstairs in two hours.

I didn't even have fresh clothes but had the forethought to wash out my underthings and hang my jeans and top in the bathroom to steam. At university, I went on holiday with a friend who would hang her jeans by the ankles every night and spritz them with water to lay the creases flat. She was a total nut job, but her jeans always looked clean. So, I gave it a go. When I came into the dining room of the MacDonald

Randolph, Dean was waiting at a table with both coffee and tea.

"Now you're going tell me that because you're from L.A., you don't do caffeine and subsist on green juice and rosé," he said with a smirk.

I sat and poured tea and milk and winked at him. Once a few sips of tea kicked in, I sat back and relaxed. The room was old world elegance with portraits and house crests lining the hunter green walls. Robed scholars rushed down the street outside the large windows.

"You looked me up?" I asked.

He scoffed.

"Of course." I raised an eyebrow. "I suppose you're not from L.A., but rather recently from there. Is that right? I am curious. Professionally and personally," he began, "what has occurred in your life in the past two years?"

I had a sharp intake of breath and made myself look at him. I used to be a morning person. When I slept at night. Dean's clean and pressed morning look bugged me. With a pang, I remembered Cadeyrn in the morning, warm and sleep-mussed.

"So, you divorced, and your dad passed. Sorry about that, Pet."

I glared at him, and he put his hands up in surrender.

"There is a blank space between then and when you picked up your Forex career ten months ago, living in Richmond. So, what happened?"

I poured more tea and picked at a scone, the liquid curdling. Why on earth did I think having breakfast with an anthropologist was a good idea?

"Well, apart from being in an alternate dimension, getting attacked by a shark, and realizing I was a long-lost princess?" I smiled and took a bite of scone, giving him wide, dramatic eyes. He folded his arms across his chest. "I rented a cottage and took a sabbatical. Not very interesting, I'm afraid."

He looked disappointed. From his ballistic nylon satchel, Dean pulled folders and notes, and scooted his chair next to me. Scents of fresh laundry and soap came off him as he reached across me to point to a notebook.

There were theories listed on borrowed time.

When a layer of time comes to a choice ending, one must collapse the layer or choose a path that takes it either up or down to another layer. Mostly, people make choices that lead to a linear progression. Thereby, it seems as though time runs along a straight and narrow.

"I refuse to entertain any questions regarding time travel. I have done too many late nights, with too much gin, where the conversation runs that way, and not only do I find it conceptually frustrating, I am not a quantum physicist. Plus, I'm not quite certain I get on with gin."

"Wasn't going to go there," I said. I forked some eggs and beans into my mouth. "So why the fascination with layered time? Debunking ghosts?"

"That's amusing. No." He drank his coffee and poured another, stirring in sugar, keeping it black. "The fascination lies in the concept of choice and consequence. Is there a point where we just subconsciously stop making real choices? Our parents, authorities, and so on, tell us how to do this, that, and the other, so it puts us on a path. When some of us go off the rails and get lost in drugs and sex and thievery, we think, 'Oh, shame about Charlie. He's gotten on the wrong path.' Did he? Or was there a moment when Charlie had no fucking concept of having a choice and stopped making decisions and found himself behind a pub in Crawley with a prostitute and a bag of heroin?" He blew out a breath and tapped his fingers on the table.

"Okay, Doctor. Take a breath, man, and back up."

He burst out laughing.

"Now, do you need to talk about Crawley?"

"Funny. No, Pet. I actually thought you would be interested in hearing more about the Goddess." He put on a pair of glasses, making him look endearingly young.

I longed to hear the voice of the Goddess. The voice of Ludek or Ewan. Cadeyrn. Always Cadeyrn. Everything in my head was so empty. I ached to be who I was meant to be. Not this shell. Dean spoke and gesticulated and joked, and I liked being around him. More than anyone I had befriended since I came back. We agreed to see each other again, but I had to catch a train back to Richmond.

Two training gyms politely kicked me out for being too rough. I was on tentative feet with the third, and tried my very best to be on good, human-like behavior. The plan had been simple. However, as with everything I seem to have messed up in my life, this simple plan of mine went awry almost instantly. The first gym I sought was tucked into a fairly rough South London neighborhood. The comments and innuendos didn't bother me one iota, as I was used to clawing my way up the hierarchy of a sparring session. I was paired with a guy called Baker Mick. He was, alas, not a baker, but had arms that resembled loaves of Challah bread. I let him put me in check once, to the snickers and jeers of the few in the warehouse. Once they'd had their jollies, I turned up the volume of my abilities and showed them some of what I could do. Within a few moves I had Mick pinned, my sword just under his jugular. I was escorted out by five large men and told not to return.

So, for the second facility, I went in talking myself down. The purpose was just to keep up my skill. Hone my strength. Paired with the owner, we joked and sparred for a few sessions. One particularly bad day, after a night of dreaming about Cadeyrn's death, I couldn't tone down my violence. The singing of the blades and sound of the movement around us brought on memories and feelings I couldn't compartmentalize. Slow motion droplets of my blood meeting Konstantín's, Kíra's wolfish grin, her sword impaling my husband over and over again. The feel of falling back through the Veil as Cadeyrn fell the opposite way. In an ending like the spar with Baker Mick, I was asked to leave the second gym. And to get therapy. For this third gym, I worked very hard to go in pretending to be human. Sane, rational, emotionally stable human.

As I was walking in to train with my new sparring partner, my phone buzzed.

"What are you up to?" Dean asked.

"About to swing a sword with a man who thinks I'm a bit mad. Why?"

"Not what I was expecting, but okay. I'm in London. Well, I was. I'm on my way to Richmond in the hopes that a lovely girl will let me take her to dinner. I know we skipped lunch and tea, but perhaps tapas toe the line? Small plates and all that."

"I can't miss this session, or they will kick me out. So, I won't be very lovely by the time you see me."

"Oh, I wasn't talking about you. But if you insist on my stopping to see you, I don't mind your grubbiness."

I could almost hear the twinkle in his eyes.

It couldn't have been more than ten minutes, because as I landed behind my partner and knocked both his knees out and pinned him to the ground, I noticed Dean standing a bit slack jawed by the shoe cubbies at the front. He politely sat and watched while I finished my session. It seemed at one point that my partner had the upper hand, but I pointed my twin swords down and swept out with my right leg, knocking him into me and allowing me to pin him again. My knee was aching, so I called it and left the ring with a handshake to my partner.

At dinner, I hit the sangria harder than was necessary. It was a gorgeous August evening, and I'd had a rough week, both financially and emotionally. I laughed at a joke Dean told, and he put his hand over mine. I stiffened, but he didn't seem to notice.

"I like you, Neysa. Quite a bit." No, no, no. Don't say that. I wanted to throw up. As it was, I was going to have a rip-roaring headache in the morning. "Could we see more of each other? Or, maybe—"

"I don't know that I can." It bubbled out from my lips before I could stop it. "I'm in love with someone else."

He snatched his hand back and finally noticed my engagement ring.

"Ah."

"It ended with him." I couldn't say he was dead. "But, I don't think I can ever get over it."

"It's worth a shot, right? We get on well."

Shit. We certainly did but . . .

"Would you like to hear a fairytale?" I asked him. "I have a good one." So, while we sat amongst the Friday night crowds who were drinking and eating and chatting and flirting, I told him my tale. I never used my own name, but as I told the story, I laughed and cried. In conclusion, I described being pushed through the Veil, seeing Cadeyrn run through with Kíra's sword.

"Where did the Veil leave her?" he asked after sitting quietly, drinking his sangria, then ordering us coffee.

"In the middle of the woods in a small town in northern Germany, called Bad Schwartau. She made her way to Lübeck, then took a flight from Hamburg, eventually making it . . . somewhere else."

"London?" he asked, not taking his eyes off me. I gave a curt nod. "That was a hell of an anecdote. Where in England did she originally come to stay?"

It was so Dean that he was still asking questions.

"Barlowe Combe. It's in the—"

"I know Barlowe Combe," he said quietly. "I was born there. My mum still lives there. Runs a tea shop." Oh, dear gods. I put my head in my hands.

"Tilly?" I asked.

He looked like the wind was knocked out of him.

"Your mum tried to hoist me on you a couple of years ago."

"Perhaps I should pay more attention to who she tries to set me up with then. You truly believe all this happened?"

"Dean, I have told you a tale. Respect that I have shared it with you."

He walked me back to my flat, where we stood outside chatting. The air blew cool, though the evening was warm. I was looking forward to cold nights. The dark days when rain kept sentry at the windows, giving me the grace not to have to see another soul. I said goodnight and started to walk into my building when he called after me.

"How do you know he didn't heal?"

I stopped short and grabbed the wall, unable to breathe. "Because I know he would have used every last scrap he had to burn her to ash."

"I don't know. I think you may have another thread to pull."

I let myself into my building and spent the night trying not to scream into my pillow.

CHAPTER 41

CORRAIDHÍN

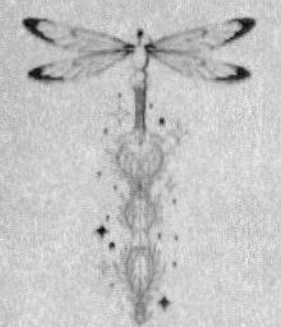

The healer pulled me aside when they arrived and said he hadn't spoken the whole journey but got up at dawn each day to train. We should have woken him earlier. Regardless, I wanted us all together for Yule, and I had two little ones now, and I wanted them to see their family. And I made a point of getting what I want. However, when they arrived, Magnus gave me eyes suggesting we were in for a treat.

I met the carriage as it came up the drive and threw my arms around my cousin. He barely touched my back in greeting. I dragged him inside to where my brother waited with Ewan. It was as strange a greeting as we had ever had. Cadeyrn's eyes kept roving the room, taking in the pine boughs and candles, the scent of cloves and mint. Laughter trickled in from the back, and Reynard and Saski came into the room. Cadeyrn was standing, looking like he had been punched in the gut. I should have thought of that. She looked so similar to Neysa. If I had to compare, I didn't favor her as much as Neysa, but maybe that was because she still pissed me off every now and again. The babes had been sleeping, but I heard their banshee-like cries from upstairs and went to fetch them.

He might have been trying not to look at my children. I understood. Really. But sometimes, we needed to saddle that horse and ride. Was that the expression? I didn't know. In any case, Cadeyrn was like my brother, and my children were to know their uncle. Silas had been here since their birth. I'd found him quite a few times, sitting and telling them stories, even though the little *moinchai* had no blasted idea what their big oaf of an uncle was on about. Ewan took the lass from me, and we walked in to sit. I wouldn't force them in his face. Gods know I hated when people did that to me with their children. He watched us sit and took his attention back to Saski and Silas, who always seemed to be sitting close. Cadeyrn smirked and shook his head.

"Something to say, brother?" Silas asked.

Cadeyrn met his eyes, and the haunted look in them had Silas regretting opening his fat mouth. I could read him like a book. Cadeyrn just pinched his nose and sat there, his hair shooting up like hands in surrender.

"Cadeyrn," Silas barked. "Tomorrow you and I are going climbing. There's a mountain nearby, and Ewan has all the ropes and such. Might freeze our balls off, but it's worth it."

Cadeyrn agreed without saying more. We had our traditional Yule dinner with spiced wine. It was dark but not nearly as late as we normally stretched the festivities. Last year, the four of us were eating and drinking until nearly four in the morning.

The babes were in their cradles on the other side of the room when they started wiggling. Not the screeching that made me want to go climb a mountain myself, but the sweet funny sounds that I never thought I would love hearing. Cadeyrn looked over and got up.

"May I?" he asked. Ewan smiled at him. My cousin walked

over slowly and looked into the cradles. There was a softness in his expression that broke my heart. He reached a hand in, and as I came up next to him, I saw that Efa was holding his finger, looking up at him with her father's olive-green eyes. Silas scooped up his niece and held her out to Cadeyrn, who had a look of terror.

"Go on. Just make sure you hold the head, aye?" He transferred Efa to Cadeyrn. Their eyes met. I knew he was seeing Neysa's eyes in her.

"Hello, *aoín baege*," he whispered, calling her 'little one'.

Ewan turned away and scrubbed his face. Silas held Pim, allowing Cadeyrn to look upon his little elfin features. He carefully touched a finger to my son's tiny ear.

"And you, *allaine balaíche*? You have your mummy's mouth. Will you use it to torment us as she does?"

Ewan chuckled. "They are calm with you."

"I think . . . I am calmer with them." He passed me Efa and bowed deeply. "Blessings to you both. I will protect them as my own." He knelt down, Silas following suit. Well, I wasn't expecting that. I leaned into the buttery warmth of my daughter and kissed her soft cheek. I didn't know how Saskeia could have let her children go. I would sooner jump out of my window. Granted, there were times when they were screaming and I needed to sleep, that I did actually feel like jumping out of my window, but I digressed. I had found a perfection in this great cruel world, and I only wished my brother and cousin could find the same.

TWO MONTHS LATER, I noticed Cadeyrn was larger than he had been. He and my brother were always formidable in their strength and size, but even Ewan commented on the breadth of muscle that built on Cadeyrn. He spent his days building and climbing, training and running. I came back to the house after a run myself. Ama was waiting with Pim, who had started giggling, smiling, and, less amusingly, pulling my hair out at the roots. Cadeyrn was swinging an axe, splitting wood and separating piles to deliver to different areas of the province.

"You won't sit still these days, cousin," I said. "Just like Neysa."

He stopped and dropped the axe. He never spoke of her. Never said her name. Silas did. In the beginning especially. He would sit and tell me stories that left a hole in my chest. Ewan, I knew, was always trying to speak to her in his mind. I could see on his face when he was doing it. As though there would be a time when it would work.

Cadeyrn glared at me. Well, I supposed now was as good a time as ever to step in some deep, deep shite.

"Darling," I said, meeting his eyes. Pim started to wiggle at my tone, so I did that funny swaying thing with my hips I never did before I had these little monsters. "Perhaps being able to say her name without growling might allow you some peace?" Pim grabbed at my hair, and I pulled his little fingers away and kissed them one by one before blowing on his little nose.

"I don't see how that would bring peace, Corraidhín." He folded his arms across his chest.

"I don't know. I suppose I see you building such a wall around yourself that no one will ever be able to get past."

"I don't need anyone to get past," he said, starting to turn, but Pim's little arm reached to him, and he didn't resist reaching back. It was sweet, really. I handed my son to him.

"I watched this documentary once," I told him, and he groaned, growling my name. Pim's eyes went wide at the sound, so Cadeyrn looked down at him and smiled. "Scientists in Switzerland were studying waves. Giant ones that smash ships. I can't think of what they are called."

"Tsunamis," he said, bored.

"Ah, yes. So, they were looking into the cause, and how to prepare for such things. They happen on islands when there are earthquakes in the ocean and the poor little sods who live on islands can get washed away. Horrible, really," I mused.

"Corraidhín," he said, pleading me to get on with it. I thought of Neysa and how she loved to stir up Cadeyrn's annoyance. I missed her too. I had never had a female friend like her. But my grief was less to contend with than the rest of these moping males.

"Earthquakes and explosions can cause these large waves, but there is something called a mega tsunami that happens every few hundred or thousand years. I can't quite remember. Watched something on meteorites after, and the timeline on both got mixed up. These scientists figured out that something big falling in the water can create a wave that splashes up hundreds of meters to wipe out coastlines."

"Yes, cousin," he said. "I should think that was obvious. When you sit the children in the bath, does the water not rise and splash?"

I waved him off. "Pshaw. Listen. There was a rock that fell into a bay in Alaska, I think. One of those freezing bloody places. It caused not only a splash, but the water built and built, and the wave that it created rose over five hundred meters. It took out trees and such on cliff tops."

"While devastating, I'm sure, I have no idea where you are going with this story." Pim was swatting at his uncle's face, vying for attention. "You, lad, are just like your mummy and uncle. Always needing attention," Cadeyrn said to my son. Gods, he would be a lovely father.

"Okay, okay. So, some years ago, this phenomenon was

being studied, and the scientists realized there is a place off Africa—islands called toucans or sparrows."

"The Canary Islands?" he asked with a patronizing smirk. At least the little shit was listening.

"Ah, thank you, darling. Yes. There is an island there. La Palma? Perhaps. If an earthquake were to hit under the water there, or a volcano were to erupt, a piece of the island, a cliff, I think—Gods, I don't know—it would plunk into the sea and the size of that plunk would cause a ripple. The ripple would cause a rise in the water. The rise in water would create a wave. The wave would get larger and larger and move across the sea, spreading out, and growing taller. They think that, within days, it would be travelling as fast as an airplane and be hundreds of feet tall. But instead of taking out trees on a cliff lining a bay, the tsunami would hit the East Coast of the United States and take out the coast from Nova Scotia down to the Caribbean. It would reach like ten or fifteen miles inland. Nothing would survive. Gods. Can you imagine?" He looked at me like I was raving. Oh, point of the story. Right. "I think you are like the mega tsunami," I said. He rolled his eyes and groaned. "Neysa going through the Veil was the island breaking apart. I think. Wait. Yes, it was. Now you are building and building walls around you, making you impenetrable, and the destruction within you is going to cause you to explode."

"If I were a mega tsunami, wouldn't this bullshit building metaphor be me destroying everyone else?"

"What do you think would happen to all of us, my darling, if you were gone?" I asked him softly. He breathed deeply and squeezed his eyes shut before kissing Pim and handing him back.

"I can't stop what's building in me, Corraidhín."

"I miss her too. No one has asked me if I am okay, but I miss her. Ewan, Silas . . ."

"I don't just miss her. She's *my* wife, and I did it. I pushed her through the Veil. I did. We don't even know where she ended up. It could be another time. It could be the middle of the fucking ocean. She could have landed in bloody La Palma. Or the desert. She hates the desert. So, you see, Corraidhín, if I talk about her—if I think about her, that's when this wave gets bigger. That's when I become a threat. I hate this fucking analogy. Gods, Corraidhín." He stomped off, and Pim started to cry. I did the bouncing sway thing to calm him and went to look for Ewan and Efa.

CHAPTER 42

CADEYRN

Just past the summer solstice was Aedtine Day in Aoifsing. According to Saski, it was celebrated in Heilig as well. We lit bonfires and paid tribute to the elements of fire and weather, for the summer harvest to be good. Ewan was sitting on the far side of one of the bonfires, staring into the flames. Silas and I had been in conversation for a great long while. I thought it might have been the first real conversation we'd had since . . . everything. It looked as if Ewan wanted to come over and talk. I knew he felt much the same as I did. Losing Neysa was like losing half of himself. When they were finally reunited last year, it was as though a seam on them which was always open had been stitched up like new. Now it was ripped open again. Except he had Corraidhín and his children. I really had nothing. I knew that when I looked at him, he could see the void in me. Sometimes I thought I would have faded away completely. Just let my immortality flake and die. In fact, I wasn't so sure it hadn't been happening anyway.

As Silas left, I sat staring into the flames. Ewan walked over to sit beside me, staring as well into the taunting lights and crackling sounds of the fire.

"What's next?" he asked.

"You're the king."

"Ah, about that. I think, perhaps, I am ready to dissolve the monarchy," he admitted. I turned to him, eyebrows raised. "I would rather not have that hanging over all our heads. I would like to perhaps be a representative and help restructure. I am not a king in my heart, Cadeyrn."

We looked out at the masses of fae enjoying the holiday.

"I grew up in the Elders' Palace," he said, pulling at a blade of grass. "Constantly surrounded by others. I dreamt my whole life of having a quiet home, perhaps a family, and not having so many fae underfoot." He looked at me—his sister's husband, pale and withdrawn, from my pointed ears to the silver streak in my dark hair.

"Whatever you decide, Ewan. Like your sister, you are the embodiment of intelligence and strength." It shocked me mentioning Neysa. I could never bring myself to say her name. Barely recognizing the compliment, I could tell he was just as surprised.

"So, I hear you're a tsunami," he said.

I snorted. A sound so like laughter it caught me off guard.

"Apparently so. It's probably a good thing there aren't documentaries here, Ewan. Surely at some point Corraidhín will have run out of references for ones she's watched in the past."

"Sometimes," Ewan said carefully, "I feel like the ceiling has come down on the world and it's crushing me. Not knowing where she went, but knowing she's gone. I come out of it because I have Corraidhín," he said. "And Pim and Efa."

I stared into the glow of the fire while he spoke.

"So, I can assure you, that what you feel—how you feel—is warranted. Because when I feel like I can't breathe, I know it's worse for you."

"Silas is bedding Saski," I remarked needlessly. We all knew that. Why I felt I had to bloody say it was beyond me.

"That's good," I said, rambling more. "That's his way. Of coping. She, though. She may love him. You will understand if I leave? That I cannot be around that?"

He nodded at me. Corraidhín was waiting for it, I knew.

"Where is she, Ewan?" I asked. "Is she okay?"

Silence answered me. We watched the dance of the flames. They swayed and tipped and flickered, looking like dancers in the sunset. The orange glow parted, revealing shades of yellow and blue, the temperatures showing up in varying colors. Low blue flames looked almost like sky. Sky over water, rippling. The orange touched upon it like blood. I couldn't peel my eyes from the flames. White swirled around the orange, a silken wash of brightness, muting the bloody tones of the drips of orange falling onto the watery azure. Behind the flames was a constellation of stars. A layer of stars upon the *Adairch a Taeoide Gaellte,* the constellation that was written upon my back and Neysa's hand. I blinked, trying to focus. Neysa's freckled hand held a stone, matching the flames. No, it reflected the flames, and pendulumed over a handwritten note, splashed with blood.

"What are you lot doing over here?" Corraidhín came over to us, shaking me from the vision. I looked at Ewan's spectral face.

"A moment, please, my love?" he asked her, voice barely audible. She saw our expressions and walked away.

"Did you see . . ."

"I think so. Ewan. I wonder if the blood—if we can open a Veil. I think that's what she did. I think that's what happened. Her power reaches between realms. She bled and sacrificed in that cavern. Then Konstantín died at her feet, and the Veil opened."

He swore at my logic, twitching his face.

I had planned to leave the next day. I was heading to Prinaer to check in with Ainsley and her lot. I had been in Laorinaghe with the representatives there for a week or so around mine and Neysa'a birthday. It was an easy escape then, everyone knew. I often went to Laorinaghe. Maybe they wondered if I had been seeing another female. I didn't think Ewan believed I had that sort of constitution. I did think he had other thoughts regarding what I might have been doing in that coastal province.

"Would you be willing to sacrifice someone to open a Veil?" he asked me.

I looked him in the eyes. I knew mine blazed with the fire behind them. The fire inside me.

"For her? Gladly. Though I do not think it's necessary. Will you help me?"

"Whatever you need, brother," he said as we clasped elbows.

Corraidhín nearly tore her husband apart when I explained that we were leaving in the morning. I said we were checking in on Prinaer, but she had seen us last night. With that gift of hers, she could easily discern our intentions from the looks on our faces. He closed himself off to her yelling and scratching. She clawed at him and said it couldn't be done, saying he wasn't stable enough to do this and he was New York and would be crushed by a tidal wave, and if there were a virus that killed the human population, the people would throw the weaker ones to the zombies and run. Eventually, he exploded with laughter, standing there, holding her hands away from his scratched-up face in the sitting room. Even I laughed until my cheeks hurt. She pulled her hands back and growled, hands on hips.

"I have no idea what kind of animal a zombie is or what it has to do with a virus," he said through a fit of giggles. "So, my love. You think that I am the weak one to throw to the zombie animals?"

She pursed her lips and splashed water in his face. I hated when she did that. It used to happen to Silas and me all the bloody time.

"Hmph. A zombie is not an animal," she answered. "Although, I suppose it sort of is. Or once was. Doesn't matter."

"And I am the sacrificial weak lamb?" Ewan asked her, smiling and prowling closer. She stepped back a bit and lifted her slightly pointed chin.

"Cadeyrn is even larger now. Though I suppose you are of equal height."

I was trying to disappear to the recesses of the room. Ewan stood before her, looking down at her face where it was lit from the low sconce and the last shards of sunset.

"I will be back within a couple of weeks. I promise. I will not leave you and the babes. I thank merciful Mother Aoifsing every day for you."

She looked away and bit her lip. I slipped through the archway and made my way to my chamber.

TRUTHFULLY, I hadn't told Ewan why we were in Prinaer. He didn't particularly like that province, I knew. As a child, he was scared to death of the Elders from there. I believed now it held memories of both the battle in which he and Neysa fashioned a magnetic field to entrap the enemy, and of setting off for Festaera with that wretched clock. Ainsley welcomed us both in her strange hall filled with ale and cider and bearded males with braided hair. It was a look, I must say. Over our third or fourth ale, I asked Ainsley—and by asked, I mean I explained to her that I would appreciate her agreement in my doing so—to visit their sacred temple to the Goddess Kalíma. She looked at me, long and hard.

"Though a lesser goddess, Cadeyrn, Kalíma is powerful. She does not take lightly to being summoned."

"Neither do I," I snarled, fire burning behind my eyes, likely changing them from green to blue and back again. "My mate was tapped by a goddess, infiltrated by *this* goddess, and taken from this realm. I reserve the right to summon her."

"Ah, but the ego in that statement alone will incur her wrath," Ainsley pointed out.

I slammed my hand down on the table. The hall quieted, a silence filled with the hard stares of a hundred or so fae who were built like bears. Ainsley's slow smile spread across her chestnut face.

"Perhaps look within a bit more and see where your link to Kalíma may lie."

I tore a hand through my hair and grabbed the back of my neck viciously. She looked at me in a rare display of sympathy. There was no masking the sorrow in my eyes these days, I knew. Ewan and Corraidhín kept commenting on what they thought was a rather impressive gain of muscle and strength in me, but anyone could see the underlying promise of a soul ready to flee its home.

"I give you my blessing to go to the temple," Ainsley Mads told me. "Be wise, Battle King."

I KNELT in the temple with its walls of pure gold and still, black pool in the center. I had told Ewan I would require only his energy and connection to Neysa to bolster my efforts. So, he stood, waiting. The air was thick with rot and something overly sweet I couldn't place. From a sack, I pulled the smoky quartz. I released my gift, and warmth, mist, pure magic, and the light of healing swirled in clouds around us. He knew my power. Knew I exuded it even when I kept it all in check. It was something I had to contend with in my long life. Something that always set me apart in the loneliest of ways.

The very walls pulsed with my power, and Ewan's responded in turn. I looked at him over my shoulder to say it was time. The juxtaposition in our powers, the situation, and my age versus the haunted, childlike look I knew I wore at that moment must have been amusing at best. He touched my shoulder and allowed his strength to seep into me. Then I touched the water and was gone. Blasted hell and shite. It was like being ripped through the ashes in a hearth. The things I saw and felt. Though the goddess never appeared to me herself as she had done for Neysa, I knew when she approved of why I had come. I could see out of the wretched dark and could see Ewan pacing, saying aloud that he never wanted to be the bloody king and would burn the world to keep his family safe.

I was cast from the pool, wet and gasping. He clasped elbows with me, and I turned back to the stone on the ground and sliced my palm open. The blood dripped onto the stone, causing it to glow and reflect in the gold of the temple. Ewan pulled his knife and sliced his palm. My eyes widened, but I knew he would blood let to find his sister. They were part of one another, and as such, it might help find her. As my blood dripped in time with his, there was a quiver in the air. A visible thread, golden and thin, shone in the expanse before us. I held my forearm out and pushed his sleeve up, revealing a matching thread. The aura around us grew hazy and soon was very clearly a Veil.

"Step away please, Ewan."

"Fair travels, brother," he told me. Corraidhín was surely going to throttle him for this. Had there been enough of my soul to care at that point, I might have said something. I stepped through, and while I expected the Veil to close as it had after Neysa passed through, it stayed, abhorrent behind me.

CHAPTER 43

NEYSA

The top of Dean's package opened, revealing what looked to be a sort of rocket ship. He had it cradled against him, a smug look on his face. I shook my head and turned back to the counter where I was purchasing my perfume. After our initial tapas dinner, we began seeing each other regularly. As friends. It was simple and comfortable to be with him. He wanted more from me than I was able to give, but for now, I enjoyed our time together.

"I thought you were buying gin?" I asked him, paying for the atomizer.

"It's a limited edition rare gin." He pulled the bottle half out and showed it to me. "My superior collects gins, and this designer launched a limited edition gin collection."

"And can you afford to pay rent now?"

"I can if this helps me keep my job after my reprimand." He winked at me and I laughed. We walked out of the back of Liberty's London and headed toward Carnaby Street. Summer was in full swing despite the rain pummeling us as we ran between overhangs, carefully angling our umbrellas to avoid the crowds.

"God, I hate Carnaby Street. Can we get this over with so we can go get a proper drink?"

I said he didn't have to come along, but he tsked. I turned right onto a side street and walked straight into a tall, broad-shouldered man. He grabbed my shoulders to right me and picked up my package. I looked up and caught my breath when I saw nearly black hair and light eyes looking at me.

"Sorry. You alright?"

I nodded silently as he walked away. Dean put a hand to my back and moved us further along. I could see the store front where I was headed, off in the distance, but had to pause before going in, my insides warring with their state of matter.

"I'm fine," I mumbled to Dean. He pursed his lips and sucked in his cheeks. "Just caught off guard."

Tentative fingers reached out and stroked my face. I wanted to swat at them. I wanted to rip them off and tell him to get away. I wanted to lean into the touch and be held by someone who cared about me. Instead, I turned and made my way to the shop.

There wasn't anything remarkable about the store. It was dim and jumbled, smelling of incense. Crystals glittered from every angle. Some seemed to vibrate toward my energy; others must have been fondled and exposed to so much they were unresponsive. An older man pushed from the back and scratched his head at us. I looked at Dean, who was standing with arms crossed, not meeting my eyes.

"Help you?" the old fellow asked. I walked to the counter and pushed over my dad's journal. The address of the shop and a name was written in the middle of one page, watercolor crystals painted over the rest of the page. The shopkeeper peered at the page through bifocals.

"That's me." He tapped the page.

"Did you know Elías Obecan?" I asked him softly.

He started and looked directly at me. "Of course I knew Elías. We were friends for many years."

I exhaled, feeling suddenly very tired and very encouraged at the same time. Dean made his way over to us.

"I am his daughter." I cleared my throat.

"Neysa." His face opened in a smile which faded as soon as it had appeared. "If you are here, then my friend has passed on." As though only just noting Dean, the old man narrowed his eyes at my friend. "Come closer, lad. I'm old and infirm and cannot see from this far."

Dean looked at me as though heading to the gauntlet, yet stepped forward. The old man looked directly into Dean's brown eyes and scoffed.

"You can wait outside."

"Pardon me, sir, but I am not inclined to leave."

The shopkeeper wheezed a laugh and slapped the counter, saying he would wager Elías's daughter could fend for herself better than any schoolboy could protect her. Color crept up Dean's face, and I had the urge to touch his cheek, yet refrained.

"You are not the right one," the man told him. He walked away, shuffled through things in the back, and we waited.

"He seems a few marbles short, Pet. Do you want me to go?"

"My marbles are all stacked, lad. Here," he announced, and set a sketch atop the counter next to a moleskin sack. "These," he said, pointing to the sketch, "are not your eyes, lad."

I clenched my fists together, counting my breaths. On the paper, outlined in charcoal, and filled in with watercolor the shade somewhere between an aquamarine and a peridot, were Cadeyrn's eyes.

"No," I whispered, touching the sketch. "They aren't. They are my husband's." The sketch did not bring any visions as I hoped it would. Likely because the bearer of those magnificent eyes was dead.

"Ah. I see. Well, I suppose you can stay," Percival said. "Tea?"

THE CLEAR QUARTZ pendulum that came out of the sack pulsed in my hand. Along with the crystal, the sack contained a torn piece of paper, yellowed with time. On the paper were two words: *Baege Maanlach*.

"Little Moon." Dean smiled, knowing it had been Dad's nickname for me. Sensing I might need to speak to the fellow on my own, my friend excused himself to drown his buyer's remorse over a pint. We sat back and sipped the proffered tea.

"In a different time, I was known as an emissary," the old man began. "My family is an ancient line who have always sworn to protect the Veil." Why was I not surprised to hear this? "My name is Percival Bryan, and I met your father about thirty years ago, when I tried to kill him."

I pitched forward in my seat. The cup rattled, sloshing tea. From boyhood, he told me, the men of his family were taught to fight and protect the Veil at all costs. Curiosity had me asking what the women did.

"They learn to summon, scry, and shield," he said, as though I were a bit thick. Long ago, a pact was made between the fae who crossed and the humans receptive to magic. Within that agreement, the humans promised to guard the Veil and dispose of any who sought to shatter the stability. Percival had been spending time around the Veil in Barlowe Combe. He witnessed my father exiting the grotto near the Veil and would have killed him outright if not for the small child he held by the hand. Because of that child, he bided his time and followed my father. Once Elías was finally alone, Percival confronted him. They fought for a time, my father eventually shoving Percival's head into a tree, face first.

"He said, 'Do not presume to know what I am doing to help the Veil. Many know the whereabouts of the stones and are readying crossing-compatible teams to seek them out. This cannot happen. Do you understand that, human?'" Percival chuckled retelling the story. "As I was a clever chap, I agreed to listen to him. I thought that either he had a good point, or that hearing him out would help me be able to kill him. So, we became friends. After about two years, I decided not to off him."

"Two years!" I spluttered.

He chuckled again and wiped the lenses on his glasses. "Oh, he knew. Your dad didn't miss a trick. Although, when you pulled that stunt in going to Spain, he was quite blind-sided. Had me fly to Barcelona to keep an eye on you until he got there."

I must have looked shocked because he smirked.

Dad became sick much earlier than I had thought. He confided in Percival sometime around my university gradua-tion. They continued to work together to secure the Veil when Dad had a vision. It was the only one he had ever had, and he guessed it had been sent to him by Saskeia.

"He loved that one fiercely, he did. I myself never married. Never saw the point. But your dad? He went to his grave with his heart across the Veil, I reckon." Once again, my heart broke for them. I told myself over and over that at least Ewan and Corra had one another. At least they were happy. I hoped.

The vision was of a man with those eyes. He said Dad didn't see much beyond the face, but the constellation of stars appeared with a braided rope. He knew the soul behind those eyes would one day belong to me, and that I would need to cross the Veil. So, they set about gathering items to help.

"I assume you crossed?" It was a simple question, yet I gripped the arms of my chair and snapped them in half from the pain in my chest. Percival didn't so much as flinch but stood and went about the shop pulling items. Small crystals, candles of varying colors, a pack of Jaffa Cakes, with a muttering of my being too thin. By the end of our visit, I was emotionally drained.

Finding Dean took me all of five minutes. There was an antiquarian bookstore a few doors down. The bell jingled when I walked in, yet no one greeted me. My friend sat on the floor at the back, a book cradled in his lap. His glasses had slid down his nose, and by the look of him biting his thumb, he was too immersed in the tome to notice. I sat next to him, keeping the silence. Without looking up, he looped an arm around my shoulders.

"Okay, Pet?"

I shrugged in answer. He nodded and placed a slip of paper between the pages, closing the book.

"Want to talk?"

I pushed at my nose and shook my head. He stood and held a hand out to me.

"Then let's get you something to eat. I'm sure a plate of cheesy chips will help."

I sniffed and took his hand.

STORIES AND SONGS of heartbreak tended to say that the quiet moments were the worst. The in between times when there was nothing to think about but the profound loss you felt. I wouldn't argue that, because all I had done since crossing back here was try to avoid those times. I would panic in the evening, knowing that within the sleeplessness that awaited me, there would be the serration of my soul as the dark minutes passed, allowing the unsolicited thoughts of my mate to infiltrate my restless mind.

So, I worked and filled my head with numbers and headlines, news tickers and investments. I ran, blasting music I had missed in Aoifsing. I trained and sparred and hoped that pushing my body to the brink of exhaustion each night would allow me to fall into slumber. However, in all those tomes of love lost, it never mentioned the fact that I could hear him speaking when my sword whined through the air in the training ring. I could hear the music of Corra's laughter in the din of a restaurant and feel the weight of Silas's gaze when the rain pounded on the roof of my flat. The louder the sounds, the faster the movement, the less control I had over the memories that would wash in, stealing my breath and leaving me stunned.

In these loud moments, I felt pain lance through me as though I were taking the sword that killed Cadeyrn. Over and over again. I walked through towns and cities, the more unfamiliar the better, attempting to keep at bay any recognition of my previous life. More often than not, it didn't work. I longed for every small moment I would never find again. The heat of his feet curled around my legs at night. The childish gleam in his eyes when he ate biscuits. The feel of having someone so imbedded in my being, I would never walk away from the loss.

I thought of the children Corra and Ewan had, and that not only would I not have any of my own, I would never meet my niece and nephew. Never see my brother again. I thought of Silas. How I hurt him repeatedly and still he loved me. Perhaps he would find love again. I had to believe one of us could be happy. The times I would have dinner with Dean, or make plans to drive out to the country, I convinced myself I was hanging on okay. And he would kiss my cheek goodnight, knowing I wouldn't offer more, and I would fall against the back of my door, tearing at my hair and pressing my nails into my palms to keep from screaming. The mask of efficiency I wore for the outside world crumbled from my face as I stepped inside my bare flat. In its place was the face of a female utterly devoid of the ability to carry on as half of what she should have been.

Waking in the predawn hours from another dream so real, I begged to get back to sleep. In the dream, my brother was pounding a pane of glass, soundlessly screaming for me. I couldn't make my limbs move to get to him, and I realized he was underwater, not behind glass. I tried to pound the ice separating him from me, but my blows were slow and soft, unable to make a difference. I cried and yelled until my eyes opened. When it was clear I was awake, my feet freezing after I kicked off my socks, I got up and showered. In my flat, with its scarce furniture and too many blankets, I had one bistro-sized dining table. I lit a red candle. It was the color for fire. For blood. Passion. Power.

Dean had stayed in town the night before. Richmond was several hours by train back to Durham. My friend planned to head up to see his mum the next day and begged me to come along. I was still deciding.

With my rose quartz pendulum, I sat near the candle's flame and wrote symbols. Nonsense and words, song lyrics, and Cadeyrn's name. Using the dagger he had given me, I sliced my palm and let the blood flow onto the paper. I had no idea what I was doing but begged the Goddess Kalíma. Begged Heícate, to whom I was heir, to help me.

It wasn't that I was no one without my mate. It was that I was somewhere wrong. I was trapped. This world was a cage. It shackled my gifts, my light, my heart. Plus, I missed him. I missed them all. My family. With my pendulum, I held still and watched as it swung back and forth without my having asked a question.

Haven't you? asked a voice in my head. *Is this all not one great question?*

If so, then what is the answer? The pendulum stopped, and much like the amethyst two years ago in my cottage, the rose quartz, the stone of love, burst from its binding and dropped onto the paper. It rolled onto its chiseled side, getting stained with blood, and the tip pointed to a drawing of an eye overlapping the lyrics to a song I had stuck in my head. *"Seems like forever when I'm near you, longer when we're apart."* The candle blew out, and I sat in darkness, wondering what the hell that meant.

Padding back to the bedroom, I reached into my closet and touched the fighting leathers I had worn when I crossed. They were clean now. Shoved to the back of my clothes. No, I wouldn't go to Barlowe Combe. Not yet. I texted Dean, knowing he wouldn't see it until later, and made a cup of tea.

At exactly 8:15, there was a buzz from my phone as I descended the steps to the street in front of my building. It was supposed to be hot today, and while I wasn't going to Barlowe Combe, I needed to be out of the flat which had no air conditioning. A halter style maxi dress made of gauzy off-white cotton dropped to my feet. Ginger colored ankle strap flat sandals completed the ensemble. I told myself I could wander the city. Perhaps get a Pimm's in a cafe, or stock up on books from a book shop. It was too hot to train, and I wasn't in the mood to work. My head wasn't in the game. I didn't have to check my phone to see that it was the persistent Dr. Preston, because he was standing against the street sign outside my building.

"Before you say no again, I want to point out that it is

cooler by the sea. Plus, mum will have cake. And you look gorgeous. Good morning."

He had a way about him, I had to admit.

"Tell her I say hello. I need to be on my own today, Dean."

He tried once more, but I shot him down again, giving him a kiss on his cheek and quick hug before walking away. His arms went around me briefly, like he might have tried to hold on. Often I felt guilty about it, but my friendship with Dean felt like my relationship with my brother or with Reynard. Not at all romantic, but lovely just the same.

The shops opened later, so I wandered about the streets seeing mums with babies in prams, people out for a morning run, and I must have stopped to say hello to ten dogs out for a walk. Eventually I wandered into a shop that had bed linens and candles that smelled of paper whites and sandy shores. I held a cashmere dressing gown in my hands. I never replaced the one I was wearing when Reynard abducted me from Cappadocia. I hoped he was well.

Near the checkout there was a small section of children's clothes and linens. My heart felt like there was a bubble in it. The babies would be seven or eight months old by now. I never kept my promise. As though an escalator were pulling my feet, I gravitated to the children's section.

Everything was white with classic little patterns and soft materials. On the shelf above the toddler quilts was a basket of cuddly toys, two having fallen out, landing on their heads. Smiling, I picked them up and had a flash in my mind. I whimpered and held on. Two small faces swam to the surface. A boy with eyes exactly like Corra's, even her rosebud mouth. A girl with peachy skin and olive eyes like Ewan's. Like mine. Both with tiny pointed tipped ears. Tears were flowing freely. They were real. Healthy. I rushed back to the cash register and placed the dressing gown on the counter.

"And will you be purchasing the rabbits as well?" She

pointed to the two bunnies clasped in my hands, one pink, one taupe, barely sacks of velour with embroidered eyes and small grins, yet tall ears. I swallowed and said of course. Really, considering the amount of money I spent, I should have stayed home to work. It was early evening, seven or eight, when I sat down to have a Pimm's and cheesy chips. Knowing the babies were fine made me feel lighter. That vision was a gift, and I sent a thank you to the Goddesses who blessed me with them. While I was still encaged in this realm, half of who I really was, just knowing those two perfect beings were thriving was a beautiful thing indeed.

CHAPTER 44

CADEYRN

Landing smack on my face in the dirt in what appeared to be a vineyard threw me. My clothes were soaked from the temple pool, and my palm was healed, though covered in dried blood. Where was I? I walked through the vineyard, hoping I wasn't in America, where I'd be shot as a trespasser. It had occurred to me to wear a fitted hat that covered my ears as I had left the smoky quartz in the temple, so there was nothing to cloak me. At the edge of the vineyard was a sign pointing into town written in French. So, I assumed I was somewhere in France. With no money, pointed ears, and soaking wet. Fantastic. In town, attached to a gambling counter, was a money wiring window. Thank the gods. Problem was that it would take a week to receive it. So in this tiny town I stayed, being a farm hand and working behind the bar at the local tavern just to have a place to stay. Utterly ridiculous to have been able to cross realms, yet I was stuck in bloody France because I had no funds.

On the first day, I asked the owner of the bar if I could use his internet. In a brief search, Neysa was nowhere, but I saw mention of her trading. The barman kicked me off the computer shortly thereafter. A few days later, I tried calling Neysa's old number, but it was already linked to someone else. After a week of wearing the same clothes that I washed out each night, my funds were finally transferred. I took a taxi into Bordeaux and got on a train to Paris so I could connect to London.

The rail journey slid me back into memories of the train we took from Madrid after Neysa and Corraidhín had gone off to Peru. Gods those two. Though my cousin had sustained a grave injury, the memory sent pangs through me of a time when there was more possibility. She wasn't mine back then, even though I was hers. But she was safe. This abyss of hell I'd been going through for a year—more, even—hadn't opened yet. It wasn't just that I missed her, or that I was pissed off with myself for pushing her through the damned Veil. It was that every sound, every action, reminded me of her laugh, her evergreen eyes, and her freckled nose. Every time I smelled the sea and the wild open water, I was crippled with remembering the way she told me stories with her head on my stomach, kissing my chest each time the story paused. I missed my best friend. My mate. My own soul living outside my body.

From London I went straight to Barlowe Combe, half hoping Neysa wasn't at the house so I could at least bathe and change before I saw her. I was going to burn these clothes. Upon arriving at the manor that used to be my home, I saw the dark windows, felt the emptiness, and immediately regretted hoping she wasn't home.

Remnants of when she and Ewan lived in the house remained. Wellies by the door, raincoats, lists and journals, chemical equations. I hadn't realized the work they put into figuring out how to collapse the Veil. She had explained the chemical makeup, but the amount of notes I could see indicated far more than I gave them credit for. Those two were brilliant.

Among the scattered notes was a dead phone. Once I plugged it in, hoping for some sort of clue, and knowing full well I'd not get one, I looked up Neysa's recently played music. I knew she missed it while in the fae realm, so I was curious what she listened to whilst she and Ewan had been here. What had she last listened to when she assumed she was heading to the Veil to die? The tune was a rasping emotional voice paired with a strumming guitar. Some male singing about the end of a relationship that had been wrong from the start. The singer seemed to have fucked up as massively as I had, repeatedly saying he was picturing her there in her wedding dress. "The Fall of Rome." Bloody hell, Neysa.

My laptop was dead. The electricity worked, so I hoped that all the bills were still being paid. It was mid-afternoon by the time I got in, and I realized that bar a half-empty jar of peanut butter that probably wasn't safe to eat, there was nothing in the house. I showered and shaved quickly, then changed to run into town and see what I could find to eat, and maybe see if my wife had been back at all.

She always teased me that no matter what I was dressed for, or where we were, my attire was the same. I pulled on a pair of trousers that I used for everyday wear, as well as training, and paired them with a light grey button-down shirt. It was stuffy and hot everywhere this time of year, so I rolled up my sleeves and grabbed the other smoky quartz before walking into town. Time didn't change much here. I'd lived in this village the better part of a century, and it bumbled along with the world, not quite growing up. I supposed that was why I loved it.

Tilly's shop hadn't changed at all either, except she had the door wide open to get some air inside. When I walked in, she beamed.

"As I live and breathe, Cade! Where have you been, love?" I smiled back at her. A man, sandy blond with glasses and a pompous smirk, snapped his attention to me. For some reason I found myself checking my dagger, though he seemed more the academic type.

"Hiya, ma'm. I've had business overseas. Just got in today and found I'm out of food. How's the shop? You alright?" Cloaking stones worked on my appearance, but my accent was something else entirely. And the English could always sniff out a false accent, so I had to focus.

"'Course. Yeah, yeah. Sit down and let me fix you something. Been loads of commotion here in town. Marriages and babies. Mike the taxi driver died. Heart attack. Shame." She was rambling, and I could barely breathe. She hadn't been here then.

"Don't fuss about for me, Tilly. Truly." I was so tired it was hard to keep my accent in place. I kept slipping, and it lilted ever so slightly. The sandy-haired fellow kept staring at me. His eyebrows were up, mouth a bit agape. I turned my full attention to him whilst Tilly heated up something for me. I didn't care what. I'd had cheese and bread every single bloody day in France. He shrunk a bit when I met his gaze, then pushed his glasses on his nose and sat up. Something about him piqued memories of a gangly teenager running into me full speed whilst playing football.

"Hiya," I said, trying to be polite. "You okay, mate?"

"Och! Cade, this is my son. My youngest, Dean." She came round and gave him a pat on the cheek before bringing me my plate. I sniffed and my eyes met his. He smelled of Neysa.

"You'll never guess who he has come across," she said like a child on Yule morning.

"Can't imagine," I answered, still locking eyes with the fellow, who was sweating now. I could smell the fear enrobing him. He was several inches shorter than I was and didn't seem like he did much in the way of training. I bet he did that cycle class nonsense I'd seen. Or yoga.

"That tenant of yours, Neysa. She's been gone too, and I missed seeing her face around here."

"Yes, I understand how you would." I took bite after bite, keeping my eyes on the man.

"Dean met her in Oxford when he was doing a lecture. He's a professor, you know. They have become close. I do wish you could have brought her today, Dean. How lovely it would have been to see her, don't you think, Cade?" I ate the entire godsdamned meat pie and bread roll in less than two minutes and felt like I was going throw up. What did I do now? Did I want to ask if they were together? Was it something I could handle knowing without burning this place to the ground? *You're not a monster.* I left money on the table, thanked Tilly, and jerked my chin to the man to follow me out. We walked a block or so to where there was a gap in the buildings along the High Street.

"Cadeyrn?" he asked. My shoulders ached from the way my body shook.

"She's okay?" I asked.

"She is. Rather, she has a lot to get through. I believed her. But it still seemed impossible. You healed?"

She told him then. Our story. I pinched my nose, squeezing my eyes shut. She would only tell him—

"She thinks you're dead," he blurted.

"You're close? To her, I mean." Of course they were.

"Not like that. I would like that. But she . . . loves you, mate."

It was as if I couldn't get enough air in my lungs. I supposed this was how Neysa felt when she had her anxiety attacks.

"Where is she?"

"Lives in Richmond. Want to call?" He pulled out his phone and thrust it at me.

"No. I want to see her. Would you mind giving me her address? Please." I felt like a child. He did, and I set off at a run to drive into the city and catch a train to Richmond. It took me another three hours until I got off the train. I didn't know Richmond well and wandered, following the directions on my phone. I turned down one particular street, as it was supposed to cross with the street on which she lived, and there were shops and cafes all along. It seemed like a nice place to live. Perhaps the closest I had seen to Laichmonde.

The sun was in that low place that seemed to dust everything in a fair light. I slowed my walk and came to a complete and sudden stop, someone slamming into me from behind. He muttered an apology and moved on. I stood staring. She was sitting at a table. Alone. Drinking what looked to be a Pimm's, an empty plate beside the glass. I would bet there had been cheesy chips on it. I was about ten meters behind her, staring at her bare shoulders where the sun was hitting. The breeze blew in from behind me, and I saw goose bumps rise on her arms and back. She stiffened and looked around. I couldn't move. Fucking hell; I couldn't move. Then she turned and saw me, and I noticed she was still wearing her ring. Her hands went to her mouth, and her nose became swollen and red. I walked over and asked if I could sit. I'm not sure if what came out was English or Aoifsing, or some degenerate mix of both, but she whimpered and stood, throwing her arms around me.

CHAPTER 45

NEYSA

For a minute I really thought it was another vision. I thought they had started back up again and here was a vision of him. It honestly took me looking at his clothes to realize he was real. Whatever he said when he walked over was gibberish, but it didn't matter, because I wanted to feel him. His hands scraped against my bare back and my blood heated.

"You're bigger," I said stupidly, running my hands over his arms and chest.

Those eyes I missed raked all over me. I put my hand flat against his stomach, and his mouth was on mine. He lifted me from the ground, my legs locking around his waist. Whistles and cheers, hoots and whoops came from all around us, and we didn't care. We were lost in the shared breath and pull of my lip between his incisors. After finally breaking apart, I dragged him to my dumb little flat with its negligent amount of furniture and stuffy air.

"I thought—thought you were dead. Say something. You're making me nervous."

"Are you happy here?" he asked me, eyebrows pinched together. I knew he didn't fully mean in this flat.

"No." I didn't even have a real couch to sit on. It was embarrassing. We perched on two dumb chairs, one of which was a desk chair where I worked. "Were you happy?" I asked, unable to look at him. He snorted.

"Corraidhín called me a mega tsunami. She said I was building like a giant wave that would destroy them all."

"That's a very serious accusation. The mega tsunami is supposed to take out the entire Eastern Seaboard."

"So I've heard."

"Was she right?"

"Well, I wasn't in the Atlantic, so it wasn't a perfect analogy." My phone buzzed. I ignored it, but a text came through as well. "Check it. It's okay." I looked. Dean, of course. He had been texting for a few hours now. No one else really contacted me. Just asking if I was okay.

"Just a friend checking in," I said, texting back a quick *Yes*.

"Tilly's son?"

I nearly choked.

"He's nice. Likes you. Knew who I was, which threw me." He was looking down at his hands. I understood now.

"He's very nice and we get on well. He's not you. No one else is you. Now tell me how you got here before I stop listening."

Arms locked around me while he spoke, not letting either of us move an inch. I sat on his lap on the chair that seemed like it was going to break.

"You're tired, Cadeyrn." I traced under his eyes with my finger and kissed his eyelids. "Want to sleep?"

He rumbled a laugh against me. His hand sat on my lap, atop my gauzy cotton dress. I touched his wedding band and couldn't help a sob that ripped out. Cadeyrn kissed my shoulder.

"I'm sorry," he said. "I'm so sorry."

I turned to him. "For what?"

"I pushed you through. The worst part was that I knew that somehow it would happen, that's why I was so horrible. I kept trying to get you away. It was too fast. Kíra and the sword. It was too fast."

I unbuttoned his shirt and ran my hands along the scar on his stomach. I knew it wouldn't have healed completely. Knew there had to be a scar. Just as there was a nasty scar on my shoulder where I had been cut.

"How long did it take to heal?" He looked down, then back to me.

"Not sure exactly. They kept me asleep for almost three months." He placed his head in his hands.

"I'm sorry," I said, touching that scar and smoothing my hands over his stomach.

He caught my lip, his incisor nicking me. I smiled against him. His hand moved to scrunch my dress until his hands were sliding along the inside of my thighs. Though any magic we had was muted, heat pulsed between us, throbbing in time to our hearts and movements.

"It's so hot in here," he murmured.

"Mmm, yes, and you've just made it worse." I was already slick with sweat as his hand slid up the sensitive inner part of my thigh then up my hip. The other hand moved along my ribs and the sides of my breasts. I laid my hand on him, stroking through the fabric of his trousers.

"Did you miss these?" I was touching the outside of his training trousers.

"Comfort is unparalleled. Fae activewear is lacking." I laughed, tracing him with my thumb. "And far too thick." He groaned. So did the rickety chair under us. I stood, pulling him to me. He untied my dress from the neck and watched it drop. I pulled his trousers off and looked at him in his undershorts, the vee of muscles pointing exactly where I was thinking I wanted to go. Every inch of him seemed bigger, cut with muscle. I wasn't complaining one bit.

His hands wrenched me forward by the hips, callouses scraping against my skin. We walked, uncharacteristically calm, to the bedroom, and he laughed at my twin bed. Before I was able to lay down, he stopped, kneeling in front of me. Oh gods. When he looked up at me, those eyes shadowed from his dark brows and lashes, I had to lean against the wall. He hoisted my leg over his shoulder and fastened his mouth to me. A thousand lights exploded in my vision and the room was fully black with pulsating white lights. Heat rose off his skin in waves, coating him and me both. My hands were buried in his hair, pushing him closer, but I was losing my ability to stand. We moved to the bed, giggling like teenagers. Once he was seated inside me, our bodies slippery in the heat, I took his face in my hands.

"I want to go home. With you. I never want to have to leave you," I told him, kissing the corners of his mouth.

He moved inside me, rocking us together slowly. I lifted my hips, grabbing his backside. We dragged it out as long as possible, kissing, touching, moving, sweating, until the pressure that built was so intense, I went over the edge, crying out his name. He kept moving, lifting my legs up, moving his mouth down the inside of my raised calves. I grabbed the headboard and pushed up my hips until he growled my name, his eyes lighting up with peridot fire.

"My God, I've missed you," I said, not letting him move.

"You have no idea." He drew lazy lines along my arms and into my hair.

"Admit it. You thought I was crazy," I said to Dean a couple days later as we sat in Tilly's shop.

"Not crazy per se, Pet. There was a question in my mind though. You're different now. Happy."

I grabbed his hand and kissed it. "I am. Thank you. For being my friend."

"Your servant, ma'am." He gave me his signature roguish smirk.

"You are a handsome thing. Go get yourself a girl, for God's sake." Tilly came by and was glum. "She's not happy with me, I'm afraid," I told him. I quirked my mouth to the side.

"Yeah, well. She'll get over it. Now, give us a kiss, Pet, and go live your life while we mortals slug through the daily, gloriously unaware of the lost princess." I rolled my eyes and kissed his cheek before leaving. "I will miss you," he called after me. "You know I was falling for you." He winked, making my heart clench.

"I think it's because of you, Dean. Meeting you. It all came together. I'll always be grateful." I ducked out of the shop and headed back to the estate to ready myself.

France was, for all intents and purposes, a pain in the ass to get to. The hope was that we could open the Veil here in the grotto, close to where the original one had been. After promising not to wear a grey jumper, I put on my leathers, and we each packed a bag as though going on holiday. From the bag of gifts the mystic had given me, I pulled a green agate that was fused together with clear quartz. We stood in the grotto, the light glowing ephemeral blue, and sliced our palms. Blood rushed to the stones waiting under us, swirling around the crystals and the etchings we had made in the dirt. I thought of home. My brother and Corra, the babies, Silas. We pressed our palms together, blood mingling, and kissed.

Take us home, I thought.

Home is us, Cadeyrn responded, though I hadn't realized our connection was intact again. I knelt and placed my free hand on the ground, the other still holding my mate's. Allowing a surge of power to release, it went into the earth. As though waking at my touch, a shimmer in the air told us the Veil had opened. Keeping our hands and arms clasped together, we stepped through.

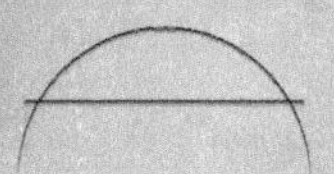

CHAPTER 46

Somebody let a herd of wild boar in the house. That was the only explanation for the amount of noise that woke me. My first instinct was to put the pillow over my head. This manor was large, but when the babies kicked off, the sound travelled. However, this wasn't the little ones. This was my sister, and she was raging. Cadeyrn and Ewan had left a week ago to check in with Ainsley Mads and her crew of hairy citizens. I consider myself a fairly rugged chap, but the amount of hair and girth on those males was astounding. Corraidhín was unusually quiet in Ewan's absence, but I suppose that was to be expected. She wasn't entirely pleased that I was bedding Saski either, so oftentimes our conversations were short.

Once I realized the noise wasn't ceasing, I pulled on a shirt and headed down the hall. Ewan had barely come in the front door, his face and hair windblown. And he was spooked. Cadeyrn wasn't with him. Corraidhín was banging him on the chest and screaming in the aulde language. He stood taking it, which had me worried. Saski came up behind me, closer than casual. Ewan looked up the stairs to where we stood and met my eyes.

"He opened a Veil," Ewan said to me.

"You helped him!" my sister screamed. "You let him go gods know where. We don't even know if she is in the same place! He could be lost, Ewan!" He grabbed her hands to keep her from beating him. He had to be fairly bruised by now.

"You knew he was going, Corraidhín," he said to her in a placating manner.

She laid her head against his chest and cried. Actually cried. She hadn't wept since . . . I couldn't remember. Not even after our parents were killed.

"I didn't think it would work," she whimpered. I didn't know what to do. I wanted to go to her, but she had her husband. I wanted to hit something. I didn't know if I was more pissed that he did it, or that he didn't ask me to help him. I knew he was bothered by this thing with Saski. Perhaps that was why, but I just didn't know.

"When, Ewan?" I asked.

"I stayed one night there, and I came straight back. So, four days. I rode hard. I don't know if you knew, but Neysa had gone to the Goddess Kalima's temple in Prinaer. The Goddess accepted her. That's where Cadeyrn went. She must have done the same."

"He offered himself to the Goddess?" I yelled.

Saski tugged at my arm and I snarled, pulling out of her grasp. She hissed.

"No. I think he called upon her for advice. She must have answered, because he came out of the pool and we bled and opened the Veil."

"You? You bled?" Corraidhín was thrumming, pulling in and out of her corporeal self. Ewan slumped to the floor where he stood and put his head between his knees. "You are lucky you didn't get thrust through with him. Did it close?"

"No," he whispered.

I walked down the stairs barefoot. They could be anywhere. The house was mostly dark; only the sconces by the door were lit. My sister was totally mist. Likely gone outside in my storm. The rain was falling in thick sheets.

"On Aedtine Day, he and I saw her," he began. I clenched my fists. "We were staring into the flames talking about her. He never did, and we spoke about her. He was almost gone, Silas. He was letting go. I could feel it. Then we both saw her, scrying and using her blood. He realized that's how she opened the Veil. Her power transcends realms much like his. It doesn't seek full authority from one realm or another. So, he thought if he did the same that he could try to find her. I helped, seeing as she and I are blood. He didn't tell you because—"

"Because of me," Saski said.

"Not everything is about you," I snapped, feeling like a toe rag for doing so.

"Because of you, yes," Ewan said. Well, fuck. Saski made an obscene gesture at me. "He didn't understand how you were able to move on."

"I haven't fucking moved on! She's my mate too!" I barked, and once again, felt like a piece of shite. "Saski," I said.

She held up a hand. "I'm not thick, Silas. You don't think I know who you want when you're with me?" She walked back through the hallway, and a door clicked shut behind her.

"Fucking hell, Ewan."

He nodded. We had no idea where either of them would have crossed, or where they would even cross back as it wasn't clear if the Veil he opened would have held. What a cluster. If only there were a topographical link to the human realm. If we could lay a map of here over a map of there and have points match up, but it simply did not work that way. When Neysa was taken in Turkey, Cadeyrn and I tried. Even if it lined up, our magnetic pole positions or whatever Neysa had said so long ago, shift. I told Ewan to get some sleep. He was a wreck.

CORRAIDHÍN WAS in the stables where they told me Neysa's *baethaache* had stayed. She was quietly rocking back and forth. By the gods, I had never seen her like this. I put my arms around her. Losing them both. I would give up being mated to Neysa for them to be safe. To return, yes, but mostly just to know that they were safe. I had likely erased any chance I had with *Trubaíste* as soon as I began this thing with Saski. I was a fool, but I was unable to stop myself. We stayed in the stables until morning. Ewan brought Pim and Efa out to us. Efa was already starting to crawl, and she was all over Ewan, trying to scramble down to her mum. I was never a baby type of male, yet these two had me wrapped round their little fingers. I liked to tell them stories about their parents and their brave auntie who had a fierce beastie. I was sure I sounded like a right tosser doing it, but it made me happy to share with them, and they babbled and smacked kisses at me, so I couldn't be that bad, I supposed.

We headed inside, and I made for my room, hoping to sleep for an hour or so before meeting with Cyrranus. Saski was coming out of her room, ready for the day. As she was passing me, I reached for her. She stopped.

"Why do you bother with me?" I asked her. "You're so beautiful. You're a queen. You should find someone less . . ." I pointed to my head as though it were exploding. She moved to me.

"I should. You're a shit to me. Well, sometimes. But I like a challenge." She leaned in and kissed me. It wasn't really Neysa

I wanted when we were together. Saski was wild and hungry, and it loosened something inside of me. Had I not been spent physically and emotionally, I might have pulled her back to her room. Instead, I kissed her back and said I would see her later.

Convincing everyone that it was safe to use their Festaeran steel again was proving to be tricky. I felt bad for Cyrranus taking on this position. Arneau did not go quietly into the night. We found folk who had sworn against him dead or incapacitated. There was nothing concrete to pin on him. I was getting frustrated; I knew Cyrranus must be tearing his hair out. We met in his new residence in Craghen, the coastal village where Cadeyrn and Neysa were married. Reynard was there too, having taken up a home nearby. They both could sense that something was up with me, but it wasn't the time to share. Especially since we didn't have a real idea of what was happening.

The day of the meeting, when Cadeyrn made Etienne piss himself, and Corraidhín and I made it all the worse, set us on a dangerous path with these two Maesarrans. They were out for blood. Cyrranus showed me notes from spies we had on the two sketchy bastards. They both were still fortifying their homes and would not let any servants outside. I felt bad for Arneau's wife. She must have been thoroughly unhappy to have brought me into their home and willingly sold out her husband. I couldn't save everyone, I knew. However, if she were being mistreated before, then surely, it was far worse now. Perhaps I could get her out. Mentioning it to Cyrranus, he said it would likely make things far worse.

"Think about it, Silas. He sees her as his property. If you

make any sort of move to help her, you will have taken from him. More so than you have already. He could strike back hard and we don't need that."

"A wife is not property," I countered.

"Yes, you and I know that. But Arneau is a prick. If you want to see it in a different light, think about it like this. I never really cared for Cadeyrn. He thinks it's because of Solange. Perhaps once it was, but I always saw him as feeling entitled," he said.

Cadeyrn never felt entitled to anything his entire existence. Even as children he moped about, trying not to get under foot.

"Though he loved Neysa, and I know he never mistreated her, if based on how I felt about him, I felt like I should go in and rescue her, what would he do? What would you do?"

This was a stupid point. We'd kill the little shite.

"I understand what you are getting at, Cyrranus, but everything you've just alluded to is a bunch of old wank. Yeah, it's diplomatically unsound to pull the wife. I get it."

I couldn't leave it alone. I knew you couldn't have everyone like you and all that, but I couldn't have Cyrranus, who always risked himself for *Trubaíste*, thinking poorly of my cousin.

"Cadeyrn was the least entitled male I've ever met, Cyrranus. I know you never saw eye to eye with him, and he puts up that wall, but I want you to know. Cadeyrn always contended with his birthright. Never relished it. And he never thought he deserved Neysa. You should know that."

Reynard came in with a book in hand, bow slung on his shoulder. His brows were pinched together, locking eyes with me.

"What do you mean *was*?" he asked, quiet as the grave. I looked up at him. Cyrranus raised his eyebrows. "Silas." Reynard stalked closer, going a bit pale. Cyrranus stood and felt Reynard's face. That was odd. "What do you mean,

Cadeyrn *was* always the least entitled male? What has happened?" Ah, fuck it all. The weasel never missed a beat.

I felt like old fabric that's been pulled and scratched and worn down to its barest threads. Looking up at these two, I realized I had missed the very obvious fact that they were a couple. I closed my eyes, then told them about Cadeyrn.

I DIDN'T KNOW if Saski was speaking to me or not. I never knew with females whether I should make myself scarce or chase them about. Most of my life, I would seek and destroy, as my sister would say. It was quick and fun and done. Then, after three hundred years of that, Neysa came in like a battering ram to the head. Saski, I didn't know. Maybe it was because she was still bloody here under the same roof, or because she looked so much like *Trubaíste*, but what little we had between us was still there. In any case, I had to seek her out and speak of bigger issues. I found her in her room. It was late in the evening when I returned from Craghen, two days after Ewan told us about Cadeyrn. I knocked, and heard the whoosh of wind, and the door opened, though she stood on the opposite side of the room.

"We need to talk," I said. I could have kicked myself. Never a good way to begin. She smirked and flipped her hair back in the way Corraidhín did when she was ready to take on anything slung at her.

"I suppose we do." I stepped in further, and the wind shut the heavy door behind me. She had on a silk dressing gown that wasn't fully done up, likely having just bathed by the heat coming off her skin.

"I've just been to see Cyrranus and Reynard. All the

subterfuge we have been expecting is starting to come to a head. With Cadeyrn's possible . . ." I swallowed and couldn't bring myself to say it. I literally stood there for a moment trying to breathe and reorganize my thoughts. She stepped closer to me and grabbed my hand. "Things could get testy. And you are heir to Heilig."

"Ah." She dropped my hand and turned to the window. "What would you have me do?"

"Are you ready to take your throne? I've sent a hawk to Basz informing him of what's happening here. I haven't mentioned my cousin. Not yet. But it may be time to take what's yours."

"Mine," she murmured. "What's really mine? I wasn't born to rule, Silas. Arik, maybe. Ludek, he wouldn't want it, but you can see how he would be the best of us. Pavla adored him, and he her. She was wilder than I am. Can you imagine that?" She looked over her shoulder with a small smile. I touched her face. She had never spoken of Pavla. "Pavla would take on the bloodiest fight. Like your Neysa, I suppose. Never asked permission. Just went in. Our mother hated it. Father treated us all equal, but when Pavla died, I swore there was a relief in father. I saw it in glimpses, and it scared me. As though he always feared that one day, she would take his throne. Or mine. If I saw it, then Ludek must have. And mother. Arik and I just kept on. Like spoiled children. Though we mourned as well. Differently. She was my sister. I know you see me as wicked." She sniffed a laugh. I didn't laugh. I went closer to her. "But I can love. I love my siblings, Silas. I would do anything for them. If Ludek hadn't killed father, I would have. Because father killed Pavla. With what he involved himself in. He killed her, and I would have killed him. What does that make me?"

I placed my hands on her hips and turned her to me, my hand going to the back of her head.

"Loyal. Determined."

"Not wicked?" she asked. I was taking in her eyes, dim and sad.

"Wicked? Surely. Evil? No. Your wickedness is what I like." I had my mouth close to hers.

"Do you? Like me?" Her voice was so small. I smiled.

"Occasionally. When you're not trying to crush my balls for one thing or another." I touched my lips to hers. "Perhaps then as well. Sometimes." I felt her smile against me.

"I don't know whether I should go back. I don't wish to take the throne. I don't want it."

"My cousin always told me we don't always want the lot we are given. We make the best of it."

She pulled back and had a knowing look on her face.

"That's what you're doing, is it not?" she asked. "Making the best of wanting what you have?"

Hell. This was why I didn't do relationships. Fuck.

"What do you want me to say, Saski? That I don't still love Neysa? That I don't think about her all the time? That I don't know if she's dead or if she will come back with Cadeyrn and that might kill me more? She is my mate, whom I cannot truly have when she is the only thing in my life I have ever wanted. Is that what you wanted me to say?"

Corraidhín would have kicked my ass for that, but it just came out.

"I am a broken male, Saski. Utterly destroyed, and there is something in me that will never be whole because I am a part of a bond that she doesn't want. You could have everything. I do like you. I like being with you. I like your wicked mouth and your wicked body, and the time we spend. But you could have someone who can love you completely. Not this." I gestured to myself. She cocked her head to the side and looked at me like a contemplative firedrake.

"I don't want anyone else," she said at last. "I want you, no matter how broken. If you truly do not want me, then I shall go. But I think you might want me and are just a bit afraid of what that might mean. Think about it."

I turned to leave, knowing a dismissal when I heard one.

"I didn't say to leave." So, maybe it wasn't a dismissal. Godsdamned females and their mixed messages. I turned back to her, and she had dropped her dressing gown.

"My wicked mouth and wicked body want to play."

Deep, poisonous shite.

BACK IN CRAGHEN, I met with Cyrranus, who was attempting to sort out trade details between Maesarra and Saarlaiche for Ewan. At some point I needed to get back home and look into readying for the autumn harvest. It was time to take on new workers. I had tried to get more of those grinder machines built. A sort of tribute to Neysa. They needed checking in on. I hadn't told Cadeyrn about them, not sure how he would feel.

The village here in Craghen was in full season, as it was a draw for wealthy travelers and those who would travel to sell their goods. I wandered the boulevard before seeking out Cyrranus at the tavern he had indicated. A family, obviously not very well off, had set up a stall across from the harbor, selling jewelry and trinkets. I gravitated toward it. There was a necklace, silver with a delicate bird stretched from one end of the chain to the next. When I looked closer, the bird had a dagger in its beak, tiny chips of topaz for eyes. It reminded me of Saski's sword. I purchased the necklace before I thought better of it, not even bothering to haggle. I walked off briskly, shoving the thing in my satchel. I had never seen Neysa on her birthday. Never gave her a gift apart from the stupid Christmas tree. I used to get gifts for females all the time. Tokens of lacking affection, apologies, parting gifts. Lina had received three or four herself. The last she had left back on my doorstep. I didn't blame her. I would have given Neysa the world, and yet, there was nothing I had bothered to get her. Time. There was never time. And she was never really mine.

Cyrranus was meeting with Alan, his minister of trade, trying to establish a presence while we worked out how many local tradesmen and seasonal workers we could take on to Saarlaiche to work the *araíran-aoír* nut orchard. I slid into the table with the two males and pulled the list they were compiling.

"Five hundred more trees were planted last spring. They may not be producing yet, but they will need tending. Perhaps part-time workers would do. Let's pull another twenty."

I had another job that needed workers, but there were many in Saarlaiche after the rebellion who needed income. Widows and children coming of age. I could not outsource anymore positions yet. We had always taken care of our own. Our orchards had sustained generations and I intended to keep that going. My heart was not in war. My heart was in Saarlaiche and taking care of its fae. Cyrranus seemed twitchy. I waited until Alan left and asked him why.

"Reynard has gone to check on his mother."

I drank from my ale and waited.

"He thinks that perhaps she would like to leave his father." Oh gods. "You can see why I might worry."

"He's a quick weasel, Cyrranus. I'm certain he will be in and out without incident." He nodded. "It isn't my business, but I'm curious. How long has it been going on?" I asked him. "Between you two." His smile was sly.

"Things were set into motion when you lot were in Laorinaghe last year." He answered with a flick of his wrist like it was old news. They suited each other. "He had a lot to sort through, though. Hasn't had an easy life, that one."

"I always thought you might have had a thing for Neysa," I said, tapping my chin.

He laughed. "Nothing beyond my thinking she was worth saving. I liked her heart. Her spirit, you get?"

"I do," I said, but it came out like a scuffle of feet on base boards. We wrapped up the meeting, and I went back with him to wait for Reynard at his home on the outskirts of town. My mind kept wandering to my cousin. I hadn't known. What Ewan said about him letting his immortality wither away. I hadn't seen it, and I should have. After that brawl we had in the hills above Laorinaghe whilst Neysa was kept under, we hadn't been close. It was torture. He was moving through the provinces like some fire beast from the hell realms, and I confronted him. What was it doing to his soul? If Neysa woke and he was ash or unrecognizable, what would it do to her? He threw it back in my face. He said he knew what was between us; what would it do to her when she found out I was dropping my trousers for bits of information? We had screamed and hit and slammed each other around until we called it quits. He was my brother, and we were at odds for a year. So, I wasn't paying attention enough to realize he was letting go.

Reynard didn't return that evening. A message was sent saying he was staying with his mother whilst his father was away for the night. Solid worry settled in my gut. Though the weasel knew how to play a game of courts and pawns, I worried he might have been blind-sided by his parents. By his mother rather. The same message came the following night. On the third evening, there was no note and no sign of Cyrranus's partner. As there was little for me to do, and Cyrranus was pacing and snapping, I slipped out and made my way to Reynard's parents' estate.

One window was lit, the rest of the house dark. I snuck in

the back garden gate and was face to face with a great, drooling, long-toothed aphrim. Fuck it all. You'd think in three centuries I would have gotten used to the stench of these fuckers. It was amazing that they made such enviable clothing and such when every bit of their body—from their palm-sized black and brown scales to their sword-length snouts—stunk of rotten fruit and diseased shite. I didn't want to kill it and leave evidence that I was there, but I really didn't want to be dinner for this slick-skinned monstrosity. It growled and sniffed, moving slowly.

I put my shield up, as I should have done earlier, blocking it from scenting or hearing me. They were blind and relied only on other senses. It was confused and went a bit wild eyed, then took off away from me. I exhaled, bending over.

The kitchen door was on a latch, so I slid my dagger in and up, unhooking it to let myself in. The kitchen was warm, so someone had made a meal. The light was likely for a servant who was still here. I opened myself to my emotions and had a light rain falling outside, then dissolved into the moisture in the air. In the daylight, I would have been visible, but in this darkened house, I was a wraith.

Room after room, there was no sign of anyone. It looked as though the lady of the house had her own sleeping quarters. I wasn't surprised. I'd seen plenty of similar situations in other houses. Especially after hundreds of years. I couldn't imagine being stuck with Etienne for that amount of time. It made me want to gag. His mother wasn't a pearl; don't get me wrong. From what I've heard, she had always been a thorny bramble, but Etienne was a fine example of a tainted soul.

I moved around the lady's room, looking—looking for what, I don't know. I felt her bed linen and pulled back the duvet. A note. The size of two fingers. *"Ballaíche,"*—*boy*—was all it said.

Was she leaving a clue? Was the clue for me or bait for

Reynard? I realized then how tired I was. How little I had slept lately. If Francois, Reynard's mother, had left more clues, they might be hidden deeper. A crystal jar sat upon her bedside table. The kind that holds creams and such. I unscrewed the lid and lifted the inner layer. Another line of script: "*Aídech á caráed*"—*help my love.*

I guessed I had to keep looking. I had nothing else to do tonight anyway. It still felt like murky water. The second clue and the notes, like the first, could have been a lure for my friend just as easily as it could have been a plea for help in saving her.

In her wardrobe were loads of shoes. She could never have worn that many. I touched a golden pair, embroidered with arrows and trees. Stuffed into the toe was another paper. "*Maíth mise*"—*forgive me.* Well, that didn't make me feel any less confuckingfuddled. I searched for a length of time and found nothing else. Slipping from the house, careful not to attract another aphrim, I made my way back across the countryside to Cyrranus.

THE TRUTH WAS that we didn't know anything yet. Francois was never what I would call a full quiver. Perhaps Reynard pulled her out while his father was still gone. Where Etienne had slithered off to begged more of a question in my mind. Cyrranus and I had both sent hawks to find the two of them, but there was a block on their magic. If my friend had been trying to hide his mother, that made sense. Etienne was a shady arse, so it didn't surprise me at all that the hawk came back to us. It took me until midmorning to reach Craghen. Cyrranus was out, which gave me time to figure out whether it was worth telling him. If it were my family, I would want to know. Even if it made me crazed. Even if it were nothing to be concerned about. Though, deep down, I felt it was a concern.

I sent messages to my shadows to keep an eye out for Etienne or anything amiss that could be linked to him or Arneau.

When Cyrranus didn't return that night, I started to panic. So, I waited. I asked his servants where he had gone, and they didn't know. I sent a male out to search for him—check taverns and inns. I called on Alan, though it was well into the evening by this point.

"Apologies, my lord," I greeted him as he stood, obviously ready for bed. Gods, I wished I were too. "I was wondering if you had seen or heard from Cyrranus since our last meeting. I am planning to set off in the morning and he hasn't returned with the information I requested."

Alan ushered me into his home. It felt empty and old. He was a decent-looking chap, and nice enough, if not a bit boring, but there was no hint of a partner here, male nor female. I wondered if that's how I might seem to some. Fuck, I needed sleep.

"I've not heard from him, Silas," he began. "But I received these. The first was yesterday, the second just this evening." He handed me slips of paper. "The first was stuck to my shed with an arrow. The second was delivered with a parcel I had ordered from a clothier in town." He turned a shade of red, and I decided I really didn't want to know what the parcel was.

Don't let it break the system. Follow the money. Shite. Reynard.

The second was penned differently. The same hand that penned the notes in Francois's room. *It is for time he will exchange my heart.*

Where was Neysa and her riddle skills when you needed her? I pulled at my chin and asked to see where the shed was. Surely enough, it was just off a small road at the edge of his property. The shot could have been made by a skilled archer, and I didn't know of any better than Reynard. There were tracks. Horse and perhaps a small wagon as the indentations weren't very deep despite the layer of packed mud that seemed to hold every imprint. All I could see was that they headed north.

Dawn light had me waking in the parlor of Cyrranus's home where I had fallen asleep against the wall, thinking that something about the clothier didn't sit well. Sometime around midday, the clop of hooves sounded up the drive. My host appeared, looking haggard and hopeless. I didn't have to ask whether he had found anything. Without a word, he thrust a note to me.

Aídech á caráed, was all its said. I followed him into the house, where he made for the kitchen to stuff his face with whatever food was lying around. I showed him the notes. He was devastated. I saw the look. I knew the feeling. I lived with it every single godsdamned day. So, I put a hand on his shoulder.

"I'll go. I'll look for him."

"When we took Neysa," he said, "from the human realm, I could see beyond what he presented. He was an ass," he laughed. "But he never let her suffer. I tried to help her. The others were cruel, but I stayed with her, and Reynard wouldn't let her out of his sight. I knew she was trying to contact you lot. It didn't matter to me, so I said nothing. Reynard saw her and said nothing as well. He gave her his own coin for ale. I don't know why I'm telling you this. I just . . . I need to go. I need to look for him, Silas."

"I can stay here another day or so before I head back to Bistaír. From there we can dispatch more eyes. Yeah?" He agreed and went up to sleep for a bit before setting off.

I pulled out the stupid bird necklace and watched the light glint from the topaz eyes and thought that it was probably a naff gift anyway.

NEYSA

When I had emerged from the Veil in the German woods a year ago, I was stunned. It had happened so much faster than I thought. My body stayed on the ground, frozen and bloody, seeing my husband's face as a sword was rammed through his stomach. The gush of blood that instantly flowed from his nose and mouth. Not being there.

For hours I must have laid in those woods. It grew darker, and I was covered in blood. Many things would start to come check out the smell of death and weakness upon me. What was more, I didn't know how much I would fight when they did. So, I made myself get up, and hid the weapons on myself.

The first place I happened upon was a fish farm. I used a tank to wash up, though I didn't smell much better for it. I had no money, and no chance at this point of charming anyone into helping me when I looked like a roughed-up pickpocket. The first thing I needed was to figure out where the bleeding hell I was. The fish farm had little signage. Some instructions in German, but that didn't mean much. I could have been in Germany, Austria, Switzerland or even middle of nowhere Iowa.

Stumbling from the forest, along a street named Kirschblütenweg, I made my way through the neighborhood into town. Night was falling. I sought out a Kneipe, which was a pub for all intents and purposes, and sat down hard on a wooden chair. The server was a young woman with a brusque manner who, I noticed, didn't look anyone in the eye. It was a very small town, so most eyes were on me. She knelt in front of me and asked what she could bring me.

"Bitte, aber wo bin ich?" I asked quietly. *Where am I?* My German was rudimentary at best.

"Bad Schwartau, Schatz. Soll ich jemanden für dich anrufen?" *Should she call someone for me?* No. No one. I shook my head and looked up at her, not bothering to hide my face anymore. It was bruised, I knew. Most of the blood I thought I had washed off, but there were bruises and lacerations from the fight. She scowled, anger flashing in her eyes. I was told to wait. After a few minutes, she came back with a plate of food and a beer.

"Kostenlos," she said. *On the house.*

She asked me where I needed to go. I didn't know. My first thought was London, but that necessitated money and a passport. The copper-haired waitress said she would drive me to the next larger town, Lübeck, where I could take a train to Hamburg. My passport was in the cottage in Barlowe Combe. If I went to the embassy in Hamburg, I would have to construct a story about being attacked, and I would be taken for medical questioning, which would be an issue as I was not human and not at all cloaked at the moment. Luckily, my hair was long enough that it covered my ears. I was so tired. If I rested, I could try to use some of my gifts. Something to get me through.

In Lübeck, I found a bar and let someone buy me a drink.

After a few, he was pawing at me, so I lifted his phone from his pocket and slipped outside to make a phone call to an old colleague in London.

"Tom," I said, relief washing over me to hear his voice.

"Neysa. For what do I owe this honor? Last time we spoke I was groveling for forgiveness for throwing up on your husband's shoes."

"Well, we're divorced now," I laughed. "So, we don't have to worry about that incident. It was a good concert, though." He chuckled and asked how I had been. "I hate to ask this, but I need a favor. A really big favor."

"Alright. Let's see if I can help."

"I've been through something lately. I can't tell you the whole story, and I am sorry for it, but I am stuck in Germany, and my passport is in a small village a few hours north of you. It's in a cottage I let. I need it sent to me as soon as possible. Once I have it, I can wire money and get to London. I will buy you a case of wine and tickets to whatever show you want to see."

"Christ, Neysa. What's happened? I know you said you can't tell me, but it seems bad."

"I'll be fine. I'm just stuck at the moment. It's safe," I added, as it occurred to me that he might be worried about getting involved. "No one is after me or anything like that."

After a long exhale, Tom agreed. So, I explained where it was and where I would be, needing to get out of this town. I left the phone in the bar. On the street, I lifted the wallet of a young woman too drunk to notice. I was not proud of myself, and I left my crystal necklace in its place in her handbag. I needed to get to Hamburg where I could pick up my passport, wire money, and get the hell off the continent. What could have been a cush hour-long train ride took me nearly four and a half on a stolen bicycle.

I scraped by for two days while I waited for the passport

and wire transfer. I could go without eating. I had dealt with plenty of that in the past year. Once I had money, I bought clothes from the nearest shop and got a cheap hotel room to wash up. Holy Christ, I looked a sight. Bruises marred my neck and shoulders, my eye. The sword wound left a three-inch scar on my shoulder, but it had healed slightly before I crossed. In a panic, I took off my clothes and looked at my forearm. The gold thread was still there. Shaky fingers traced it, wondering where Silas was. Knowing Cadeyrn was dead. Wondering if there was any reality in which I could survive being here. Being without them.

London was the vortex it had always been. My first crush. It lured with its history and glamour. Its decay and growth. In my ulcerative state of being, it was perfect. A way to immerse and disappear. It took me a month to be able to cloak myself. Well, my ears only. Every other semblance of my gifts was gone. Every link I had to my true self. To my mates and family. Gone. All I had was a gold thread. I was drinking and not sleeping. Going out and meeting men, leading them on until the last possible minute, then leaving. Never intending to so much as let any of them kiss me. I was cruel and promiscuous. It took one final night of stupid amounts of alcohol and too much flirting and innuendos. I led one man on too much, and he followed me home, pushing me into my flat. As he laid his hand into the door and shoved me backward, I took it. For the slightest of pauses, I stood there waiting for it. I had brought all this violence on myself, hadn't I?

Then, in my head I heard Reynard's voice saying I was no one's prey, and Corra's voice telling me I was a hellcat like her. All it took was a few well-placed moves and a flick of my small knife across his face and hands to have him backing off. I called 999 and had the man restrained while I waited on the police.

The next day, I left that flat in central London and moved to Richmond. Living a putrefying existence such as I had been was not helping, nor sustainable. Once I settled, I opened my trade accounts back up and jumped back into the market as my funds would run out sooner or later. With my first big paycheck, I got a tattoo matching Silas's just under the gold thread. As promised, I added a beastly wing arcing over the top of the original arch, a single pine bough resting on one side. It embodied who we were to each other, a disastrous love. My mates and me.

CADEYRN HADN'T SAID anything about the tattoo since he found me. I waited for it. I wanted to hear something, but he hadn't said anything regarding Silas either. As we crashed onto the hard floor of Kalíma's temple, I panicked.

"Is he okay?" I pleaded with Cadeyrn with my eyes. "Silas. You haven't said."

He traced my face. "He's fine. Working with Reynard and Cyrranus."

Relief washed over me. We stood in the temple, looking around. I pulled a tiger's eye stone from my pocket and left it with a thanks to the Goddess. We emerged from the temple to a small crowd of horned and hairy warriors with their imposing female leader at the center. Every single one of them had shock on their face—from their pointed ears to their dark, glowing eyes. Ainsley held her broad sword aloft and knelt on the leafy ground, immediately followed by all of her compatriots. Cadeyrn and I looked at one another in confusion.

The hall was bustling with chatter and ale. We wanted to get home. To get somewhere. We were told that the Goddess had never appeared there before and to have both gone and crossed back across realms was a benediction. We were revered and waited upon, and all we wanted to do was leave. Cadeyrn explained to Ainsley that we were in need of horses and it was pertinent that we get back to Bistaír.

I wasn't aware that's where we were going, I said to him. *I have never been.*

He paused.

Sorry. Didn't think that far to tell you. I'm not running at full force right now. Is that okay with you?

It had been only two days since he found me. Ten since he left here and scrounged for work and food in France. I threaded my fingers through his. *Of course.*

Ainsley finally let us go with repealing her bid for the dissolution of the monarchy. We rode off at a clip and began to slow by nightfall. I had been gone a year. There were babies and politics, likely lovers, and changed dynamics. My breathing sped up, heart rate following suit.

"What's wrong?" Cadeyrn asked, coming closer to me as we rode.

I wasn't entirely sure how to express my concerns without sounding like I was afraid of being kicked out of the junior high lunch table. Except that was not dissimilar to how I felt. What if they didn't want me back? Not really. Surely it was easier without me. Less complicated. I should think the memory of me would be better than the reality. It was still unbelievable that I was able to sleep beside him again. Curling my legs and body into his delicious warmth when we made camp, I closed my eyes. He traced the tattoo as I started to fall asleep.

Do you like it? I asked. I heard him swallow. *All I had left of us was the gold thread. I was afraid, every day, that it would disappear one day. So, I had this done. It's all of us.*

It's beautiful. You're . . . so beautiful.

I kissed his shoulder and allowed myself to fall asleep with our gifts intermingling between us.

I could feel Bistaír as we neared. The pull of a place that held the memory of my parents. Held the imprint of my brother. Nerves fired in me, tumbling my stomach in a washer of fear. Outright fear of seeing everyone. Oh, God.

Before we reached the cypress-lined drive leading into the estate, my brother was there, wild-eyed and reaching for the reins. I slid from the horse and embraced him. Pictures in his mind. I saw pictures. As though he were too overcome with emotion to speak to me. In the pictures, I saw the children. Corra.

Cadeyrn had the horses and walked alongside us as my brother led me up the drive to the house. Ewan called for Corra. She popped round the wall to the foyer and clutched a baby closer to her than might, perhaps, be comfortable for the poor thing. I covered my mouth and smiled, reaching for her.

"By the gods, Ama! Take the children. Cannot force them on Neysa straight away. It's uncouth!"

Ama came in, shocked, and took the child from Corra.

"Come, darling. Thank the gods you're still you. And Cadeyrn. I thought I'd lost you both." To my eternal surprise, tears rolled down her face. She swatted herself and stood straighter, grabbing me and smacking my cheeks with kisses.

From the top of the grand staircase, Saski's face appeared, and I knew. I knew she and Silas had been together. She greeted me politely, but fear was rolling off her. My eyes must have been darting around, because Corra told me Silas was in Craghen with Reynard and Cyrranus. My heart sunk a little. I needed to see him too. But I was here and could wait. We sat in the drawing room, Corra insisting I did not have to see the babies yet.

"Don't be stupid, Corra." I held my hands out to Ama, who obliged and placed a squirming child in my arms. She looked at me like I was glowing and grabbed at my hair. I held her little fingers and saw Cadeyrn lift a sleeping child from his cradle. Until this moment I could never have imagined him with a baby. Yet, in this moment, I couldn't imagine why I hadn't. I leaned into the milk warm scent of the one I held and kissed her. Tears fell freely, and she wiggled and babbled.

"I don't know their names," I whispered, ashamed. Ewan walked over.

"This young lass is Efa." He touched her nose, and she giggled. "And this one," he said, tickling the foot flopping in my mate's arms, "is Pim." Pim picked at his uncle's face, and Cadeyrn bent to blow a raspberry on the boy's cheek.

"I had a vision. The only one. The day you came to me, Cadeyrn. I was shopping. I saw their faces. I saw them and I knew they were okay. I thought . . . that it was a gift. To have seen them. Know that they were safe."

Feeling the solid weight of the child in my arms, I thought it might just be the most wonderful feeling in the world.

OUTSIDE, on the edge of the kitchen garden, I sat marveling at the property and just being back in Aoifsing. Feeling like the shell I had been was gradually filling back up. I knew I shouldn't bother Silas, but I had been gone a year, and that entitled me to a few annoyances. Although the last time I'd felt entitled to such, our reunion wasn't so pleasant.

You're probably going to say something along the lines of, "Holy fucking hell." I hope you don't hate me, and I know you're busy, but when you have a moment, it would be nice to see you. I left it at that. I didn't want to rush him. I was here. I was content to be here, breathing in the air I never knew was so different.

Early evening breezes blew, balmy and calm. Things snuffled around in the garden. I walked in to look. To see what grew here when what was inside of me had weathered away systematically while I was gone. Potato vines climbed, and tomatoes grew over a trellis heavy with fruit. Late summer berries and aubergines filled the space. The palm-sized velvet leaves rustled in the increasing night breeze.

"Nice?" Silas asked, a smirk in his voice. I moved so fast I tripped on a cluster of courgette vines. "Just nice to see me? I did not say what you said I would. Mine was far more colorful."

I literally ran and jumped on him, sobbing. Not the silent tears that fell when I saw everyone else. Deep, embarrassing, sobs.

"So snotty, *Trubaíste*. Good to know some things never change." He held me against him, his face in my neck and hair. Moments we stood, creating a cage of arms around each other.

"You're okay?" I pulled back, looking my fill, patting his arms and shoulders. He laughed, then grabbed my arm.

"This is new." He barked a laugh and brushed his thumb over the tattoo. "I like the additions." Then I let it all out. I told him about London and the would-be rapist, Reynard's voice in my head, my drinking and being awful. Finally getting away from it and trying to settle. About Dean and Tilly and thinking I was in a collision course with letting go. I hadn't told Cadeyrn yet. As though I hadn't wanted to spoil being together. I was ashamed at my behavior in London. Silas sat me on his lap, holding my hands while I told him.

"There is nothing at all to be ashamed about." He grabbed my chin. "Nothing."

"There is. I was . . . a different person, Silas. Horrible. I got kicked out of training gyms! I was leading men on and walking away just because I could. Who does that?"

He looked skyward and shrugged.

"I couldn't feel anything of myself."

"And now?"

"It's like I was a shell and being back here . . . Being with you lot, with my own gifts . . . The shell is filling back up."

"You haven't told him? Any of it?"

I shook my head, and he took a deep breath, pressing his forehead to mine.

"You should. Tonight. Don't wait. You don't want your shell to fill then you crack like a splattered egg."

I pinched him. He kissed me once. A brush of lips against mine.

"I am very glad you're home."

Home. Yes, I was home.

"You've been with Saski," I said. I couldn't judge. "I understand."

"I thought you might."

I rested my head on his shoulder. Footsteps sounded, and I knew from his scent that it was Cadeyrn.

"I can go if you need . . ." he said to us, at a bit of a loss.

I held my hand out to him and smiled, standing. Silas smiled as well, then wrapped Cadeyrn in a bear hug, pounding on his back. They stood like that for a minute or so. I didn't know what had happened while I was gone, or even before that, as things had been different between them. But it seemed that here, now, it was mending. Because they were the most beautiful males, because they were mine, because I needed them, and just because I could, I ducked under one of their arms and included myself in the embrace, pulling them both in as tight as I could possibly get.

"Reynard should be here for this," Cadeyrn said, and I laughed because it didn't seem like something he would say.

"Ah, about our friend," Silas said, pulling away, though I refused to let him go just yet. "Och, I love you too, *allaíne Trubaíste*," he said, kissing my head. "But we do have a problem. Let's go in so I can tell everyone at once."

I groaned but let him go.

NO ONE DARED SPEAK as Silas told us what he and Cyrranus had been dealing with the past week. We were all in a state of shock. I was in no shape to go after him yet but offered immediately as Reynard was my friend. What was more, it was his voice that had me fighting back in London. Silas had sent hawks to his wraiths all over Aoifsing. We sent a hawk to Ainsley, letting her know of the situation. I sat, breathing slowly, holding both Silas and Cadeyrn's hands, not wanting to let them go. Wanting to rage at Reynard being in his father's hands. I stood and asked quietly where the bedchambers were. Another home that wasn't mine. Everyone looked at one another.

To Cadeyrn, I asked where I would be sleeping. Everyone looked at each other, causing my fingers to tingle, my stomach to slosh.

"Let's get a fresh room made up for you," Corraidhín said. Cadeyrn's eyes met mine, and I didn't understand the look. "That way you two can start over with your own space."

I followed her up, a housekeeper joining us. Corra stood with me in the bedroom that was being fluffed and readied. The room had two large bay windows, a tufted seat beneath each. In the center of the room was a canopied dark wood bed, covered in layers of white linens. The housekeeper left to run a bath for me, and I slumped into a settee.

"He's quieter," I said to Corra. "Should I worry?"

"He was fading, Neysa," she said quickly, kneeling before me.

I sat up.

"I thought he was getting better. Then Ewan told us. Silas and I didn't realize. I think he was giving up. Then they saw a vision of you and then they left. So, yes. He's quieter. For now. He'll be back to normal, I'm sure."

She left the room, and I undressed for my bath, pondering what she had said. We had both started to fade, then. I came out of the bath in my cashmere dressing gown. It was too warm for the balmy night, but it was all I had with me. Once again, a vagabond with no clothing. My husband was sitting on the settee, wine in hand, in fresh clothes and damp hair. He must have bathed in his previous chamber. I sat next to him and couldn't resist leaning over for a kiss.

"I have to tell you something." Then I began the horrid details I had given to Silas. After I finished, he set his wine down and took my face in his hands, pressing his cheek to mine, much like that first time I let him in to my visions and memories so long ago. I held on like letting go would have me adrift forever.

"I have a question." He looked at me with those aquamarine eyes aflame. "Did you ever get Tom tickets?"

I pushed him back and laid on top of him, relishing that lazy smile and the smokiness in his eyes.

"Quite good ones. Cost me a bomb. Plus the case of wine."

"Do you need to talk to anyone? About anything?"

"I'm okay talking to you."

"I want to start over. I want us to have a home. Not somewhere I have lived, or we get stuck. A proper home, where your clothes are. And the dogs. I just want to start over with you."

"I love Saarlaiche. I would be happy there. Make that our home."

He looked as though he were wrestling with whether to say something. In the end, he put his hands into my hair and pulled my face to his.

CHAPTER 48

NEYSA

The clues were mostly a mother's plea for her son. None of us knew how to take them. Francois never seemed less than frigid with her son, and she had let him suffer for so many years. Centuries, even. The main question I had was, could we trust her? Were they pleas for us to find her or her son, or were they a horrid manipulation of Reynard's complicated feelings for his mother?

"It is for time he will exchange my heart." I read it out loud to the room.

Silas and Corra were staring at me, which had me twitchy.

"Yes?" I asked. Everyone in the room turned to me.

"Weeell, it's just that you figured out the note from Cadeyrn here. We thought you might have some insight on this one," Silas said with a clap on my back.

I groaned, but Cadeyrn snickered.

Don't laugh, I told him. *I still have nightmares about all that nonsense.*

Apologies. I thought you needed a project. His answer barely controlled the amusement underneath.

Yes, because I didn't have one already.

I'll give you a project later. He laughed into my neck, wrapping his arms around me.

I reached for the notes and touched the one Silas was holding. Our gifts intermingled, playing and zapping at each other, and then I was thrust into a vision.

Spinning arrows. Time counting down. Pale eyes being covered with a blindfold. Francois holding Reynard's hand as he bled in a wagon. Cyrranus walking into a room with at least twenty guards, preparing to fight.

"We have to get to Cyrranus," I blurted. "He won't hold out against all of them. Something keeps blocking his magic." They were all looking at me for more information. I grabbed both Cadeyrn's and Silas's hands and projected the vision to them. They swore.

"Etienne wants the clock." Yeah, not a chance. I turned to Silas, a question in my eyes. "I sent it with Ludek. He seemed the most able to get rid of it. It's in Heilig with him."

"I'll go back." Saski spoke up for the first time. "I'll make sure he knows it's being hunted. I suppose it's time for me to go."

She was looking at Silas. He was staring at the notes, pointedly not looking at her.

Silas, I said to him mind to mind. *Say something to her.*

He exhaled slowly.

"You're ready then?" he asked, not quite meeting her eyes. She just watched him curiously.

"I've been here long enough." She left the room, and we heard her go upstairs. Silas muttered about getting ready to go after Cyrranus.

Bistaír was my family's home. This place—more than a manor, not quite a palace—was similar, I thought, to Hever Castle in Kent. Corra and Ewan seemed to be happy here. White-washed plaster walls and large bay windows made it so that the place was always shining and bright. A lovely place for the babies to grow up. A library covered the third floor, and I walked the packed bookshelves. From the window I could have sworn I saw movement in the trees, but it faded as soon as I focused. Being back here, all my senses were on overdrive. The basic ones like sight and scent had me spinning. Perhaps it was the light playing as the sun dappled through the branches. Stacks of books sat on a desk in the corner. All magical texts. I touched them and saw Ewan pouring over them, most likely when I was in Heilig. A year. Nearly a full year had passed since that day in Festaera. Before that, it hadn't been so long since I died. What an absolute mess. Pulling a book on time and another on goddesses of the realm, I claimed a seat nearest the window.

For time he will exchange my heart.

We all knew what Etienne wanted. However, what he planned to do with the blasted clock was beyond me. We needed to get to Cyrranus and not let him enter that trap. I wasn't ready, and if I were honest, I was terrified of Cadeyrn going, but we owed it to Reynard.

"From chaos we make haste, thus erring in the thread that we pull from the tapestry of time itself . . ." I read. Then reread. Holy burning hell. Dean said nearly the exact same thing. "It is from discord that we choose a path which follows simplicity in its linear progression. One might halt, digressing in his escape from upheaval, to make the decision to move away from the linear segmentation of his existence. It should be noted that once a linear cord is in motion, it is predisposed to stay in motion along that linear progression. However, time itself does not move in and of a singular dimension. It adheres to no realm or rule. We observe time and events differently from our particular standpoints. We are but moving time-pieces, altering the shape and furtherance of our development. Who is to say that we have no mechanics intrinsic to our being, to alter the threads we choose? Time itself is relative."

Magic, physics, philosophy, and a bloody great headache all wrapped up in one maddening ancient fae text. There. Out past the trees. There was motion. It was a man, stumbling. I stood and looked out and he was gone. Head throbbing, I turned back to the text but found my head pounding even more. The room felt stuffier, and I tried to angle my head away from the sunlight.

What catalyst had pushed me to attend Dean's lecture that day in Oxford? Even though the topic of discussion wasn't exactly what had been disclosed. He had even received an official reprimand from his employer for the deviation. My eyes popped open, sending a searing pain through my head. I ran from the library, looking for a toilet. Shit. I didn't know the layout of the place. I began flinging doors open, trying to push the nausea away. Out of options, I hurdled for the window at the end of the hall, swung the latch out and vomited from the third-floor window. God, I hoped no one was under me.

"*Trubaíste*?" Silas asked from behind me. He came to stand next to me, a hand at my back. I vomited again, the pain in my head lancing. His hand steadied me. I pulled a handkerchief from my pocket and wiped my mouth.

"Your head?"

Yes.

I was afraid if I spoke out loud, the pain would worsen. He steered me away from the window and down the hall. I noticed he was dressed to leave, swords strapped and weapons all visible, but he brought me to a room and sat me on a bed. I laid back, and he brought a cool cloth for my forehead, then laid beside me, a hand over my heart. Cool power flowed into me, coiling and nudging at mine. I let go, allowing it to intertwine with my power. Already the pain was lessening. I looked at him.

"Where are you going?"

He brought his face to mine, close enough to kiss if he dared.

"To find Cyrranus."

Oh, no, you aren't. Not without me. His power trailed through me, lighting my veins and filling my empty shell. I turned to him and wrapped my limbs around him, getting frustrated at all the weaponry to get around. We were glowing in an ombre of light and dark. Distantly, I registered his breathing being ragged and strained, and I clutched him closer. Energy shot from us both, and we arched off the bed together. The pain ebbed away like a retreating tide.

"There is a dagger digging into my groin," I said after a time. He huffed and murmured that it might not be a dagger, and I pinched him, which did no good because he was covered in fighting leathers.

"Were you in pain like this while you were away?" he asked quietly.

"No. I felt nothing. Just hollow. I would have relished the pain if it meant . . . I was connected to you." He squeezed my hands. "It doesn't smell like her in here."

"I never brought her in my room." Yet I was here. "Before I head out." He got up and pulled papers and ledgers from a drawer and sat next to me with them.

"First of all, you aren't going without me. I owe it to Reynard."

He nodded, not insulting me by insisting I stay.

"I have a present for you." He ran a hand through his hair. "It's probably a stupid present. Like the damned Christmas tree, but still."

I smiled at him and kissed his cheek. He laid a palm on the

papers and pointed to them. I looked down and recognized the blueprints for the grinders for the araíran-aoír nuts. On the sheets and ledgers were listings for manufacturing of thousands of the machines, a warehouse to house them, and purchases for the machines from both private residents and provincial officials. He even sent one back with Arik. I covered my mouth with my hand.

"I couldn't put a ring on your finger, or give you anything really special, but this seemed important to do. Because I thought I'd never see you again. You were still a living thing in me, and I needed to have that thing represented, aye?" I just gaped at him, tears spilling over. "Now that you are back . . ." His voice stuttered, and he took a breath. "It's all yours. The plans are in your name. You can do with them what you want."

I looked them over and saw how it brought more jobs to the people. More revenue to the province. Words failed me completely. I stared at him, feeling that thread we wore on our arms pulsing between us. A living thing indeed.

"Know that if I could have . . . If things were different . . . I would have given you a ring. Because there has been no one who has ruined me so thoroughly as you, and I wouldn't trade that ruination for a thousand years of peace."

"I want so much to kiss you until you can't see straight, but I was just throwing up and I'm so gross."

He roared a laugh, pulling me in for an embrace instead, and kissed my cheeks.

"Thank you, Silas."

Once the crushing pain had subsided, I remembered that I needed to speak to everyone regarding that antiquated text. We left the room hand in hand, and I ducked into my chamber to freshen up before meeting them downstairs.

Corra was staying on with the babies, which made her testy and bitter. We all met in the sitting room downstairs. The late summer heat had me plucking at my shirt, not looking forward to being in leathers. Explaining the text I'd found and the discussion I'd had multiple times with my human friend, I elaborated on the parts I thought had been relevant to my finding a way home—or at least a way back to Cadeyrn.

"It doesn't entirely make sense to me," Cadeyrn began, his voice haughty and cool. "You say you aren't speaking of time travel, yet this pulling of a different thread seems to do just that. What is it that Dean knew that relates to this realm and to the issue at hand?"

I leveled a stare at him, wondering why the frostiness, but Ewan spoke up.

"Starting from the point of the linear progression, the author speaks of an event that occurs, causing the forward progress to be on a roll, so to speak—"

"Oh! That is the first law of physics," Corra said. "Like the meteorite documentary I watched. An object set in motion stays in motion unless an outside force steps in to stop it. Like a meteor hitting a planet."

Ewan smiled at her and bent over to kiss her so thoroughly we all looked away and at each other. She was right, though. It was the same for an object at rest. I said the same, stating that if a thread hadn't been chosen, or there was a suspension in the weaving in the tapestry, things would be stagnant.

"It doesn't make sense," Cadeyrn said, reiterating his previous sentiment. "So what you are saying is that a suspension in a decision can alter the progression of reality? Then how would we all not be living in separate continuums?"

I said that in essence we were, and he pinched his nose in annoyance. My own head was spinning, but thankfully the headache was gone, thanks to Silas.

"Two or more events that occur simultaneously for one of us may not be simultaneous for another if we are in a different progression or chose a different layer within the continuum."

Everyone groaned. I stopped speaking for a moment, honestly thinking I might just go run and leave them to it for a while. But Reynard and Cyrranus needed us. So, I walked to a pitcher of cool water on a pedestal table and poured a glass, nearly moaning at the feeling of the liquid in my throat. Cadeyrn's eyes were on me, and I met his stare, feeling bare. For a moment, I stood sorting out how to explain what I was thinking, almost wishing Dean were here to help me out.

"The clock," Cadeyrn said after a time. "That's what you're getting at." I nodded. "We all felt different pressure within the headway we had to make. The countdown was different for all of us. I thought it was just an aulde spell. You're saying differently?"

"I'm sure it was an aulde spell, as the reality of it couldn't be perennial without magic. Which is why it works here. It is a harbinger of options for our own tapestries. A relic of both realms as it functions on both human physics within the space-time continuum and the magic here. A bridge of sorts. Hence the GMT on the chronograph. We all saw the same time as it was in the human realm. Or at least where I came through."

"That's why it seemed to be moving," Ewan noted. "It looked fluid."

"It was moving," Cadeyrn said, paling. "It only stopped once we all chose a thread." He looked like he was going to be sick. I felt much the same. "We chose the events that came to pass. In a normal circumstance, things would have played out as the events dictated. When we brought the damned clock in, it became its own—"

"Gravitational force," I said, looking directly at him.

We let the clock be its own dimension, making us all work independent of one another. I had seen the Veil. Cadeyrn saw his pushing me through the Veil. Ewan seemed to think he saw himself not returning. I turned to Silas.

What was your countdown? What did you feel? I asked him.

"Nothing at all," he answered, face slightly green. "Just nothing." He walked outside, barely making it from the room before dissolving.

There was silence amongst us. I noted Saski's absence and realized she must have left as there was no feeling of her in the house. She was in love with Silas. I could sense it. The four of us in the room were looking in different directions, trying to figure out how to process the information. I walked to Cadeyrn and took his hand. His clenched in mine, face looking out the window.

Together, remember?

Neysa, what we are saying is with that damned clock, we chose what happened. I chose to push you through. Because of what you saw, it was a Veil. But I chose to send you there. How do we get past that?

I turned him to me, holding on with both hands.

You made a decision based on slivers of information. What you chose to do was push me away from Kira. You chose to see me while I was away. You chose to find me. Look at me. His eyes shifted but settled on mine. Gods those eyes. I had missed them. I put my hand on his cheek and lifted on my toes to kiss him. *We always choose each other. I chose you. I will always choose us.*

Scuffling and a door thrown open pulled us out of our

little bubble. Silas entered and tossed a heap of a male onto the rug in front of Ewan.

"Found this wandering the woods, Majesty," Silas said in a growl. My eyes nearly popped out of my head as I dove for the heap. "I take it you know the human, *Trubaiste*?"

Holy shit. Semi-conscious, laying there, he looked like a man who had been singing through a beating. Blood ran from his nose and mouth, but his lips puckered in a lopsided grin. He adjusted his glasses.

"Halloo, Pet."

CHAPTER 49

Dean's eyes looked to Cadeyrn, who was visibly counting breaths.

"Really, it's uncanny how well you described them all."

"Neysa?" Ewan asked.

Helping Dean to his feet, I stood, an arm around his waist, which was marked by both my mates.

"Oh, please you two. Take the threatening male vibe down a few notches," I said to them.

Silas came to stand in front of us and made a show of bending over into Dean's face. A slow, devious smile spread across his stubbled face.

"He has that boyish charm, *Trubaiste*," Silas said, sniffing from Dean's shoulder to his neck. The boyish charmer stiffened at the fae warrior so close to his throat. He had heard my stories of Silas and Cadeyrn and what they were capable of. Especially when it came to me. I rolled my eyes at Silas.

"He does, doesn't he? And you are being a pig. You can admire him from the other side of the room. Now, before *I* start threatening you. Dean. What the hell are you doing here?"

Could he cross? Was he going to get sick? Cadeyrn moved to my side with the speed and grace of a wraith and looped an arm around me.

You. Don't forget that you only found me because of Dean. So don't be a pisshead now.

I would have found you. It may have taken longer, but I would have found you. His thumb swept over my lip.

"Was that just a conversation?" Dean asked. I raised an eyebrow at him. "Okay. So, I kept thinking about the threads. Your yarn ball drawing, and the different realms, and that clock you mentioned. They kept nagging me. Then the Goddess. I wanted to see how it all really connected."

"Funny, we were just putting all this together ourselves," Corra said, circling Dean. He looked even more unsettled than he had with Silas. I smothered a laugh and felt Cadeyrn rumble a bit behind me.

"I followed you. When you lot crossed. I know. I'm a complete nutter for doing so. I didn't really think. I just went through once you had opened it."

"You didn't come out when we did—or where we did."

"I came out in a field. It was on the edge of a seaside village not too far from here. Landed right on my face. I walked into town and asked where I was. Dropped a few of your names."

"Someone told you to come here?" Cadeyrn asked, deathly quiet. Ewan folded his arms over his chest.

"I was held in a storeroom for a . . . clothing shop, perhaps? Someone called Arneau told me and said to give you his regards. He told me how to get here."

Ewan swore. Silas snarled, the sound making Dean jump. Silas dispatched a hawk to Craghen to track down Arneau. He had to be within a day and half's ride from there.

I moved to the shelves near Corra and opened a bottle of

wine. I didn't care that it was early afternoon. Once I poured my own, everyone else came to join in. Dean stood awkwardly until Ewan waved to him to help himself. On the light caramel leather sofa, I pulled my feet under me and sipped at my wine, my knees pressed against Cadeyrn. He angled his head so that it tucked over my own, and our sides fit together. A sigh escaped me, answered by my husband's free hand covering my knee and stroking the underside through my leggings. Ewan asked Dean to continue explaining why he was here.

"That clock. I know, Neysa, you didn't know what became of it whilst you were with me," he began.

There was a snap of electricity in the room, and a flash of heat. I didn't really blame them on this one. Dean was too bright a guy to not have realized what he said. The implication of it—however innocent the reality was.

"I think it needs to be destroyed. Or somehow dismantled. I think it is an object in constant motion, making the choices you make irrelevant."

We all sat drinking. Dean wasn't used to the stillness we could all adapt, so he was shifting foot to foot. Ewan asked him to explain further.

"When I first met Neysa in Oxford, she asked whether it would be possible to back track on a thread within the layers of time."

Next to me, Cadeyrn inhaled sharply.

"Yes, and he made fun of me for wanting to regain unrequited love."

Silas snorted at me and patted my shoulder, leaving his hand there. I shot Corra a look as if to say, 'What is with these males?' She gave me a shit-eating grin back.

"Sorry, Pet. Well, I wasn't totally off though." He winked. "It did get me thinking. From her questions to what she described in the events that led to her being pushed through the Veil."

The pusher himself on my right went rigid. I smoothed a hand down his leg to calm him.

"It seemed like while the clock led you to the vessels—is that what you called them?—it had begun a systematic configuration of a separate time dimension."

"Fucking hell, man. Are you saying we are in a separate dimension? That everything that has happened, hasn't really happened?" Silas asked. I was wondering the same.

"Not really, no." We all exhaled audibly, making us chuckle. Dean pushed his glasses up and ran a hand through his hair. He was filthy and looked exhausted. We hadn't even offered him the toilet, for God's sake. "I think that because the clock is its own gravitational force, and it is always in a state of motion, teetering on the edge of both realms, instead of there being a tightly woven tapestry from which to pull threads, it's like a sieve or a screen."

"Our decisions transfer back and forth?" Ewan asked. "So, the clock, in its movement, causes time to be different for each of us. Our sense of urgency thus scripted by the differences we experience. Neysa has visions and sees glimpses of things, past and present. Because of her link to Cadeyrn, he can often see what she sees. However, due to the clock, what they saw, though perhaps the same exact images, caused an aberration in how they saw them?"

"Making us victims of our own selves?" I asked. Cadeyrn leaned forward and put his face in his hands.

"I think it can be weaponized," Dean announced.

"It helped us in finding the vessels," Silas stated.

"Maybe . . . it really didn't," I said. "Maybe, because I had seen it in my vision, we—I—assumed it would help us, so we used it. Perhaps my vision was a warning. It was leading us to the clock to get rid of it. Perhaps Etienne was already trying to claim it. It must have been spelled—"

"It has the same spell signature as the vessels," Cadeyrn

said, looking at the floor. "I hadn't noticed it. It was all too much. Everything. Once we had the clock, I should have noticed it and put it all together, but I was distracted."

I got up, filled our glasses, and sat for a moment. How could we dismantle the clock without reactivating it? Not to mention, it was all the way in bloody Heilig. All we had going for us was that Etienne didn't know where the clock was. Ama came in and showed Dean to a room for him to clean up. I disappeared into the kitchen and was shooed away by the cook, so I stood by the door waiting as he piled trays of cheeses and summer berries, a danafruit paste, nuts, oysters on ice, and iced white wine. Once the cook and I were laden with food, I called everyone in. Cadeyrn was outside.

"Her answer to everything is food," Corra said to Dean as we sat on the rug next to the coffee table.

"I've noticed," he replied. I shrugged and squeezed lemon over my oyster, slurping it down. Corra was staring daggers at me. I finally met those daggers head on and asked point blank if there was something she wanted to know. Ewan pinched his nose the way Cadeyrn does.

She's wondering if you and Dean . . .

I know exactly what she's wondering.

He threw his hands up.

"Okay, for the record, busy bodies. Dean and I did not date. We never slept together, and there is nothing more to say."

"Well, we sort of dated," Dean dared, likely emboldened by the two very large fae males of mine being out of the room. I groaned and shot him a look.

"Excuse me, Dr. Preston, but I was quite clear about our friendship."

He laughed and said he was messing with me.

"Och oysters. Can't hack them," Silas said, coming into the room and picking up a nub of cheese. "What's got you pissed off, *Trubaíste*?" He handed me a deep red strawberry and sat behind me, legs on either side of mine.

Ewan began asking Dean questions about his life and such, saying how much he enjoyed Tilly's shop. Once they were speaking, Silas put his lips to my ear and used his hand to press my face closer.

"Cadeyrn has gone to intercept Saski. I think she wouldn't listen to me right now. He has a force following Cyrranus's tracks, and we will meet them on the road tomorrow. Not sure I trust your friend here, but if what he's saying is true . . ."

I turned, pushing my face closer, angling away from Dean. I felt Silas's heartbeat against my back.

"We need to move quickly and come up with a fucking good plan," Silas said. His fingers curled into my hair where he held my face.

Anything else, or do you just want to cuddle with me? I teased. He smiled against my ear and wrapped arms around me to reach for more food. I drank my wine and slurped more oysters. As the light dimmed in the window-bright room, most of the food had been cleared, the wine drunk, and Cadeyrn was not back. Corra and Ewan left to be with the babies, as they had been away from them most of the day. I was wine addled, still lounging against Silas. As I brushed my fingers against the oyster shells, pictures formed in my mind of the ocean floor, the sway of seaweed and tides pulling back and forth. Reaching up, I touched Silas's face and showed him what I saw. His lungs filled, and I felt him smile before kissing my head. Opening my eyes, I saw Dean looking at us. He blinked slowly and gave me a small, lopsided smile as if to say he understood now. Reaching out with my gifts, I sent the images from the ocean to Cadeyrn. I felt a relieved, soft amusement come through.

One of the servants came in and began lighting sconces, washing the room and all of us in a warm glow. Before the last sconce was lit, I tapped into my gifts, willing a glow of white light to come out and darkness to glitter from my feet. Dean's eyes went wide. Finally. Finally, I could use my magic. Release that built-up pressure. Silas reached out like we had done on the street in Laichmonde; we created a cyclone of light, dark, mist, and electricity.

"She's showing off for your benefit, lad," Silas said to Dean.

I snapped my teeth at him playfully. Dean reached out tentatively. Silas pulled back, and I offered my magic to Dean, caressing him. He looked like fingers ran down his arm. Silas chuckled. One sconce above a desk in the corner illuminated a stack of books and ledgers. I tried to stand to walk to it, but Silas growled softly, holding onto me.

"I'll get it. Which one?"

"The top three." He waved his hand, and the books appeared before me. I turned, stunned. He shrugged. They were provincial ledgers and trade agreements. Silas said he had brought them back from his meeting with Cyrranus and Alan. While I waited for Cadeyrn to come back, Dean excused himself to go to his chamber, and I sat with Silas flicking through the ledgers.

"Is he full of shite?" Silas asked after a time. I didn't think so and said as much. Dean couldn't let things go. It was his personality and nature. Following us because he had to offer us his theory fit in his method of operations.

"Do you remember when we were looking for clues in the library at your mum's?" Silas asked. I did and nodded. "I know you always say that I pick you up . . . and I said some horrible, fucking horrible—" he scrubbed his face "—things to you back after Heilig. But you picked me up that night. It was a complete clusterfuck what happened after with Cadeyrn, but . . . yeah."

Closing my eyes, I leaned back against him.

"Are you in love with Saski?" A whoosh of air as he stroked my hair.

"Maybe? I like her. I do. I really do."

"Maybe . . . that's worth exploring further?" I stroked his arm. "I mean, you were involved this whole time? A year?"

"Yeah, more or less. If you call involved just . . . you know." We threaded our fingers together. "Still, it was longer than I've ever stuck to one female."

A sharp pain lanced through me, and I doubled over. Silas asked if I was okay, and the pain happened again. Cadeyrn had been hit with something. He wasn't responding to me. Silas was pacing and snarling, saying he should track him, which I thought would take time away if he didn't find him and we needed Silas here. We faced off in the foyer of the receiving room, snarling in each other's faces, as the door banged open and Cadeyrn shouldered through, holding his side. Both of us turned to him, our teeth still bared.

"Gods, you two. Stop snarling," Corra called from behind us, Pim on her hip. Silas pulled his cousin to the sitting room. I unstrapped his weapons and opened his jacket. Pim was squawking in Corra's arms, wiggling to get out. I pressed my hands against a stab wound in my mate's side, meeting his eyes.

"It's healing, but the blade was rusty, so I'll have to clean it out before it closes."

I wanted to scream and throw things. Ama came in and waved at us all to move away. We followed them to our bedroom, where Ama had Cadeyrn lay down. She wiped at the wounds—there were two—and used a scalpel-like knife to open the wound where it had healed.

"Stop fussing, you lot. I'm fine." I saw his lip was a bit swollen as well. I leaned down, touched it, and he winced. Yep, definitely a bruise.

You're actually pissed off at me? I just glared back. He

rolled his eyes and stared at the ceiling while Ama dug out bits of rusted metal.

"Saski is fine." He looked to Silas, who nodded curtly. "Alan is dead."

"Fucking hell," Ewan swore. I didn't think I've ever heard him swear that much. I felt like a sailor in comparison. "Who?"

"Arneau's henchmen. They cornered me in Alan's house. I stopped to check in after seeing Saski. I knew something was wrong and perhaps I shouldn't have gone in." He hissed as Ama dragged a long shard from his side. I grabbed his hand. "I smelled blood. I found Alan in his toilet chamber, throat cut. They pushed me in then. There were five of them. One was able to cut off my air supply, so I wasn't fighting well."

The healer took a long thin spoon-like utensil and began scraping the shallow bits of the wound. His face was calm, but I could tell by the set of his mouth that the pain was considerable. Ama gave him the all-clear to let his gift take over and motioned for me to step closer to him. I laid beside him on the bed and let my mind and magic open up to him. Let that same unspooling as I had done with Silas, that healed my headache and released my tension, flow into Cadeyrn. The others left the room. Watching the wound stitch itself back together was mesmerizing.

I can't lose you. I just can't. His answering squeeze on my hand didn't reassure me. "I'm serious. Don't go off like that." He was falling asleep, but his lips twitched upward. I gave a mighty humph and placed my hand over his wound.

EWAN WAS in his study when I slipped out of my bedroom in the middle of the night. I'd been thinking of how we could curtail the escalating violence. As I approached my brother, he was looking at Alan's ledgers. The same ones I'd perused earlier.

"A trade embargo," I said. He looked up with red rimmed eyes. Between the situations he had been dealing with, the babies, and me, I was sure his sleep was minimal. "You should impose an embargo on all trade from any of Etienne's holdings. Even seize whatever assets he has in a bank—I don't know how it works here."

He turned a paper to me, written in his hand, of all representatives in Aoifsing and Heilig. It declared trade with Etienne and Arneau an act of war. Any holdings either of them had in another province would be seized and trade with Festaera heavily sanctioned. I sank into a chair, too exhausted to stand anymore. At least we were on the same page. Earlier he had sent another letter, which turned out to be a disclosure to Ainsley Mads requesting her support in the embargo. As she operated as a sovereign province, it seemed in bad faith to declare sanctions and embargoes without consulting her.

Etienne's operations included aphrim skin clothing and wagon coverings and aphrim themselves, which should have been noted as a red flag much earlier as it was, in essence, a militia, or, at the very least, a weapon. He and Arneau jointly manufactured weaponry from Festaeran steel. In closing off trade, no one would purchase from him, and he could not purchase steel from Festaera. In fact, Sergo would now be required to pay heavy tax on exporting the steel. In an effort not to sink the entire province, fluid trade would be opened for Festaera's other resources. Like Prinaer, it had many mines, Festaera's being rich with granite, slate, and marble.

The goal, as my brother and I sat through that long night, was to ensure the self-sufficiency of every province while keeping trade open. Additionally, since our visit to Heilig and the eradication of Konstantín, Ewan and Arik had been in talks about trade agreements. The idea being that trade with Heilig would broaden the reach of each province's cash crop.

"Gods, you two." Corra's voice rang like church bells, stirring me.

I struggled to open my eyes in the watery morning light coming in through the study window. I must have fallen asleep with my head against the bottom of the settee in Ewan's office. He was across from me, barely awake with his head tipped back against the polished wood of his desk. Ledgers and trade agreements were spread across the floor. The babies were in Corra's arms, trying to get down. Ewan reached for Pim, his eyes still closed. I sat up, rubbing my eyes, not quite awake. Efa crawled to me, pushing her little hands on my thighs. I lifted her and brought her to my chest for a hug. She looked at me and put her head against my shoulder, her thumb in her mouth, and stilled. I closed my eyes again and leaned back, holding her. Images of me, of Ewan, of Cadeyrn making faces at her, swam into focus. Silas talking, waving his hands around in an animated story. It took me a sleepy minute, but I realized that my little niece was projecting to me what she saw. Or what made her happy. I tried to show her images as well. Ewan and me as children, my beastie snuggling Ewan, the dogs, the sea. We both must have fallen back to sleep sharing our thoughts, because the next thing I knew was Cadeyrn touching my shoulder. I blinked at him and saw the most beautiful smile across his face, lifting all the way to his eyes, where they shone in the morning light. He leaned in and kissed my cheek and the top of Efa's head on her mop of dark hair.

How are you feeling? I asked him. He lifted his shirt to show me the healed wounds, only a faint pink line where they had been.

Back to normal. Shall I take her so you can get some tea? I debated it. She seemed awake but still clung to me. Until she turned and saw her uncle and began scrambling for him. I laughed and passed her off with a kiss.

Oh, I found these. They tumbled from your satchel. I figured you might want them. He handed over the two bunnies. I held them out to Efa, asking her which she would like. Pim, who had crawled from Ewan to us, was pointing. I held them to him as well. I tried to hand him the pinkish one, but he was saying, "Uddah, uddah," making me giggle. So, I gave him the taupe, and Efa took the pinky, immediately shoving the bum end to her mouth.

As I stood amongst the mess Ewan and I had created last night, I sighed. First tea, then explanations.

CHAPTER 50

NEYSA

In Greek mythology, Achilles was sent by his father, Peleus, to train with the great centaur warrior, Chiron, in the foothills of Mount Pelion. Trudging though the northern part of Maesarra, en route to intercept Cyrranus, I felt like Achilles making his way through Thessaly to get to the cave of the famed Chiron. The landscape here was of rocky forest and unforgiving foliage. Plants looked close to juniper, cypress, and rosemary. The trek north started after breakfast and a rundown of what Ewan and I had managed to lay out the night before. With Etienne's assets tied up, we already had a foothold. Though it was around seven or eight at night, the golden hour of sunshine was only starting, indicating that nightfall was still a couple of hours off. Rocks and boulders became more plentiful, the tree thicket greater, as we climbed the rising elevation. Brambles had scratched my face and neck incessantly, making my mood sour with every footfall.

Ewan was pissed at me. I had refused to let him come along. He had tried pulling the king card, which I had laughed at, and he had stormed off. Perhaps I was barely up for the task, but there was no question as to my going, especially since

Silas and Cadeyrn were suited up and ready. Corra, who had been slightly frosty with me after our initial reunion, privately thanked me for insisting he stay. However, walking out of that home with my brother stewing in anger with me and Corra less than friendly had me unsettled. Leaving Dean behind felt wrong somehow as well.

Five guards accompanied us. A company of twenty went ahead, a separate unit of spies fanning out in a large perimeter, and a host of twenty a half day behind us. We had to move as swiftly and silently as possible while covering our backs. And fronts, as it were. Lifting a conifer branch to duck under, I was whacked in the face by another, and swore colorfully before tripping over a rock. Cadeyrn caught my elbow just as my knees hit the ground, taking a bit of sting from the fall. Silas paused ahead and looked back with an 'uh-oh' look on his face. He was wearing a third or fourth day of stubble, making his features darker, but I saw the look nonetheless. Cadeyrn came round the front of me where I knelt, holding my eye.

"Bloody hell," he said under his breath. I held up my hand in annoyance and waved him off, fumbling blindly through my pack for a handkerchief. "Don't be stupid. Let me see it."

"I'm fine. Keep going; I'll catch up." I pressed the cloth to my eye and saw it came away with blood and sap. Fabulous. He rolled his eyes, kneeling in front of me.

"Not in the mood to be patronized, so give me a second and I'll catch up."

He quirked his lips to the side and knit his dark brows together.

"What? I'm fine. Just go. I'm not a damsel in distress."

His mouth was twitching. My temper flared seeing it. I stood quickly and stomped off, only one eye working at the moment, which started to feel like I was in a strobe light from the sun dappling through the trees.

"I know you've been mountain man gym rat for a year,

and maybe you think I've been sitting on my ass for a year, but I have been training. Not in this blasted man-eating forest, but don't treat me like a child." An amused cough sounded behind me.

"Your pyre," Silas muttered to him as I pushed past him and led them both. Cadeyrn chuckled. Boots caught up to me.

"Saski wanted aphrim skins like yours, by the way. She said they did your ass a great favor." I growled, glaring at him through one eye. One, because I didn't even want to think about her right then. I felt like her scent was everywhere. All over both of them. Two, because my aphrim skins died when I had. Three:

"So, is the implication that these leathers do no such favors, or that generally speaking, my ass is in need of such dispensations?" I bit out at him.

There was a very male silence since I knew there was no right answer to that. As I kept walking off, I kissed my fingers and touched them to my ass for good measure. Both males chuckled behind me. Okay, the sap was stinging. Nothing was improving my mood. Every stupid branch and thorn bush I stepped over lent itself to greater moodiness. I wouldn't admit that a year back in the human realm softened me. As I had suspected, after an hour or so, the sun dipped lower, crouching under clouds and slipping behind the mountain. We made camp near a cave mouth within which Cadeyrn searched for any hiding beasts. Or fae.

"Chiron's cave indeed," I muttered, gnawing on some bread and cheese.

"Is it the time of night we start associating our woes with human mythology?" Cadeyrn asked, cleaning his blade. "Are we theorizing that we all have an Achilles' heel?"

I scoffed.

"That is below my pay grade," I sneered. Silas smirked,

munching an apple. "Though true, I was more thinking of the presumption of men."

Both males raised an eyebrow at me, which would have been quite cute had I not been in a horrible disposition. Cadeyrn urged me to elaborate. The wry smile he gave me was like a warm arrow to my core, but I was too nettled to give in to my better nature.

"Achilles's mother, Thetis," I began, "and his father, Peleus, assured he trained with Chiron to be the legendary warrior it had been prophesied he would become."

"If memory serves," Cadeyrn drawled, interrupting me, "Peleus was rather self-serving, and Thetis a tad overbearing." I glowered at him, still pressing the cloth to my eye. "Thetis was impossible to be around, always in a fit, shifting this way and that, making trouble for people and gods alike." Oh, he was pressing his luck. "In fact, wasn't she always that little bit unhappy about having to have just Peleus after Zeus and his ilk had originally been courting her?"

The little shit was baiting me. Silas was smothering a laugh, and my temper was rising.

"Zeus and 'his ilk' rejected her because they couldn't handle the prophecy that her son would be stronger than his father. Typical male bullshit. I wouldn't have put up with it either if I were Thetis."

"As a sea nymph," he said. "She was likely used to having both men and gods at her disposal. To be stuck with Peleus must have really vexed her." In the flickering firelight I could see him trying not to smile as my fingers crackled with energy.

"Watch yourself, brother," Silas warned.

"Who is to say she was stuck with just Peleus? He was mortal and she was a daughter of a god. She married him, yes," I said sweetly. "Mythology doesn't follow her story much past the Trojan War." He stiffened ever so slightly. "The reason Thetis chose Peleus was because he was told he would have to accept her many forms. So, he called her from the sea and held her."

I opened my thoughts to both shit stirrers sitting with me and allowed images of how I pictured it going down with Thetis and Peleus.

"As he held her, she became water, slipping through him as he lay there, trying to grasp her." In my mental snap shots, she looked like Corra and Silas in their mist forms. "Then fire burst forth and still he held her flaming skin, accepting her wrathful nature."

Thetis's fiery manifestation recalled Cadeyrn, when he encapsulated the camp with his fire so that he could carry me to his tent after the spar with Bestía. Cadeyrn swallowed, looking at me, his hands stilling on the knife he had been cleaning.

"She became beast," I continued. "Snarling and turning hideous and unforgiving." It was not a stretch that my mind's eye produced a beast much like my *baethaache*. "Yet he held on, pulling her beast closer to his mortal body, wounding him even, until she became fluid once more, washing over Peleus with the salty kiss of the ocean and all its violence, serenity, and unpredictability. Once she became a beautiful nymph once more, he made love to her against the lap of the ocean, and they married."

Both males were looking a bit peaky.

"So, you see, she was quite thorough in choosing Peleus. Christian scholars like to suggest that she was subservient, and Peleus asserted his male dominance over her." I smirked, though I was quite sure it looked dumb because I was still one-eyed Neysa. "I should think it quite obvious that Thetis would never be tamed. She was her own beast. It was only a question of whether Peleus could handle it."

"Holy bleeding hell realm, *Trubaíste*. Now I need a cold bath." I laughed at Silas as he thumped over on his side, facing away from the fire. Cadeyrn's eyes were glued to me. He came over deliberately slow and forcefully turned me to him. Raising both eyebrows, he pulled the cloth from my eye. His nostrils flared as he brushed a thumb over my eye and moved it down my face. It tingled where he touched, all the minor scratches healing, the eye stinging less and less.

Perhaps we should see if Master Chiron is in his cave?

It would be rude, I answered truthfully, though I really, really wanted to go into that cave with him.

Ah.

Don't "Ah" me.

Hmmm. There will be payback, Neysa, he said with a whisper of mischief, brushing a kiss to my eyelid.

Quite sure. Looking forward to it. He got up to pick up his weapons and rearrange the sleeping area.

In my head to Silas I said, *I'm sure there will be payback on your end as well.*

A crackle of his power shot through me, alighting my own magic. Yeesh. Sensitive males.

Maesarra was much larger than I'd anticipated. Ewan's intelligencers had spies who located Cyrranus in northern Maesarra and had spotted Etienne on the border of Veruni. Making our descent from the mountains, everyone was pissy. Silas seemed twitchy about Saski, Cadeyrn was acting pompous, and I wished I were alone with him to warm that frost. The guards with us tried to keep it in check, whereas the three of us made no such effort. My knee was killing me. I had twisted it in a throw at the second training gym I went to in England. It had never been the same, but I ignored it most of the time. Until hiking for hundreds of miles. Downhill. With weapons.

Silas was scratching at his face, complaining of the heat, though the temperature dropped the further north we came. Cadeyrn commented that perhaps the scruffy beard wasn't working for him. His cousin got in his face and said he didn't feel like making the effort to shave on a rescue mission. So it went for the entire next day. And night. Waking that third morning, my knee was so stiff I could barely stand from my bedroll. The males were off taking care of their own business, our guards already waiting as I sat, acting like a damned princess. Which I was, but still. Finally, I stood and yelped with the pain, my leg wobbling. Crap.

I didn't want to make a fuss, but I pulled my husband to the side and asked him to look at my knee.

"I can't seem to activate the quadricep muscles," I said. Behind a tree where there was a bit more privacy, he told me to take down my trousers. I did, holding on to his shoulder for support as he knelt before me, feeling the knee and surrounding muscle. His fingers felt upwards into the wobbly quadriceps and stopped just above the kneecap.

"There," he mumbled, his gift seeping in. My gift responded, braiding itself with Cadeyrn's. He looked up, confused, and I shrugged. White light shone around us as he prodded the knee and muscles.

"There's a detachment in one of the quadriceps, and there is fluid under the kneecap. When did it happen?" He stayed kneeling, his hands wrapped around my leg.

"Maybe six months ago?" He choked, asking why I hadn't said anything earlier. I waved my hand. "I got used to it."

He was taking longer than usual to heal the knee, and I wondered if he was drained. Back against the tree, my arm braced on his shoulder, he brought his lips to the inside of my knee and a zinging sensation went all the way through me.

Silas appeared from the copse of trees just in front of me. He stopped dead, eyes wide. I knew how this looked. Though I was with Cadeyrn, who was my husband, and even if it were less innocent a situation, it would be appropriate. He silently walked off, dissolving into mist. Cadeyrn stood and motioned for me to pull up my pants. I cocked my head to the side and looked at him. Really looked at him.

"That was for a show?" He grabbed the back of his neck and looked at me sidelong, green eyes burning. "To make him feel jealous? You don't think he feels like shit anyway? You're an asshole." I tromped off, gloriously pain free, and told the guards to follow. Another day in discord then. Great.

Cadeyrn was absolutely unrepentant, wearing a smug male look all day. Silas was mostly mist, moving along the streams and ponds we passed. There was a flicker in the light. Silas appeared, searching the area, when Corra moved in.

"Fucking hell, sister," Silas yelled. For a second I was so worried I couldn't feel my legs from the adrenaline rushing through me. Cadeyrn reached for my hand and I pulled away. Then Corra smiled and flipped her hair back over her shoulder.

"Halloo, darlings. Thought I'd drop in to help."

I flopped to the ground in a languid heap. "

"Sorry, Neysa. Everyone is fine. Well, except poor Reynard, but that's what this about. See, I was faster than you lot, and caught up with Cyrranus inside Veruni. Our hawks all found him, but he's a stubborn arse, determined to find Reynard. I told him he must wait for us to get to him or else he would die a bloody death at the hands of twenty backwoods soldiers just as Alan had."

"Delicately put, Corraidhín," Cadeyrn said, voice flat.

"Yes, well, he is hiding out in a hunting lodge. I can show you when we get there. What's with you all? Everyone looks like shit and smells like frustration." We all groaned and began walking again. The twins went on ahead, heads together in conversation too quiet for even our fae hearing. Silas shook her off, and she glared back at me or Cadeyrn, I don't know. I looked away.

As we camped that night, Corra explained that Etienne had taken a stronghold in Bania, usurping Analisse's manor house. I was breathing through my nose to calm down. We would have to go back there. Catching Silas's eye, I could see he was thinking the same. Slipping between the trees to have some privacy before settling down for the night, Corra intercepted me, wrapping a slender hand around my arm and towing me further away without saying anything. A rushing stream drowned out our voices when she rounded on me.

"Listen, I am so very glad you are home, Neysa."

"But?"

"You're making a muck of things, darling," she stated simply. I barked a laugh which contained no humor whatsoever.

"Yes, well, I'm sorry to have interrupted your perfect life, Corra."

"Pshaw. It's not that," she waved, mist streaking through the air. "The children love you. Thank you for the bunnies. They are positively disgusting with dribble, but Efa won't let hers go." My heart ached hearing that. "You have to figure out this thing with my brother. It's going to kill him."

I was silent.

"So?"

I met her eyes, the same as her brother's, and stayed silent.

"What will you say?"

I crossed my arms and shook my head. "Tell me you didn't come all this way to bully me."

"I'm not bullying you, darling. I'm informing you of a crisis situation within our family and asking what you intend to do about it. My cousin and brother are both hurting because of you. Cadeyrn was letting go, and he and Silas were so distant for so long. Silas was getting on with Saski. Not that I love her, but . . ."

"But maybe if I had stayed gone, he would have gotten over me?" That was the question that hung in the air. The question that followed me day and night. "Perhaps you would have found another look-alike for Cadeyrn to bang for a few years until he got over me too?"

She slapped me, and a rush of darkness cocooned me, moving me back from her.

"That is what you meant, wasn't it? I was stuck in that realm long enough to give you all just enough space to deal with me being gone. Appreciate a lag in my chaos? Maybe had I faded completely it might have released them both from our bond and they could have been free. That would have been ideal really." I raised my voice slightly, darkness and light twirling around me.

"That's . . . not what I meant," she said.

I snarled. "Of course it was. You just didn't want to say it in so many words. I'm sure each one of you has thought it, if only briefly. Well, I'm sorry. I came back, which likely saved me from fading. If it's such an inconvenience to have me around, I can leave once I find Reynard. Do you think I meant for any of this? God, Corra! I would take a knife to my own heart right now if it would spare either of them from dealing with me. Even godsdamned Dean got sucked into my vortex. So just as I said to Silas after I was brought back from the fucking dead, there is nothing you are saying that shocks me, because I know it all. I. Am. A. Nightmare. Slap me again. Hit me. Drop kick me. I don't care. I love them. I am married to Cadeyrn and I want to stay that way forever if he can handle me. I love Silas and want him to be happy too. I am mated to them both, Corra. I didn't do it. It was done to us. Yet, somehow, it's my fault? What do you want me to say? I would leave if I thought they would be truly happy. I would. It would kill me, but I would do it. So if you really think they could be happier, then ask it of me."

She stood, chewing on her lip and tapping her foot. I walked away, noting the yellow eyes watching me from a distance. Bowing my head, I bid the wolves watch over the camp while I made my way out. I got about a half mile before I realized what a dumbass I was being and stopped. Truly, Neysa, get a grip.

Steeling myself to walk back, I was greeted with a sound kick in my ribs. Another blow missed my head when I blocked it with my forearm. Dazed, my forearm barking, I flipped in a crouch, one leg out. No one. Where did it come from? A blink, and a golden-haired male appeared before me, no weapon in sight. I knew him. He had attacked us in Bulgaria. Two others filed in behind him, swords at the ready. Shit.

All I had on me was my forearm dagger. What was I thinking in leaving without my swords? The golden male blinked behind me. I felt his magic as it moved through the particles of the atmosphere. Just before he could be out of reach, I swirled my darkness around him, trapping him in a sort of particle vacuum. The other two advanced. Bloody great. Keeping the golden boy trapped, I was able to fight the others. As they rushed me, I dropped and rolled to the right. Jumping up, I released my dagger and ran at them. When it seemed I was going to meet my end on their swords, I caught a tree branch overhead and swung over it, dropping onto one's shoulders. He didn't have time to react as I stabbed the dagger into his neck. I willed a jolt of electricity into the other, dropping him to the ground, unconscious.

Of course, the kilometer back to camp took forever pulling an unconscious male and one wrapped in magical darkness. When I made it to the edge of camp, I dropped the male and electrocuted the golden one for good measure because I needed to sit down. All eight fae in our camp were at attention, wondering what the hell had happened. I said there was one dead a half mile out, and to deal with these two, as I was going to sleep.

Replenishing my magic didn't take very long. It seemed like it was heightened by my adrenaline and general mood, so I felt like it was depleted more than it actually was. I found myself joining my mates and the others as they interrogated the two I had dragged over.

Golden boy broke every time Cadeyrn brought his knife to the male's face. The other told us Reynard would be killed if they didn't return.

"He's lying," I said. "That would have been voiced only if they had been sent to negotiate or retrieve one of us. They tracked me, and their only intent was to kill me. Not a word was exchanged. Gut him."

"Wait! I know where he's being kept," the assassin said, shooting a sidelong glance at his companion. From the look in golden's eyes, I knew the assassin was lying. So did Corra.

He's lying. That fast, Silas put a dagger through his temple. I turned away.

"You?" I addressed golden boy.

"It's a job. I don't care about the particulars of who does what. I can give you information in exchange for sparing my life. Etienne is a bastard anyway, so it doesn't worry me."

We gave our word, and for that he divulged where everyone was, and what was happening.

"If I catch a whiff of your worthless mercenary ass again— ever—you will see that what I did to your friend here was a mercy." Silas leaned closer. "Starting with that pretty face of yours." The male swallowed and agreed before disappearing. Everyone turned to me. I gave a nonchalant gesture and swigged from my water skein.

THEIR CHATTER WAS like the buzz of cicadas from where I sat, still holding that darkness around me. I wondered what it really was. I pulled it around me like a shield, but it wasn't one. Perhaps it was a way for me to recognize my need to protect myself. Fairly certain my rib was broken, and something was damaged in my arm, I pulled a tonic from my bag and drank it to ease the pain. Cadeyrn's face turned, likely from the smell of the tonic. He started to come over, but Corra put an arm on him, saying to leave me alone. Instead, she walked to me and sat beside me on a tree stump.

"I would never ask that of you." She twirled a lock of my hair around her finger. "Foremost because I do not think it necessary. Loads of other reasons as well. But, selfishly, I would not ask it because while you were gone, I missed you too. A great deal. We are friends and we are sisters. My concern lies for all of you. Do not think for one second that there would ever be a time that you wouldn't be missed. Do not think there is any amount of time that shall pass in which either of your mates would be free of you. I simply ask that you make up your mind as to how to be at peace with both. Now, I could wager a full set of aphrim skins that the male contingent has been doing a fabulous job of pretending to not listen to this conversation. I suppose I have been the only one speaking, so it's more of a lecture, but I needed to say that to you. If you need to talk, you can seek me out. I saw this documentary about this woman who always felt she was being watched and followed, and she started seeing a psychologist, and after a time —wait. No, she killed the doctor. Don't do that. Let's just be sisters, yes?"

I nodded, still in my swaddling blanket of dusk. Dawn was

a few hours off, and we all needed sleep. Who knew what tomorrow would bring. As I slid into my bedroll, I felt Cadeyrn lay behind me and put a hand on my ribs, allowing them to heal. I breathed in fully, allowing the murkiness clouding me to subside. With a kiss pressed under my ear, he left.

CHAPTER 51

SILAS

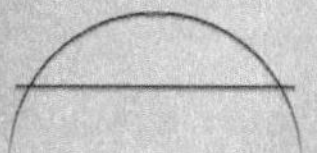

Looking like a trapped beast, Cyrranus was where my sister had left him. The cabin was small, only large enough for a couple of males to grunt and piss in. This had been one of the worst treks I had had to make, between the terrain, the heat, and our personal situation. I still was not sure if my sister showing up caused more trouble or helped. Ultimately, it helped flush out those mercenary bastards, though it showed how thick we all were that *Trubaiste* had left. Gods that one. The death of me for sure.

Cyrranus paced the cabin while we told him what we knew. Once we had all rested properly and eaten, we set back off for Bania. Truthfully, if I never had to be in that fucking manor house again, I would have been grateful. I should have known Etienne, that sneaky shite, would go there. Just one more godsawful night sleeping on the road until I could shed a little blood. Saski would have enjoyed sorting the place with us. I probably should have gone to get her rather than sending my cousin, but I honestly thought she would have maimed me. Plus, it was time she got back to her lands. She was to be queen after all. Not a country squire like me.

We sent a hawk both forward and backward to our soldiers, telling them where we were going to enter the city limits. There would likely be all sorts of obstacles, but at this point, I welcomed them. It might make me the basest of creatures, but I needed to run, kill, and fuck until the heat on my skin went away. At least I'd be doing one of the three shortly.

Shields and wards were up over the grounds of Analisse's compound. The orchard seemed unfazed, which meant that it was teeming with snipers in trees and likely some sort of magical traps here and there. Cadeyrn could sense the abhorrence in the atmosphere as though it were a virus in the air itself. Once he knew where and what we were dealing with, he could begin to dismantle it. While he worked, my sister and I dissolved into the omnipresent mist in Veruni and moved through the orchard. I hated to say it, but it felt good putting my dagger through every piece of shite who was guarding this place. Dissolve, reestablish self, gut the fucker, dissolve. That was our course of action for an hour or so, trying to not raise any alarms before Cadeyrn had a chance to break the spells.

Once we cleared the orchard, there was a straight shot to the back of the manor, lined on either side with a smaller grove of trees, full of their late summer leaves. Corraidhín and I moved back through and reappeared at the back edge where everyone awaited our task. She was grinning like a mad hatter, almost as crazed as I felt. The slightest sound of grass underfoot had me dissolving again and retreating into the orchard after a straggler. He loosed an arrow at me which missed, then another that hit me as I was coming to my corporeal self. I kept pace after him, and just as he flung open the door to the house, I drowned the shite before he could call out. Now I was inside. Fuck it all to never, I wished I could speak to *Trubaiste* the way she could speak to me. Making the best of the situation, I moved through the bottom of the house, the way we had the night we escaped. The night Reynard helped us. Now it was our turn to get him out. Slipping in and out of rooms, under cracks and through pipes, I searched for our friend.

Of fucking course he had to be in the room I had shared with Neysa. Reynard's attention snapped to the door as I drifted in. As I came to my form, I saw him staring wide-eyed and battered, bound to the bedposts with aphrim skin ropes. Careful not to make any noise, I made my way across the room. As I pulled the gag from his mouth, I knew my mistake.

"It's all spelled," he choked. The golden-haired teleporter I let go last night appeared beside me, and knocked me upside the head.

CHAPTER 52

As an experiment to see if my touch heightened his power, I laid my hand on Cadeyrn's back and willed the slumbering magic from deep within me, where a beast should be, to transfer to him. Ripples flowed between us then. As he unwound the spells warding the grounds of the compound, my power separated the strands of darkness and light, willing them to do my bidding. Corra and Silas came back and appeared before us, smiling as though a bit mad with bloodlust. Silas's eyes found mine before he tore back into the orchard where he sprinted after a straggling guard. Corra called after, but he was gone. We heard the whizz of arrows and the thump of one hitting just as I felt a knock on my left arm. Silas was hit.

Are you okay? Just a moment longer and we could all converge on the place. My impatience was making me jumpy, and Cadeyrn growled at me to calm before it undid what we were attempting. But Silas was hurt, and he wasn't back yet. Then the wards dropped and like puppies, we all ran through the orchard, weapons at the ready. Corra reached the doors fastest, and I went down hard as everyone began filing in.

Cadeyrn was ahead, but Cyrranus yanked me up. My head was spinning like I had been knocked.

"Go!" I yelled at him. "I'm fine. Get everyone in and find them." He saluted me and ran after the small group of soldiers who went in. The rest stayed outside, where there was now an entire regiment of aphrim closing in around the perimeter of the house. By my estimate, there were at least two hundred of the feral infantry, moving on us in their clumsy, labored way, each of the large scales on them shifting with the movement. Our follow up regiment was close behind, moving through Bania, but for these beasts, we had roughly fifteen soldiers, and me with a dodgy head.

Reeking, eye-watering slobber sprayed everywhere when the aphrim moved. It was a wonder they made such enviable clothing, because these creatures were downright nasty. Slow moving and mostly blind, they were simply a means to slow us down and wear us out. As long as the others could get Reynard, and now Silas, out. A long saliva-covered tooth caught my arm before the beast it belonged to met its end on my sword. I yanked my arm back, pulling the wound open. Disgusting. That would need tending quickly. I was sure the bacterial level in the spit was insane.

You're hurt. A statement. His voice in my head was clipped, so I knew he was fighting as well. I spun between two aphrim, then crouched down, causing them to crash into each other and angrily battle between them.

Aphrim. I'll be fine. Get them out.

Bloody hell. Pretty much. Losing the strength in my injured arm, I kept swinging and slashing, felling the beasts as I went. Our soldiers made a point to keep me flanked. There was a sound to my right, a spray of blood. The solider next to me crumpled under the jaws of a huge aphrim. My knees wobbled slightly, yet I rammed my dagger straight through its eye. Distantly I could feel blows to my ribs and chest, and I knew Silas was taking them wherever he was.

Silas, I know you're probably fine, bloody great warrior and all that, but on the off chance the blows I'm feeling are finding their mark, just hang in there. Doubled over in pain, I had to swipe out maniacally to kill an aphrim. *The good news is that we are killing so many aphrim, I can get some new skins made so my unremarkable ass can look better.* There was a brief, painful sliver of amusement on the other end.

The tail regiment broke the boundary on the property and were within view. Somehow the sixteen of us managed to get though most of the oily beasts, with only ten or so more left. I was drained and needed water desperately. My relief was short lived as ballistae started firing arrows and spears into our soldiers, taking them down in impressive numbers. I ran toward the ballistae and the accompanying fae who manned them, spearing my own power into them. A couple fell as my electricity hit them and the metal of the unit. Reaching the unit itself, I tried willing more power to my body to release the energy and take out the other gunners, but simultaneous blows to my mates had me falling over. I was hauled up and slammed into the wall of the house, my teeth singing with the contact. The male wrenched my arm behind my back, tearing the aphrim wound. I screamed and kicked back, making him bark and backhand me, my head bouncing off the concrete wall again, one of the carved bird reliefs dancing in my vision.

"Got me a prize," he whispered in my ear, kneeing me in the kidney. I vomited with the pain and went slack. He sniggered, grabbing my other arm back. My shoulder jolted with pain and I grunted, but he had me bound and was pulling me away. I'd taken out one of the ballistae, though I wished I had managed both before getting caught.

What's happened? Where are you? Cadeyrn questioned through our connection.

I'll be fine.

Damn it, Neysa. Where are you?

Where are you?

That's not funny. Fuck. Ugh. Then the sound of a sword singing and the roar of fire in close quarters. I wished I were there to see it. *They aren't here. Silas and Reynard aren't in this house. He went in but he's not here.* A feeling of cold dread went through me as the guard who had me bound dragged me away from the property toward the city proper.

Cadeyrn, get out of there. Get everyone out. Now. Hysterics began walking in my mind as I kept yelling at him to get out. I tried turning around to see back, but the guard elbowed me in the ear. Christ, I was going to have a compound concussion.

Where. Are. You? he demanded.

Get out of there! I kept screaming at him. Then the entire manor disintegrated like it had been a house of ash, touched by a mighty finger. All that was left of the plaster and birds, the wooden shutters, the stones, was ash on the wind. I couldn't think straight. *Cadeyrn—*

I threw up again, and the guard swore and kicked at me. Had he made it out? Had any of them?

Cadeyrn.

I reached in myself, searching for a tether and finding nothing but a spark of our bond.

We dropped through the ground into what must have been a root cellar. Once at the bottom, there was a tunnel leading deeper to the east. We walked maybe a mile or so, every part of me aching. Though my aphrim wound had stopped bleeding, it stung and felt puffy. I would worry about that later. After a time, a doorway led to a steep ramp with a wooden grate overhead. The guard used my head to push it open, which, if he hadn't been on my to-kill priority list before, he was riding shotgun with Etienne now. Dim light greeted us as we emerged into the kitchen of a modest house.

Through another set of doors, flash bulbs pulsed behind my eyes, distorting my vision from the concussion. Then we stopped. He tossed me to the ground like a sack and put a boot on my back. A surge of power went through the room and knocked at my battered self. I looked up to see Etienne standing before me, his son and Silas behind him, both barely conscious.

"You stink of sick, Princess," Etienne sneered.

"Blame the guard," I spat, head throbbing. I was so out of practice, I wanted to punch myself for letting these two-bit guards take me. Don't pass out. Whatever you do, Neysa, don't pass out. I looked at Reynard, his clothes torn, face slashed and bruised. They must have kept beating him as he healed. His own father. Silas's eyes found mine. He was enraged, eyes wild and translucent, as though it were the only part of him that had turned to mist. Gags filled their mouths, and they hung from shackles on the wall.

"You'll find that in this room I've suspended access to all your gifts. Though my son is fairly useless to begin with, being that he has no real gift, apart from speed." Bastard. Godsdamn bastard. "Now, what I want is simple. How this shall play out is simple. What you need to do to survive and to save your mate is simple."

He walked to Silas and grabbed his throat. I opened my mind, trying to let my power come to me, despite the restrictive feeling.

"Give me the clock, and together we can use it. Tell your brother to abdicate. There. Simple, no?"

"What do you want with the clock? Surely, you must know it doesn't play to your own agenda."

"For starters, I plan to bring my daughter back."

Oh.

Acknowledgments

Shout out to Matt Wallace for taking a couple hours to help me understand magnetic fields, some basic physics, and how one might use crystals and temperature variations to create a weaponized magnetic field. Definitely flexing that I have a JPL rocket scientist on speed dial.

About the Author

Jessika Grewe Glover grew up along the humid shores of South Florida, eventually marrying her British husband and moving to Los Angeles, where they live with their two teenage children and rescue bulldog. Jessika writes multiple genres from literary to speculative fiction. When she is not writing or reading, she can be found traveling, creating art,  making chocolate dragons, and bantering in song lyrics. She is the author of the *Another Beast's Skin* contemporary fantasy series. *Stars Like Gasoline* is her first contemporary fiction novel.

Stars Like Gasoline

Another Beast's Skin

A Braiding of Darkness

Of Chaos and Haste (coming soon)